"Have you no desire to attend the Devine ball?"

"No," Madelyn blurted out.

His eyes narrowed in disbelief. "Come now, doesn't everyone want a chance to be a duchess?"

"It is not a matter of whether or not one wants to be a duchess, but rather one of principle."

He raised a dark eyebrow. "And what principle would that be?"

"That innocent young ladies should not consort with wolves."

"Indeed?" He leaned in closer, an ebony lock falling over one eye. "And you believe the Devine men are both wolves then?"

Good Lord, he looked like a gentleman pirate. "No," she continued in a whisper, ignoring a foreign stirring deep within her body. "It's my opinion that the duke is the worse of the two."

Other **Avon Romances**

Coming Soon

And Don't Miss These
ROMANTIC TREASURES
from Avon Books

AT THE
Bride Hunt Ball

OLIVIA PARKER

AVON

An Imprint of HarperCollinsPublishers

This is a work of fiction. Names, characters, places, and incidents are products of the author's imagination or are used fictitiously and are not to be construed as real. Any resemblance to actual events, locales, organizations, or persons, living or dead, is entirely coincidental.

AVON BOOKS
An Imprint of HarperCollins*Publishers*
10 East 53rd Street
New York, New York 10022-5299

First Avon Books paperback printing: June 2008

Avon Trademark Reg. U.S. Pat. Off. and in Other Countries, Marca Registrada, Hecho en U.S.A.
HarperCollins® is a registered trademark of HarperCollins Publishers.

Printed in the U.S.A.

10 9 8 7 6 5 4 3 2 1

In loving memory
My grandmother,
Celia Garczynski, 1921–1992

And for my mom,
my rescuer, my therapist, my audience,
my friend, my inspiration.

Acknowledgments

My heartfelt gratitude goes to the Jaguar, the Panther, the Rabbit, and most especially, our Annie Bee.

AT THE
Bride Hunt Ball

Chapter 1

"**D**on't fret, my dear. Perhaps one day you'll blossom into a beauty like my Harriet."

Miss Madelyn Haywood nibbled on her bottom lip as she weighed her choices. She could scream, making a frenzied dash for the French doors in the adjoining room, or she could retain her composure and nod agreeably.

"Ah . . . thank you," Madelyn replied. Politeness won.

"Don't look so forlorn." Lady Beauchamp waved her fan vigorously in a vain attempt to mask a belch. Her aunt's stale breath was a clear indication the woman was good and foxed. "There are still two more cards to be presented, yes? *You* could be so fortunate. It's said miracles happen all the time." She started to giggle, but a hiccup cut her short.

"Let me assure you I haven't the slightest inclination to receive one." Madelyn lifted her chin and pretended to look about the room.

"Oh dear," Lady Beauchamp exclaimed, closing her fan with a snap. "That's why you're here, why we're all here. What great fun is this! Just think, soon even you could have a chance to be a duchess!" Using her fan, her aunt made a stabbing gesture toward four young ladies chatting excitedly by the foot of a grand staircase. "Look at them . . . smiling like simpletons. If my dear Harriet hadn't just received an invitation to the ball, I'd think they were deliberately flashing their cards so that I might see. What an atrocious display! Such a lack of decorum!"

Madelyn gave a short nod in response. Though anxious to quit her aunt's company, she prayed her association with her father's sister would forestall any strange possibility that either of the Devine brothers should come near. Lady Beauchamp had a habit of imbibing large amounts of wine at social functions—really, at any function save breakfast—and people seemed to avert their gazes, deftly avoiding the loud, opinionated woman as if she were a knot of rats.

Madelyn rose on the tips of her slippered feet, hoping to spot her friend amidst the crush of guests. "Aunt Lucinda, do you see Miss Greene?"

"Do you mean to say Miss Charlotte Greene? Good heavens, *she's* here? However does her mother think her scrawny, milk-and-water miss would ever land an invitation to His Grace's estate? Oh, I pity the girl and her mother for they will certainly walk away this evening disappointed. Charlotte Greene, you say?" Her aunt tossed back her head, bursting into unladylike guffaws.

Incensed, Madelyn opened her mouth to defend her friend when the ostrich plumes tucked inside the folds of her aunt's blue turban tickled the nose of the gentleman standing behind her. He erupted into a sneeze, then glared at the back of the viscountess's head. He was still looking at her thus when her aunt turned around, apparently to see what had collided with her headwear.

Madelyn stifled a small grin, satisfied the gentleman managed to give her aunt a scornful glare, encapsulating all of what Madelyn needed to say in defense of her dear friend.

The stout woman slurred her apology, then promptly excused herself from Madelyn's company with a swish of her skirts. She watched her aunt wander directly into the very crowd of young women she'd just admonished—no doubt to find some other young lady to perk up.

After a brief inspection of the room's occupants, Madelyn located her stepmother, arms linked with Lady Beauchamp's Harriet. She made a wide arc around the pair as she passed, putting scores of guests between them. She felt her stepmother's arctic glare prickling the back of her head as she slipped into the adjoining room.

In the ballroom, she was about to give up hope of ever finding her friend when she spotted Charlotte, executing her best impression of a tea rose on the hand-painted Chinese wallpaper at her back. As Madelyn made her way through the sea of people, talk of the duke and his brother rippled around her.

" . . . such a scandalous way to find a wife for the presumptive heir, don't you agree? All those innocent ladies locked away with the Devine men for a fortnight . . . "

" . . . very clever of the old Wolf, wish I thought of it first . . . "

" . . . strange he isn't taking a bride himself and wants his brother to carry on the family line . . . "

" . . . I say, it's damned unfair. He's likely to choose only the best of the lot for his brother, leaving only the seasoned nags for us to pick from . . . "

Seasoned nags? She turned and gave the man who uttered that particular phrase a good glare.

This being her fourth season, Madelyn thought she could pen a novel cataloging the names of all the crafty rakes and pompous heirs she'd come across. Naturally, at the top of her list of insufferable men would be the Brothers Devine.

Arrogance and wickedness never before blended to form such tempting packages. For in the heart of every romantic female of the *ton* lurked the secret desire to spark the interest of one of the proud Devines. Of course, it helped that they were members of one the wealthiest, most ancient lineages in all of England. With Lord Tristan's wicked recklessness, and the Duke of Wolverest's brooding arrogance, eager mamas looking to marry off their hopeful debutantes rallied to the challenge. Unfortunately for them, the Devines' questionable pursuits didn't include virgins or marriage. Until now.

However, Madelyn was no fool. She could well imagine the brothers held this ball for some darker purpose. She knew men like them well—the sort who gave little more care to a woman's heart than they did the roast pheasant they had enjoyed for dinner. Lord Rothbury was one, and her stepmother had ordered her to accept it along with the earl's proposal last season. Madelyn had flatly refused. She had been locked in the wine cellar for a day as punishment. It would have been longer had their butler quit sampling the Haywoods' stock of spirits as he had promised.

Charlotte smiled as Madelyn approached. "Clever girl. I didn't think you'd ever leave your aunt's side."

"Yes, and you could have used her as a shield of sorts as well. Your companionship would've lessened my suffering," Madelyn teased.

Telltale red splotches bloomed on Charlotte's cheeks and neck. Her smile faltered and her gaze dropped to the floor.

"Is something wrong?" Madelyn asked, knowing Charlotte had high hopes of receiving an invitation to Wolverest Castle. Perhaps she was now feeling the effects of rejection.

The poor dear, Madelyn thought when her friend answered only with a tiny shake of her head. She was quite sure Charlotte would make a suitable wife for any man—just not Lord Tristan. Unfortunately, Charlotte considered herself half in love with the pompous rake already—along with every other romantic lady of marriageable age.

A flash of crumbled white peeked out of Charlotte's fist. Madelyn's brow rose. "What's that you're holding?"

"Oh, 'tis nothing." Charlotte looked up but failed to meet Madelyn's gaze. "Did you know Wolverest Castle is in Yorkshire? I don't know exactly where, but not far from West Burton, my mother said. Perhaps near your mother's cottage."

"Indeed." She gave a short nod. "Willowbrooke is on the outskirts of the Wolverest estate. Speaking of our host, midnight is nigh upon us and I haven't seen His Grace. Though I doubt I'd recognize him anyway."

"Quite." Charlotte nodded her agreement.

Between the both of them, they were only marginally acquainted with Lord Tristan. And as for the Duke of Wolverest, not at all. When His Grace came to town for the parliamentary session, he only attended a scattering of highborn functions to which Madelyn would never in a hundred years find herself invited. Which suited her fine. She certainly didn't need another stuffy aristocrat wagging his finger at her for her lack of sophistication.

"To be sure, I'm beginning to think His Grace isn't here at all," Madelyn remarked with a touch of hope. "Well, he has only two more ladies to invite to his castle and then this horrid evening will finally be over."

"There's only one more left now." Charlotte pressed her lips together so hard they turned white.

"Oh?" Madelyn prompted, curious about Charlotte's odd reaction to her query. "Did you see who she was? Do we know her?"

"N-No. I'm not certain," Charlotte stammered, suddenly finding sincere interest in something across the room.

She cleared her throat delicately to garner Charlotte's flagging attention. "To think he has his sister and his solicitor pick the potential brides," she said, widening her eyes. "Scandalous, wouldn't you agree?" Charlotte didn't answer, so Madelyn followed her friend's line of vision.

Across the room a young woman sat plucking an enchanting melody on a harp, though the hum of conversation nearly drowned out the sound. Still, Madelyn suspected there must be something other than a harpist holding her friend in this state of distraction.

Behind the musician, Lady Rosalind leaned down to speak with the duke's solicitor. Acting as hostess for her brothers, Lady Rosalind had swept from guest to guest, making light conversation throughout the evening. After speaking with the solicitor, she would disappear for short periods, slipping through a pair of tall doors underneath the sweeping staircase. It was then Mr. Ashton would present the next invitation.

As there were to be seven potential brides, there was only one invitation left.

Perhaps Lady Rosalind was consulting with her brothers. Madelyn imagined they lounged in their private rooms, sipping claret as they waited for their sister to return and divulge just who their next unwitting victim was to be. She shuddered visibly.

"Are you unwell?" Charlotte asked with concern.

"Just my cursed imaginings 'tis all," Madelyn murmured, returning her gaze to Lady Rosalind and the messenger of doom.

She observed the pair until Lady Rosalind excused herself from Mr. Ashton's company after casting a glance in her and Charlotte's direction. The duke's sister smiled briefly, then exited through the tall doors under the grand staircase.

If the pattern held true, there would be another invitation presented shortly. The tension in her shoulders eased as a wave of relief washed over her. The evening would be over soon. Her stepmother would surely make a fuss and declare her lack of enthusiasm as the reason she wasn't chosen. But perhaps there was a chance she could manage to persuade her way into traveling to Yorkshire with Aunt Lucinda and Harriet. With the both of them preoccupied with the hope that Harriet would catch the interest of the younger Devine, she could plan an early return to Willowbrooke Cottage. Husbandless yes, but her heart would remain her own.

"He's staring at you."

Madelyn looked up and caught the solicitor's gaze. Mr. Ashton's smile resembled the starry-eyed gape of a besotted fool. He straightened the spectacles on his thin nose without breaking eye contact. Indeed, he *was* staring. A knot of dread as heavy as a cannonball dropped in the pit of her stomach.

"It's quite unnerving, isn't it?" Madelyn struggled to keep her voice sounding bored and disinterested. "He very well could be staring at you."

"I hardly think so." Charlotte giggled. "I've been watching him for several moments. I believe he's on his way over."

"You're jesting with me?" Madelyn asked with swelling panic. She looked to where Mr. Ashton once stood and found him gone. Her eyes skimmed the crowd for a moment until she spied him weaving through the guests. He held a white note card to his chest, his eyes flashing with what she assumed was anticipation of the recipient's elated swoon.

"Oh, dear. This cannot be happening."

"Don't panic. Just graciously accept the invitation like everyone else," Charlotte offered. "I must say, Maddie, you're my dearest friend, but I don't quite understand why you wouldn't want to attend. It's wildly eccentric and all very exciting."

"It's arrogant madness." Madelyn looked left then right without turning her head as she weighed the easiest route of escape. Guests loomed everywhere, their gazes locked on the solicitor and his progress across the room. Her heart thudded madly within her chest. She couldn't very well burst through the swell of people—she'd be caught swiftly by Mr. Ashton for sure. She was well and truly trapped, unless . . . She turned, her gaze drawn to the candlelight's luminous reflection on the French doors at her far left.

"Let's split up. I'll try losing him by running into the garden. If 'tis me he's targeting, he'd never think to find me there standing amidst a downpour."

She didn't wait to see if Charlotte chose to flee or not. Instead, she dashed toward the rain-streaked glass doors, taking an indirect route around a row of potted lemon trees marking the entrance to the conservatory. Realizing too late that she'd walked herself into a corner, she plucked one of the hard balls of unripe fruit as she raced past. She pushed mightily against the door of the conservatory, losing precious seconds, before realizing it pulled open instead.

"Miss Haywood!" Mr. Ashton called out, panting. "Miss Haywood, I beg you, wait!"

With one last glance over her shoulder at the nearing solicitor, she ducked inside the humid room. Zigzagging around rows of exotic blooms, she nearly crashed into a small fountain with a water-spitting frog in its center. Rounding it, her feet skittered on the smooth floor, panic creeping in as she realized there might not be another exit. But in another moment she spied a fogged glass door across the room. Fairly flying, she sprinted to the other side, praying it would open to the garden.

Reaching it, she yanked the door open and flung herself outside. She looked over her shoulder and breathed a sigh of relief. Ashton was no longer in sight—only his muted shouts proclaimed he still hadn't given up chase.

She didn't care if she was making a scene; she was leaving this mansion tonight secure with the decision she would no longer do her stepmother's bidding. She would not waste any more time chasing after titled men with hefty account ledgers—and insatiable appetites for young flesh—just to appease her stepmother. She would live her life the way she deemed fit, alone with her memories at Willowbrooke Cottage.

Thankfully, the rain had taken a respite, but the flashes of lightning nearby declared there would be another bout of rain and wind ahead. Upon hearing the door of the conservatory creak open, her hope sank. Apparently, Mr. Ashton was as persistent in his pursuit of the fairer sex as was his employer.

She spied a flagstone path, which disappeared somewhere underneath a curtain of branches of a willow tree. She headed for the cover it would provide. Glancing down at the knot of fruit in her palm, she tossed it in the air and caught it swiftly, her lips curling into an impish smile. At least she had a weapon.

Gabriel Thurston Devine, the seventh duke of Wolverest, rested a hip against the balcony railing, his arms crossed over his chest. Looking down into the shadowed garden, he inhaled the scent of wet earth and exhaled it on a low growl.

The rumblings of conversation merged with the soft thrum of plucked harp strings—the sound rising from the open French doors of the ballroom beneath his rooms.

He shook his head in disgust. Twenty highly desirable ladies down there, only seven of whom would be singled out to audition for the bride of Devine. It would be quite the miracle,

Gabriel mused, if the evening concluded without producing a scattering of catfights. They were all very keen on marrying into his family. Silly creatures. If only they realized what a fool's heart Tristan possessed.

Gabriel had gone to great lengths composing a list of eligible ladies of impeccable beauty, decorum, and wit from which his younger brother would choose a bride. It was a nearly impossible feat, as Gabriel lost several early candidates to marriage along the way. It took nearly a year to finish the ever-changing list, with the assistance of his sister and his aging spinster aunt, who lorded over their affairs as the self-appointed voice of cultivated reason. During this time, Gabriel struggled to convince straight-from-Oxford Tristan that he must marry, produce heirs, and maintain the family dukedom—for Gabriel himself wouldn't marry. He knew he simply did not have the compulsion to inflict that sort of aggravation on a woman.

After all, he expected nothing less than perfection, and such a creature didn't exist. And even if she did, he thought it highly probable that the very flawlessness that first attracted him to any future bride would turn him into a bored, resentful beast in his married life. The thought of sending his wife to waste away the hours at some obscure property, forgotten, lonely, and unwanted, filled him with a very real, very familiar uneasiness. His mother had been such a woman, and he still harbored a bitter resentment toward his father for the emotional torment that man had created.

A door slammed in the distance, followed by a string of muffled shouts. "Miss Haywood! Miss *Haaaywoood!* Pray, halt!"

A wisp of pale yellow fabric flickered down below, followed by a feminine gasp. Someone was in his garden and that someone was decidedly female. And as it appeared, she was being chased. If he didn't know that Tristan, at the last possible minute, decided to await the arrival of the party in Yorkshire, he'd have assumed his brother had lured one of their female guests into the shadows.

But who would wander in the rain-soaked garden? The ground was surely saturated, quick to ruin silk shoes and the hems of dinner gowns.

A dark cloud released the full moon, casting silvery blue light behind the mansion. He winced as the figure tripped and fell over the same uneven flagstone he had stumbled over this morning on his way to his favorite spot to read the morning paper. Gingerly, she brought herself to her knees with a mild curse. Gabriel's scowl deepened.

Standing, she looked over her shoulder toward the doors of the ballroom, the light revealing her face. She seemed of average prettiness, he guessed, dark hair and pale skin were the only details he could discern in the shadows. A sudden obliging gust of wind plastered her gown to her curves.

One dark eyebrow lifted as Gabriel contemplated the curve of her hips and backside. She was narrow-waisted and small, but one wouldn't describe her as skin on bones. From his vantage point above her, he could hardly deny noticing the deep valley between her breasts. Voluptuous. Yes, that was it. She was voluptuous. He had always preferred small breasts on a woman.

A shout rang out. The girl jumped, looked about, then slipped under the cover of the sweeping branches of a willow tree.

To his amazement, a man, who looked quite like his solicitor, came sprinting across the courtyard, slipping to a halt in the mud. His mood darkening further, Gabriel braced his hands on the banister, leaning over to get a better look.

"You're not thinking of jumping, are you?" Gabriel's sister called out from behind him.

He straightened with a crooked grin. "With my luck I'd only break an arm."

"I worry this will not go as planned," Rosalind warned. "Tristan might enjoy this too much."

"The young pup's more likely to imitate me and waste the entire time finding fault with them all and end up choosing no one."

"But what about you?" She heaved a frustrated sigh when he didn't answer. "You, dear brother, are incredibly stubborn. I know we have talked about this at least a hundred times before, but I had hoped you would change your mind. Why do you insist on being unmarried?"

He rubbed his brow, growing irritated with this vein of conversation. "You were too young to remember."

Apparently judging his mood, Rosalind didn't press for a more descriptive answer, and he was thankful for it.

A flash of lightning offered him another glimpse of the figure below. The young lady emerged from under a curtain of branches, but before she could break free from her cover, a branch snagged a curl atop her head. Busily, she worked it free, then leapt behind a tall hedge.

He shook his head. "Tell me, have any of our guests gone missing?"

With a grumble, Rosalind folded her arms across her chest. "You're bored," she said over her shoulder, ignoring him. "This *could* have been enjoyable for you had you bothered to pick one for yourself."

His hands tightened on the railing. "There is a woman down there I would like you to make certain we invite," he replied, indicating the garden with a nod of his head.

Turning, Rosalind placed her hands on her hips and eyed him speculatively. "Down there? 'Tis done, Gabriel. I just picked the last of the seven."

"Then make it eight. I must have this one."

Rosalind tried peeking above his shoulder, even hopped twice to see over, but to no avail. With a small, sisterly shove, she pushed in front of him for an unobstructed view of the garden.

As if on command, the young lady peeked out from behind the hedge. Either she'd grown six feet tall, Gabriel thought with a reluctant grin, or she had made use of the stone bench to peek over the top of the hedge.

"Ooh," Rosalind almost crooned. "Miss Madelyn Haywood has caught your interest?"

Haywood? Why did that name stand out in his mind? She wasn't that half-American maladroit miss who lived her life teetering on the edge of social disaster, was she? Their domineering Aunt Eugenia had specifically ordered the chit removed from the list, and he had heartily agreed.

Rosalind straightened her spine, a knowing smile dancing upon her lips. "You will be pleased to know I have already invited—"

"Your Grace! My lady!" Mr. Ashton called out from down the hall before running into Gabriel's study. His solicitor's shoes were caked in mud, smeared on the sides where he obviously attempted to wipe them off in haste.

"I beg your pardon, Your Grace," Ashton said before pausing to catch his breath, his bald head gleaming in the firelight. "The last invitee—she eludes me, sir. I cannot believe it myself, but I almost think, I believe—"

"Spit it out, Ashton," Gabriel nearly growled.

"Well, sh-she's running from me. I—I don't understand it myself. To think she doesn't want . . . that she feels compelled to run . . . how dare she!"

"How indeed." Shrugging on his black frock coat, Gabriel plucked the invitation from Mr. Ashton's grasp, then tucked it into his inside coat pocket and headed out of the room. "If you'll excuse me, Rosalind. And thank you, Ashton," he said distractedly over his shoulder at the doorway. "I'll manage this little minx myself."

* * *

A sharp crack of thunder clapped in the distance, followed by a deep, earth-trembling rumble. Madelyn felt its resonance through her thin satin slippers and upward through her bones. The former gentle breeze was now steadily rising, swirling leaves around her in twirls of air.

After fighting with a sweeping branch for the possession of the hairs piled atop her head, she stepped out from under the willow, certain that Mr. Ashton had given up hope of ever finding her, and even more certain that standing under a tree was the surest way to get lightning to strike it.

What a disaster! Her knee throbbed terribly from her fall, so she hobbled over to a stone bench on the other side of a tall hedge. Lifting her hem, she stepped atop the bench to peer over. Relieved to discover that Mr. Ashton had indeed apparently given up the chase, she plopped down, cringing as she felt the cool stone dampen her backside through the thin fabric of her gown.

She let out a small laugh as she noted her appearance. It gave the impression ruffians had accosted her. Her hair had come loose of its chignon, and fat burgundy locks hung down in her face and curled around her shoulders. There was a tear in her mud-dotted hem, and her shoes were soaked through. She turned her gloved hands over in her lap and saw growing red speckles of blood seeping through small snags in the fabric, surely from catching herself on the stones. Her stepmother was going to kill her. If not for eluding an invitation to Wolverest, then surely for ruining her dress.

As she lifted the hem of the gown to inspect her knee, she heard a shuffling sound and the hairs on the back of her neck stood up. Someone was approaching. She sprang from her seat, clutching the unripe lemon in her palm.

A man emerged from behind the hedge at the exact moment a flash of lightning speared through the sky. Pulling back her arm, she launched the hard lemon in the air, nailing her target square in the forehead.

He stumbled back. "What the hell was that?"

Madelyn stared at the tall shadow, her eyes adjusting, focusing on wide shoulders, wind-tossed black hair, thick bangs tumbling forward and nearly reaching his high cheekbones. He was dressed almost entirely in black, except for the stark white of his cravat and shirt. She leaned forward, peering into the shadows. Why, he rather looked like he'd stepped from the pages of one of those gothic novels Charlotte's nose was always buried in.

He looked . . . familiar, but she couldn't place him. Unfortunately, she did know for certain he was *not* Mr. Ashton.

"Oh . . . no," she groaned.

"And good evening to you, Miss Haywood," he said, with a slight bow of his head, his sultry mouth tugging into a smile.

A glint of silver brought her attention to his eyes. His gaze was so direct, so soul-reaching, she imagined he could read her thoughts. She took a backward step. "G-Good evening." Unexpectedly, the pain in her knee throbbed and her footing faltered. She stumbled forward. He caught her at the shoulders.

"Are you hurt?" he asked, his deep voice a thick whisper.

"'Tis nothing. A scrape on my knee is all." She shivered as the heat from his hot hands fairly scorched the skin of her naked shoulders.

He guided her back onto the bench, his face so indecently close to hers, she could feel the heat from his body on her cheeks, across her collarbone—everywhere.

"Better?" he asked once she was settled.

She nodded, watching him closely. His serious gaze dipped to her bodice and wavered there for a moment before rising up to drift across her neck, her cheek, her hair, and finally returning to her eyes. His perusal wasn't disapproving nor a predatory leer, but more of a general inventory of her appearance. Still, the heat of embarrassment inflamed her skin. She must look simply horrid.

"I must confess," he replied, looking to the sky and squinting against the wind, "this is a peculiar spot to find one of the guests, considering the state of the weather. May I ask what you're doing out here? That is—besides hurling objects at unsuspecting wanderers."

"Oh. I—I thought you were someone else."

"A walking bull's-eye," he suggested with half a smile. "You've quite impeccable aim. You're a terribly brilliant archer, I presume."

"You're half right. Just terrible, I'm afraid."

"I don't believe you," he said, rubbing his forehead.

She laughed. So did he—a deep masculine rumble that rolled through her like the thunder had earlier. The sound of their mixed voices made her feel warm and—strangely—giddy.

Silence stretched between them and her smile fell away as she stared up into this man's glorious face. His sun-kissed cheeks were taut, his strong jaw bearing the slightest shadow of bristles.

A small voice inside her head warned of the dangers of talking to handsome men in moonlit gardens . . . alone.

She stood abruptly. "If y-you'll excuse me, m-my stepmother must be looking for me and I believe quite another storm is brewing . . . " Good Lord, the man was making her stutter.

"Indeed. Mr. Ashton is looking for you as well."

"I haven't the faintest idea why," she lied.

His expression turned stern. "I believe you've been invited to Wolverest."

"How did you know my name?"

"Pardon?"

"When you first . . . you called me by my name after I threw the lemon."

"Was that what it was? I was quite sure it was some sort of rock."

"How did you know my name?" she urged once again, suppressing a smile.

He clasped his hands behind his back, rocking on his heels as he studied her with a cool, assessing gaze. "It wasn't hard to deduce, I'm afraid. You've made yourself quite memorable with the guests."

The solicitor *had* been shouting it across the ballroom and through the garden. She hadn't realized until now the gravity of the scandal she had caused. Madelyn blushed, looking to the ground. Why did she always let her emotions provoke her actions?

A charged silence fell between them. Words jumbled up in her mouth to fill the awkward silence with something, anything, but she bit her tongue, unwilling to fall victim to nervous babbling. The smooth edge of the bench brushed against the back of her knees, but to take a step forward would put her directly under his chin. He stood indecently close and she wondered if he was aware of it—if he did it on purpose to intimidate her.

"Have you no desire to attend the Devine ball?" he asked, his tone mildly curious.

"No," she blurted out, right before good sense told her to keep her opinions to herself.

His eyes narrowed in apparent disbelief. "Come now, doesn't everyone want a chance to be a duchess, an exalted peeress of the realm?"

"It is not a matter of whether or not one wants to be a duchess, but rather one of principle."

He raised a dark eyebrow. "And what principle would that be?"

"That innocent young ladies should not consort with wolves," she murmured.

"Indeed?" He leaned in closer, an ebony lock falling over one eye. "And you believe the Devine men are both wolves, then?"

Good Lord, he looked like a gentleman pirate. "No," she continued in a whisper, ignoring a foreign stirring deep within her body. "It's my opinion that the duke is the worse of the two."

"M—the duke?" He straightened, his eyes flashing with surprise. "And why is that?"

"Arrogance."

"And you believe Lord Tristan is absolved from this sin? The lad has proclaimed he'll not settle for a woman looking any less beautiful than the goddess of Venus herself."

She shrugged. "Simply a case of a younger sibling aping the disposition of the elder. The inclination is a common one, I'm afraid," she added, nodding.

His expression darkened as his intent gaze fairly fastened her to the bench. "Tell me, Miss Haywood, what makes the duke worse in your eyes?"

"Only that this bride-hunt event, this *game*, is by *his* design." She raised her chin. "Pray, sir, what manner of man thinks nothing of herding a group of young, harmless women to his private estate like we were nothing more than prized sheep? The nerve, I say."

"Indeed."

"I shan't be surprised if the duke surveys them all with a monocle and gives them all an assessing pinch as they cross his threshold."

He nodded slowly, his mouth turned downward, as if actually contemplating the very thing. Regret zinged through Madelyn for painting such a vivid picture.

He cleared his throat and offered calmly, "Perhaps he's being creative."

"Or," she countered, "perhaps he finds some absurd pleasure in having so much power, when any other man holding the same contest would be ostracized from society simply for being . . . for being . . . "

"Yes?"

"Cork-brained."

Her comment prompted a funny sort of sound from him, like a cough shrouding a chuckle.

Madelyn's heart hammered against her ribs. Talk of the duke's impertinence had clearly unnerved her more than she would have liked to admit. Silence stretched before them as her pulse thudded back to a more sedate pace.

Abruptly, he knelt down on one knee before her—as if about to offer his love in a heartfelt proposal. She stared, wide-eyed, at the top of his dark head as his assessing gaze slowly rose up the length of her body, finally meeting her blinking eyes.

"Sir?"

"May I?"

"May you what?" She gulped.

"Assess the injury to your knee?"

"No!" She plopped back down on the bench, clamping her hands atop her knees. The motion sent stinging shards across her wounded palms. She cringed. He noticed.

Gently, he turned her hands over in her lap, his broad shoulders blocking out the rest of the world.

"You're bleeding," he said as he started to peel off her gloves with his long, tapered fingers.

Madelyn gasped and pulled her hands away. "I assure you, I am well." She adjusted her gloves. He waited silently for her to finish, then pulled out a handkerchief from the inside pocket of his coat and softly placed it into her palm.

"Come. Allow me to escort you to the kitchen entrance and have my staff take a look at you."

"Your staff?"

He opened his mouth to respond, pausing for a moment, as if carefully selecting his words. "No, no. That would be Wolverest's staff, of course. I'm afraid I never introduced myself . . . I'm Gabriel Devine."

Her eyes narrowed. Perhaps this was why his face had appeared familiar to her. Wolverest's family name was Devine. And they were known for their dark, exotic looks. She blinked up at him. "Mr. Devine, is it?"

"Hmm," came his noncommittal reply. With his hand cupping her elbow, he assisted her to stand. "And perhaps you'll want someone to attend to your hair before rejoining the party," he drawled, his gaze flicking to the top of her head.

Bringing up his hand, he froze, hesitating in the act of reaching for her hair. His features sharpened in a contemplative frown and he sighed, a strange mix of resignation and gruffness. It appeared he'd come to some sort of private decision. Tentatively, he looped one of her heavy curls around his finger and tried tucking it back atop her head. It resisted his urging and bounced back to the middle of her forehead. Apparently determined to bring it under control, he tried once again and ended up with the same result. For a moment his eyes twinkled warmly with the reflection of the moonlight.

Madelyn forgot to breathe. No wonder the Devines were so sought after. Up close, whilst this particular Devine studied her untidy curls with his beautiful face, logical thought did not process. Truth be told, if he bent down to kiss her, she might do the unthinkable and go limp within his arms like a wet goose.

Distant thunder rumbled like a boulder rolling down a hillside. She knew she should act more demure, that her gaze shouldn't be so direct, only she was quite certain he meant to tell her something but thought better of it. He shook his head, barely, and the spell cast between them broke.

"The invitees will be announced shortly," he said quietly. "Once they're publicly declared, there's no turning back." He looked away, a muscle working in his throat as he swallowed. Taking her hand, he linked her arm with his and led her toward the back of the mansion.

To Madelyn's relief, the clouds waited until they reached the door before soaking the earth again.

Mr. Devine turned to bid her farewell as soon as they stepped inside. Gently, he took hold of her fingertips and kissed the air above her knuckles. His smile was tight, polite. As if she were already dismissed.

Using the light from the bright fire in the kitchen hearth, Madelyn discerned the color of his eyes—an uncommon shade of sparkling blue, offset by an outer ring of dark blue. How did anyone manage to concentrate under his attention? They were quite utterly . . . mesmerizing. Thinking of her own brown eyes, she was almost envious.

"Thank you," she said, finally.

His smile fell away, his gaze serious, distant. "No, no," he said, his pensive gaze caressing her face, his mind clearly in another place. "Thank *you* for being so . . . refreshing."

Blinking, she jolted out of the heady enchantment. He thought her *refreshing*? A greedy swallow of cool lemonade after eating a dry biscuit was *refreshing*. Had she gone around the bend? What had she expected? That their shared glance was akin to love at first sight? The man was simply being courteous. Was she such a green girl to consider any show of kindness from a handsome man to mean he was enamored of her?

Annoyed with herself, she broke into a polite grin of her own. At her smile, he turned, gesturing to a young maid whom he introduced as Anne. He proceeded to bark a few orders to the staff about what was to be done for Madelyn's comfort. Catching the cook by a tap on her elbow, he pulled her aside, murmuring in her ear. At the cook's nod, he turned and left the room.

If the servants were at all surprised to find Mr. Devine in the Duke of Wolverest's kitchen distributing orders, they made no mention of it. They bustled about placing glasses of wine on silver trays and arranging various sugared cakes on plates and three-tiered servers.

Others folded linen napkins far from where the cook stood merrily rolling dough onto a large worktable. The plump, rosy-cheeked woman looked perfectly happy to have all the organized chaos zipping around her kitchen.

Anne urged Madelyn to sit on a stool at one end of the table so she could take care of the wounds to her palms.

"Oh, miss! I see you'll be leaving in a sennight."

Madelyn returned her attention to Anne. "Pardon?"

"Wolverest Castle, miss," Anne replied. "You'll be sure to have a grand time, if I may say so. The grounds are quite lovely." She unfolded the handkerchief Mr. Devine had pressed into Madelyn's palm in the garden. "There's an orangery, a splendid topiary garden, and a gleaming ballroom fit for a . . . "

Anne continued to speak, but Madelyn was no longer listening. Glancing down, she groaned. Tucked inside was the invitation Mr. Ashton had failed to present himself. Exasperated, she shook her head. "Oh, that Mr. Devine."

"Mr. Devine?" Anne asked, wide-eyed.

"Yes," Madelyn said. "'Twas his name, no?"

"N—" Anne gasped as the cook bustled past, elbowing her in the ribs. "Y-Yes, of course, Miss

Haywood, Mr. Devine he is," she rasped, rubbing her side.

Trailing her fingertip across the red wax seal, Madelyn whispered to the now blushing maid, "He's as sly as a fox."

"Aye, miss. That he is."

Chapter 2

"You're throwing me to the wolves?" Madelyn's heartbeat tripped as she swallowed past a lump of panic.

With a thump and a lurch, their modest carriage rumbled down Grosvenor Square, away from the speculative glances and hissing whispers of the Devine dinner party guests and on toward the Haywoods' decidedly less opulent residence across town.

"Calm your nerves, child," her stepmother replied from the seat across from her. Priscilla's short gray and blond curls bounced with a forgotten youthfulness as a carriage wheel found a loose cobblestone in the road. "Certainly, I'll not *throw* you to them."

A relieved sigh whooshed out of Madelyn. "Thank the good Lord . . . "

"More like . . . dangle you in front of their gaping, salivating mouths."

Madelyn eyed the carriage door and contemplated jumping out.

"Don't look so panicked," Priscilla advised. "It's not a flattering look for you."

Madelyn closed her eyes for a moment and took a deep breath. Priscilla's insults never penetrated. Or rather, she'd like to think they didn't. "But I do not wish to attend," she managed calmly.

The baroness waved away her plea. "You should count yourself fortunate I intercepted you before you had a chance to rejoin the party. To think you ran from an invitation," Priscilla said, giving a condescending huff of laughter. "Do you realize what a great honor it is even to be on the list, much less *invited* to Wolverest?"

Madelyn looked down in her lap, folding the invitation Mr. Devine had smoothly tucked within her palm into another small, thick square. Maybe if she kept folding the thing it would simply disappear, she thought with a grim smile.

"Your behavior was atrocious. You should count yourself lucky His Grace missed the entire episode. He arrived for the formal announcement of invitees sometime after you had disappeared. I've no doubt had he or his sister witnessed your outlandish behavior our invitation to Wolverest would've been withdrawn." She folded her slim arms across her chest, studying Madelyn with a cutting glare.

A decade ago, when her father titillated the *ton* by marrying his lover, her new stepmother was known as a striking beauty who slinked across ballrooms with provocative grace. Blessed with beauty, but cursed with a sour demeanor, Priscilla grew into a resentful, envious creature in the years after Jonathon Haywood's death. Never satisfied with her lot in life as an aging widow with depleting funds, bitterness ate away at what youthfulness was left. Though her shiny blond hair had dulled with gray and the wrinkles of a frown never left her face no matter her mood, Priscilla still dressed and arranged her hair like a woman half her age.

"Just look at yourself." She indicated Madelyn's hem with a sharp nod of her head. "Must you forever be such an impetuous creature? Look! You've ruined my gown. You've even managed to burst the seam under your bosom . . . "

As her stepmother droned on, Madelyn blocked out the steady stream of her inadequacies. Looking down, she absently noted the gaping tear just under her breasts. It must have started out as a mere slit for her not to have noticed it before and then grew from the strain—the borrowed gown *was* too small for her curvy figure. She remembered how Mr. Devine's eyes had drifted there.

" . . . and to think I lent it to you with the hopes you'd make a fine impression," the baroness finished, turning to stare out the window. "How are we ever to compete with the likes of you as our bait?"

"Bait? Me? How can you expect—"

"How can you refuse? You would be a laughingstock to shun an invitation such as this. To be sure, the scandal sheets would read heavy with your antics again. I cannot withstand any further ridicule. Money is dwindling, Madelyn. We cannot expect to be ever fully enveloped within the bosom of the upper crust. We're simply tolerated as it is. However . . . " She turned, pinning her cool gaze on Madelyn. " . . . I can and shall use you."

"What of our agreement?" Madelyn asked, dreading her stepmother's answer. "Father had said I was to return home to Willowbrooke."

"It was only a suggestion. If you recall, as the cottage wasn't entailed to his estate, your father had presented it to me years ago on our wedding day. And I have no intention of allowing you to stay there."

The carriage floor seemed to drop away from Madelyn's feet. "But you . . . you said this was my last Season. That I could live at the cottage."

"I changed my mind. I might even sell the pokey old thing."

"It holds no significance to you and means everything to me."

"You're barely twenty. I'll not waste your potential by letting you fade into spinsterhood. Is that really what you want? To hide away in high country with no company except for servants while you spend your afternoons cutting pictures for the bourgeois?" She made a snipping motion with two fingers.

"I'm a profile miniaturist," Madelyn corrected.

"Whatever you want to call it." Priscilla shrugged. "No one has become rich from being one."

Since her coming out, Madelyn had been mercilessly thrown in the path of every available nobleman in the peerage. Her stepmother even hinted she should allow certain "liberties" with men of substance to entice them to propose. She refused, of course, but Priscilla had assured her that this behavior was normal, that even she had approached the marriage mart at the time of her own debut with the same unprincipled tenacity. This, however, did not comfort Madelyn in the least.

"Really, Madelyn," Priscilla said, the corner of her mouth lifting into a smirk. "What woman of good sense would refuse an opportunity to snare a Devine?"

"Me," Madelyn answered matter-of-factly. "You might find me completely out of my head, but I *would* prefer a safe man, perhaps a country gentleman, who just might fancy my company to that of his mistress."

Priscilla shrugged, clearly unmoved by Madelyn's declaration. "Well, *I* have a plan. Whilst the other girls are tripping over one another, vying for the attention of the younger pup, *you'll* pull the rug from underneath them all when you snag the duke himself!"

Clearly the woman had stepped out of reality and into a realm of her own making—one that inspired title-hungry stepmothers into thinking a big nobody such as she could attract a fastidious, ill-tempered duke.

Madelyn shook her head in disbelief. "It is *Lord Tristan* who is choosing a wife. The duke cannot make his intentions more plain. He means not to marry."

"Humph. We will endeavor to change his mind. Honestly, I don't see why this comes as such a shock to you. A chance of landing a duke is every young girl's dream. A veritable happily-ever-after."

"I can hardly see how luring a man into an unwanted marriage could bring happiness for either party."

"Maybe so, but just think, you have a chance to be a *duchess*! Think of the prestige and respect it will bring us! And the money. Oh, just think of the gowns!"

It took great strength to sit still and not lunge across the carriage, grab her stepmother by her perky little nose and squeeze until she admitted her insanity.

Instead, she sat forward, staring intently into Priscilla's eyes, hoping simple logic would set her stepmother on the path of good sense. "I must ask you," she started, her voice low, "have you seen the sort of women the duke consorts with? Utterly flawless. They smile, laugh, and pout with precision. Thin, upturned noses, cold eyes always patronizing. I daresay, the immaculate creatures probably all employ bejeweled chamberpots—"

"Yes, but you *were* chosen. I can't believe our luck myself, but the fact remains. *Someone* overlooked your inelegance and believed you might interest the younger Devine."

Shoulders slumping, Madelyn swallowed hard, startled by the sting Priscilla's words brought forth. Her stepmother was indeed a fool if she believed she would go along with her twisted plan.

Besides being a practical, sensible woman, Madelyn was well aware that she didn't possess the physical attributes to lure a confirmed bachelor into an urgent desire to be wed. She was clumsy, graceless, and known throughout society since the year of her debut for making hasty decisions often resulting in bodily pain—hers or someone else's. Not all of them were her fault, of course. Sir William's ankle wouldn't have been sprained had he believed her when she informed him that waltzing wasn't her forte.

"I *will* take my rightful place in society," Priscilla announced bitterly. "I deserve it. And if I must use you or withhold things from you to get what I want, so be it. If you want to return to the cottage, you're going to have to do as I please and snare that duke. At least try, Maddie."

"You've inflated hopes," Madelyn said on a loud sigh, which made the tear under her bosom rip a bit farther. She should have known that Priscilla would use her attachment to Willowbrooke as clout for her own personal gain. It left her with little choice. If her presence was needed to secure a residence at the cottage, she'd go to Wolverest, only she wouldn't be happy about it. She knew very well that Priscilla could go back on her word, but she simply had to take the chance. She had been born there, grew there, lived and loved there, far from the society that snickered behind their silk fans about her American mother's questionable comportment. In fact, her Yorkshire home carried all her memories of her beloved mother.

She looked up from her lap to find her stepmother watching her closely—which was never good.

"You owe me," Priscilla nearly growled.

"Whatever for?" Madelyn asked, her tone incredulous.

"For refusing Lord Rothbury's suit. Imagine my disappointment when I discovered you gave away what was your best offer as of yet. The man is an earl."

"The man is a cad."

"They all are. And now this opportunity falls into our lap and you fault me for it? Just think of what we could accomplish!" Her eyes gleamed in the darkness. "With my help, I'll turn you into quite the tempting treat for the duke. His Grace shan't be able to keep his eyes off of you!"

A thought popped into Madelyn's mind. She knew who the other six invitees were: the Fairbourne twins, the infamous flaxen-haired daughters of a powerful marquis; Miss Laura Ellis, another blond, dainty in all respects; Madelyn's cousin Harriet Beauchamp, a beautiful brunette with lovely eyes the shape of almonds; Julienne Campbell, a raven-haired beauty with untitled parentage, but from a wealthy, respected Scottish family with lineage almost as ancient as the Devines'. And she herself, the seventh and final invitee. But she had skipped one. *Who was the sixth?*

She vaguely remembered discussing who it could have been with Charlotte just before Mr. Ashton . . .

Her mouth fell open. Opening her palm, her eyes narrowed as they settled on the folded invitation. She recalled her friend's tight-fisted grip around the same crumpled white shape back in the Devines' ballroom.

"Who was the sixth invitee? Do you know?" Madelyn blurted out the questions.

"You mean you don't know?" Priscilla shook her head in a patronizing manner. "I can't wait to tell you for you shan't believe the name tumbling from my lips!"

"Pray, tell me," Madelyn said, suspecting she already knew the answer by her stepmother's response.

"Miss Charlotte Greene! Who would have ever thought? Now there's one to stump the betting books at White's!"

"That's not fair," Madelyn said quietly. "She has the same chance as anyone." She closed her fist around the invitation again and inwardly groaned. Charlotte actually *liked* Lord Tristan. The sweet girl was probably in raptures upon receiving her invitation, but instead of seeking her out to share her excitement, Charlotte felt compelled to restrain her enthusiasm because of her own obvious dislike of the whole affair. Now she *had* to go to Wolverest. Someone *had* to protect Charlotte. Sweet, trusting Charlotte. Those wolves would gobble her up in one bite.

For reasons unknown to Madelyn, the image of Mr. Devine kneeling before her in the garden entered her wayward thoughts. With the wind tousling his black, rakish locks as trees swooped and dipped behind him in the wind, she thought he had quite the handle on his own wolfish charms. And he had tricked her. It seemed that an untitled Devine was equally as dangerous as a titled one.

Although, she thought with a pensive tilt of her head, he did seem genuinely concerned for her well-being. Attentive . . .

Oh dear. What sort of backbone did she possess? He was just another scoundrel and they were all the same. She had come to that conclusion after Lord Rothbury. She had vowed then to never allow herself to entertain the idea that she—or anyone, for that matter—could reform a rake.

Madelyn closed her eyes for a moment, inwardly cringing. She couldn't secure her dearest friend's safety from hundreds of miles away. There was no way around it; she simply had to attend the ball. She couldn't sit back and let Charlotte make a dreadful mistake.

Settling into her seat, she leaned her head against the frame of the windowpane, her traitorous mind sinking into the blue depths of a daydream—a shade remarkably similar to the eyes of Mr. Devine.

Chapter 3

Yorkshire
One week later

Gabriel took one look at Miss Haywood and instantly regretted inviting her.

From one of the tall windows of his private office that overlooked the front terrace, he had surveyed the relentless procession of carriages pass through the two-story gatehouse since the hour of ten. Their guests were arriving one atop another within the inner courtyard, making him suspect they all had considered it a veritable race to be the first welcomed into his ancestral home.

For a moment his mood darkened at this intrusion into his private world, but it was of his own making and simply had to be done. He reminded himself he'd predicted the sense of invasion, the orderliness teetering on a peak of chaos. However, what he did not anticipate, Gabriel mused, was the sense of impending dread settling in his bones as he stared at Miss Haywood stepping down from the Greenes' carriage.

He didn't believe a bloody word she said about not wanting to marry his brother. A young woman of moderate means and full possession of her sanity would never run from an invitation others would do anything short of murder to obtain. Indeed, her aversion to being a Devine bride could be part of a marital strategy, he thought. Perhaps she had hopes Tristan wouldn't be able to resist such a challenge.

Hell, he was scarcely able to stop himself from pulling her against him in his garden in London and brushing his mouth against hers. Strikingly beautiful, she was not. However, he had to admit she was adorable in such a beguiling way he had half a mind to say it astounded him.

A grin tugged at the corner of his mouth as he remembered that evening and how her rich, burgundy locks tumbled from the pile atop her head. Certainly, she wasn't the most graceful of creatures. In fact, she was wholly unacceptable. And full of flaws. If she were his ward, he'd hire a team of finishing governesses and lock them all in Wolverest's tallest tower for months, maybe even a year.

Gabriel reached back, massaging the back of his neck in frustration. Miss Haywood had a reputation scattered with clumsy happenings at public functions, which he had begrudgingly deemed permissible, and a bold stepmother who nearly had her ward compromised a number of times. "She is a shameful, vexing creature who cannot dance or even play," his Aunt Eugenia had declared—repeatedly. By those accounts Miss Haywood's name should not have remained on the list. But Rosalind insisted the chit be placed there, claiming to admire a frank openness in her gaze and an intriguing sense of the unexpected, and, by God, his sister was spot on.

Gabriel shook his head in bemusement. Why the hell did he give in to Rosalind? Miss Haywood did not belong here.

He took a step closer to the tall window, heat from the afternoon sun warming his face through the glass. Miss Haywood stood there on the cobbled drive, a serene smile upon her lips, her round, dark eyes giving the impression she hid a deeply sensual nature. It was unintentional, for sure. Had the silly chit known she possessed such a bewitching gaze, he was sure she would have learned to use it by now to gain numerous advantages in life.

With his back to the study door, he heard his brother enter, the sound of his footsteps telling him Tristan headed straight for the fireplace.

"Let us review our agreement," Gabriel threw over his shoulder.

"Spare me the idiocy of details," Tristan remarked from his position in front of the gilt-framed mirror above the mantel. He stood dusting imaginary lint from his shoulders, but Gabriel knew what his little brother was actually doing: Tristan Everett Devine was inventing things to do that would award him more time to admire his own reflection.

"I realize I cannot foist maturity on you, but damn it all, stop using your banal criticisms as a crutch to keep from taking a bride." Gabriel frowned at his ridiculous brother, who was now examining his teeth.

"I only base my scale of judgment by your example. Every man has his own preferences."

"Preferences? You find a flaw with every marriageable woman who crosses your path. This one too chatty, too pale, too skinny, too plump, too short, too tall," Gabriel finished, nearly running out of breath. "You agreed to be less discriminating."

"Come, come," Tristan drawled. "That's certainly no way to talk to the man who agreed to give up a life of content debauchery to make certain the title remains in our grasp. Besides, if you will recall, there always seems to be a stunning beauty by your side. You are as guilty as I."

Gabriel's scowl deepened. "I do not mislead them with inane flummery."

Tristan gave a short bark of laughter. "No. *You* drop them like a fireplace poker left to close to the hearth should you spot a freckle." He dug in his waistcoat pocket, but came up empty-handed for whatever it was he was looking for.

"I don't like freckles," Gabriel grumbled, remembering the ones on Miss Haywood's nose. And the pale, tiny one just above the corner of her upper lip.

"Do you have any more of those peppermint drops?" Tristan asked.

Without answering, Gabriel turned to his massive mahogany desk and opened the top middle drawer. He grabbed a handful of the candy and tossed it atop his desk. One rolled off and fell soundlessly to the rug. He shook his head, then remembered his task and turned back to the set of windows overlooking the front lawn.

The Marquis of Fairbourne was handing down his flaxen-haired twin daughters from their carriage. As three servants rallied around a second conveyance laden with trunks, Fairbourne linked a daughter to each arm, puffing out his chest with apparent pride.

Gabriel smiled grimly. The man obviously thought he had this thing already won—he did have double the chances. Indeed, and double the worry.

"Ah, the twins," Tristan remarked from behind Gabriel's shoulder.

"Remember your gentlemanly manners," Gabriel warned in a slight mocking tone.

"Mine or yours?"

"Both," Gabriel muttered as he stared past the twins. Miss Haywood was in the peculiar process of removing pins from her bonnet. What the devil was she doing?

"They are rather delicious looking, aren't they?"

Gabriel nodded absently, answering a question he wasn't listening to. A footman moved, obstructing his view. Impatience pricked at his nerves. Finally the robust man stepped aside revealing a cheery looking Miss Madelyn Haywood patting the locks tumbling from the loose bun atop her head. Didn't she know a lady wasn't to remove her bonnet in public?

But the disapproving furrow in his brow gradually relaxed. In the daylight, her dark red hair looked positively glorious. The very shade of a glass of claret held up to firelight. Ah, hell. He decided to forgive her. They were in the country, after all.

Finishing her task, she stood with one gloved hand shielding her eyes from the sun, the other resting on her hip, the yellow ribbons of her bonnet entwined within her fingers. The bonnet swung back and forth in the breeze, batting against the sky blue muslin of her dress as her assessing gaze took in Wolverest Castle.

"I've heard they've a particular fondness for Frenchmen."

"Who?" Gabriel asked, the word mostly air. He suddenly had no idea what his brother was talking about.

"Who else? The Fairbourne twins." Tristan popped one of the peppermint candies into his mouth. "If they like zee French accents, I think I weel 'ave to indulge them, *non*?"

Gabriel closed his eyes momentarily, shaking his head. Tristan, on occasion, could be downright absurd.

His brother chuckled at his own jest, swaggering away from the window. As he passed a glass-paned bookcase, he paused to use the reflection it provided to smooth his dark hair away from his face. "Where's that French poetry book Rosie was reading last night?"

"I have no idea," Gabriel answered. With any luck, Rosalind anticipated Tristan's ploy of seduction and threw it in the pond.

"Pity," Tristan said ruefully. He swept his fingers across his forehead. "I do know, however, that I don't envy you and the unsightly mark on your face." The bruise had faded to a hideous shade of chartreuse. "How'd you come about that again?"

"I had a . . . a mishap in the garden back in London," he answered distractedly. He continued to watch Miss Haywood.

"Brother? If you haven't noticed, the house is rapidly filling with women who desire my attention and I must be on my way," Tristan said, straightening. "Quite a striking bunch, the whole lot. My only regret is I must choose only one."

Gabriel turned to find Tristan now leaning inside the door frame. "Use your head," he began. "Do not show favoritism. Do not insult anyone. Make your preferences and aversions known only to Rosalind and me. If you happen to make your choice before midnight on the night of the ball, you would be wise to keep it to yourself. Again, there is to be no indecent behavior, Tristan, no fake French accents, and for God's sake show some restraint."

"I will if you will," Tristan remarked casually as he inspected his fingernails. "Are you done? I'd like to get a head start and seek them out, you know."

"Seek them out?" Gabriel chuckled. "You just might have to hide."

Tristan stood, straightening his coat. "Well, thank God *you're* not choosing a bride, Gabriel. With all your rules of manner and dress, no doubt you'd kill her with boredom."

Gabriel's smile froze, then fell into a scowl. His little brother had no idea of the gravity of his flip comment.

With an exaggerated bow, Tristan quit the room with a jaunty step into the hall. And a good thing he left when he did, Gabriel thought—just before he was about to throttle him.

But it would have been wrong to blame his brother for his poorly chosen words. Tristan was too young to remember the happy, vibrant woman that was their mother . . . and how their father changed everything with his thoughtlessness.

A high-pitched shout pulled Gabriel's attention back to the window. He looked to the grounds for a dog, for it certainly sounded akin to a canine's yip.

But it was no dog. It was Miss Haywood.

Her pretty little bonnet went aloft as she ran to and fro, flapping her gown as if it were on fire. Miss Greene tried desperately to keep up with her friend's mad dash, but Miss Haywood was just too quick.

"What the bloody hell . . . " Gabriel took a step closer to the window and blinked a few times after he thought the crazed woman accidentally afforded him—and the small crowd forming about her—a view of her shapely calves, not to mention her knees.

She continued to flap about the drive in such a frenzied manner, she crossed the short expanse of lawn, attracting curious onlookers who began to follow.

She was headed straight for the pond. He watched her edge closer to where the lawn sloped toward the water. If the girl wasn't careful, she'd fall in.

And given what he'd heard had happened at the Montagues' garden soiree last spring, she didn't know how to swim.

He swore, running his hand through his already tousled hair. "Doesn't that woman ever stay put?" Turning away from the window, he strode out the door. He had wanted to divulge her of his true identity privately before she embarrassed herself by addressing him improperly in front of everyone. But he couldn't let the chit drown either.

In the hall, Gabriel spotted his butler standing like a marble sentinel by the open front doors. Trunks and bags of every size and shape were heaped in a pile across from him as servants rallied to take them up to the correct rooms.

"Your Grace," the butler intoned, his face expressionless. "There seems to be a disturbance on the lawn."

"Yes, Gerard. I'm aware of it."

"Of course, Your Grace."

"Order a bath to be readied for Miss Haywood." When the tall, silver-haired butler acknowledged the order with a slow nod, Gabriel strode out the front doors, down the multilevel steps of the terrace and onto the drive.

An image of Miss Haywood lounging in the hip bath, water lapping against her glistening skin, rose unbidden in his mind.

With a shake of his head, he pushed the thought out of his head. If he didn't curb his imagination, he'd need a dunk in the frigid pond as well.

* * *

One moment she was admiring the lavender-lined path snaking around the castle—the long, grayish-purple sprigs bouncing up and down as heavy bees collected their fragrant pollen—and in the next she was jumping about like a madwoman because one of those pesky little creatures found its way under and up her gown.

"A bee. A bee. There's a bee," Madelyn cried in a frantic whisper, rushing about.

"Where?" Priscilla spun about, looking. "There's no bee."

"Under my gown," Madelyn cried, flapping at her skirts. "It'll sting me."

"Well—then let it," Priscilla said through gritted teeth. "Better to stand still and comport yourself as a lady than to flail about like a loon."

"Are you jesting?" Madelyn asked in disbelief, shaking and swatting her gown as she crossed the lawn. "The last time I was stung, my hand remained swollen, red, and painful for five days. There isn't a salve in existence to save me."

"Stand still so I can help you," Charlotte urged, following Madelyn.

"The Fairbournes are looking at us," Priscilla whined, trailing behind them. She looked over her shoulder. "And following us."

"I say, young lady!" Lord Fairbourne called out. "What is the matter?"

The baroness smiled tightly. "Not a thing, my lord." She whipped around, growling through her teeth. "Madelyn, I demand you stop this instant."

And Madelyn did—directly at the top of a gentle slope.

"Wait, wait . . . " She stood perfectly still for the barest of a second. "I think . . . it's gone." A sigh of relief poured out of her. "It is." Her shoulders easing down, she turned around, only now noticing how the lawn slanted sharply to a large pond. "Well, it's a good thing I didn't fa— *Yeeow!*" An acute jab stabbed her left buttock.

She whipped around, swatting at her bottom, then mistakenly stepped on her hem. And then she fell, or rather, rolled, directly into the lake.

Priscilla screamed. Charlotte gasped. And Madelyn, dragging herself out of the knee-deep water, tossed herself upon the grassy bank and broke into a laugh.

"Oh, Maddie!" Charlotte skidded down the hill. "Are you all right?"

"Yes, yes, I'm fine," Madelyn sputtered, wiping at a swag of hair that had fallen into her eyes. "C-Cold. But f-fine. At least the water wasn't very deep over here."

"I should have known *you'd* do something like this," Priscilla hissed. "You clumsy cow."

"I'll get help," Charlotte said in a quiet voice, throwing a disapproving glare at the baroness.

Madelyn looked up, noticing the small crowd forming on the crest of the slope. The Fairbourne twins smirked down their noses at her—though she had to admit they had no choice, as they were standing above her. And their father, the ruddy-faced Lord Fairbourne, blinked at her as if she were a newly discovered bug specimen.

Standing, Madelyn gathered handfuls of sopping fabric in her hands and began to ring herself out. She looked up from her task to see a young footman start down the hill. He took one look at the front of her gown and turned on his heel. "If—If you'd like, miss," he said with his back to her, "I'll fetch a blanket." And then he took off running.

"Thank you," Madelyn replied, a question in her eyes. She wondered what made the servant so uncomfortable. Of course, it probably wasn't every day that a silly woman jumped in their pond. Or . . . she looked down. The water had plastered the gown to her skin, making the pale blue fabric appear wholly see-through. Each rib bone, each *breast*, was shockingly visible in startling detail to anyone who would care to notice.

Wrapping an arm across her chest for modesty's sake, she began to trudge up the hill, her sopping skirts clinging to her thighs and hampering her progress.

She realized that any normal young lady would be perfectly mortified to have fallen in a pond after such dramatics in front of a half-dozen people. And really, she expected to be more embarrassed tomorrow than she felt right now. But somehow she couldn't summon the humiliation. Maybe it was because she didn't care what these people thought. Or perhaps it was because after an exhausting ride in a carriage for four days with her stepmother and her wealth of criticisms, the splash in the pond felt downright revitalizing. Or maybe . . . she wasn't surprised. From an early age she had accepted the fact that things just happened to her. Yes. That was it. Now if she *hadn't* fallen into the pond, *that* would have been a surprise.

She stopped short when a rather large-sized pair of polished Hessians came into view.

Her gaze traveled up the length of the man's legs, from his knees to his athletically toned thighs covered in fawn-colored breeches—which were sinfully snug—and stopped somewhere around his lean hips and flat stomach.

"Why is it, Miss Haywood," came a familiar deep voice, "that every time I meet you, you're quite damp and speckled with mud?"

Never the one to be shy, Madelyn raised her head to meet Mr. Devine's beautiful stare, which promptly stunned her to silence. He was so remarkably handsome. How in the world did his acquaintances manage to concentrate on anything in his presence? She couldn't say anything. Her mouth just opened and shut like a fish. She probably smelled like one too, now that she thought of it.

After a moment longer than she would have liked, she managed a wobbly smile. But the effect she hoped it had on him was ruined when the same wet swag of hair fell again, covering her face. He chuckled softly, smoothing it out of the way for her.

She had half expected to see him here, as he was related to the Devines and they were certainly going to invite more than the potential brides and their families to even out the numbers, but she would have preferred he didn't observe her so . . . so soggy.

His eyes sparkled with suppressed laughter. "What exactly was the problem, dear lady?" He crossed his arms over his chest. "*Was* there a problem? Or did you just feel like going for a swim?"

"Y-Yes—I mean no. There was a bee."

The footman appeared, saving her from further stuttering, and handed her the blanket. Mr. Devine pulled it from her loose hold and wrapped it snugly around her shoulders.

"I'm angry with you," she declared, suddenly remembering he had tricked her with the invitation.

"And why is that?" he asked after he finished wrapping her up.

"You snuck the invitation into my grasp." She sniffled. "Did you think I'd forgotten?"

"Nonsense, it would have made its way into your possession somehow. I was simply helping out my man."

"Your man?" Her brow knitted together.

"Come. I'll walk you inside." He surprised her by taking her hand in his large one as he guided her up the hill. "I must explain something to you, in private, and after, you can tell me just why you felt compelled to test the waters."

Nearly to the top, she found her voice again. "I would very much like to change first." Something slimy, which she hoped was simply mud and not a leech, slid down her calf. "That is, if you think the duke will tolerate me traipsing through his castle dripping muddy pond water everywhere."

"I can assure you it's quite all right," he said, a flash of warmth in his icy-blue gaze. "But first you must allow me to clarify something that was said—"

"Mr. Devine," Madelyn said on a loud sigh, trying to free her hand from his firm grasp. "I should like to freshen up a bit fir—"

For some reason unknown to her, everyone standing on the hill collectively gasped. And Madelyn could have sworn Mr. Devine groaned under his breath.

When she opened her mouth to speak again, a blushing Charlotte shook her head hurriedly as if she were trying to send Madelyn a signal. Puzzled, Madelyn's brow furrowed. She looked to her stepmother, whose alabaster skin turned positively crimson.

Priscilla stepped forward, grabbing the wrist of Madelyn's free hand. "Please forgive her, Your Grace. The water must have influenced her sense of propriety. I'm quite certain my stepdaughter meant to address you properly and I—"

"Your Grace?" Madelyn eyed Mr. Devine suspiciously. "Why did she address you as if you were . . . "

Her voice trailed off as she studied the fading yellow crescent of a healing bruise on his forehead, then dropped to the family crest embellished on the buttons of his dark green jacket. Her mouth fell open, her eyes opening wide as the connection dawned. No. This man standing before her exuding an easy confidence was not *Mr. Devine*. He was a rascal, a schemer, a fraud, and she should have known better than to believe in his glittering gaze.

Her skin prickled with embarrassment. "You're the duke." She breathed the words in a whisper of disbelief. She felt like an instant fool. "In the garden . . . you lied. Why would you lie?"

"Don't be silly, darling." Priscilla squeezed Madelyn's hand painfully so that all four fingers and thumb were smashed together within her own. "His Grace hasn't a need for untruths." She settled her apologetic gaze on the duke. "Please, let me take her inside so I might talk to her, settle her down. She's normally quite endearing, if you just give her another chance."

"Baroness," the duke stressed, his eyes seething with anger as they fixed on Priscilla's pleading gaze. "Kindly loosen your hold. I believe your grip is cutting off the flow of blood to Miss Haywood's fingers."

Priscilla let go instantly. With a bow of her head, she backed her way up the hill like a chastised child.

As soon as the duke returned his attention to Madelyn, his eyes softened. "I did not anticipate this. Really, how could I," he said quietly, giving her hand that was held within his a gentle squeeze. "I had planned to capture your attention privately before—"

"Before what?" Madelyn asked, struggling to keep her own voice low. "Before I could humiliate myself?"

"I dare say," he said with a dark look, "you seem to be doing a fine job all by yourself."

"You mock me." She whispered the words, but they still held the heat of censure. Looking at their joined hands, she pulled hers from his hold. She shot him one last reproachful glare, then grasped the blanket threatening to slip off her shoulders. With a sniff, she trudged up the hill. He beat her to the top, blocking her path.

"Wait," he ordered, his austere expression telling her he was a man accustomed to having people do exactly as he commanded.

She refused to look at him any further, choosing to fasten her angry glare at the center of his chest. For a moment there was nothing, no words, no whispering from the other guests, just the sound of her angry breathing, her chest rising and falling with the exertion it took from slogging up a steep hill in a drenched gown.

Finally his cultured tones broke the silence. "I didn't lie to you," he said quietly, for her ears alone to hear. "That is my given name."

"We both know that is not how you should have introduced yourself," she bit out. "And it's certainly not proper for me to address you so informally."

"If you care to remember, your manner of behavior that evening did not lead either of us to comport ourselves within the rules in which the stricture of society insists."

She looked up at him, her expression incredulous. "Why did you lie? Was this why I was chosen?" She glanced at the faces of those who stood about them, though at some distance. With the exception of her stepmother and Charlotte, everyone else grinned like imps, leaning an ear forward in desperation to overhear more of their conversation.

"For a game? Am I the joke?" She swallowed hard, defiantly ignoring the voice inside her head telling her she was behaving coarsely. After a moment of silence she shook her head, disappointed—in herself, in him. She made to take a step around him.

He anticipated her move, his broad shoulders impeding her path yet again. "Indeed, I tricked you into receiving the invitation," he said, keeping his voice low. "But if I had not, you would have run from me as you are trying to do now."

"Mr. De—" Madelyn stopped herself, attempting to take control of her emotions. "Your Grace," she said with forced sweetness, "did it ever occur to you that there could, possibly, be a woman in all of England that *doesn't* wish to marry into your family?"

"No, quite frankly," he said with an arrogant arch of his brow. "If there were, I'd consider her the silliest of fools."

"I see," she said, affronted.

With a sharp tug, she grasped the slipping blanket tighter across her shoulders. Taking a cleansing breath, she forced a brilliantly fake smile as she started to tremble, not knowing if it was from anger or cold.

"Please, let me pass," she said, her mask of composure slipping.

In response he looked down at her like she was

a faro box and he the gambler waiting to see which card sprung next. After a long minute, he stepped aside. "Of course."

Madelyn strode past him, feeling strangely bereft that he'd given up trying to stop her. Then, thinking that a very odd feeling for her to have, she broke into a run, dashing across the lawn and on toward the castle, never slowing her pace.

Halfway across the lawn, however, it occurred to her that she didn't even know where she was going. She just knew she had to get away from him and the crowd of onlookers. Oh! How the Fairbourne twins must be enjoying her mortification.

A doe-eyed servant girl appeared at her side, applying a running curtsy as she tried to keep up with Madelyn. "Miss, I've readied a bath for you. Your bags have been taken up." She continued to run alongside. "I'm Jenny," she panted, "and I'm to show you to your room."

Madelyn stopped abruptly. She turned to Jenny, who seemed more than relived for the respite. "My bath? Do you mean to say, that man," she gestured behind her with a sharp nod of her head, "that conniving rogue, *anticipated* me falling into the pond?"

"I don't know, miss." Jenny looked uncomfortable, quite like she wished one of the other servants had been assigned to see to Miss Haywood's comfort. "It would seem so. My father says the master's always thinking of things ahead of time. It's a sign of a great leader. He's very watchful too. He probably took one good look at you and knew you'd end up in the pond."

Madelyn didn't know what she thought about that. But speaking of ends, she mused with a cringe, the pain in her own end had begun to throb fiercely.

"Tell me, Jenny," Madelyn prompted as she continued toward the castle at a decidedly slower pace. "What remedies do you know of to soothe the pain from a wasp's sting?"

"I don't rightly know, mum, I've never been stung myself. But I could find out."

"Please do," Madelyn said as she stopped at the base of the multitiered steps leading up to the castle's main doors. Well, there was no other way to get up them without putting one foot in front of the other. She took a step. Cringed. Took another step. Cringed. "Why do there have to be so many steps?"

"Pardon?"

"The steps. You see . . . " Madelyn paused to look over her shoulder, making sure no one else could overhear. "I've been stung back there." She pointed vaguely to her backside. "Every step produces a twinge of pain."

Jenny's mouth quirked with a suppressed smile.

"Whatever you do, Jenny, please do not speak of the whereabouts of the sting to another soul. I've been embarrassed enough for one day."

"I shan't, mum. I promise."

Chapter 4

By noon the entire household knew exactly where Madelyn had been stung. It was a spectacular feat, she supposed, taking into account the vastness of the castle.

"You must consider the fact that there are hundreds of servants," Charlotte said, following Madelyn across her bedchamber. "Certainly enough to keep a steady wave of gossip flowing strong."

"Yes, but if I encounter another giggling Fairbourne twin or one more well-meaning servant armed with a secret smile and another poultice for wasp stings, I'm leaving." Madelyn plucked a small blue pillow from her bed, fluffed it, then placed it atop the cushioned bench at the foot of her bed.

"But you mustn't go," Charlotte cried, removing the pillow before Madelyn could sit on it and tossing it back upon the bed. "Remember your agreement with your stepmother." She pointed to the blue and yellow striped chaise lounge across the room. "You'll be infinitely more comfortable there."

Madelyn nodded. "It wasn't an agreement. It was blackmail." She shuffled over, gingerly settling down on her side, her head resting on the curved arm.

"Still, you must pretend to try and snag the duke. And Priscilla shan't believe you are, based on what happened when we arrived."

"Then perhaps I'll simply find the castle's dungeon and hide in it for the next fourteen days. Charlotte, I'm positively mortified."

Charlotte, deciding to sit on the lounge near Madelyn's feet, was bent halfway down to sit when her dark blue eyes grew wide. She bolted across the room, catching her dozing mother's empty teacup just before it hit the floor.

"I don't think Wolverest has a dungeon any longer," she said, settling the cup back on the tray on a nearby table. "But really, how in the world does addressing His Grace improperly outshine falling into a pond and exposing yourself?" She paused, sticking out her own nearly flat chest. "I mean, *revealing* yourself, Madelyn?"

"Nonsense. I had a blanket."

"A blanket that kept gaping open."

Madelyn groaned. "Thank you for pointing out that added facet of my humiliation. At least the deceiver pretended not to notice."

"Your deceiver noticed, all right. His gaze dropped down every time you blinked."

Madelyn sat up, her backside aching with a knot of pain. "He's certainly not mine," she said, patting the loose bun atop her head, still damp from her bath. "And I don't believe you."

"You should," Charlotte said. "*I* observe everything." She turned, studying her napping mother for a moment, then looked at Madelyn with a cheeky grin. "I've something to show you." Reaching inside the front of her bodice, she pulled out a folded sheet of paper.

"What have you there?" Madelyn asked.

Unfolding the paper as if it was made of spun sugar, Charlotte held it directly beneath her nose, her eyes skimming the lines. "It is a list of Lord Tristan's favorite things."

"Wherever did you get that?"

"Myself." She smiled proudly at Madelyn. "Through careful observations—not to mention heavy eavesdropping—I concluded several of his lordships predilections. I made a list and I've been studying it."

"Charlotte, I'm amazed."

Her friend's playful expression turned doubtful. "Do you think it strange?"

"Absolutely."

Charlotte tried to sigh with vexation, but smiled instead. "Well, I figured it couldn't hurt. Would you like to hear them?"

Madelyn smiled at her friend's show of remarkable trust. Anyone but Charlotte would hoard such vital information, disbelieving her claim to dislike Lord Tristan. But not Charlotte. They had an unbreakable bond sewn in childhood on threads of unconditional love and a mutual obsession with snooping about, books, and anything covered in, baked with, or drizzled over with chocolate. Besides, they both had a family member who criticized them to excess, only they each handled it differently. Madelyn pretended the barbs didn't hurt, while Charlotte constantly altered herself.

"Yes, please, read on," Madelyn said. "Words cannot express the extent of my interest."

Charlotte raised a skeptical brow before reading aloud. "His favorite color is red; his favorite fruit is strawberries . . . " Charlotte paused, her nose scrunched up as she squinted to read the next line. " . . . his favorite flower is the Papodee—no, oh goodness I've forgotten the pronunciation. The Pahippo—no, that doesn't sound right either . . . Oh! I've got it. The Paphiopedilum orchid." Looking mightily pleased, Charlotte smiled briefly to herself, then her pale brows knitted in thought. "Whatever do you suppose that looks like?"

"I have no idea," Madelyn commented with a grimace as she tried in vain to find a more comfortable sitting position. "But I'm willing to wager five young women will be wearing them in their hair at dinner this evening."

Charlotte's face fell. "Do you really think so?"

Madelyn smiled, finally settling in. "No. But I do think you'll positively go blind if you insist on not wearing your spectacles."

"About that . . . " Charlotte looked down, her tone turning glum. She began twirling a pale coil of hair around her finger. "Harriet told me Lord Tristan doesn't like spectacles on women. She said that she overheard him say so at the Atkinsons' ball last spring—that they make a woman look older than she is and . . . intelligent." She mumbled that last part.

"And he considers intelligence a flaw? Charlotte, why would you seek the interest of a man who—"

"Don't be silly, Madelyn," Priscilla broke in. "A man like his lordship deserves whatever his heart desires." She nudged Madelyn's foot as she walked past her to stand beside Charlotte.

"How did you get in here?" Madelyn asked, since she hadn't seen or heard her door open.

Priscilla peered over Charlotte's shoulder, her eyes darting over the sheet of paper she was holding. "Our chambers share a dressing room. Besides, I have a key."

"But I don't even have a key."

Her stepmother's shrewd gaze lifted briefly to meet Madelyn's. "Of course *you* don't. Lady Rosalind presented all the chaperones with the key to our own room and our ward's rooms so we might lock you in at night. To ensure the obvious propriety and safety."

The fact that Priscilla said "might lock you in" didn't slip past Madelyn.

Priscilla shrugged. "You can't get out. And obviously, no one can get in, unless they have the key."

Throwing a hand to her throat, Charlotte gasped with masked delight. "Even his own sister believes Lord Tristan would ravish us in our very beds!"

"Exactly," Priscilla agreed. "Lady Rosalind assured us there was only one key for each room. And more importantly, my lady has informed all the chaperones that anyone caught outside their bedchamber without proper escort after midnight will be swiftly eliminated." Reaching out, Priscilla snatched the sheet Charlotte was holding. "Tell me where you obtained this paper."

"'Tis mine," Charlotte answered, looking like she feared that Priscilla just might lunge across the space between them and bite her on the hand.

"I can't see how any of this scribbled nonsense is going to help *you*," Priscilla scoffed.

Madelyn stole a glance at the newly awakened Mrs. Greene sitting in a chair across from the fireplace. Charlotte's mother had demonstrated a rather remarkable hold on her temper, having been forced to witness Priscilla's catty impertinence in such close proximity in the past few days. However, if the pinched set of her lips were any indication, Mrs. Greene's restraint was at its limit.

"Humph," Priscilla said haughtily, pulling Madelyn's attention back to her. "Just out of curiosity, of course, has anyone made a list of the duke's favorite things?"

The room fell silent.

"I don't believe so," Charlotte offered finally. "And why would they? He isn't taking a bride." She looked to Madelyn, giving her a slight what-else-was-I-supposed-to-say shrug.

The baroness's keen eyes skimmed the page, making short work of the list. She then crumbled it up, tossed it to the floor, and rounded her attention on Madelyn. "There are things of which we must discuss. Things I wasn't aware of until today. We must have a chat." Her frigid blue eyes widened momentarily as she attempted to stress the point.

Madelyn knew what her stepmother wanted. Priscilla was very likely ready to explode with curiosity as to how and why it seemed she had met the duke prior to coming to Wolverest. As far as her stepmother knew, Mr. Ashton had been successful in hunting her down in the garden, and that she, having been intercepted by her stepmother in the hall across from the kitchens, missed her introduction to the duke with the other invitees.

There was a knock on the door, and Madelyn arose from the cushioned bench with care for her backside. "I imagine it's Jenny with another compress for the sting," she said, shuffling across the room. She opened the door, revealing the maid. The girl bounced a quick curtsy.

"Yes?" Madelyn asked.

"His Grace expresses his interest in your welfare and desires your immediate company in the orangery."

Madelyn's eyes narrowed.

Priscilla sidled up to her, whispering in her ear, "What a boon." The baroness then smiled wickedly down at Jenny, whose pallor turned positively ashen before she shrank back. "Well, what are you waiting for, girl? Take us to him."

"Ah . . . His Grace specified Miss Haywood was to come alone."

"Alone, is it?" Priscilla turned her back to the maid momentarily to smile smugly at Madelyn. "Well, then, by all means, hurry along." She tried scooting Madelyn out the door by tugging on her elbow.

"Why?" Madelyn asked, her limp arm held captive in her stepmother's grasp.

"Pardon, miss?"

"Did His Grace disclose the reason for his request?"

"For your interview," Jenny responded gently. "The master and Lady Rosalind mean to have interviews with all of his lordship's prospective brides. You are the first."

Madelyn pulled her arm loose. "Tell him . . . " She paused, tapping one finger on her chin in thought. "Tell him I've a headache. And I . . . acknowledge his concern. Perhaps we'll speak another time."

"Are you sure, miss?" The poor maid looked as if she was already dreading the message she'd have to relate.

"Quite."

Madelyn waited for Jenny to leave, then tried to quietly shut the door, but Priscilla stopped her short by jamming her foot inside before it could close.

"Wait!" Priscilla called out to the maid before turning back to Madelyn. "Are you mad? You barely escape from insulting him at his dinner party by running away from an invitation, you address him improperly in front of his guests, argue with him, and now you shun his request to see you? Have you lost your mind, child?"

Madelyn thought about it for a second. "I think so." Rubbing her temples, she moved to step around her stepmother.

"Where do you think you're going?" Priscilla

matched her stride. "You're to march straight to His Grace and beg his forgiveness."

"I certainly will not," she answered incredulously.

Priscilla came to an abrupt stop, one corner of her mouth pulling into a smirk. "And what of poor Charlotte? You would have her chances of winning Lord Tristan reduced by being so closely associated with an ungrateful, rude, bluestocking such as yourself?"

Madelyn looked at Charlotte, who sat, brows furrowed, struggling to straighten out the wrinkles in the list Priscilla had so carelessly thrown to the floor.

She sighed. Charlotte had harbored a school-girl's affection for Lord Tristan ever since that day the Greenes' carriage tipped over when their horse became spooked by an irate street vendor. His lordship had freed them from the twisted vehicle and even managed to settle their horse with expert hands and a bit of whispering. That was five years ago, and the girl's cap had been set for Lord Tristan ever since.

Charlotte was vulnerable and quiet—certainly not the sort of young lady Lord Tristan was known to consort with. He'd bring her gentle friend to tears in no time. And the coxcomb didn't deserve her tears. But Charlotte's mind couldn't be swayed. She fancied herself in love with him. This was a dream come true—a chance to win the man of her dreams. Her hero.

Madelyn couldn't force her friend to see the lecherous rake for who he truly was, but she knew she could do everything within her power to steer the wolf away. And she couldn't very well protect Charlotte if the duke sent her packing for her blatant impertinence.

Swallowing her pride like a swig of sour milk, she glanced at a smug-looking Priscilla. "I'll go. I'll . . . behave. But I will not beg if he chooses to send me home."

"Now, that's a good girl," Priscilla chirped, patting her on the hand. She leaned in, whispering, "We must get you out of this horrid brown frock you chose to wear and get you into something more . . . appealing. Something of mine, perhaps."

"But everything of yours is too small," Madelyn pointed out, following her stepmother as she waltzed toward the dressing room.

Turning, Priscilla smiled like a hungry cat. "Exactly."

"Why did I listen to that woman and not bring my shawl?" Madelyn asked no one in particular.

She hugged her arms around herself, following Jenny to the orangery by way of a narrow brick path bordered on both sides with low hedges.

A sudden burst of wind took Madelyn by surprise. She gasped as the cold air shot straight through the thin, peach-colored jaconet dress. Jenny looked over her shoulder, giving her a sympathetic smile.

Shivering, Madelyn looked down at the dress she had unwillingly borrowed from Priscilla. She tried to quell the wicked feeling of being a juicy morsel about to wander into the woods, all to lure a wolf for her avaricious stepmother.

Indeed, it would have been fitting if she had brought a shawl, Madelyn mused. Or a cape. A nice red one, with a hood.

Her arms covered with goose pimples, they rounded a bend and finally reached the orangery, which Madelyn noted was four times as big as their home in Chelsea. They stepped inside the south facing building and were instantly enveloped with warmth and the cheery scent of orange blossoms.

"My word," she remarked in awe as Jenny led her down a tiled path in the middle of orange and lemon trees. "It's a veritable forest. There must be four hundred of them."

"Three hundred and seventy-seven to be exact," came a husky feminine voice ahead. A beautiful woman, closer to the duke's age than Madelyn's, stepped out from behind a silk screen and smiled warmly at Madelyn. Her hair was glossy black just like the duke, but her round, blue eyes revealed a sweet softness, unlike her eldest brother's frosty azure.

"Lady Rosalind." Madelyn curtsied.

"Miss Haywood," Lady Rosalind returned. "Come quickly. Let us sit and talk by the fountain." Dismissing Jenny, she linked her arm with Madelyn's and walked around the silk-covered screen used to separate a seating area from the rest of the large room. On the other side sat a pair of ornate garden chairs situated next to a fountain with two opposite-facing fish at its center.

With care for her bottom, Madelyn took a seat, instantly feeling the fabric tighten around her chest. She folded her hands demurely in her lap, all the while fretting whether the seam under her bust would hold out. With her luck, her dress would bust open the very moment Mr. Devine—no, *His Grace*—walked into the room.

"Tea?" Lady Rosalind gestured to the tea tray set out on a nearby table.

"No, thank you," Madelyn replied. Her throat was dry, but her stomach was doing strange flip-flops at the prospect of encountering the duke at any minute.

"I can see you're nervous, and I don't blame you, or any of the ladies for that matter. My oldest brother isn't the sort of man who inspires one to feel at ease. And, naturally, as all of you are trying to impress him for Tristan's sake, I thought, since your interview was first, I'd talk with you before my brother joins us."

"I don't understand," Madelyn said, perplexed. She had harbored the thought her interview was first so she could be either properly chastised or eliminated because of that morning's event, but Lady Rosalind seemed unaware of her recent social blunders.

"You see," Lady Rosalind replied, looking over her shoulder as if making sure no one was near, "my brother . . . he can appear rather cold and . . . arrogant. Please, do not be led by your first impression."

Do not, indeed. In the garden Madelyn believed *Gabriel Devine* to be an agreeable man equipped with a sincere concern for her welfare. The only fault in his possession at the time was that he oft stood too close—though even that wasn't so horrible. But she'd been wrong. Now she lumped him together with all the other pompous aristocrats of her acquaintance.

"It might help you to know . . . " Lady Rosalind paused with apparent indecision about her thread of conversation. "Underneath that facade, I believe, a heart in need of—" She stopped, shaking her head sadly, tenderness for her brother heavy in her gaze. "I suppose it isn't at all fair of me to speak of his private feelings. However, I do feel pressed to explain his reserved nature in hopes to forestall any imagined slights by his lack of presence for the next two weeks. Other than this interview, one might never lay eyes on him again until the night of the ball."

"Forgive me, my lady, but I fear your advice has come too late." Madelyn sighed softly. Perhaps the duke would hesitate about sending her away if she explained the situation to his friendly sister first, winning her compassion. She took a deep breath and continued. "I met His Grace back in London at the dinner party."

"Oh yes," Lady Rosalind replied, nodding. "I remember. My brother spotted you from his study." She leaned in, her exotic eyes showing keen interest. "He went after you, didn't he?"

"Yes, well, basically. But I . . . I don't believe *I* made a good first impression."

"Pish! My brother spied you in the garden, Miss Haywood, and insisted I invite you—unaware that I already had."

"Really?" Madelyn asked, her curiosity stirred.

Lady Rosalind nodded. "To be sure I have a mind to think—" She stopped and shook her head, "Nevertheless, I'm sure whatever you did was overlooked. You were invited beside the point."

"I accidentally threw a lemon at him," Madelyn blurted.

Lady Rosalind's mouth fell open. "You didn't!"

"Yes, knocked him square in the forehead, I'm afraid. But I didn't know it was him and he didn't bother to ex—"

"That's what the mark on his forehead is from? He told me . . . oh dear." The look of surprise in her eyes was quickly replaced with a flicker of anger. "He didn't try . . . that is to say . . . there weren't any untoward advances, were there?"

Madelyn shook her head. "It was dark. I didn't know who it was. So you see—"

"Oh my." And with that, Lady Rosalind leaned back in her seat, her dark head thrown back as laughter overtook her. "Y-You, goodness—" She tried to speak but fits of giggles kept bursting forth. "I can't tell you how many times . . . knocked some sense into him, I hope." Her laughter crumbled away and she wiped the tears from her eyes with the trim on her gloves. "Thank you. Oh, you are precious."

Madelyn didn't know what sort of reaction to expect from the duke's sister, but hysterical laughter was definitely not one of them.

"Good afternoon, Miss Haywood." The duke's deep, rich voice broke in as he walked around the screen.

Lady Rosalind cleared her throat, pulling herself together with surprising quickness.

The sunlight shining through the floor-to-ceiling glass walls made the duke's obsidian hair positively gleam. He was dressed impeccably in a dark blue jacket and matching waistcoat, his snow white cravat tied in a gentle cascade. The dark, almost exotically handsome man radiated affluence, confidence, and effortless charm. He looked precisely like someone who would, by no means, *ever* find someone like *her* appealing.

Suddenly overwhelmed with a nagging inadequacy, Madelyn shifted in her ill-fitted gown. Whoever thought she'd do well as a candidate for the bride of Devine was sorely mistaken.

The duke pointed to a nearby lemon tree without removing his ice-blue gaze from her. "I trust you are unarmed?"

Madelyn nodded, ignoring his deliberate taunt.

Lady Rosalind made a choking sound at the same time. Her lips were pressed together tightly and her eyes shut as if she was severely concentrating on not laughing.

"Rosalind," the duke said, glaring down at his sister with one dark eyebrow raised. "The event sheets."

She cleared her throat delicately. "We discussed this earlier and decided I'm handing them out after dinner."

"I would like them now. Would you ask Miss Sparrow to retrieve them?"

"I dismissed her, just." Her eyes narrowed. "She must have passed you on your way in—"

"Then please, see to it yourself. I'd like to speak with Miss Haywood alone."

Lady Rosalind's gaze swung from her brother to Madelyn and back again. "You'd like me to leave you both alone?"

"Yes."

"Here?"

A muscle in his cheek twitched. "Would you have me state the obvious?"

Lady Rosalind worked her jaw. "You are aware of how improper this is. You risk jeopardizing her reputation, Gabriel. We have promised the chaperones the strictest propriety."

"Miss Haywood is certainly safe with me," he intoned, looking down at his sister like he was ready to toss her out himself. "And no one needs to know."

"Still—"

"Leave."

"I think—"

"Now."

Lady Rosalind stood, giving Madelyn an apologetic smile. "Miss Haywood, if you would, please call me Rosalind. You are simply delightful. Oh! I almost forgot. I'd like to commission your most desired services. I'd fancy you to present each female guest with her framed silhouette before the night of the ball. Your accuracy is stunning."

Madelyn returned her smile, pleased at how friendly and pleasant the duke's sister turned out to be—so very unlike her brothers. "Of course," she said. "It would be my pleasure. And please, you must call me Madelyn."

The duke's sister nodded with a smile, giving Madelyn's arm a little squeeze as she passed. With that, she left them alone.

The room fell silent and the insufferable man continued to stand there, staring down at her. She looked everywhere but at him. One would think a duke would be aware of how impolite it was to stare. Her nose twitched as the alluring, woodsy scent of his shaving soap wafted through the air between them.

His dark presence was nearly overwhelming in the bright atmosphere of the orangery. The air suddenly felt stuffy, her dress too tight, the room too quiet. Just when she thought she couldn't take the silence any longer he spoke.

"There needn't be any animosity between you and me."

Madelyn took a breath to speak, but her mind was uncharacteristically blank. Being the sole object of his attention was unsettling. She shifted in her seat, one side of her tender bottom throbbing. Part of her wanted to crawl under her chair and cower, and another part wanted to stomp on his foot for being such a rascal. Both actions, she decided, were childish, so she sat there, clasping her hands tightly in her lap, hoping her eyes wouldn't betray her thoughts.

"I will speak of this now and never again," he said. "That evening in London, I was only thinking of averting your initial embarrassment. I realize now that I was only delaying it."

Her brow furrowed. "I don't understand."

"Come, Miss Haywood. Surely you recall. You did not know who I was. You spoke of me with such venom, such disgust. You called me . . . arrogant and . . . what was the other?"

Cork-brained. "I don't recall," she muttered, shrugging innocently.

"In any case," his eyes sized her up, contradicting his next words, "the gentleman in me couldn't bear your mortification should you realize at that moment the very man you expressed such abhorrence for was, in fact, standing before you."

"I can assure you," Madelyn expressed calmly, "embarrassment is something I would have preferred to suffer in front of only you instead of a score of people."

"Your point is made." He bowed his head slightly.

Pulling her lips together thoughtfully, she supposed that was about as close to an apology as she'd ever receive.

Flipping the tails of his coat out of the way, he occupied his sister's empty seat. Leaning back, he entwined his long fingers like a basket across his flat stomach, his lean-muscled legs stretched out before him. He looked her square in the eye and her heart felt like it jumped to her throat. Here comes the elimination, she thought.

"I believe you," he said.

"You believe what?"

"You do not want any part of this," he stated. "And I certainly did not want you to be either. But by some scrap of mercifulness on my part, here you are. Certainly not as attractive as the others and glaringly unfit, but somehow I find you deserve a chance."

His bold snobbery almost made her laugh. "I thought—"

"You thought you were summoned here to be eliminated," he finished for her.

"Am I, Your Grace?"

Gabriel thought the girl looked ready to scream . . . or cry. Either one, he didn't like the way she so obviously felt ill at ease in his presence. Inwardly, he told himself it was a mistake, to trust this one, but in truth he did believe the chit. Certainly, he wouldn't absolve her person of any possible future transgression, but hell, after what happened today at the pond . . . only an imbecile would doubt her motive. Leave it to his sister to pick the one woman who wanted nothing to do with Tristan.

He studied her until she squirmed in her seat, which he knew must be painful considering recent events. "No, you're not eliminated." A knowing smile played upon his lips. "You'll not escape that easily."

"Escape? I have no idea what you're talking about," she answered, her coral-colored lips pursing in a charmingly thoughtful manner.

"No? You informed me in London that you do not wish to marry a Devine. Your incident this morning in the pond only proved to me how desperately you want out."

"I will not pretend to misunderstand, but I didn't jump into the pond in the hopes to be eliminated. I tripped. I had been stung by a bee."

"Yes, you had said as much."

Her suspicious gaze studied his face as she worked something over in her mind. Gabriel tried to remain cool, detached, to hide his grin, but failed miserably. "Who told you where I was stung?" she blurted out, accusation flaring in her eyes.

"The maid."

"I asked her not to tell anyone."

"Don't blame the poor girl. She's paid to listen to me, not you. I asked. I was told. Which reminds me." He reached into his pocket and pulled out a key. "Press this to your . . . affected area. It should take away the swelling and numb the pain."

"A key?" She blushed prettily. "You're jesting?"

"Quite serious, I'm afraid." He shrugged. "My grandmother insisted it worked when I was a child. Though I've never managed to be stung on . . . on such a delicate area." He held it out to her. "It's worth a try."

Madelyn eyed his offering skeptically. It might work, she mused. But then again she'd be shamefully thinking of him while pressing it to her bottom in the privacy of her room. Or worse, she'd be thinking of *him* thinking of *her* pressing it to her bottom in the privacy of her room. "No, thank you. I'll suffer in silence."

He shrugged again, dropping it back into his pocket. "Do you know, Miss Haywood, you have something none of the other ladies possess."

"Pray, what is that?"

"My attention." Gabriel felt a surge of satisfaction at the surprise in her gaze. "You are an enigma to me. Here in your hands lies the opportunity to marry far above your station. A marriage that would not only offer you all the comforts of life and social acceptance imaginable, but a marriage to a young, handsome . . . " He paused, withholding the word immature. " . . . well-connected man."

"And a man who clearly doesn't have the capacity to cherish a woman's heart. At least not yet anyway."

"Why do you run?"

"I told you," she said. "I do not wish to marry."

"At all?"

She kept her silence, dropping her uneasy gaze to her lap. "One might propose the same question to you. You're still young, a duke no less. Why do you shun marriage, shirk your responsibilities, and let them fall to your brother?"

"No one will ever accuse you of holding your tongue," he drawled, his eyes dropping to her mouth. He allowed his gaze to linger there only until he felt a surprising twinge of desire. He then focused on her round, brown eyes and realized the action did nothing to dissolve the feeling.

"Perhaps I have not a woman of my acquaintance who can hold my attention longer than a day," he continued, a bit too sharply. "Perhaps my requirement of perfection in a woman is so high that it is unfeasible to imagine she even exists. Or, perhaps it is only that I would not enjoy surrendering my mistress." At the stunned look on her face, he couldn't bear to taunt her any longer. "I'm teasing, Miss Haywood. You needn't look so chagrined."

"You misinterpret my thoughts, Your Grace. Why would I care about your mistress or *mistresses*? I only returned the same question asked of me. I certainly haven't a care for your personal matters." She looked him in the eye. "After all, I'm not here to win your affections."

Gabriel ignored a twinge of annoyance at her response. "I see we understand one another. You and all the others reside within these walls for the single purpose of competing for my brother. Your presence means little else."

"That's perfectly plain. There's no reason for you to explain."

"After today, one would be hard pressed to set eyes on me for the next two weeks."

She surprised him with a bright smile. "Whyever would you condescend?"

"Exactly." He shifted in his seat.

"I imagine you have many important tasks to attend. Duties to uphold. Why, you might even see fit to leave." She smiled sweetly, a blasted dimple creasing in her cheek.

"Quite right." He rubbed his chin distractedly. "It is not as if *I* am looking for a bride, of course."

"Of course," she echoed, looking more at ease every passing second.

So then why was he feeling steadily more vexed?

Damn it all, she really was quite pretty, Gabriel thought, while watching her pretend to be comfortable. Her burgundy hair was pulled into a loose topknot, and he found himself wondering how in the world the maid managed to tame all her glorious red curls into such simple elegance. She sighed, bringing his attention to her bosom. There, her skin was pinkish, flushed. He couldn't help but notice that her breasts, again, nearly burst over the square neckline. The gown was obviously too small, and he wondered why the baroness would choose to stuff her curvy ward in such a gown. Perhaps to attract Tristan's attention. Miss Haywood might not fancy herself a bride, but that said nothing of her stepmother's aspirations.

He cleared his throat in an attempt to clear his head. "I must warn you of two things, Miss Haywood. First, I expect as little trouble from you as possible from this moment on."

"I'm afraid I have to disappoint you once again. Misfortune follows me everywhere."

"And when was that?"

"When was what?" she asked, blinking.

"When did you feel you disappointed me?"

She hesitated, looking at him like he was crazy for not understanding what she meant. "In London, and this morning."

"You haven't disappointed me at all. Intrigued me, quite. Disappointed me, certainly not." Her gaze was so clear, he felt if he stared at her long enough she just might be able to see his soul. He stood, not trusting himself any longer. Hang her interview; he had to get out of this room.

"What is my second warning?" she asked.

He ran a slow hand through his hair, concentrating on maintaining his distance when all he really wanted to do was cross the space between them and grab her up by the shoulders. The funny thing was, he couldn't be sure what he'd do with her when he got ahold of her. Would he haul her to her feet and scoot the impertinent miss out the door, or would he hold her lush body against his own and make love to her with his mouth? The latter, of course, startled the hell out of him. He was accustomed to maintaining a certain level of passionate constraint, and the things he found himself thinking about lately . . .

Using a finger to loosen his constricting cravat from its stranglehold on his neck, he cleared his throat. "My second word of caution, Miss Haywood . . . I am unusually capable of persuading others to alter their opinions."

"It sounds as if your warning is a disguised threat."

"Choose whichever inspires you to behave."

Footsteps echoed in the distance, approaching quickly.

"I've returned," Lady Rosalind called out, rounding the screen. "I brought the sheets listing the planned events for the entire fortnight and I . . . " Her voice trailed off as she glanced at Madelyn. "Are you all right, Madelyn? You're as pink as a kitten's nose."

"Yes, quite," Madelyn answered, her voice small.

"She's fine," Gabriel snapped. Strange, but he hadn't heard his sister open the door.

"Well, I for one don't believe you." She fanned

herself with the thin stack of papers in her grasp. "Dreadfully stuffy in here, it is. I think we should cut our meeting a little short, don't you agree?" She looked to her brother.

"Of course, if Miss Haywood is unwell . . . "

And then his sister nearly yanked the young lady to her feet. "I'll walk back with you." After she ushered a flushed Miss Haywood in the direction of the door, she turned to glare at her brother over her shoulder. "The poor thing," she said softly. "What did you do to her?" She didn't wait for an answer and stalked away, catching up to their guest.

"What have I done to her?" Gabriel muttered to himself as he crossed the room to crank open a window. Cool air washed over his skin. "What the devil did she do to me?"

Chapter 5

Four days later Madelyn was forced to admit that the Duke of Wolverest was a man of his word. Truly, she hadn't caught a glimpse of him since the abrupt conclusion of her interview. The man had seemingly dissolved into a mist quite like the ever present haze that perpetually clung to the various domes and chimney stacks of his castle. And like the mist, the duke's brooding existence was always sensed by her, always considered.

She thought, or hoped, that perhaps the deceiver had simply left, that maybe he went to a hunting lodge miles and miles away. Sometimes she thought he might have gone to London to hunt down an actress or an opera singer. Mostly though, she thought that she shouldn't be thinking about him so much.

And what was it again he had said in the orangery? Oh yes, his intriguing statement that implied he had thought it necessary to give up a mistress for a wife. Could he have meant that? Or had she misconstrued his words? Well, she did know one thing: she really shouldn't care.

With black paper and scissors in hand, Madelyn reflected on this as she stood in her bedchamber studying Charlotte's profile. Her impatient friend sat in a Hepplewhite chair before one of the tall windows overlooking the topiary garden and the great expanse of the south lawn beyond.

"Are you almost done?" Charlotte asked, throwing an anxious glance toward the window. "The archery lesson is to begin in nearly five minutes. We'll be late."

"One more minute, now shush," Madelyn replied, her concentrated gaze bouncing from paper to profile as she busily snipped her friend's silhouette.

"Madelyn," Charlotte pleaded. "You promised this wouldn't take long. I've a mind to think you're doing this on purpose."

"Oh, for heaven's sake! I'm not keeping you from Lord Tristan," Madelyn insisted, continuing to concentrate on her work.

"See! You knew exactly what I was thinking. You *are* trying to keep me from him, admit it."

"Don't be silly, Lottie. Besides, the ever-courteous Lord Tristan will surely wait for you."

"Do you know," Charlotte said quietly, "I find it rather unfair none of the other girls like him as much as I do yet he awards them more attention."

Madelyn gave a disbelieving huff of laughter. "That's not true."

"Oh, it certainly is! When we were on our way to the picnic yesterday and we encountered that old footbridge with a rotted plank . . . he offered a hand of support to each of them in turn but failed to assist me."

"You are forgetting that you and I used our own good sense and simply stepped over the last board." Madelyn made a final snip. "Certainly, had you fretted like a pea goose, he'd have aided you across as well."

Her spine straight with indignation, Charlotte hesitated, then nodded stiffly. Clearly, she was loath to relinquish the imagined slight.

"There, 'tis finished," Madelyn said, holding up the profile of her friend seated in the elegant chair. "After I've finished the rest of the silhouettes, Lady Rosalind claims she'll have them all framed."

The bedchamber door opened behind Madelyn. She turned to see Priscilla sweep into the room, tugging on lace gloves.

"Still cutting pictures, Madelyn?" Priscilla shook her head in disdain. Her stepmother was obviously still a bit irked with her abbreviated explanation of her initial run-in with the duke. But if anything, Priscilla was ever hopeful the interlude put her ward a step closer to marital entrapment.

"The other girls have already begun to assemble," Priscilla said with an expectant look. "'Tis not so wise to disregard the Devines' schedule. As I recollect, were you not late in coming to the picnic yesterday afternoon?"

"That was no fault of my own," Madelyn answered, returning her scissors to its case. "I explained that to you yesterday."

"Nonsense! Couldn't find your shoes?" She clucked her tongue. "Come now, you can produce a better excuse."

"Someone hid all of my shoes."

"That's ridiculous!"

"I agree!" Madelyn cried out. "I drank the posset left out on the table with a note from the house-keeper advising me to drink up, as it would relieve any lingering swelling from the sting. Strong stuff, that was. I fell asleep within an instant. When I awoke—*poof*—my shoes were missing. If it wasn't for Jenny happening upon them in a vacant room down the hall, I'd be barefoot right now."

"Well, you shouldn't have wasted time looking for them and simply borrowed a pair from me."

"They wouldn't have fit. Just like every borrowed—"

"Pardon," Charlotte exclaimed. "But it seems we'll be late for the archery lesson as well."

Priscilla gave Charlotte a squinty look before she turned back into the hall. "Come, girls. We'll fetch Mrs. Greene and walk you both down on our way to tea with the other chaperones."

Charlotte immediately rose to follow the baron-ess, but hesitated after realizing Madelyn hadn't joined them.

"You *are* coming?" her friend asked, worry evident in her gaze. "I shan't survive without you there. No spectacles, you know. I'm very likely to kill someone by mistake without you there to guide me."

"True. Very true." Madelyn looked about the floor, noting the black slivers of paper dotting the cream and blue rug. "Go on ahead. I'll tidy up a bit first. *Don't* aim at anything until I get there."

"Please, hurry along," Charlotte said with a beseeching glance, then turned to leave, shutting the door quietly behind her.

Madelyn sunk down to her knees to pluck the scraps from the rug. Using one hand like a bowl, she collected the bits of paper.

There was a clicking sound at the door. Assuming it was an anxious Charlotte, she didn't bother turning around when she called out, "Almost done." She stood, walked over to a tray set on a nearby table and dusted the bits onto a napkin.

Bending to tighten the laces of her half-boots, she plucked her pelisse off a chair, then hurried over to the door and turned the handle. The door wouldn't open. She jiggled the handle and jerked with all her strength for a second time, but it remained firmly shut. Someone had locked her in her room.

And the only person who had a key was her stepmother. But why would Priscilla lock her in her room?

Her brows knitted together, Madelyn went to the door of their connecting dressing room, thinking to leave through her stepmother's chamber. She reached for the handle and groaned in frustration. It wouldn't budge either.

She sighed, slumping against the wall. What an odd predicament she found herself in. She had quite unexpectedly become imprisoned—for a short while anyway. For a moment she contemplated shouting at the top of her lungs, but the inner castle walls were much too thick. No one could possibly hear her screams. Besides, there was no one *to* hear her. The chaperones were meeting with Lady Rosalind for tea in her salon, and no one else would be returning to their rooms until after the archery lesson. And who knew how long that could be?

Pushing off of the wall, she strolled back into her room. In truth, she wouldn't have minded the solitude, the brief respite from the nausea brought on by Lord Tristan's practiced sincerity and his gaggle of silly admirers . . . and Charlotte could surely handle the other girls.

But not Lord Tristan. All he'd have to do is give Lottie a lopsided grin and a crook of his finger and her friend would go wherever he led. The man presented a wicked assortment of dangers. No, she couldn't leave Charlotte alone in that man's company for a second.

Madelyn's fingertips tapped at her chin while she weighed her options. She could simply sit here, like some cow-eyed fairy-tale princess, and await someone to rescue her from the castle tower or . . . or . . . her fingers stilled as her gaze swung to the tall windows. A breath of excitement whispered within her breast. Would she dare?

A seed of an idea blooming in her eye, she strode over to her bed. Flipping the coverlet out of her way, she tugged at the underlying linen sheets. Her room was only on the second floor. And she certainly wasn't so silly as to be afraid of heights.

* * *

Yorkshire was incomparable, Gabriel thought as he sauntered through the topiary garden upon returning from surveying his grounds. Oh, there were many who found the vacant moors desolate and dull. It had none of the conveniences of London, nor the splendor of Bath, but it was here that he played as a child, well before the responsibility of being the heir to a dukedom took over his choices. And well before the task of acting "father" to an impish, young Tristan took over his life.

When he returned to Wolverest from a tedious session of Parliament, the serenity and familiarity of the land quieted his mind, assured his being. But what kept him coming back, what kept him from retiring to one of his other numerous properties instead, was this high country's hidden treasures.

Indeed, Gabriel knew it wasn't all just empty green fields of moorland grass for miles around. Tucked within the wide landscapes of these uplands was an unpredictability that a less observant person might never be aware of. There were waterfalls concealed in swaths of wilderness, rocky stream beds rambling in deep valleys, and . . . knotted sheets?

"What . . . in . . . God's . . . name?" Gabriel blinked. And blinked again. No, it wasn't a trick of his imagination. Knotted sheets *were* being lowered out of a second floor window of his castle. Breaking into a sprint, he dashed down a row of hedges trimmed into the shapes of various waterfowl and stopped just beneath the window.

A dark green pelisse flew from the open window, sailed down and slapped him in the face. He removed the offending fabric, which he noted possessed an alluringly feminine scent of rose and mint, and tossed it over a hedge.

A stocking enclosed leg swung over the sill, followed by the other, both feet successfully finding a foothold in the old stone tower. Astonished, Gabriel's sharp gaze settled on familiar red tresses with thick, wild curls escaping the top bun. His jaw tightened in response. *What the bloody hell was she doing now?*

He took two steps forward in an effort to be in the most beneficial position should his little "deserter" fall.

To his surprise, Miss Haywood continued to unerringly shimmy her way down the wall, using the knotted sheet as support. As he admired her agility, he realized the back hem of her pale yellow dress had been joined with the front, then yanked up from the bottom to her waist, affording her the benefits of makeshift breeches . . . and insurmountable modesty, considering the luscious view a fluttering skirt above his head would have afforded him.

About the time her booted feet were at his eye level, the toes of her right foot searched in vain for a proper foothold. It must be difficult, he mused, to be able to see down over the swell of a gathered skirt. He grinned as her toes pointed left and right, scraping back and forth against the stone as they hunted for a niche in the wall.

She let forth a mild curse, then, without further warning, pushed off from the wall with her other foot. Apparently, Miss Haywood was giving herself ample room in preparation to jump the rest of the way down. He had only half of a second to react, bracing his legs wide apart.

She jumped directly into him, her back colliding with his chest. His arms reflexively wrapped around her middle as the two of them flew backward onto the lawn, his body cushioning her fall.

Letting out a shriek, she spun within his hold, but remained sprawled atop him—her thighs straddling his hips, her breasts pressed tightly to his chest, her nose an inch above his own.

"Good Lord! What are you doing here?" she asked.

"Apparently, I'm saving you from a broken ankle . . . to the detriment of my health," he said with a grunt, unable to ignore how well she cradled the mold of his body. Reflexively, he slid his hands up and then back down the span of her back. She squirmed, unknowingly nestling him farther within her thighs. His breath hitched.

"Are you all right?" she asked with sincere concern.

One corner of his mouth lifted into a grin as he realized she was, as of yet, utterly oblivious to their erotic position. Unable to trust himself, Gabriel reluctantly loosened his hold, then released it, dropping his hands to his sides. "I'm fine, I believe. You?"

She nodded. Surprising him, her gaze warmed, traveling down to his mouth. An urge ignited within him to lift his chin and take possession of her mouth, her lips. But he suspected he wouldn't be able to stop there.

"May I ask what you were trying to do?" he asked instead, the tone of his voice just above a throaty growl.

"The . . . ah . . . archery lesson," she said softly. "It's starting. I—I was late and my stepmother must have accidentally locked me in my room."

He glanced at the dangling sheet. "You must have *really* wanted to go."

His comment brought her gaze back up to connect with his. Pressing his lips together, he fought valiantly to keep from laughing. But in the end he couldn't keep a low chuckle from rumbling in his chest. The movement of his mirth made her entire upper body bounce up and down.

Her face burned red with a feverish blush as she only then noticed their wicked position. "Unhand me!"

"Miss Haywood, if you paid any attention at all," he said, a smile softening his words, "you would have noticed long ago that there is nothing keeping you from getting off of me."

She glanced down, realizing with a visual start that his arms, indeed, remained at his sides. She rolled away, scrambling up to stand.

"Aren't you going to thank me?" Gabriel asked, raising up to lean back on his elbows. Something shifted inside him, his heart felt lighter and he realized he no longer sounded like himself. By God, he was actually teasing the woman. Again.

Patting at her hair, she raised her chin to a haughty angle. "For what?"

"Saving you."

"I'd sooner marry your brother."

"Promises, promises," he mumbled.

With a loud sigh she presented her back to him and marched away.

"You've forgotten something," Gabriel called out.

She turned back like an angry whip. "What have I forgotten?" Not waiting for his answer, her eyes flew to the hedge where he had thrown her pelisse. She collected it, then stomped off again.

"That's not what you've forgotten," he said, crossing his ankles and smiling like a scoundrel.

She stopped, turning to face him with an annoyed glance. "Yes?" she asked, clearly vexed. "Are you going to tell me or is this some sort of game and I should guess?"

He cleared his throat, blinking slowly. "Your skirt."

After a small gasp, she looked down at the knot of fabric pinned to her waist and her exposed stocking-enclosed calves. Hurriedly, she released the pins, allowing the skirts to fall into the proper place.

For a moment Gabriel regretted pointing out her predicament so boldly. Good Lord, if she started to cry, he didn't know what the hell he'd do. But then she looked at him, and instead of embarrassment, irritation, or a pout—real or practiced—her mouth wobbled with a suppressed bubble of laughter. Any other woman would have burst into tears or swooned with mortification.

"Well, thank you," she mumbled. Presenting her back to him, she walked on stiffly, swinging her coat at her side as she tried to pretend nothing out of the ordinary had just happened.

Gabriel let out an airy whistle as he observed the sway of her hips while she made her way up a far hill to join the assembled group of women. The memory of the unexpected spark of heat forming between their bodies as she lay sprawled atop him would surely plague him for the remainder of the day and into the depths of the night. But it was nothing he couldn't manage to restrain. His willpower was strong.

Frustrated, he looked away from the sight of her, choosing instead to focus on the knotted sheets swaying in the breeze. Plenty of women had "thrown" themselves at him for years. Some he had welcomed with open arms—others, the naive innocents, he gently declined. But no woman had ever dropped out of a window into his arms, knocking the very air from his lungs and forcing him to acknowledge an attraction he'd rather ignore. He'd never seen anything like Miss Haywood in his life. He'd never felt so unprepared.

He shook his head. Foolish woman, nearly got herself killed. And all for an archery lesson? It didn't make any sense. She told him herself she had no interest in marrying into his family, then she went and risked her life—her bones at the very least—to make certain she got to attend a function with Tristan? Simply illogical. Perhaps he was wrong to believe in her disinterest. He rubbed his chin in thought. Perhaps he would keep a closer eye on Miss Haywood. Starting right now.

He stood and brushed himself off. Glancing over his shoulder, he caught one more glance of her retreating form before she crested a hill and slipped out of his line of vision. Illogical and dangerously intriguing. He must keep his distance, he told himself, and yet find a way to observe her every move at the same time. He could do it. All he needed was determination, discipline, and . . . a lot of brandy.

Chapter 6

"**A**rming oneself with bow and arrow when one's rivals are poised so temptingly across the lawn is not the wisest of exercises," Charlotte announced. Sulking, she dropped down in one of the chairs beneath a sun canopy.

Returning from the refreshment table, Madelyn handed her friend a glass of lemonade. "That is, if you chose to wear your spectacles. Without them, I wager you'd miss your intended female competitors and tragically pierce the heart of his lordship instead."

Charlotte accepted the drink with a distracted thank-you. Her envious gaze was fastened at a point across the lawn where Harriet Beauchamp was currently standing on tiptoe, whispering into Lord Tristan's ear.

He wore the flamboyant costume of his Archery Society: a dark green frock coat and cape, white shirt, cravat and breeches, and a rounded hat adorned with a plump white ostrich plume. He was dressed to impress, Madelyn surmised, and from the numerous admiring glances—with the exception of herself—he was doing a smashing job.

Bernadette Fairbourne, her cupid's bow mouth pursed in an insistent pout, waited impatiently for his assistance, while her sister Belinda stood with arms crossed over her chest, glaring at Harriet, who shot answering daggers out of her eyes. Madelyn was instantly reminded of a picture in a book she once saw of a pack of lionesses, snarling at one another over the carcass of a felled gazelle.

Laura Ellis and Julienne Campbell huddled together some distance behind them, giggling into their gloved hands while sneaking glances at the duke—the same man Madelyn had landed on an hour ago. Presenting a handsome picture, he sat upon a marvelous black stallion on a far hill, watching them all for the past fifteen minutes as his horse stamped impatiently at the soft ground.

"Look how they all hover around him!" Charlotte cried out, effectively pulling Madelyn's attention back to Lord Tristan. "They've not a stitch of modesty between them. So flirty, so brazen. Can you believe it, Maddie?"

"Frankly, yes," Madelyn responded matter-of-factly. "And I dare say, he's rather enjoying their artful maneuvering . . . " Her voice trailed away when, out of the corner of her eye, she saw the duke urge his mount into a trot. Her heartbeat skittered as he turned toward the sun canopy. She'd managed to avoid him earlier while she and Charlotte attempted to try their luck aiming for the targets, and now fretted that he was coming over to speak with her.

"I mean really, how *do* they expect the man to

breathe?" Charlotte cut in, fairly slamming her glass atop the table. "Upon my word, his lordship must be annoyed beyond repair!"

"I rather believe he's in his element," Madelyn remarked with a wry smile. "Just look how he smiles, all lopsided and lazy. He drifts from lady to lady like a bee amid a cloud of honeysuckle." Making a stab at subtlety, she pretended to look at a copse of trees to her right. The duke had disappeared.

"You're right," Charlotte said dismally. "Lord Tristan has been more than attentive to everyone's archery form but mine."

"Yes, I noticed that as well. But you must consider he responds well to their boldness. You, dear, have no reason to feel lacking. Your sense of discretion is charming—a credit the right man will undoubtedly appreciate. They have only their shamelessness to recommend them."

Charlotte sighed, her face an image of pure dejection. "I mustn't blame them," she said, still staring across the lawn. "'Tis not their fault but my own. I fear I cannot help the fact that he finds me so very, very dull."

"Nonsense," Madelyn answered, hating the fact her friend was already falling into the depths of self-pity, and this only their fifth day at Wolverest. "If you whimpered at his heels for attention like a neglected hound, Lord Tristan would be fawning over you as well. The Devine men simply prefer forward women. That *you* should like such a man fairly rattles my sensibilities."

The jangle of a harness and movement in the corner of her eye turned Madelyn's head. The duke's horse was being led to the stable by a groomsman, the duke now nowhere to be seen. *And just why should I care to notice?* Looking down, she adjusted the laces of her protective gloves with sharp tugs. "I say, I don't know where His Grace went off to, but if he plans on coming anywhere near me, I'll shoot him in the foot . . . providing I have my bow and arrow in hand."

"I find that exceedingly improbable, even at close range."

Madelyn turned to see the Duke of Wolverest, shockingly minus his coat. He leaned his back against the thick trunk of a nearby oak tree, his discarded coat resting on a low branch. Sunlight filtered through the leaves above, rendering his tousled, raven-black hair dappled in shades of light and shadow. His white shirtsleeves were rolled up to just above his elbows, and his tanned hands rested on his lean hips. He looked windblown and alluringly refreshed, like he only just returned from a vigorous ride.

Reluctantly, Madelyn acknowledged the surge of anticipation that made her pulse quicken, her breath catch from being the focus of his attention. She was attracted to this handsome, sleek, virile man—had suspected so ever since their first encounter. She'd be an idiot not to admit so to herself. But that didn't mean she should act upon her attraction. Surely he couldn't be the only man in England who could make her flesh grow peculiarly warm under his gaze. Besides, he was a Devine. A name famously associated with shattered hearts for as long as she could remember. It was even reputed his own dear mother died of a broken heart.

Her gaze pulled to his snug black breeches as he bent one knee to rest his booted foot against the tree trunk. She wondered how much he had heard of her and Charlotte's conversation.

"How long have you been standing there?"

"Just." He crossed his lean-muscled arms over his chest. "Miss Greene, if I may offer you a little advice . . . "

Wide-eyed, Charlotte turned in her seat at the sound of the duke addressing her, so caught up was she in studying Lord Tristan's interaction with the other ladies. "Y-Yes?" she fairly squeaked.

"Timidity is beneath his detection. If you want to gain his notice, you'll have to step up to the challenge."

She nodded, her lashes fluttering in apparent astonishment at his casualness. "Ah . . . thank you."

He inclined his head, his intent blue gaze swinging back to Madelyn.

As she returned his stare, she wondered why he chose to grace them with his noble presence after claiming he'd do otherwise in the orangery. Perhaps he joined their party to plague her with further mortification. Surely he must be aware that his presence here only reminded her of their encounter in the topiary garden the hour before.

"You were saying?" he prompted.

"Was I saying anything?" she rushed out, worrying if she'd spoken her thoughts out loud.

"As I remember, you were threatening to impale my foot," he stated, a spark of humor in his eyes.

"Oh. It was an empty threat, Your Grace. You needn't worry."

He laughed, flashing her a peek at straight white teeth. "I assure you, love, an arrow shot by your hand would never find its mark."

She straightened. "Is that so?"

He nodded his head slowly, smiling like a scoundrel as he reeled her in effortlessly. "You jerked the shot and your positioning is poor."

It wasn't at all surprising someone noticed her clumsy performance. But it was surprising that *he* noticed. "*You* were watching *me*?" she asked. "All these women here and you managed to stay focused on *my* poor archery poise? I must say, I find you quite talented."

He grinned. "Ladies have said as much in the past." Clearly he was left unscathed by her sarcasm.

"Yes, but were any of them true *ladies*," she muttered under her breath.

"Pardon?"

She blinked like an owl. "What?"

"I believe you said something."

"Hmm?" She smiled brightly.

He shot her a narrowed glance, his eyes vividly blue and vividly disbelieving.

She cleared her throat. "We were discussing my

shortcomings . . . " A topic she was well acquainted with.

"You close your eyes just before release," he said. "A dangerous flaw, to say the least."

Somehow, hearing *him* say she was flawed hurt. It was certainly a different reaction than when Priscilla or her aunt pointed it out. "And you are an expert?"

"I am a second-generation member of the Toxophilite Society."

The name of the archery society that the Prince Regent himself belonged to did little to impress Madelyn. She supposed the club was probably only created as an excuse to socialize and drink spirits to worrisome excess.

"And I belong to the Company of Scottish Archers," he added.

He just had to throw that in. Fine. So he might know what he was talking about.

He studied her for a moment, then pushed off the tree. "Would you care for a demonstration?"

She shrugged.

"That is, if you think your *sensibilities* shan't be rattled," he challenged with a playful grin.

So, he *had* been listening to their conversation . . . "Surely I can handle your tutoring, Your Grace."

"I doubt that," he murmured. Striding over to the canopy, he ducked under it and offered her his arm. "Miss Greene, if you'll excuse us?"

Charlotte nodded quickly. Madelyn wondered if her friend's eyeballs would ever return to normal size.

Hesitantly, Madelyn placed her hand on the duke's arm, instantly feeling the heat of his skin, even through the thickness of her glove. He escorted her toward Lord Tristan and his giggling gaggle of females and paused at one of the tables to retrieve a bow and the quiver full of arrows.

"Brother? Whatever inspired you to join us?" Lord Tristan approached, the white plume in his hat bobbing with each step. "Is the dear Miss Haywood in need of assistance?"

"Nice hat," the duke said over his shoulder, walking with Madelyn past the small crowd.

"Er . . . thank you," Lord Tristan returned, his tone clearly questioning his brother's sincerity.

Madelyn still on his arm, the duke spun on his heel, apparently remembering protocol. "Ladies," he said in general greeting to the group at large before bowing his head briefly.

A ruffling of fabric ensued as five young women sank into deep curtsies accompanied by a chorus of "Your Graces."

Turning, he directed Madelyn at a brisk pace down the row, past the last remaining target post, and through a copious group of birch trees.

Just where was he taking her? she wondered. All the targets were set on the very part of the lawn which they were walking away from. Surely he didn't mean to instruct her somewhere private. That would be exceedingly improper.

She glanced over her shoulder with concern. "Must we be so very far away?"

He looked down at her with an are-you-kiddingme expression. "The farther away you are from living beings, the safer I feel. I wouldn't want any unnecessary injuries dampening the festive mood."

She gasped, offended. "Don't be silly. I'm not that bad."

"I'm never silly. And yes you are."

"That's preposterous! Charlotte nearly speared the gardener . . . and he was twenty meters to the right!"

"Yes, but you must consider the fact Miss Greene failed to bring her spectacles. Had she wore them, I'm quite certain she'd have hit the bull's-eye every time."

"How did you know she wore spectacles?"

"Her interview."

"Oh." It was all she could mutter at the moment, her mind now busy with thoughts of the other girls' interviews. Had theirs been cut short as hers was? Had Rosalind been sent away as well? Did he fancy any of them for himself? That last unforeseen thought jolted her out her musings as quickly as if someone pinched her.

Looking about, she saw they had stopped just on the other side of the clump of birches. To her left, about fifteen meters away, sat another target completely blocked from view from the other guests by the collage of trees.

She turned, meeting his suddenly serious expression with a suspicious one of her own. "You must forgive my directness, but as I'm sure you are aware of the reputation of the Devine men, and seeing as how the chaperones are taking tea with your sister at the castle presently . . . d-do you mean to seduce me?"

A smile tugged at the corner of his mouth. He took a step closer, leaving only enough space for the tube of arrows between them, the bow being held at his side. A cool gust of wind sifted through them, sending his clean soapy scent and a hint of leather in her direction.

"I—I mean, we are rather separated from the rest of the group," she said, trembling a bit.

He tilted his head in an assessing manner, examining her with such a charming grin tugging at the corner of his mouth, she fought the urge to smile back and bask in his attention.

Good Lord, why will he not say something?

He leaned forward a touch, as if about to indulge her of a wicked secret. "Do you want me to?"

She threw a hand to her throat. "Of course not!"

"I thought I should inquire. You looked almost hopeful," he said, his eyes sparkling with mischief.

"I certainly did not!" She swallowed, secretly worrying that she *had* looked pitifully expectant. "You must have mistaken my concern for personal security for anticipation. Your reputation *is* rather tarnished."

Nodding like he'd made up his mind about just what sort of woman she was, he said, "Guilty by association, is it? Tell me what you've heard and I shall venture to enlighten you. Really, Miss Haywood, I've no ulterior motives where you are concerned."

"Humph. I've a mind to think it's all part of the Devine plan—to appear innocent and lure your victims in."

"If I were going to seduce you," he said quietly, "would I increase your odds of deflecting my advances by arming you with weapons?"

Blushing, she gave a short, soft laugh. "Well . . . no," she said, her embarrassment so strong her skin felt prickly.

Why in the world did she think, even for a second, this man would want to seduce her? A little nobody with little money, a small dowry, and even less in good looks. Of that she could have no doubt—Priscilla constantly reminded her that her curves bordered on too generous, her thick red hair too, well, red. Oh dear, what an idiot he must think her. She rummaged around her thoughts, looking for a way to change the subject. "I'm wondering . . . "

"Hmm?" He looked so handsome, gazing down at her expectantly.

The wind stirred the thick black locks curling around his collar, and his eyes matched the color of the sky today. She knew it was her imagination again, or some trick of his, but he had the appearance of . . . well, he almost looked as if . . . as if he enjoyed her company.

She smiled tightly, reminding herself not to fall again for his effortless charm. "At my interview, you said you'd stay away, and now here you are, standing in front of me." And shamefully too near, she added to herself.

"Indeed, but that was before . . . " He paused to

shake a lock of black hair out of his eyes with a toss of his head. "You see . . . I couldn't resist."

"Resist what?"

"You."

She supposed he meant only to tease her again, but his intent gaze and the intimate timbre of his voice flushed her traitorous body with heat. Swallowing hard, she realized her protective wall was cracking under his onslaught of subtle flirtation.

However did this man manage to both infuriate and charm her with only his presence? One minute she steadfastly assumed she could ignore him and the next she warmed to his gentle teasing.

He continued to stare down at her, his body blocking out the rest of the world. The wind dislodged a lock of her hair and the breeze took it, tickling her cheek. She reached up to rub the curl away at the same time he did, only he got there first. Her fingertips brushed the back of his hand. To an onlooker, it would appear he was caressing her cheek, and she was encouraging him. She let her hand drop away thinking he'd do the same, and he did, but not before tucking the coil behind her ear.

His heavy-lidded gaze dropped to her mouth. She wouldn't fall for that ploy again. Reflexively, she licked her lips, then fixed her attention on his shirt, which did little to calm her nerves. A slit between button holes offered her a peek of his golden skin. She nearly gulped.

"Shall we begin the lesson?" she asked, somehow finding the courage to look up at him again.

He nodded slowly, his pensive expression pulling into a scowl. Finally, he tore his fixed stare away from her lips and threw a glance at the stand holding the bull's-eye across the way.

"This one's only fifteen meters away," he said, sounding a bit cross. "Turn around."

She blinked a few times, not quite sure she understood him. Making a circle in the air with her finger, she looked at him askance.

"That's right, turn around."

With her pale muslin dress fluttering in the breeze, she did as he commanded, presenting her back to him. He stepped in close behind her, the folds of her dress billowing in and around his legs. Instantly, the heat emanating from his body spread across her back.

"First, one must find a proper stance." His deep, cultured voice sounded just above her left ear. She tried to ignore the tiny ripples of shivers running down her neck to her shoulders. "Your initial instinct was to turn in and face your target, but this will only cause you to shoot low."

"Then how is it I should stand?" she asked, her voice shaky.

"Were you not observing the other ladies?" He stood so close to her back, she *felt* every word he wrapped his lips around.

"No. I did not."

"Too busy watching my brother?"

She closed her eyes, her neck bent slightly to the side, secretly allowing his breath to feather across her skin as he spoke. Lord, she'd lost her fortitude.

"If I had been listening to his lordship," she murmured, "I gather I would have known how to stand. Besides, you of all people know I have no interest in Lord Tristan."

"Hmm," he said quietly. "Which makes it all the more likely he'll choose you."

Her eyes flew open at his words, but before she could ask him what he meant, he slid one booted foot in between her feet.

She gasped. "Your Grace?"

"Please cease the formality and address me by my Christian name."

"Thank you, but no. I'm not falling for that again."

"At least in private, then."

She shook her head.

"I insist."

"It wouldn't be proper."

"Neither is climbing out a window with your skirts hitched up to your waist. Come now, let us be friends. I daresay, I've seen more of your body in the last couple of days than any ma—"

"Stop," she said curtly, her face flushed with heat. "That's enough. Fine. I acquiesce. Gabriel it is." *Friends, he says.* Why did that irk her so?

"And may I call you by your given name?"

"No," she said flatly. The deep sound of his answering laughter rumbled behind her. She smiled freely, guessing he wouldn't be able to see.

Placing a warm hand on the swell of her hip, he gently nudged her feet apart. "Slide your left foot back a bit," he said, a smile in his voice.

She complied. Then her breath caught as his knee brushed the back of her thigh.

"Once you've mastered this stance, you can choose from countless others." His tone changed.

Although it was a tone of simple instruction, the air dripped with sensuality—like he was no longer speaking of archery but of some dark, sinful delight of which she could only imagine.

"Are you paying attention?" he asked.

"Mmm-hmm," she managed softly.

"I ask because you've closed your eyes again."

"Wh-What?" She blinked herself out of a stupor and straightened her spine.

"Is the wasp sting still bothering you? You should have tried my key."

"It wasn't necessary." The last thing she wanted to discuss with him was the state of her bottom. "I've fully recovered."

"Good." He cleared his throat. "Practice each position over and over. Compare the results of your release. And with time you will discover which one is more pleasurable for you."

"What are we talking about?"

"Your stance." Without retreating from his wicked nearness, he reached around her, offering her the bow. "Take it," he said, his breath feathering her earlobe.

She grasped the bow, holding it tightly between her thumb and index finger.

"Relax your grip," he said softly. "Take the arrow. Raise it . . . draw . . . hold."

The man was positively on fire. The presence of his body heat was distracting her thoughts. As her hands shook, she regretted appearing so visibly apprehensive. As attentive as his brother was to the other ladies, she had never seen him take the liberty of standing so sinfully near. Truly, if she were to take a step back, she'd be pressed up tight against him. The thought secretly thrilled her.

"This is why you jerked the shot," he said, removing his hand from her hip to settle it over her drawing hand. "Relax."

"Calming myself at this point is out of the question. You are standing too close," she finished quickly, as if running out of air.

After a brief hesitation that felt like an eternity, he took one step back. But it wasn't nearly enough. Her heart still palpitated and she felt undeniably overheated.

"Look at your target. Concentrate on keeping your eyes open," he said while manipulating her fingers underneath his into the correct position. "Allow the string to slip off your fingers without moving your hands." He finally stepped fully away from her, allowing a rush of cool air to race up her back.

Madelyn held her position, allowing time to regain her senses. "I'll miss, I know it. I'm simply too clumsy for this sport," she said after a few steadying breaths.

"Nonsense. When you're ready, release."

Taking a deep breath, she aimed the shot.

"Eyes open," the duke playfully reminded her.

"Yes, yes, my eyes are open." She deliberately widened them for emphasis.

There was a flicking sound—not a twang, as she'd

heard earlier—and her arrow flew through the air, hitting the outermost ring. It wasn't a bull's-eye, but she hit the target. Not the lawn or a bush or an ill-fated gardener's bottom, but an actual target. Astonished, she whirled around to face him.

"Well done," the duke said warmly, giving her shoulder a gentle pat.

"I can't believe I did it," she said, beaming up at him.

He smiled at her enthusiasm, the skin around the corners of his eyes crinkling. "Of course you did. I instructed you."

She rolled her eyes. "I know for you it must seem a rather insignificant triumph, but for me . . . " She sighed, satisfied.

For the next quarter of an hour she continued to practice and Gabriel continued to instruct. He grinned and patted her shoulder when she did well—after she stopped jumping up and down in celebration, of course—and offered her further coaching when she did poorly. He continued to stand close enough to brush up against her every now and again, but she soon became used to it and often found herself seeking the shield of his broad chest when a chilly gust raced across the lawn.

All too soon they ran out of arrows and agreed to retrieve them together.

"My stepmother wouldn't believe it if she witnessed it with her own eyes."

"Come now, Miss Haywood. Surely you discredit yourself."

The statement came from Lord Tristan, who emerged from the trees with a swagger, his pastel entourage following in his wake. With dark auburn locks, long straight nose, and a strong, squared jaw, there was no denying Lord Tristan was handsome—in a romantic sense. But Madelyn thought his cool blue eyes exemplified an adolescent shallowness. Mayhap in about five years his mind would catch up to his outward appearance. Except for the blue eyes, he looked very little like Gabriel—he of the dark and brooding.

It struck Madelyn that maybe it was why she found Gabriel so charming. He didn't have the appearance of a man who smiled warmly or often. But when he did, it seemed to knock the breath straight out of her. It transformed his entire face. Truly, if he'd frequent London ballrooms and quit sulking so often, she rather thought all the ladies would be flocking at his feet, instead of scurrying from his scowl.

"The ladies are distressing," Tristan said, straightening his hat, "that you might be changing your mind about this whole not-taking-a-bride thing."

"Don't agonize, Tristan. Seeing as how your hands were so delightfully full while tutoring, I chose to lighten your task and assist Miss Haywood myself."

"Why would I agonize? It's not as if you're a challenge to me."

"And a challenge would trouble you?"

"Of course. I would feel horrible when you embarrassed yourself trying to prove you were a better shot."

Madelyn watched the exchange between brothers with avid interest. She wasn't sure how it started, but the spark of competition flared between them seemingly out of nowhere.

"All right, then," Lord Tristan said, pointing east. "The apple tree next to the Rose Pavilion."

And what a sad little apple tree it was. Madelyn squinted, barely making out a single red apple hanging high on an otherwise naked branch. Poor thing stood separated from the rest of the orchard, which was enclosed with walls for protection from the wind and the rain.

"About forty meters away," Lord Tristan informed the group. "First one to hit that lone apple gets to escort Miss Haywood back to the castle."

The duke inclined his head, accepting the challenge. He swept his hand forward, indicating his brother go first.

Madelyn wasn't sure how she felt about being someone's prize, but she wasn't about to let it go to her head. After all, she surmised, surely they weren't fighting over her. That would be preposterous.

Lord Tristan stepped forward, giving himself ample room. He held out his empty hand, waiting a moment before Harriet murmured "Oh!" and flounced over to him, handing him his bow and an arrow.

"Thank you, Miss Beauchamp," he said without

turning to look at her. Taking up his stance with great ostentation, he drew back, held, aimed, and released.

Madelyn was certain his lordship would win as she watched his arrow. A series of rapid whacking sounds rent the air as it slapped through a scattering of leaves on the branch just below the apple, then flew to the ground, jabbing into the dirt. Lord Tristan's throat convulsed in apparent vexation.

Silence enveloped them. Madelyn pursed her lips and glanced around the group.

Belinda Fairbourne stepped forward. "'Tis a shame the sun went behind the clouds, my lord. A distraction, for sure."

"And that bird chirping above our heads is quite irksome," her sister Bernadette added, pointing above her head. "Don't you agree, ladies?"

Overly sincere choruses of "Yes" and "Indeed" followed the query.

Lord Tristan turned, white plume bobbing, and grinned at them quite like he wholeheartedly agreed.

A chuckle bubbled up inside Madelyn, but she managed to contain it. Her laughing eyes met Gabriel's as he took the bow out of her hand, his lingering touch skimming across her knuckles.

He slid an arrow out of the quiver, then handed Harriet the tube. She took it, looking mightily pleased, leaning in close. Gabriel nodded his thanks distractedly, then strode over to stand next to his brother.

Without any of Lord Tristan's pompous flair, he

set his arrow, drew back and held. Madelyn stared, transfixed, at his bare forearms. The muscles flexed and tightened as he aimed his shot.

A whizzing sound rent the air as his arrow cut through the sky, ripping through the wind and slicing into the apple. The fruit dropped to the ground. Gabriel's arrow had split it in two.

"Satisfied?" he asked, turning to his brother.

Lord Tristan removed his hat, swooping down for a low bow. "I am humbled," he said, straightening and returning his plumed hat atop his head.

Gabriel nodded, slapping his brother on the back. Lord Tristan then took the bow from him and sauntered away, a Fairbourne twin on each arm, Harriet in the lead and Laura and Julienne on the ends, cooing in conciliation.

Gabriel held out his arm to Madelyn. "My prize?"

She placed her hand on his arm. "I'm not so sure I'm fit to be anyone's prize."

"Come now, Miss Haywood. Tell me you're not the sort to fish for a compliment."

Her face flushed with heat. She wasn't sure why she'd made the comment, but baiting him for praise wasn't one of them. "No, of course not," she replied, forcing a small laugh.

"Good," he said, sliding a glance at her. "Because a beautiful woman should never plead for flattery."

Taken aback, she glanced at his handsome profile. He was frowning, looking ahead as they walked on. *Beautiful? Just the other day he claimed she wasn't even pretty.*

They entered the copse of trees, Lord Tristan and the other girls already far ahead. "I'm quite impressed by your accuracy," she said with sincerity.

"Truth be told," he replied, still looking forward, "I'm surprised he missed. He's quite a good shot, really."

"It's the feather. Perhaps it threw him off balance."

To her surprise, he threw back his head for a short bark of laughter. "You could be right, love."

They emerged from the trees, making their way across the lawn, Lord Tristan and the others far ahead. Madelyn turned toward the castle but was jerked to the left as the duke veered in the opposite direction.

Her brows drew together in a frown. "Are we not to return to the castle?"

He nodded. "Are you not forgetting someone?"

Her mind drew a blank, then suddenly she gasped. "Charlotte!"

Together they approached the sun canopy, startling a daydreaming Charlotte. Gabriel bent low, offering her friend his other arm with a smile and a "Shall we?"

Caught unawares, a pleasantly surprised Charlotte rose from her chair with a nervous smile. As the trio made their way back to the castle, Gabriel made polite conversation with Charlotte about the weather and its effects on his orchards, but Madelyn kept quiet.

Two nagging concerns had wormed into her thoughts. The first was the shame she felt for forgetting that Charlotte still sat alone. And the second was the surge of reluctant admiration thrumming through her that the duke had remembered.

Chapter 7

He couldn't stop thinking about her. And all the different ways he wanted to bed her.

"Bloody, weak-minded fool," Gabriel muttered the next day as he sat on the bench before the pianoforte in the music room.

He assured himself it was only a smidgen of lust he felt, nothing more. Certainly no more than what he'd have experienced had any other attractive woman thrown herself atop him. But then there was his archery instruction . . .

And she *was* in dire need of assistance. He was only being accommodating. True, he shouldn't have teased her or stood so close. But she shouldn't have smelled so sweet, smiled so openly. He had half a mind to think she knew how to shoot a straight arrow all along.

He ran a hand through his hair, tousling it further. He knew the best course of action would be to quit Wolverest for the duration, perhaps even return to London and catch himself a new mistress. But it would only ensure that Tristan would remain single by the end of the fortnight, and God forbid he should kick off before his brother produced an heir with a suitable bride. If he didn't get this business taken care of now, the next duchess of Wolverest could very well end up being a beautiful woman with a perfect shape, straight teeth, a flawless complexion—and about as clever as a rock.

Besides, he had a nagging suspicion that Miss Haywood had a plan of her own. And he believed it had everything to do with keeping her friend Charlotte away from Tristan.

He'd realized it only yesterday as he watched Miss Haywood from atop his horse. She shadowed Miss Greene the entire time, ushering her friend under the canopy when Tristan tried to converse with them. She was behaving like an overprotective mother hen determined to keep her baby chick far from jaws of the fox. The meddlesome woman would do well to stay out of his affairs. And damn her for looking so adorable while she was doing it.

Gabriel's fingers slid upon the keys, finding a familiar position, then broke into a distracted rendition of a long forgotten Mozart lullaby he'd played as a child. But after a few measures his mind ceased to concentrate on the keys, and his fingers danced through the rest of the piece by memorization alone.

His mind drifted again to the day before, when Miss Haywood stood with her back to him as he instructed her poise. He recalled her alluring scent—rose and mint—and the freckles scattered across the back of her neck tempting him for the brush of his lips. His body ached anew remembering how difficult it had been to restrain his hands from easing her short cap sleeves down her arms, to slip his fingers down the front of her bodice, to sink his teeth into the flesh just above her collarbone. If she had known what he was thinking, she'd have run away for sure. And all the better for her.

He stood, pushed away from the bench and walked around it, heading for the door. Perhaps if he looked over his accounts in his office he'd forget about her for the time being.

Truthfully, the fascination he felt for her bewildered him. She was the exact opposite of the sort of women he preferred. She was clumsy and outspoken, often disheveled and more than often impulsive. He was a man accustomed to surrounding himself with beauteous young women equipped with the disposition and decorum befitting their elevated station in life. Their skin was never dotted with mud, their hair never out of place, and their clothes always fit them to perfection. Easy to dismiss, they were often cold, distant females, and his carnal relations with them were straightforward, passionless encounters—by his design. He preferred it that way. There were no emotions other than the mutual will to fulfill a need. He was at all times in complete control. But none of this explained why Miss Haywood's smile continued to persuade his own.

You would never tire of her.

Ah, hell. He ran his hand through his hair, ignoring the bang that often fell over one of his eyes. He entered his office, striding down the long, narrow room toward his desk in the far right corner adjacent to the hearth.

Miss Haywood deserved someone who would cherish her, protect her, admire her forever-child spirit and revel in her spontaneity rather than fault her for it. She deserved much more than he could ever offer her. She deserved, he hated to admit, better than his impetuous brother.

He sat at his desk, opening a ledger his estate manager had left out for him. Thinking to look over his projected expense for an annual town fete he sponsored, he soon gazed up, knowing his chance at concentration was lost. Rubbing his brow, he ordered himself to stay detached, no matter how badly he craved more of Miss Haywood and her ill-fitted gowns.

Madelyn loved to snoop. It came naturally to her, which was why, she supposed, she did it so very often. Recognizing that most would consider this a flaw, she preferred to think of herself as a victim to an insatiable curiosity inherent at birth. Charlotte told her she was just plain nosy.

Although her inquisitiveness got her into trouble and more often presented her with startling results—at fifteen she'd discovered what *exactly* their footman wanted to do with the new upstairs maid—she couldn't seem to stop herself. Only now she had a tangible reason for her snooping: someone was having a jolly good time playing tricks on her and she intended to find out exactly who.

First an overly strong posset which, she suspected, was designed so the guilty party could hide her shoes, nearly making her miss the first scheduled picnic. Second, she'd been locked in her room, again, nearly keeping her from attending the archery lesson if not for her ingenuity. And third, just this morning, when they were all to gather for a late breakfast with Lord Tristan, someone slipped her a note under her door. It read:

Dear M—

Meet me in the orchard at the base of the old mill tower posthaste. I have something of great significance to relate.
Awaiting your swift presence,

C—

Perplexed, Madelyn had a difficult time trying to figure out which tower was an old mill, so she thought to walk the entire perimeter of the inner courtyard, which would have taken her the rest of the morning. Thankfully, a liveried footman spotted her, pointed out the tower and told her he hadn't seen another living soul since dawn—except for His Grace, who was due to arrive from his daily morning ride at any moment. Not daring another meeting with him, she shouted her thanks over her shoulder and sprinted back inside.

Naturally, she'd missed breakfast. Priscilla and Charlotte filed in the room upon returning and

Madelyn questioned them, but to no avail. Her stepmother only accused her of not attending by design, and Charlotte stated she hadn't any idea about a note. It was then Madelyn came to the conclusion that one of the other bride-hopefuls had it in mind to knock her out of the competition. Funny, but they were wasting their time. She wasn't participating. And even if she were, she'd be the first to admit she didn't stand a chance.

A trip to the kitchens was in order. Someone ordered that potent posset the other day, and perhaps someone there would tell the truth. Jenny claimed she didn't have any idea, she'd only delivered it, but Madelyn knew better than to believe that clanker.

And so, early afternoon on the sixth day at Wolverest, Madelyn snuck out of her room. The other girls were supposed to be resting before changing for tea, and the men, she'd overheard, were in the billiard room with Lord Tristan. She did not, however, know where the duke was, and that thought pestered her as she crossed the marble hall.

As she approached the massive hearth with a roaring fire burning brightly, she contemplated which deep-set, dark corridor led to the kitchens. There were two, one on either side of the hearth. She bit her lip for a spell, then chose the one with a gold-tasseled tapestry depicting a hunting scene hanging above it. Hunting equals game, equals food, equals cooking, equals kitchen. Simple enough. And if she was wrong . . . there was little else she loved to do in a four-hundred-year-old castle than snoop around.

Turning the corner, her eyes took a moment to adjust to the shadows. After a moment of blinking and squinting, she spied a lone sconce down the hall and ambled toward it. The berry-colored walls were lined with various paintings, mostly of men in battle or men on the hunt. There were others where the shadows yet clung and she couldn't make them out. She paused and admired a few and strolled by others, finally arriving at two sets of doors. The first set were locked, but the second opened easily. Ducking her head inside, she breathed in the scent of leather and mild tobacco. It was certainly not the kitchen, but the strong, masculine presence ignited her senses. What would hurt should she take a peek?

Books lined the walls from floor to ceiling on the two parallel sides of the long, narrow room. The gleaming floor was of polished wood with intricate Turkish rugs placed underneath groups of furniture gathered to inspire one to sit, read, or converse. At the far end, a cheery fire crackled in the grate behind two wing-back chairs, a red lap blanket thrown over the back of one. To the far right, in an alcove, crouched a huge mahogany desk. The mullioned windows behind it showed a gray day, offering little help in lighting the deep chamber. It occurred to her then that the room was designed to intimidate. Anyone sent to walk down the long room to stand before that desk and receive a reprimand had to be in possession of great courage.

She squinted into the shadows dancing within the room, thinking she saw movement behind the desk.

"Do you need something?"

She jumped a foot. "Oh dear," she said breathily with a hand thrown to her throat. "I didn't know . . . that is to say, I hadn't imagined—"

"Miss Haywood," Gabriel called crossly, looking up from a stack of ledgers upon his desk. "Do you need assistance?"

"Ah, no," she answered firmly.

He looked the stuffy, arrogant aristocrat today, scowling as he was at her. Dressed almost entirely in black, he was nearly invisible in the dimly lit room. His cravat was twisted in an intricate knot, his obsidian hair tousled around his face. He exuded confidence, business, and . . . a touch of wickedness.

She was glad for the shadows in the room for she was certainly as red as a ripe Yorkshire apple. Leave it to her to wander directly into the lair of the one man she was trying to avoid.

Her hands shook and she wasn't certain why. Only yesterday she laughed and joked with him during the archery lesson. He was amicable, playful, flirtatious, *dangerous*.

And now he was as approachable as a foaming mad forest creature. She wasn't sure which was worse.

Up to this point in her life, she had never felt comfortable in her skin. But Gabriel changed all that yesterday. When he was near, she secretly *loved* being in her skin—especially if that meant she could revel in the shivers spinning down her spine while he stood near, or bask in the warmth of his attention.

Whether his actions were practiced or simply a product of her imagination, Madelyn couldn't help but feel drawn to him, addicted to the heady sensations he stirred within her starving soul. And that was the very reason she knew she needed to stay away from him. Being near him made her second-guess herself, her opinions. Particularly her stand on pompous noblemen.

"Are you going to stand there, letting the cool air rush in?"

"N-No. I'm so sorry." She backed out the door with a wobbly smile. "I'll be on my way."

"Come here."

"Ah, no thank you." The last thing she needed was to be alone with him in a dark room. Besides, Priscilla had squeezed her in yet another one of her tight-bodiced gowns and she'd forgotten her shawl.

He straightened in his seat. "Are your feet fastened to the floor?"

Poking back into the room, she shook her head. "Of course not." Insufferable man.

"Are your muscles insufficient?"

She shook her head again.

"Is that no or shall I ascertain the suppleness of your legs with my bare hands?"

"My legs are just fine, thank you," she stated calmly, though the picture he painted flushed her with unwelcome heat.

"Then come here," he ordered.

Obviously out of her head, she stepped back into the room. Surely this wasn't as risky as her conscience was screaming to her that it was. She'd been alone with him more times than she dared count, and he'd never tried to ravish her. *And why would he want to ravish you?* Funny, but the voice inside her head sounded suspiciously like her stepmother. She wanted to strangle that voice.

Pursing her lips, she shuffled over, the swoosh of her pale blue walking dress the only sound in the room other than the occasional pop and hiss of the fire. She came to a halt two feet in front of his desk.

"I must ask," he said, his silvery-blue gaze glinting in the firelight as he perused her from the top of her head to her waist and back again, "what prompted you to invade my private office?"

She looked about her. "I had no idea. Y-You see, I became lost."

"Really?" he asked, disbelievingly. He leaned back in his chair, studying her face with hooded eyes.

"Mm-hmm."

His gaze dropped to her bodice and stayed there a long time. She was suddenly acutely aware of the strain on the fabric.

"Your stepmother dresses you abominably."

Her face flamed with embarrassment. He was telling the truth; in fact, she agreed with him. But only an unfeeling, selfish beast of a man would have the audacity to point out to a lady that he didn't admire her fashion.

In that moment she fairly thought she hated him—just as she should have from the start.

"Like almost all the others, this gown is on loan from my stepmother," she bit out, "which is why, I suppose, it doesn't quite fit properly. I *am* aware of the limitations of my wardrobe."

"Unfortunately . . . " He rose out of his chair and rounded his desk to stand before her. " . . . so am I."

He grinned at her. Grinned! He insulted her, very nearly made her cry and then he grins? Blinking up at him, she prayed he couldn't see the moisture gathering in her eyes. Many people had insulted her, and with her clumsiness, she had to admit she supplied them with ample ammunition, but his criticism cut straight to her heart. And the realization that this man could hurt her so easily, so casually, unsettled her. She knew he was arrogant and she should have expected snide remarks and dark glances, but at some point an uninvited flicker of hope had come to life within her. The hope that she was wrong about him.

Madelyn bit her lip in agitation. "Is this why you asked me to come to you? To judge my attire? Did you need the light of the fire to be certain?"

"No," he said. "I told you to come here for an entirely different reason." He reached behind her with both arms. She leaned backward as he leaned forward. For a moment she thought he meant to kiss her.

Heat radiated from his strong, solid form onto hers. Her skin felt pervaded with his warmth, her only view that of the underside of his slightly bristled chin. A small gasp came from the back of her throat as the heady sensation of having him press into her enveloped her.

"Sir?" There was a soft swishing sound as he pulled the red blanket from the chair behind her. Slowly, he slid it up her back and around her shoulders, his movements slow, lingering.

"You'll catch cold," he whispered, stepping back only enough so he could look at her face.

Their gazes met and held. She had no idea what to make of him at that moment. First he insulted her and then he covered her up in an unlikely chivalrous gesture, staring into her eyes as if he would very much like to kiss her.

And she very much wanted to kiss him. This wasn't supposed to happen. *He* wasn't supposed to happen. Titled, devilishly handsome men were rotten. They were selfish, boorish, arrogant rogues with no care for the tender feelings of the fairer sex, only for the next bit of muslin they could catch. This, she kept reminding herself as she watched the skin around the duke's eyes crinkle when a small smile crept across his face. Was he even aware of how he was looking at her? No one had ever looked at her like that before.

"I—I have a problem," she muttered.

The sparkle in his eyes faded. "And what is this problem?"

You're chipping away at my resolve. "Someone's been invading my room, stealing my shoes, leaving me overly strong drinks, locking me in, there was a letter . . . "

At the look of astonishment on his face, Madelyn regretted bringing up the subject.

"Never mind. I must sound mad."

"Miss Haywood," he remarked with interest, "are you suggesting one of the other guests has sunk to subterfuge?"

She summoned up some concentration and reiterated the events of the last few days with surprising clarity. Gabriel nodded at the appropriate times and appeared to be taking her concerns seriously, although . . . no matter what they were talking about, his light eyes seemed to bore into hers with wicked promise, as if he knew some undiscovered dark, secret about her. Like he was only half listening to her while his mind played out sinful imaginings—something like what her footman had wanted to do with their new maid.

She felt flushed, and hoped *he* was listening to the words pouring out of her mouth because *she* could no longer remember what she was talking about. "I should go," she blurted out.

"Please. Sit," he said, gesturing toward the chairs at her back with a sweep of his hand.

She glanced over her shoulder at the cozy chairs and felt tempted to risk the odds and remain in his presence. But her sense of self-preservation set her back on track.

"It isn't proper to be alone with you," she uttered in a breathy whisper.

"We'll talk. No ravishing. I promise," he said, grinning, with his hand over his heart.

She took a good look at him. So darkly handsome, exotic in appearance, his steady eyes concentrating on her, tempting her for one second to imagine he would take her in his arms. Perhaps he'd rip this blanket from her grasp, toss it to the floor, and yank her hard against his sleek body, holding her in complete possession until she succumbed. She imagined his sculpted, warm mouth covering hers . . .

She shook her head. "I must go." Grasping at the blanket, she strode for the door without a backward glance.

It felt like an age before she reached the doorway. And she could have sworn she felt his smoldering gaze follow her the entire way. She stepped into the corridor without bothering to shut the doors, her mind concentrating on stifling the urge to return.

Halfway down the dark corridor, she swore under her breath. In her befuddlement she'd turned down a different hall. She spun in a circle, smothering a pang of panic. What if that wolf stalked her in the dark? Heaven forbid, they'd be found together. She'd be considered compromised. There would be no other course of action except a hasty marriage. Priscilla would be ecstatic. Charlotte would be shocked, but secretly thrilled. And she herself would kiss her heart good riddance and kick it in a ditch.

She turned another corner and soft, pale light beckoned her farther. The hall opened on her right, presenting a series of alabaster columns. She turned, her jaw falling open. It was the most magnificent ballroom she'd ever seen.

The eggshell-colored room was enormous, slightly longer than it was broad. She stepped through a pair of tall columns, her slippers sliding on the glassy parquet floor. Five shimmering glass chandeliers scattered reflected sunlight about the room. Every so often a shard of light sparkled a rainbow on the walls. Madelyn almost needed to squint from the glowing radiance. The entire back wall was a series of French doors, above them gleaming windows covered with sheer, cream-colored drapes.

She moved deeper within the room, her attention drawn above. Her head dropped back to gaze in wonder at the soaring ceiling. Naked gods and goddesses frolicked, unabashed, across the wide expanse. Some with only a trail of hair or a strategically placed arm as their only badge of modesty.

It was hard to smirk with the predictability of it all when one's mouth was gaping open. Leave it to the Devines to hold a seemingly proper ball while amorous beauties passionately cavorted above everyone's heads.

Suddenly dizzy, Madelyn gave her head a shake in order to regain her balance. She returned her attention to the room at large and, lifting her arms, swung around in a graceful arc—or what she pretended looked like a graceful arc. She was never any good at dancing. Her timing was off, her rhythm jumbled, and she always managed to stomp on her partner's toes. She shrugged. Perhaps it was because she always fretted that others were watching, comparing, judging—like her stepmother. But there was no one here. No one to tell her that her movements were as fluid as a polluted river. No one to laugh at her sincere attempt at elegance. No one but the gods and goddesses above, and they were too busy to care.

Closing her eyes, she smiled to herself as she raised her arms in the position of the waltz. She counted off in threes, eyes still shut, and began gliding across the floor. The blanket the duke had wrapped around her slipped, swishing to the floor. She ignored it, so caught up in the steps of the dance. Even so, she opened her eyes a slit, just to make certain she didn't go crashing through the French doors.

And that's when she saw him. He stood just inside the room, his face a mask of serious concentration. She stopped, her arms slowly falling to her sides, her skirts swooping back into place. Too embarrassed to even utter a gasp, she looked to the floor, summoning up the courage to either speak or run away. Neither happened. She continued to stand there, frozen.

He sauntered forward, stopping when he reached the red blanket pooled on the floor. As she looked up, he bent to pick it up, his eyes never leaving her face.

"Explain this to me," he said softly, his cultured tones so befitting the atmosphere. "For someone who claims the Devines are nothing better than the lowliest of scoundrels, I must ask why you think nothing of coming to me, dressed to tempt the holiest of saints?"

Her cheeks flamed. "I have done no such thing," she muttered, hating the way her body thrummed with delight at the hint of the slightest compliment. "Tempt someone?" She shook her head disbelievingly. "The only tempting I might inspire is provoking someone into hiring me a reputable modiste."

He quirked a brow. "And the person who gave you this warped sense of yourself is . . . the baroness, I imagine?"

"I guess . . . I don't know. I never thought of it as 'warped.'"

"Have you a mirror in your possession?" he asked, stalking toward her with the red blanket thrown over his arm.

"Of course," she said, eyeing the blanket and anticipating being covered up with it once again.

"Do you utilize it quite often?"

Actually, no, Madelyn mused. She tried to avoid her reflection at every turn. Oh, she checked her hair and face from time to time, but just a passing glance, nothing more.

"Just as I thought." Without breaking his gaze from her, he tossed the blanket on an ornate chair positioned against the wall.

Madelyn shivered, feeling incredibly exposed.

He bowed deeply, then took her free hand in his. "May I have this dance?"

A giggle bubbled forth. "You're serious?"

He straightened, a feigned look of offense in his features. "Indeed, I am."

"But . . . there's no music," she said hesitantly, a smile in her voice.

His broad shoulders rose and fell with a shrug. "I shall hum a waltz."

"Oh, no," she said, backing away. "The last thing you need is to waltz with me. I'm quite dangerous, I'm afraid."

"Really?" he asked, raising a brow.

"I'm sure you've heard what happened last Season to Sir William?"

He blinked in mock astonishment. "That was you?"

Heat flooded her cheeks. "You've heard?"

"No," he said flatly. With a teasing light in his uncommonly blue eyes, he escorted her to the middle of the room.

"Your Grace, I—"

"Gabriel."

"Gabriel, I cannot waltz. I cannot keep time and I cannot keep from trampling upon my partner's toes."

He took her right hand with his left while his other hand sat heavy and firm on her waist—just a notch lower from being entirely proper.

"And who told you this?" He began to hum, the reverberation of his deep tenor vibrated through her bones.

Madelyn hesitated, partly because the sound of his low voice was mesmerizing and partly because she thought he was asking a question he already knew the answer to in order to make a point. "My stepmother," she said finally. "And I believe her."

He pulled her closer, their hips brushing as he moved her across the floor.

"Nonsense," he drawled between humming. "You were doing a perfectly fine job of it by yourself when I came upon you."

Her blush bloomed anew as she imagined what a sorry sight she must have been when he came upon her.

"You danced like an angel," he said softly.

"It was different. I wasn't worrying about making a mistake *and* I had an imaginary partner who, naturally, hadn't any feet."

"A gentlemen is responsible for guiding his partner," he said, pausing between humming to speak. "Did you ever consider it was your partner who caused your missteps? Or your stepmother's critical eye, distracting you from keeping time?"

"I don't know," she said, pausing in thought. "I suppose . . . "

"You seem to be doing a smashing job presently."

And she was. *They* were. And she hadn't even realized they were in the steps of the dance until now. He controlled her every movement with ease and confidence. A bubble of laughter escaped from her chest and she smiled the widest, most uninhibited smile she had ever managed in her entire life.

With each swirling step across the expanse of the ballroom all of her insecurities and misgivings scurried and hid from the light in her laughter, the joy in her heart. And with a dizzying sensation, she surrendered herself to the glory of her partner's masterful control. The rhythmic rise and fall was mesmerizing, and with Gabriel, incredibly easy and natural.

He spun her faster and she felt as if she were flying and he, her anchor, her guide, keeping her safe from falling flat on her posterior.

His soft humming ceased, his gaze locking into her own. They continued to twirl about the room, in perfect time, in perfect silence. Constantly whirling. She felt elegant, graceful, and very much like laughing again.

It bubbled forth and she closed her eyes, laughing without reservation. And he joined her, his deep chuckles heartening her further. Effortlessly, Gabriel repeated the turns, her feet never colliding with his, their rhythm never faltering. When her fits of giggles crumbled into a delighted sigh, she opened her eyes and realized that they'd stopped right where they had begun. Madelyn breathed deeply, trying to catch her breath. It was hard to do while Gabriel's azure gaze sparkled with such heat into her own.

"Your smile is enchanting," he whispered, a sense of wonder in his voice, "and when you laugh, you are utterly captivating."

Her wide grin wavered then fell, so stunned was she at his compliment. She gave her head a tiny shake, thinking to dispel the charm of his words.

"Dizzy?" he asked, the exertion of the dance apparently not affecting his breathing as it did hers.

"No, not at all," she said on a sigh. "Oh, Gabriel. That was absolutely wonderful."

He retrieved the blanket from the chair and she felt it being swept around her shoulders again, his hand holding it tightly closed between her breasts. Blinking as if coming out of a trance, she sobered and met his steady gaze. Gone was the teasing light, the arrogant gleam, and in its place was a penetrating stare, making her desire nothing more in the world than for him to touch her.

And then his voice washed over her, low and smooth. "I do not know how . . . " he said softly, his gaze centered on her mouth, "and you certainly have no idea . . . of the effect you have on me." Swallowing, his expression changed to one of confusion, as if in the act of sorting out his thoughts, he'd come upon some new discovery.

"Gabriel," Madelyn whispered, trying to draw him out of his thoughts. Infernal man, why did he have to say such nice things, why did he have to go and make her dream of a life shared with him, of loving him? "We are alone again," she said, staring at his mouth. A sensual pull grew between them. Her mouth parted slightly.

"Indeed," he agreed. With a sharp tug, he pulled her to him using the blanket still in his grasp. His mouth an inch above hers, he brushed his lips across hers in a maddening, achingly slow, feather-like sweep. Back and forth and once again.

Instead of shock, tingles of shivers shimmered down her body, down her breasts, her stomach, her legs. Almost to the point of whimpering, she felt her muscles threaten to go limp, so willing was she for his touch.

And then his mouth sunk into hers for a brief yet lingering taste. His lips felt smooth and hard and Madelyn struggled with the urge to stand on her tiptoes for more pressure, for more of him.

But he pulled away too soon, releasing his grasp

on the blanket. She nearly stumbled back, but he steadied her shoulders. Then he cupped her face in his hands as if she was fractured glass, gazing down at her in that peculiar fashion of his.

"It isn't right for you to look at me like that," she murmured.

"Like what?" he asked, his hands falling away.

It had to be false, for he seemed stunned by her declaration and his arrogant mask slid back into place.

She dipped in a curtsy, bowing her head. "Thank you for the dance. I enjoyed it."

He bowed. "It was a pleasure."

She bit her lip and looked down, unable to meet his gaze any longer. Whether the reason was because she doubted his sincerity or because she feared he could somehow tell how much she wanted him to kiss her again, she didn't know. With that scandalous thought inside her head, she tightened the red blanket around herself and dashed out of the room.

Chapter 8

Perhaps if he banged his head hard enough on the mantelpiece, Gabriel thought, he could knock himself out cold, thereby relieving his ears the punishment of having to endure the sounds coming from the mouths of the Fairbourne twins.

'Twas a shame, really. Though they sang a piece from Rossini's *Semiramide*, the pair could have been singing in Finnish for all the care they took to enunciate their Italian properly.

Tonight marked the commencement of the bride-hopefuls' talent performances. Not that Tristan gave a horse's ass whether any of them could hold a note, play a tune, or read for that matter—his brother's expectations began and ended with what abilities any one of them could offer him inside his bedroom, or in any room. But for one—torturous—evening it gave the musically talented a chance to show off their skills. Unfortunately, it also gave him a blasted headache.

Pushing off from the wall next to the hearth, Gabriel let his gaze drift across the dimly lit room until it affixed to his target: Miss Haywood. Damn, but his body yearned for the taste of her lips, for the feel of her supple body so close to his own. The sight of her made his entire body as taut as a drawn bowstring. Dear God, and her freckles. He wanted to memorize where each one was located and kiss them all.

Dressed in a dark blue silk gown, she smiled placidly as the cats continued to screech not five feet in front of her. A less observant person would have believed she was, in fact, enjoying their performance. But every so often, when the harmony of the Fairbournes wavered and clashed, her eyes crinkled at the corners and the apples of her cheeks would lift a touch.

He shifted his stance. This one was remarkably good at feigning indifference. She was mischievous, all right. So discreet, such a good actress, he rather thought she'd do well in the theater.

He had suspected she was trying to keep Charlotte away from Tristan, and tonight, not more than five minutes ago, his suspicions had been further solidified when he watched Madelyn choose her seat.

Tristan had asked Miss Greene if he could take the seat next to her on the settee. Quick as a whip, Madelyn squirmed her way in between the pair, plopping herself in the middle before Tristan had time to bend at the waist. Smiling innocently up at his brother, she had gestured for him to take the empty seat to her left.

Gabriel shook his head. How long did she think this was going to last? In all probability, she was making it worse. The longer she kept his brother from conversing, strolling, or sitting next to Miss Greene, the more determined Tristan would become. She was unknowingly baiting his brother's appetite. However, in the end it didn't matter. Gabriel had decided that he wouldn't let her win this game of love.

Oh, he would have his brother married at the end of the fortnight, and if Charlotte Greene managed to catch his brother's interest, then he wouldn't let anything stand in the way. And that included the cheeky miss with the penchant for getting under his skin and making him smile, tease, trip over his words, and chuckle like he was . . . well, like he never had before.

Just before Gabriel reckoned the glass chandelier was indeed vibrating and on the verge of exploding, the Fairbournes completed the act and everyone clapped politely while the twins grinned in response to the praise. He managed a quick touch of his fingers to his palm, inwardly proud that he had the strength to resist the urge to jump forward and shout in triumph that they'd finished.

A small refreshment intermission was announced, and here and there guests began to stand and circulate about the room. Gabriel hung back, waiting to see what Miss Haywood would do as she rose from her chair. For at the same time Tristan reached behind her to tug playfully on the thick satin ribbon Miss Greene wore around her waist.

But before Madelyn could intercept the play, her

attention was immediately snagged by her stepmother, who pulled her forward with a not-so-gentle yank on her arm.

The baroness's mouth was pulled tight as she spoke sternly to her charge. With her fingers wrapped around the crook of Miss Haywood's elbow, she urged her farther forward, inadvertently leaving Tristan and Miss Greene standing next to one another. Gabriel laughed to himself as Madelyn attempted to turn back to look over her shoulder but failed as the baroness demanded her full attention.

Just as he suspected, Tristan initiated a conversation with the fair Miss Greene, using the trick of pretending he could not hear what she said in order to take a step closer and dip his head close. The ploy was hardly necessary. Bereft of her spectacles, Miss Greene was already standing closer than was safe.

Poor Miss Haywood, Gabriel mused as his gaze swung back to her. Whatever shall she do now? Inadvertently knock Tristan to the floor? Swoon in a desperate attempt to gain Charlotte's attention?

He smiled to himself . . . then stopped cold. On Madelyn's arm, red, fingerlike marks emerged where her stepmother had gripped her moments ago. Anger, hot and tangible, rose up within him. He angled toward them, his hands clasped behind his back to reduce the probability that he'd reach forward and toss the baroness out of the room by her scrawny neck.

" . . . perhaps if you wore the gown I had laid out for you, he'd have sat next to you instead of standing— Oh! Your Grace!" Priscilla dipped into a fluid curtsy, then urged Madelyn to do the same with a nudge of her foot.

As Madelyn sunk into the gesture, Gabriel halted her movement by taking her gloved hand into his own.

"Miss Haywood." He kissed the air above her knuckles, his lips aching to press onto her mouth instead.

"Your Grace," she murmured, her eyes flashing with a peculiar blend of mild annoyance and distress. He released her fingers.

"You look . . . " Ravishing, adorable, voluptuous, tempting. ". . . good in blue." *Good in blue?* What the bloody hell was wrong with him? "The shade . . . it is my favorite," he said, feeling utterly silly for the first time in his entire life. "I've something in my possession the exact color."

"Pray, what is it?"

The color matched the velvet drapes hanging high above his bed to near perfection. This, of course, made him think of her lying in his bed, which made him imagine her minus the blasted gown, which made him think she'd be rather cold, lying there without any clothes and all, and this made him think of settling himself atop her to warm her up, which made him imagine sinking his—

Damnation. He couldn't very well tell her it was his bed dressings that were blue.

During his hesitation, Tristan had joined them, Charlotte's hand tucked into the crook of his arm.

Madelyn instantly spotted it and her expression altered with a twinge of panic.

"Perhaps the shade matches your eyes," the baroness offered awkwardly.

Gabriel turned and looked at the baroness crossly. The daft woman obviously imagined he gave them a riddle to solve.

"No," Madelyn answered, drawing his attention immediately. "They're too luminous to be compared to the dark hue of my gown." Her studying gaze bore into his for only a moment, and then she blinked away their connection and smiled tightly. She turned to Tristan and Charlotte.

"Charlotte," she called sweetly, "do come with me." She held out her hand. "Let's get some refreshment."

"Thank you, I do not want any presently," Charlotte said with a meaningful side glance at Tristan.

"But—"

"Perhaps," Gabriel interrupted, "you would allow me to accompany you?"

"N—" Madelyn started to decline his offer, but a bump in the hip from her stepmother cut her short. She threw a brief glance at the baroness, who narrowed her eyes in a threatening manner. Madelyn nodded dolefully. "Yes, that would be grand."

He held out his bent arm. After a brief hesitation, she took it, her touch as gentle as a butterfly. In silence, they approached the side table laden with refreshments and various cakes and sweets.

"Have you no musical talents to display this evening, Miss Haywood?" Gabriel asked, handing her a glass of punch.

She shook her head, taking a sip. "None at all. I've always longed to learn, but I fear I have neither the patience nor the discipline."

"You can draw and cut remarkably detailed silhouettes. Rosalind showed me the ones you've done of the other guests. She said you completed them with remarkable speed and dexterity. They are quite remarkable."

Her brown eyes flashed with reserved pleasure and she blushed prettily. It had become apparent to him that she was unaccustomed to compliments and they made her uncomfortable. "Thank you," she murmured, staring into her glass.

Gabriel placed the tip of his index finger under her chin, gently tilting her head so he could look into her eyes. "Perhaps one day you might do one of me."

She nodded, rubbing her arm in a fashion he had first assumed was a nervous gesture, then realized her fingers smoothed over her skin as if something had irritated it.

And then he remembered how the baroness had squeezed her there. Knowing it was forward to touch her again, but unable to stop himself, he trailed his finger over the fingertip-shaped marks above the crook of her elbow.

She snatched her arm away, cupping her palm over the spot he'd touched.

"Who did this?" Gabriel asked.

"Ah . . . " she said, hesitating. "The archery lesson?"

The woman was an abominable liar. Her statement sounded like a question.

He frowned. "I abhor lying."

"It's nothing, really."

And he truly believed she thought that. He gave a slow nod, a scowl sliding into place. Taking a step closer, he bent to whisper in her ear. "If you confided that someone, whoever it was, made those marks on your person, they would deserve nothing less then a sound thrashing. Or at the very least, their guardianship would be stripped and you would no longer suffer from their company."

"Yes, but then who would then have to suffer mine?"

"I'd see to it myself." He pulled back, searching her large eyes.

Her cheeks turned pink and she looked about the room. A stab of regret jabbed him for wording his answer unflatteringly. But he wasn't about to correct himself at the expense of sounding like a buffoon.

"Tell me, and it shall be done," he intoned.

"Please, let us return to Charlotte," she said softly.

"Of course."

After she finished her drink, Gabriel guided her back to their small group, nodding at acquaintances as they crossed the room. Untwining their arms, she made to step between his brother and Charlotte, but he gently steered her across from them with the pressure of his hand at her lower back.

"Has anyone seen Mrs. Greene?" Tristan broke in.

The group turned in unison to the window seat where Charlotte's mother had settled herself, snoring softly. Rosalind stood at her side, apparently noticing only just then that the woman she was conversing with had fallen asleep.

"Right. Well, Charlotte had expressed an interest in my collection of botanical volumes," Tristan stated.

Gabriel didn't miss Madelyn nearly jolt out of her stockings at his brother's familiarity with her friend's given name.

"After we finish up here I thought I'd take her down to my private library . . . "

"I—I don't think that's such a good idea," Madelyn blurted.

"Rosalind would chaperone," Gabriel intoned.

"Take no offense, but it only took a bit of prodding for her to leave you and—" Madelyn pressed her lips together, masking a wince.

Gabriel knew she had almost blurted out that the two of them had been alone. But were they really? He suspected Rosalind hadn't actually left. Besides, Rosie knew Tristan couldn't be trusted for one minute alone with a female. Charlotte would be safe enough.

"Leave you and who where?" Priscilla asked with keen interest.

Gabriel scowled at the woman. Her eyes shifted from sharp curiosity to indifference in a matter of a second. Pursing her lips, she reverted her gaze to some point across the room.

"Wolverest. Tristan."

Gabriel turned at the sound of Adam Faramond's voice. The Earl of Rothbury stood behind Madelyn—who looked like she'd just been spooked by a ghastly apparition. Her eyes were large and unblinking as she stared straight ahead. And from the rapid rise and fall of her chest, her breathing had increased twofold in a matter of seconds. She must still be fretting about the prospect of his brother showing Charlotte his private library, he thought. She'd do well to put her plan behind her now. Whomever Tristan wanted, he would make certain the opportunity was there.

"Rothbury," Gabriel returned with a nod. Truthfully, he was a little surprised the earl had shown after he had already declined the invitation. Tristan's school chum abhorred *ton* functions, and if he was at one, it was because he was in pursuit of some unsuspecting female. Many a protective guardian steered their daughters or wards away from Rothbury. Gabriel had set him straight without hesitation when the insidious man had the audacity to set Rosalind in his sights not too long ago. Rothbury didn't have a conscience, as far as he could tell. The man delighted in the art of seduction—whether it be a blushing debutante or his best friend's wife.

"I see you've changed your mind," Gabriel said to him. Perhaps he came to discuss horseflesh with Tristan.

Rothbury inclined his head, ignoring Gabriel, and instead focused his attention on Madelyn's back.

Gabriel thought to introduce Rothbury to the group, but stalled as the earl stepped around Madelyn. And from the spark of recognition in her eyes, Gabriel became aware that they knew one another already.

"Miss Haywood." Rothbury bent low. "I trust you are well?"

Tentatively, she curtsied, her eyes flying from Rothbury to Gabriel. She masked it well, but he could see the uneasiness there.

A series of chords on the pianoforte broke the questionable silence as Rosalind drew everyone's attention to the front of the room. Miss Beauchamp, armed with a violin, announced the Mozart concerto she would be playing, accompanied by Miss Ellis on the pianoforte.

It was time for Gabriel to leave. As the guests took their seats, he excused himself and made for the door. Reaching it, he looked over his shoulder to find Tristan and Charlotte sitting side by side at the settee. He smiled. It would suit Miss Haywood well to realize sooner rather than later that one couldn't control whom one fancied. Though he had just learned that lesson himself when she waltzed into his life.

Hesitating, he watched Rothbury and Priscilla lead Madelyn toward another settee. As the trio took up their seat, placing Madelyn in the middle, he noticed she glanced about the room, hunting for someone. Then her searching gaze connected and locked into his.

He blinked, dismissing the fear he thought he spied in those dark chocolate depths. She was overreacting. Tristan certainly wouldn't try ravishing her friend in a room full of spectators. And if at the conclusion of the music demonstrations, Tristan insisted that Charlotte see his books, Rosalind would be certain to chaperone. Turning, he left the room before the urge to spin on his heel and return to Madelyn overcame him.

Gabriel didn't give a damn if his guests considered him a rude lout for quitting the music room for the serenity of his library down the hall. After all, he thought he'd rather surprised them that he'd even attended in the first place.

Staring into the fire in the grate, he shook his head slowly as he balanced his glass of brandy on his knee. This task of watching Miss Haywood was more perilous than he'd imagined. He had been wrong. He couldn't disregard her any more than one could ignore the sun shining in one's eyes. She had a light, an aura of quiet beauty, and he couldn't keep from imagining he could capture it and make her his own. But he knew how volatile that action might prove, so he gritted his teeth and told himself to simply forget her already. She was just a woman, and an imperfect one at that.

Throwing back his head, he took the last swallow from his glass, then eyed the thing crossly. "You're certainly no help."

Fortunately, there wasn't a reason to watch her any longer now that he knew what she was up to. Having figured her out, he could keep his distance, as he had originally planned. After he had Tristan well and truly hitched, he'd plan a trip to his hunting lodge in Scotland and Miss Haywood would pack up with the others and return to wherever it was they called home. Which was a good thing. A great thing. Distance between Miss Haywood and himself would surely keep his imagination in check, his hands to himself, and her clothes on. All he had to do now was make certain Charlotte had every opportunity to be with Tristan as the other girls did. Certainly, this slip of a girl couldn't outmaneuver him. He proved it tonight when she tried keeping Charlotte by her side and away from his brother.

He rose from his favorite wing-back chair and made for the crystal decanter on the side table, then cringed as the duet by Miss Beauchamp and Miss Ellis took a wrong turn and ended on a discordant note.

A minute later a sigh emerged from the doorway, making Gabriel pause in pouring his drink. He looked over his shoulder to find Tristan leaning against the door frame.

"Still planning on taking Charlotte to your library?"

"If her mother ever stays awake long enough to chaperone us. I'm afraid Miss Haywood managed to coerce Miss Greene to insist upon it."

"Don't be surprised if the little minx follows you, sketching your every move," Gabriel muttered.

Tristan shook his head. "I still don't understand why you had to go and invite Rothbury," he added gruffly.

"Come now," Gabriel said. "Did you expect to have them all to yourself all of the time? Rosie insisted we even out the numbers. Seems we can't have a bunch of pouting women standing around waiting their turn to dance with you at the night of the ball. Besides, Rothbury's not looking for a bride, last I heard. Drink?"

He took Tristan's grunt for yes, poured his brother a glass, and handed it to him as he returned to his seat. Closing his eyes, he sank back into his chair, choosing to forgo stroking Tristan's ego by telling the young man he had nothing to worry about. Maybe a bit of jealousy would do him good. Perhaps it would spur his fickle brother into choosing a bride more quickly.

Tristan gave his glass a swirl, then tossed the liquid down his throat. "I'm surprised, is all," he said through a grimace. "Considering the fact he's been panting after Miss Haywood since last Season. But I'm sort of glad he's here. I did want to take a look at that Arabian beauty of his."

Gabriel sat up, nearly spilling his drink. "What did you say?"

"Rothbury. Arabian."

"No. What of Miss Haywood?"

"Ah." Tristan nodded. "Wants to marry her, or bed her. I'm not sure. Supposedly, he proposed last spring, but she refused. Said he suspects she was only testing his sincerity. Playing hard to get." He shrugged. "He's not giving up, you know. Man's as determined as a bull in heat. Hell's teeth, what are you scowling at me for?"

Gabriel blinked, easing back into his chair, every muscle pulled tight. So Rothbury wanted Madelyn. And it certainly wasn't her dowry he was after. He closed his eyes for a moment, hoping the rumble of jealousy wouldn't come, but it did. And it fairly roared in his ears. He flexed his fingers, hoping the movement would pacify the ache to throttle Rothbury with his bare hands.

He knew he had to get away from here, away from her. "How does this make *you* feel?" he asked in attempt to control his unfounded jealousy by focusing on his brother's emotional response.

"That another wolf is in the mix, sniffing around?" He shrugged again. "I'm not sure. I can't say I'd ever considered Miss Haywood before Rosie invited her to Wolverest. She's a peach and all, but a diamond of the first water she is not," he finished derisively.

His brother's comment provoked a twinge of protectiveness in Gabriel, but he managed to keep silent, choosing to ignore it.

Tristan sighed. "I don't know. Truth is, I haven't made my decision. Not even close. I think I'm still hoping you'll change your mind and pick one of them for yourself so I can continue being a lazy, reckless, debauching, wastrel of a second son." He laughed. "Just surprised, is all. That you invited him knowing he was bent on pursuing the chit."

"I didn't know," Gabriel muttered.

"I guess it doesn't matter. Just don't know if I can concentrate with Rothbury panting about, is all." His brother shrugged, placing his glass on the side table. "I best return." He grinned. "Charlotte's to play a minuet."

Gabriel gave a slow, distracted nod. Without her spectacles? He hoped she had the piece memorized for it could be disastrous otherwise.

"You know," Tristan offered. "I could tell Rothbury he's free to pursue Miss Haywood, that I have no intentions toward her."

"Somehow, little brother, I don't think whether or not *you* wanted her for yourself would make a bloody difference to him."

Chapter 9

The next afternoon, Madelyn was still recovering from the astonishment of seeing Lord Rothbury again.

Walking down a dark corridor in silence with Charlotte, she tightened her Spanish blue shawl around her shoulders and tried to ignore the ache in her belly. The pair were on their way to a scheduled tour of Wolverest Castle, the guests assembling in the marble hall. It seemed miles away until she remembered that Lord Rothbury could very well be there. And then it felt as if Charlotte was running, dragging her along, when in actuality their pace had slowed.

Last Season, Rothbury had pursued her with all the finesse of a deranged hunter. He had the habit of showing up wherever she went, which made her suspect he was bribing one of their servants for the information. And he simply wouldn't take no for an answer.

Being an earl with over thirty thousand a year, Priscilla had practically begged Madelyn to allow him to court her. The plain and simple fact was that she had no interest in the man. He had the reputation of a rake, the persistence of a skilled huntsman, and the impudence to offer her the position of being one of his mistresses when she refused his proposal.

She had to admit he was handsome, with his tousled ash-blond locks, tall form, and easy smile. Only, there was something about his amber-colored eyes that reminded her of a lion. A pursuing, methodical, flesh-eating lion.

And now he was here. She certainly hoped he moved on, though doubt weighed heavy on her shoulders.

For all the nervous fluttering going on in her stomach, it was no match for the memory of Gabriel standing over her, kissing her in the ballroom. Coupled with this new and wondrous feeling was the nagging voice inside her head reminding her of how disappointed she felt when Gabriel quit the music room last evening. In the ballroom, he had been so kind, so gracious. He'd managed to stop her from worrying about the steps of the dance, and she'd felt graceful for the first time in her life. She rather thought something was blooming between them. Be it friendship, or something else she'd do well to dismiss. Because then he had changed.

In the music room he was quiet, distant. When he kissed the air above her knuckles, she found herself longing for the heat of his touch. When his finger skimmed across the crook of her bent elbow, shivers fell in cascades from her shoulders to her knees. And when his hand pressed at the small of her back . . . she felt all her senses heighten, but when she turned to look at him, he'd appeared bored, as if his thoughts were far off, unreachable.

How irrational she was turning out to be. She came to this castle with a plan: keep Tristan away from Charlotte, and keep Willowbrooke within her grasp by pretending that she was trying to win the duke. The former was a juggling act, though she felt she was succeeding somewhat in that end. But the latter needed some work: she fretted that if she spent any more time in Gabriel's company in order to make Priscilla believe she was actually trying, she just might do the unthinkable and fall in love with the man.

Gabriel was in a foul mood.

Half hidden by a velvet drape, he leaned a hip against the polished oak handrail of the balconied corridor overlooking the great hall. Crossing his arms over his chest, he continued to scowl down at the gathering pool of ladies and their chaperones as they awaited the commencement of a guided tour of Wolverest.

One of the reasons for his current state of vexation was that Julienne Campbell had been eliminated last evening. No one informed him until the lass and her grandparents were well on their way to Edinburgh this morning. This wasn't supposed to happen. No one was to be sent away before the night of the ball. Tristan was a damn fool.

But the second, more pressing reason for his foul mood was walking straight toward him from down the darkened corridor, matching strides with Tristan: Rothbury.

All his life, Gabriel had distanced himself from any sentimental emotions connected with women. It was a surprisingly easy thing to do. *Was.* The stock he once put in his indifference wavered and shattered. His hands curled into fists and all he wanted to do was pummel Rothbury to the ground, then drag the rakehell down the stairs and throw him out of the house. All this and Madelyn wasn't even his.

Early this morning, after he breakfasted alone, he had amassed a small hunting party, which included Tristan, Rothbury, Lord Fairbourne, a local farmer and friend, and himself. The crisp air seemed to have cleared Miss Haywood straight out of his head until Rothbury started chattering away about her physical attributes. Gabriel had grinned down at his gun, thinking how easily the man could have been mistaken for a partridge.

"I wonder," Rothbury drawled now as he approached. "Are you going to follow them about, making certain no one steals the silver?"

Gabriel answered with a grunt. Dismissing the earl, he turned to Tristan. "Why did you eliminate Miss Campbell?"

"Because she had a crooked bottom tooth," Tristan said casually. "Besides, she bored me."

So that's why he wasn't told. "You can't eliminate them because of your asinine imagination."

"Imagination? Every time I looked at the chit, I couldn't help but stare at her mouth. Distracting, it was." At Gabriel's silent glare, Tristan added in defense, "I certainly didn't tell *her* that . . . exactly. And it shan't happen again. The not-telling-you-first part, I mean. Indeed, you can't expect me to marry a woman with such an evident *flaw*." Ignoring his brother's scowl, Tristan joined Rothbury in leaning over the handrail to ogle the ladies below. "I say, what a lovely view."

The Fairbourne twins spied them first, awarding them flirtatious smiles and a wave of their lace handkerchiefs. An eyelash-batting Harriet noticed Tristan second, followed by Laura Ellis, who giggled behind her gloved hand.

"Hmm . . . It seems there are two missing," Rothbury surmised. "Shall I investigate?"

"No," Gabriel and Tristan barked in unison.

"Let's see," Rothbury said, rubbing his jaw. "That would be Miss Greene and Miss Haywood?"

Gabriel grunted.

At that, Tristan straightened, his face pulled into an expression of contemplation. "Do you know, I think I quite like Miss Haywood."

Rothbury turned to Tristan, his lips straightening to a thin line. "Is that so?"

Gabriel's eyes narrowed. Was that a quirk of a taunt he saw in Tristan's eyes? "And why is that?" he asked, hating the curiosity niggling at him.

"Come now, Gabriel," Rothbury stated. "As I remarked this morning, I for one quite enjoy the elegant turn of her neck."

"And when have you had the time to gawk at her neck?" Gabriel asked.

"During dinner last evening," Rothbury answered.

"Should've been there, Gabe," Tristan replied, smiling like an imp. "Her gown was of the palest pink, her skin looked like a ribbon of poured cream."

Gabriel took a deep, calming breath. Since when did his brother wax poetic? He thought of the scattering of dots on the back of her neck and shoulders he had spied during her archery lesson. "She has freckles," he said in an annoyed tone. "Lots of them."

Tristan only shrugged.

"Like me, you never liked freckles, remember?" Gabriel pointed out.

"I don't mind them much now." Tristan waited for his brother to look at him, then raised a challenging brow.

Gabriel nodded slowly. "So your admiration of Miss Haywood is solely founded on creamy skin and freckles?"

"There's more," Tristan said in defense.

"Lord, help me."

"She smells simply delicious."

Gabriel said nothing, bothered as he was that his brother had also noticed her alluring scent.

"And her hair is such a gloriously dark, rich red."

"You've been partial to blondes since birth," Gabriel reminded him.

Tristan responded to his comment with another shrug, but Gabriel hadn't missed his lips twitch with a smile. It seemed that Tristan was deliberately baiting his jealousy. And he'd fallen for it like a stumbling imbecile.

"I must agree with your brother," Rothbury interjected. "She's quite unlike the others."

"And I agree," Gabriel said with exasperated certainty.

"I find enjoyment in her reservation," Tristan continued. "She's serene."

"What? Serene? Reserved? She's impudent and rash."

Tristan grinned. "She has none of the wealth or noble connections as the other ladies and yet holds herself with such quiet dignity, it's as if she fancies herself as superior."

"Miss Greene can be placed in that category as well," Gabriel drawled. "Why not count off her qualities?"

"Ah, here they are now," Tristan replied. "I think I'll go wish them well and express my eagerness for their return." Turning with a grin, he bounded down the stairs to join the growing crowd.

Walking with Miss Greene, Miss Haywood looked decidedly comfortable in a light green muslin that was undoubtedly one of her own, as her breasts appeared contained. And thank God for that. Gabriel didn't think he could handle such a delectable sight from his current vantage point, especially with Rothbury leering down at her like a starved wolf.

Rubbing his stubbled jaw in his hand, Rothbury nodded to himself, apparently making up his mind about something.

"Rothbury," Gabriel growled, a warning in his tone.

The earl pushed off the railing. "I think I'll be on my way."

"Hold." Gabriel stayed him by clamping a hand over his shoulder. "I didn't invite them here to be ravished by you."

Rothbury shot an affronted glare at the hand on his shoulder before shrugging it off. "I'll not ravish them all."

"You'll not place a finger on a single one."

"Come now, Gabriel," Rothbury began, the devil in his gaze. "You know as well as I it wouldn't hurt should I pluck one straggling sheep into a darkened corridor and sample her wares. After all, shouldn't Tristan know if he's choosing a cold fish or an eager student?"

"Stay away from her," Gabriel warned. They both knew he spoke of Miss Haywood.

"Tsk, tsk. I am a guest in your house," Rothbury taunted. "If you recall, I was invited to tour this pile of rocks along with them." He threw what he said next over his shoulder as he sauntered away. "I heard about your little interviews. What would you do? Schedule another one and ask her if I sunk my tongue down her throat?"

An angry growl rose from Gabriel's throat as he threw one arm out, catching Rothbury by the back of his coat and fairly dragging the man to stand before him. "If you do not want me to cut it off with a rusty broadsword, you'll manage to keep it in your mouth." Abruptly, he released him.

The earl stumbled back a bit, but his features yet held an amused expression. "My, my, Gabriel. A little overprotective, are we?" He dusted himself off. "Seems I've some competition. This could be fun."

"I'll be watching you," Gabriel said, stalking away, heading for the wide steps.

As he descended the stairs, he stole a glance at the crowd of women assembled across the hall. Before turning the corner, his eyes instantly connected with Miss Haywood's. She was smiling at something one of the other ladies had said. She bowed her head slightly in acknowledgment of his presence, but Gabriel looked away, leaving her gesture unreciprocated.

"The restoration of Wolverest Castle began in the late fifteenth century," the butler intoned, "and continues today with the exception of the west wing and its original chapel . . . "

As the butler's bored tone droned on and on— mercilessly—Madelyn stood in the back of the crowd, pretending to admire some enormous smoky green vase of which they were told there were only three like it in the world.

She hated tours of great houses. Adversely, it was something the Greenes loved to do whenever they traveled. Throughout her adolescence, Madelyn had accompanied them to more halls, abbeys, castles, and sprawling manors than she could ever count. And if they were reputed to be haunted . . . well, that was all the better.

What Madelyn disliked so fervently about tours was being told where she was allowed to wander and where she was not. It was the forbidden staircase she wanted to explore, the barred dungeon the mistress of the house deemed their sensibilities too fragile to withstand, that frustrated her. Simply put, being herded into room after room in which they were *allowed* to observe did not fascinate her anywhere near as much as a single room they were banned from viewing.

With that in mind, she sighed, thinking of the locked doors barring them from a viewing of the Devine family's private art gallery. When the butler searched through his ring of keys for the last time and then explained he had misplaced the one belonging to that room, Madelyn had to restrain herself from waving madly from the back of the group, volunteering to go and fetch it herself.

The crowd shuffled farther down the hall, the enthusiastic Greenes in lead with the butler. Not surprising to Madelyn, Charlotte chose to wear her spectacles for the tour, hiding them in her reticule until Lord Tristan bid them farewell. There was no way her friend would chance missing a single detail because of her silly reservations about Lord Tristan catching her with her spectacles on. Besides, he wasn't supposed to be joining them again until supper that evening.

As the group of young women made their way into the sculpture room like a pack of sheep bored into a trance, Madelyn held back. In her mind's eye she retraced their steps, thinking there must be at least one other door to the art gallery that might be unlocked. Making a mental map, she pieced the rooms they had visited with their connecting hallways.

"The duchess's parlor," she whispered, glancing over her shoulder down the candlelit corridor behind her. She recalled a pair of tall, white paneled doors behind the butler's back as he launched into his soliloquy of the benefits of the Adam brothers' graceful design. If her calculations were correct, those doors should lead, if not directly, to the private art gallery. It was worth a go.

She peeked around the heavy oak door into the enormous sculpture room, making certain Priscilla hadn't taken notice of her departure. In the far corner, her stepmother stood in deep conversation with Lord Fairbourne. Satisfied, Madelyn turned back and slinked down the corridor, heading for the last room on her left. With one last glance over her shoulder, she ducked into the room.

"My dear Miss Haywood," Lady Beauchamp exclaimed, her voice echoing loudly within the immense gold and cream parlor. "You're not having a good time of it, are you, my gel?"

Madelyn inwardly groaned. "Aunt Lucinda," she said in cautious greeting. Her aunt had apparently spied the row of decanters on the side table when the party visited the room earlier. Obviously, she must have thought to stay behind and sample their contents.

Giving a quiet sigh, Madelyn realized that backing out of the room, though easier than talking to her aunt, wouldn't appease her burgeoning curiosity about those doors. She slipped farther into the shadowed room, lit only by the small fire smoldering in the hearth.

Draining the last remaining drop of wine in her glass, Lady Beauchamp settled it on a small table in front of the crimson settee she lounged upon. "Oh, how my heart breaks for you, child. Oh, a little anyway. This is a competition, after all."

"Whatever do you mean?" Madelyn asked, when in actuality she didn't give a hoot. She casually made her way across the room toward the pair of white doors.

"Good heavens! My meaning is clear," Lady Beauchamp said with a drunken chuckle. "Falling in the pond, addressing His Grace improperly, and to top it all off, you argued with him *and* presented him with your back. By the Fairbournes' account, you've done little to entice his lordship and only raised the ire of the duke by your performances."

Her aunt laughed again. This time the movement threw her off balance and she teetered where she sat. If the woman hadn't been sitting, Madelyn mused, she would have most probably ended up face first on the Aubusson rug.

"I'm not worried," Madelyn replied, walking past the rain-streaked mullioned windows. "If they chose to eliminate me, so be it."

"Oh, I hope not, child. You might not catch yourself a husband but you've done well giving us all something to giggle about."

Halfway to the doors across the room, Madelyn

feigned an interest in the elaborate scrollwork of the ceiling, partly because the detail was astonishing and partly because the distraction kept her from becoming irritated by her aunt's words.

"Such visits to the country . . . *hiccup* . . . I find them dreadfully boring." Lady Beauchamp blotted her handkerchief across her chest. "Awfully damp in here, is it not? That tiny fire does little to chase away the shadows, and warms the room even less."

"Perhaps it is so because it has been raining since just after noon," Madelyn suggested, hoping her aunt wouldn't ask her why she was about to jiggle the handles of the set of doors. To her surprise, they turned easily. She smiled, the thrill of a pending exploration making her heart race.

"Got lost, did you?" Lady Beauchamp asked, rocking back and forth in an effort to scoot her robust frame to the edge of the settee.

"Er . . . yes. Do you need assistance?"

She shooed Madelyn's question away with her handkerchief. "Those doors will lead you to a corridor connecting back to the sculpture room," her aunt said, pausing in the act of standing so she could regain her sense of balance.

Madelyn's shoulders slumped in defeat. "Thank you," she said politely, swinging open the doors.

"You thought those would get you inside that private art gallery, didn't you, child?"

Eyes blinking in surprise, Madelyn turned back, catching her aunt's conspiratorial wink.

"You're not a very clever one are you, child? I'm sitting here chirping merry and even I could figure that one out. Maybe that's your trouble. You need a drink."

Simply at a loss for words, Madelyn managed a shaky nod and half a smile. The woman had been offending people for years—herself since birth. Most blamed Lady Beauchamp's loose tongue and slanting remarks on her fondness for taking frequent dips into the brandy decanter; however, Madelyn knew her aunt, drunk or sober, simply did not have the continuity of thought to see beyond her opinions to the implied insult.

She slipped out into the dark corridor, shutting out what little light the parlor provided once she closed the doors at her back. As her eyes adjusted to the darkness, a rosy glow of candlelight pooled onto the floor at the end of the hall. She strode toward it, disappointed she had to rejoin the group and cut her exploring short. The sound of hushed voices reached her ears, stalling her footsteps.

" . . . so blue, they're like those of an angel . . . "

"He's so tall," someone said on a sigh. "His shoulders, strong and broad. I thought I'd swoon into his arms when he looked at me."

"Were you not overcome with envy yesterday as he so obviously tried to pretend not to be looking at me? A subtle flirt, he is."

Madelyn instantly recognized the whiny tone of Miss Bernadette Fairbourne. It seemed Lord Tristan's admiring flock was in the process of counting off his various attributes. She inhaled, preparing to clear her throat as she rounded the corner into their line of vision. The next comment stopped her cold.

"To think we'd want Lord Tristan when such an impressive specimen as His Grace is around," Bernadette proclaimed. "His lordship's a veritable schoolboy compared to the duke. His looks so brooding, his presence so commanding. I believe his apparent disinterest in marriage hides a deep craving for feminine attention. And I should think any one of us could change his mind."

"Quite. At least one of *us*, anyway."

There was a pause as the group did their best to smother a rush of giggles.

"Hush. She'll hear you."

"Who? Charlotte? She's too busy in the corner, hiding from Lord Tristan," Bernadette crooned. "Poor dear, it's too bad she put on her spectacles. Did you see the look of panic on her face when he surprised us all and entered the room? It's obvious she didn't think he'd actually *join* the tour." She paused to giggle. "He keeps turning to look at her and she keeps revolving so that he can't."

"Well, she can have him," someone added with dramatic conviction, perhaps the other Fairbourne girl or Laura Ellis.

"Oh, I'm not certain." Harriet. The high-pitched, singsong voice belonged to her cousin, Madelyn was sure. "I still prefer Lord Tristan."

"Nonsense, Harriet," Bernadette said with a laugh. "None of us should put much credence in the fact His Grace wouldn't change his mind and take a bride himself. It would be too late then, should one of us marry Lord Tristan. Dreams of being Duchess of Wolverest would vanish in a pinch."

"Still," Harriet whined.

"Perish the thought! We need your concentration. We've got bigger game to fell," Bernadette instructed. "But remember, ladies, this is a friendly competition, discretion is the key."

Their chattering continued, but it was obvious they were moving to rejoin the tour as their voices faded away, as did the weak candlelight that had accompanied them.

Madelyn's breath rushed past her lips in a soft whoosh. They wanted the duke, not Lord Tristan. For a few moments she just stood there and blinked, not knowing how or if this recent discovery even affected her. She needed to go back to her room and think.

She turned, choosing to retrace her steps back down the corridor and through the parlor instead of making her presence known. Each step brought her further into the inky darkness.

The wispy hairs on the back of her neck stood up as a shiver trickled down her spine. She could have sworn there was someone else in the darkness along with her, echoing her every step. She shrugged the notion off, blaming her nerves on her newfound discovery.

Had those women been feigning an interest in Lord Tristan while secretly hankering after the duke? Or did this just come about? And what was she going to do? And why must something be done about it? Funny, she actually felt a twinge of sympathy for Lord Tristan.

The corridor seemed darker, longer, and without the candlelight behind her from the sculpture gallery, Madelyn could barely see her hands in front of her face. Halfway down she made out a sliver of light emitting from the doors that were now partially open. Strange, she could have sworn she'd shut them. She slowed, reaching out until her fingertips brushed the cool door handles.

She hesitated. Her aunt was very likely still in the parlor, and Madelyn knew she would have to assuage her curiosity with an explanation as to why she had returned this way. Then she dismissed the thought. Her inebriated aunt wouldn't remember her passing through in the first place. With a click and a moan, the doors opened farther. The room was empty.

In a flurry of movement, a shadow swooped from behind her and she was yanked back inside the dark corridor by large hands molding around her shoulders in an unrelenting grip. In a space of a second she found herself pinned to the wall by a hard, unyielding, masculine body.

Chapter 10

Madelyn looked up into eyes of blue flame and a face framed by a tousled mane of ebony locks.

"Gabriel," she breathed.

"Ah, hell." His dark head dropped down. "Mistook you for someone else, I'm afraid." He looked up, his face dangerously close.

"W-Would you mind telling me who?"

He shook his head slowly, not to negate her request, she supposed, but out of irritation with himself. Whomever he had expected her to be, Gabriel's entire body was tight and ready to pounce.

He looked a bit disheveled. Bristles dusted his chin and jaw, telling her he hadn't shaven today. And his cravat lay untied and loose around the corded muscles of his neck.

"Just leaving the sculpture gallery, then?" he asked with a flicker of anger. He leaned in, his hands splayed on the wall, framing her shoulders.

"N-No."

"Then what were you doing tiptoeing in the dark?" His gaze affixed on her mouth. Without breaking his concentration, he shifted his weight. But the action did little to make their position less scandalous if any one should happen by the room.

She swallowed, distracted by her initial fear and the feel of his warm, long body so close to her own. "I became lost— Oh, there's no sense hiding it. I was looking for your art gallery. Your butler had forgotten his key."

Bitterness stabbed at Gabriel's insides at her bold lie. On his way through the castle, hunting for Rothbury, he had happened by Lady Beauchamp, who claimed he could find a wandering guest beyond the double doors in the parlor. He didn't believe the woman, as she smelled heavily of spirits and swayed where she stood as if aboard a sailing vessel. However, he felt compelled to inspect her assertion to be sure it was not the earl watching and waiting to strike. Once inside the dark corridor, he had overheard the bride-hopefuls concocting a secret plan to have a go at him instead of Tristan.

And now Madelyn stood before him, apparently just coming from a talk with the others. He shook his head, staring down at her, hoping his glare intimidated her into admitting the truth.

With a stony expression, he watched her swallow convulsively. "Where did you come from?" she asked.

He lifted the corner of his mouth in a disbelieving smirk. "Is there something you'd like to explain to me?"

"Well . . . no," she muttered, perplexed by his question. Perhaps she should explain to him the effect he had on her body by standing so sinfully close, she thought. With each breath she took, her bodice brushed against his chest. She tried not to notice, but the sensation was hard to ignore.

"It's not safe to wander alone in the dark," he replied darkly.

His warning made her curious. "Why? Are there hungry beasts afoot?" she asked with a nervous chuckle.

"Indeed, there are."

Startled by his quiet words, she wanted to meet his gaze, to discern if he was teasing her again as he often did, but she couldn't stop staring at his mouth. She closed her eyes. All she had to do was stand on the tips of her toes . . .

He leaned in closer and whispered, "Go. Now. Return to the others."

But Madelyn didn't want to leave. A yearning, sudden and unbidden, rose up within her and she shivered, realizing she wanted—no, needed—him to kiss her again.

"You're right. I should go," she began, not caring that she was speaking her thoughts aloud. She stared at his lips. "It isn't at all proper for me to want a kiss."

She had only enough time for a short inhalation before his mouth swooped down and caught hers once, twice, and again for a series of separate, thorough kisses, each one robbing her of her breath. An acute, all too short surge of pleasure stung her senses, prompting a surprised but sleepy-sounding moan from the back of her throat.

Gabriel pulled his mouth away, inhaling slowly, deeply. She wanted more, he instinctively knew. And there was nothing he wanted more at that moment than to taste her again as well. She smelled so sweet, her lips so soft, so eager.

Only he wanted more, much more, than he had a right to coax this woman to give. Her luscious breasts rose and fell against his chest, triggering a molten desire, which raged in his veins like nothing he'd ever experienced before. His mouth, his teeth in particular, itched to graze the soft skin swelling above her bodice.

"You need to leave," he whispered hoarsely.

Oh, but it had ended before it began, Madelyn thought. He made her feel light, feminine, desirable, and her mind and body craved more of his attention. "Please, not yet," she pleaded, tilting her face up to his.

He closed his eyes on a low groan, as if knowing she wanted more of his touch caused him physical pain. She watched his throat convulse as he swallowed. On the wall, bracing her shoulders, his hands trembled under the pressure of supreme self-control. She wondered if Gabriel thought he'd made a mistake and was, in fact, repulsed by what he'd just done.

On the contrary, he was wondering if the bewitching woman realized the power she wielded over him. At this point, she could have asked him for anything in the world and he would have no choice but to grant her wish. He'd never felt so utterly weak.

At his hesitation, Madelyn's bravery wavered and she turned her face away, ashamed by her behavior. Closing her eyes, embarrassment flooded her thoughts. She wanted him to kiss her, and he apparently wanted nothing more than for her to leave.

Damp heat fanned down her neck toward her breasts, and she opened her eyes a slit to see that Gabriel had lowered his head to her bodice. Shivers of delight scattered across her as his smooth lips brushed the skin at her neckline. He exhaled a low growl and raised his head, gritting his teeth.

"I want you. Dear God, how I want you. I can't—" He cleared his throat. "Go."

She took a deep breath, summoning the strength to turn and walk away. He was right. She should go, but that didn't stop her from feeling a shameful twinge of disappointment.

But then his sculpted lips brushed across the apple of her cheek. Her eyelashes fluttered closed. "Please, Gabriel," she whispered.

With his hands still braced on the wall at her shoulders, Gabriel held himself back, not allowing any part of his body to touch hers except for his chest as they each took a breath. "Please Gabriel, what?" he asked, his words mostly air.

"Kiss me again," she breathed.

"As you wish," came his dark whisper.

And then he leaned down, smoothing his slightly stubbled chin down her cheek as his warm lips hunted for hers. He smelled mildly of brandy and leather, and she swallowed, feeling drunk with sensation, her arms hanging boneless at her sides. A shiver ran down her spine, and she tilted her head, raising her chin. He gave it a small, silent kiss, then, with a breathy moan, he pressed his lips onto her mouth in gentle exploration.

They stood there in the dark corridor, his mouth slowly, methodically, slanting across hers again and again. He tended to her mouth as if she were a rare, delectable sweet. As if he had all the time in the world, he savored every honeyed nook of her mouth with each dip and swirl of his tongue. And he kept his hands planted on the wall the entire time. Vaguely, she was glad for that. The power of his kiss alone nearly made her knees buckle.

In the darkness, she felt consumed by him. Liquid heat coursed down her body, settling into a gentle ache at the center of her being. She had no idea what to make of the sensation, only that he provoked it and she wanted it to continue.

As he continued to explore her mouth, one of his hands fell away from the wall and his long fingers smoothed along her naked collarbone, making her nearly jump out of her skin with delight. He moved gently up her neck to cradle her jaw within his large hand. She felt as delicate as a porcelain doll. Her arms felt heavy, but she lifted them, grabbing the lapels of his jacket and pulling him toward her to deepen the kiss.

Her small act of insistence unleashed the beast within him. Their kiss turned into a torrent of passion. Gabriel's groan and Madelyn's answering feminine sigh broke the dark silence of the corridor and she slid her arms around his neck, bringing him even closer to her. He intensified the kiss even more, thrusting his tongue deep inside the sweetness of her mouth as his hips pushed against hers, echoing the motion in a maddeningly wicked way. He continued his thorough and steady siege of her senses, wordlessly coaxing her on as she shyly tried to match the cadence of his passion. Boldly, one of her arms snaked under his coat and around his waist, and she pulled him closer, desperately trying to fulfill a need burning inside her that nearly drove her out of her head.

Gabriel groaned, pinning her hips tighter against the wall with a sudden push of his. She grasped at his strong back, wanting to feel more of him, wanting to crawl inside him. The kiss steadily escalated, his lips moving hotly, his tongue stroking hers, making her nearly cry out.

Running her hands up the sleeves of his frock coat and then his shoulders, she sunk her fingers in the thick, silky black curls at the back of his head. He stopped cold.

Breaking the kiss, Gabriel shifted his weight off of her. Panting, he looked into her eyes, and she recognized the power of his restrained passion. With their chests rising and falling from exertion, Gabriel turned his head away, glancing at the open parlor doors where he'd yanked her from minutes ago.

"Wh-What . . . " Madelyn began shakily.

"Return to your chamber." He shook his head, still not looking at her. "And lock the door. If I knock on your door within the next couple of hours, by God, don't let me in."

"I—I don't have the key."

"Then push something very heavy in front of the door," he commanded gruffly.

She stood there, catching her own breath, her mind reeling with what had just happened between them.

"Go," he ordered, his sharp tone an unexpected bite to her fragile state.

Hot tears stung the back of her eyes. Blinking them away, she ducked from under his ridged arm next to her shoulder and, without a backward glance, hitched up her skirts and broke into a run, her wobbly legs not breaking rhythm all the long way to her assigned bedchamber. Once there, she slammed the door behind her and leaned her back against it. She gasped for air, trying to catch her breath while willing her heartbeat to slow and steady itself.

Her legs trembled. Bringing her fingers to her lips, she touched them as they yet throbbed with the faint memory of the duke's tender onslaught. She closed her eyes and slid to the floor. What in the world had just happened? She knew better than to allow herself to be lured onto a scoundrel's web of seduction.

She had borne witness to her father's indifference to her mother in adolescent confusion. Her mother appeared unmoved by this chink in her marriage. Seeing that had made Madelyn fume. If she couldn't have the whole of a man's heart, she told her mother with all her eight-year-old fury, then she didn't want anything to do with it. Her mother had smiled, leaned down to ruffle her unruly locks, and told her never to set her sights on a man who had too much money and too much free time. "Marry your best friend," she had advised her, "be he a stable lad or the King of England, for he'll never think to break your heart."

Madelyn pushed herself upright. Gabriel's unwavering attention, his subtle flirtation, his insistence that she address him by his given name . . . why, he must have purposely followed her into the dark corridor. Tomorrow, she would demand an apology and that he leave her be. He should be able to control himself. Or she hoped so because it seemed that she could not. If anything, tonight she had discovered a part of herself that she never knew existed. A shocking part of her that desperately wanted to return to Gabriel and offer her mouth and anything else he wanted for his possession.

Leaning her head back against the polished wood of the door, she sighed, her traitorous mind replaying their kiss. His touch was so tender, so intense. And Lord, she wanted him to do it again. With a lurch of fear she realized how fortunate it was for her that he had still been in possession of his senses and was able to stop himself from further ravishment. Her body, it seemed, did not listen to her mind. Who knows what would have happened if he hadn't stopped? She could only imagine.

Rothbury had tried to kiss her. But she was never so swept away to allow him to do so. She'd duck, dash, or push him away, her mind never dreaming of what his kiss would be like.

There was a click and she heard as well as felt the door rumble behind her as someone tried to open it. Her back pressed to it, her heart palpitated. Dear Lord, Gabriel had come!

Swallowing, she looked longingly over to the armoire across the room, wishing she had scooted it to the door when she first entered her chamber. The door rumbled again. How in the world was she going to keep him out? Her puny weight would never be able to keep him from opening it.

"Madelyn?" Priscilla's muffled voice came from the other side of the door. "Madelyn? Are you in there?"

The breath she had been holding rushed out in a loud whoosh. It was only her stepmother, not the duke. She was relieved. And strangely disappointed. "Yes . . . yes, I'm here."

"Wherever had you run off to?"

She turned about and opened the door, encountering Priscilla's deceptively angelic beauty. "I felt ill," she lied. "So I returned to my room."

Her stepmother glanced at the door with disgust. "It's so humid; the door must be sticking." Turning, she studied Madelyn. "My, you are flushed. Your lips . . . they almost look swollen. You'd best not be getting ill on me, now with only a sennight left to sway the duke. Remember . . . your mother's cottage."

Madelyn nodded, shuffling over to her bed.

"I'll allow you half an hour to rest, then we'll have Jenny dress you for supper. I hear the duke might be in attendance," Priscilla added with excitement.

Madelyn groaned, plopping down on her bed,

instantly enveloped within the cushy, ivory-colored coverlet.

Priscilla took a long, assessing look of her, then flounced to the dressing room door. "Let's take advantage of this opportunity. It's time you wore my dark green velvet gown."

Madelyn whimpered, covering her face with a pillow. It was Priscilla's best, newest, slinkiest gown. It had a low, scooped back and, of course, would fit tight across her ample bosom, nearly pushing her breasts up to her nose.

"If this doesn't manage to catch the duke's attention," her stepmother stated, a wicked smirk on her pale lips, "then nothing will."

Madelyn snuggled farther within the blankets. Little did Priscilla know exactly how much of the duke's attention she already had. Hang the apology. She was going to act mature and do the right thing from now on. She was going to hide in her room.

Chapter 11

"**P**sst. Wake up, Madelyn."

"I'm not sleeping and go away," she said, her voice muffled beneath her pillow. The bed dipped to the side where Charlotte sat.

"Whatever happened during the tour? One minute you were standing there and the next you were gone," Charlotte said, wresting the pillow from Madelyn's grasp. "And you missed supper. Priscilla's furious. Here. You must be starved. I brought you an apple."

"No, thank you," Madelyn replied, still spread out on her stomach across her bed. "I feel quite ill." And that was the truth. The duke had kissed her, passionately, and she hadn't wanted him to stop. The memory of their encounter was burned into her mind.

Indeed, missing supper was a mistake. As she lay in her bed, all she could think about was him. If he had come to her room as he warned her he might, she wasn't sure she would have sent him away. What did that say about her inner strength, her resolve? Years of alternately avoiding or scolding self-centered scoundrels did absolutely nothing to prepare her for Gabriel. And what compounded matters, what turned her stomach to knots, was the fact that apparently she wasn't the only one who was attracted to him. From what she'd overheard hours before, there were at least four other females under this roof who were thinking about changing Gabriel's mind about marriage.

"Maddie? Did you fall asleep?"

Rolling onto her back, Madelyn opened first one eye, then the other, her eyes adjusting to the low light emitted from the small hearth across the room. She eyed the green velvet gown slung over the silk dressing screen. "So how was it?" Madelyn asked. "The rest of the tour and dinner, I mean. Did Lord Tristan speak with you, look at you, confess his undying admiration and swear off all other women?"

Charlotte sighed, spinning the apple she held by its stem. "He surprised us all and joined the tour. Saw me in my spectacles, I'm afraid."

"Oh, Charlotte," Madelyn murmured with sympathy. "Chances are he has already seen you in them prior to this occasion. He did pull you from that carriage accident years ago."

"Yes, but he wasn't looking at me then as a potential bride. And listen to this," her friend said, leaning forward. "Harriet told me he eliminated Julienne Campbell because one of her bottom teeth turned inward." She smiled wide, baring her teeth. Then she spoke while barely moving her lips, "Peas luk. Ahrrre 'ine cruked?"

"Your teeth are fine, Lottie," Madelyn said with a shake of her head. "And I'm sure Julienne's are as well. 'Tis Lord Tristan whose *mind* is crooked."

"You think I'm silly, don't you? Well, if he'll cross off a beautiful girl with one crooked tooth, he very well will think nothing of axing a pale, flat-chested, spectacle-wearing dullard."

Madelyn whacked her in the head with a pillow. "You are not a dullard."

Charlotte shrugged, sobering. "I would have enjoyed your company at supper. I was seated between your stepmother and Laura Ellis this time."

A twinge of guilt stabbed at Madelyn's conscience. She had pleaded a headache to a furious Priscilla as she returned from their dressing room, holding the velvet gown that now hung on the dressing screen. Her stepmother had been so angry, she'd even forgotten to lock her in her room before she left for dinner. But after hearing that Gabriel was scheduled to attend, she couldn't fathom sitting down to dine, squished in a snug dress while he scowled down at her, or worse, ignored her.

"I'm sorry, Lottie," Madelyn replied with sincerity. In addition, she knew she couldn't handle watching the ladies keep one eye on Gabriel while they pretended to maintain an interest in Lord Tristan with the other. She wouldn't have been able to keep from rolling her own eyes and throwing up her arms with the absurdity of it all.

"Well, I don't blame you. Could hardly eat myself. I was nearly overcome by Laura's perfume," Charlotte said, crinkling up her nose. "The girl must have fairly drowned herself in lavender."

"Lord Tristan's favorite perfume?"

"No, actually," Charlotte said, sounding surprised herself. "In fact, Lady Rosalind mentioned after the tour that the duke rather enjoyed the lavender-lined path in the courtyard."

"I see."

"Change your mind about the apple?"

"No, thank you."

Charlotte tilted her head to the side to bite into the fruit, but paused and spoke instead. "His Grace was there, you know."

"Yes, Priscilla had said as much," Madelyn said, trying hard not to needle Charlotte with questions about Gabriel. Had he teased the other girls like he did her? Or, did he seem out of sorts? Thoughtful? Did his smile come easily and often like it did when they spoke? Did he ask—

"He inquired after you. Priscilla told him you were unwell, and he expressed his desire that whatever it was that ailed you didn't keep you from the riding jaunt to the falls tomorrow."

Madelyn groaned. She hoped he wouldn't be joining them. If it was the same cascading falls she frequented when she lived up here as a child, she certainly didn't want the sinful duke to intrude upon her decent childhood memories—let alone face him in the daylight.

She sat up, holding her bent knees to her chest. "I'm a coward, Lottie."

"Don't be silly, it is *me* who always hides. In fact, that's why I came to see you now. They're all down there, the chaperones, drinking Madeira and playing charades. I daresay, the entire lot is top heavy. I pleaded an upset stomach, told my mother I was off to bed when in actuality I am too shy to play their game."

"I don't blame you. I wouldn't want to play with them either." Madelyn grimaced. "No, Charlotte. I am a true coward. Do you remember how we had that conversation back in London, the day after the ball?"

"Of course." Charlotte stood, and twirled the apple again by its stem. "After scolding me for keeping my little secret, you told me you had met a bull-headed but devastatingly handsome scoundrel who had fooled you into accepting the invitation when you ran into the garden."

"And do you remember why I ran?" Madelyn prodded.

"Because you despised the Duke of Wolverest and his brother and you did not want any part of their 'arrogant madness.'"

"I thought so. I think so." Frustrated, Madelyn rubbed her temples. "I suppose there is an underlying reason. Perhaps I was afraid if I joined in the bride hunt, I might be painfully compared to the other, more sophisticated, infinitely more desirable women, and be forced to confront my own blinding inadequacies."

Charlotte smiled warmly, still twirling the apple. "That is perfectly understandable. I felt that way at times."

"How could you say that? You are beautiful."

"I hardly feel that way," Charlotte scoffed. "Why do you think I worry so and purposely walk around nearly blind? There's a welt on my shin the size of Cornwall from all the times I walk into the legs of furniture."

"You try to change yourself to fit someone's . . . some *man's* ideal . . . I cannot do that. I will not live my life trying to be something I am not." Gabriel was making her so confused. If he thought her so unfit, so unacceptable that he *mercifully* allowed her to attend this stupid ball, why had he kissed her, why did he look at her in that unnerving, yet thrilling way, and why had he not sent her home a long time ago? "I'm sorry. I should not have said such a thing."

Charlotte shrugged. "It is true. I will not hide from the fact. We want the same thing from life, from love, we just have a different way of going about it. We all need to marry well. I need to wed, Maddie, and if looking a certain way or acting a certain way will get me there, so be it."

The stem of the apple weakened and the fruit Charlotte was holding dropped to the floor. A soft knock sounded at the door at the same time.

The friends shared a glance. "Who could it be at this hour?" Charlotte asked.

Indeed. Everyone was downstairs and according to Lottie were all deep in their cups. Besides, Priscilla wouldn't knock, she'd just barge in.

Madelyn swung her legs to the side of the bed at a second round of knocking. Grabbing her thin robe, she shrugged it on and tied the sash. "Your mother could be looking for you," she said, standing. "Perhaps she went to check in on you and found you gone. This would be the next logical place she'd look."

Charlotte agreed, then loped over to the chaise lounge to feign not feeling well.

Madelyn padded toward the door, picking up the apple. She hesitated before the closed door. "Who's there?" Silence. She looked over her shoulder at Charlotte. "Perhaps they've gone."

Turning the brass knob, the door opened with a groan. A tall black shape stepped forward.

"Forbidden fruit," Gabriel murmured with dark amusement.

Madelyn glanced down at the apple clutched to her chest, then hastily hid it behind her back. Giving the appearance of temptation to a man who kissed her senseless hours before was certainly not an intelligent idea. She took a deep breath and instantly regretted it. He smelled warm and alluring, and she struggled with the compulsion to step closer into his aura of heat.

"What are you doing here?" she asked, trying to appear nonchalant. In truth her entire body fairly thrummed because of his nearness. His black locks were tousled, as if he'd just run his hand through his hair, and the top three buttons of his shirt where undone, his untied cravat hanging loosely around his neck. He looked adorably rumpled, which softened his cross expression.

"You don't listen," he drawled, slowly waggling one long finger. His azure eyes glittered with the reflection of the firelight coming from within her room . . . and with something else, something darker, dangerous. "You weren't supposed to open the door."

The deep timbre on his voice made her shiver. "If you weren't expecting me to open the door, why did you bother to knock?"

"A test."

"And I failed."

"Miserably," he said, his slow, appreciative gaze feasting on her scantily attired body from the top of her head down to her toes and all the way back again.

Never in her life had a man looked at her so thoroughly, as if he wanted to consume her. Now that was a silly thought. However he could have looked, she must have imagined it, that was all there was to it. Swallowing loudly, Madelyn crossed her arms over her chest in a shielding gesture that she hoped came off as indignation.

"All right, then," she said. "Seeing as the test is complete, I bid you good eve—"

He took a step closer, raising a hand to press firmly against the door. "Are you alone?"

She took a step back. "No."

At his skeptical look, she stepped aside momentarily, revealing Charlotte lounging on the chaise. Or she hoped, anyway. There was a chance her timid friend had gone into hiding upon hearing Gabriel's voice.

But he didn't remove his piercing eyes from her face to see for himself if she was lying. So she stood there, shivering as the heat from her room escaped into the drafty hall.

"What do you want?" she asked, tossing a long, loose lock over her shoulder.

He gaze was direct and unflinching. "A confession."

Her brow furrowed. "Whatever for?"

"You are playing a dangerous game, Miss Haywood." Gabriel's deceptively quiet voice vibrated through her.

Whatever did he mean? "I'm not playing any sort of *game*." She placed both of her hands on her hips. "I've a mind to think *you* are the one playing a *game*, sir. I didn't come knocking on *your* door in the middle of the night."

Straightening, he shook his head slowly, a hint of irritation shining in his eyes. "I will not profess innocence. I came here knowing you'd be abed."

"And I was," she said with a brisk shrug, stating the obvious.

"I came here thinking you were alone."

"And I'm not," she pointed out flippantly.

He ducked his dark head down, close to hers. "Miss Greene sits fifteen feet away and 'tis the only reason my hands remain at my sides and not sculpting over your naked, quivering flesh."

Her heart skipped as the burn of a blush crept up her throat to her cheeks. Some traitorous part of her body delighted at his words, but then her rational mind took over. Prior to his threat of ravishment, she'd thought that maybe he would come to apologize for his part in their unexpected kiss, but it had become evident he entertained no such benevolence.

Her ire rejuvenated by her thoughts, Madelyn straightened her shoulders. "Please step back. I'm shutting the door now." She hoped her voice sounded more convincing than it did to her own ears.

He gave her a slight bow of his head and turned to leave. "Don't forget about tomorrow afternoon," he said over his shoulder.

The ride to the falls.

"You'll be happy to know I shall be in attendance." He smiled, wide and arrogant.

"Thank you for supplying that piece of information," she said sourly. "Perhaps I shall have a headache tomorrow afternoon and spend the day resting in my room."

He turned, walking backward down the hall, his swagger matching his roguish smile. "And perhaps I'll carry you down to the stables slung over my shoulder. I'll spend the rest of the day relishing the memory of having your—"

"Stop!" she called out, throwing up a hand. "Do not say another word. I don't want to hear—"

"I think you do."

"I certainly do not," she said flatly, before rushing to shut the door.

It suddenly dawned on her why so many otherwise prudent women turned to milk toast from one devilish glance, one soul-searing kiss: being good and proper took hard work, and being bad was . . . sinfully easy.

An unreachable concern hung just above her present thoughts. What had Gabriel said that confused her? Oh yes, he had wanted a confession. It was the second time he had asked for one. And whatever for? For this *game* he claimed she was playing? Had he noticed her plan to keep Charlotte away from Lord Tristan?

Leaning her back against the door, she sighed and threw an exasperated glance at her friend. "I'm sorry," she said shakily.

Charlotte's expression was of pure astonishment. "Was that who I thought it was?"

Clutching the apple to her chest, Madelyn nodded, thankful for the solid support of the door at her back. Surely temptation awaited in the hall.

Gabriel stalked down the hall, mindless to the cool drafts haunting the corridor like floating specters, mindless to the deep shadows swallowing the carpet before him. His alert mind and body was yet fully focused on Miss Haywood. She had answered the door in her blasted night rail.

The infernal woman had no idea the picture she had presented standing in her thin gown with the firelight at her back. She might as well have been naked.

Muscles tense, his blood threatened to boil over unless he appeased the lust coiling within his ravenous soul. His body ached for her touch with a fierceness he'd never known he possessed. And his anger at the prospect of her betrayal only amplified his hunger. Some low and wicked part of him seethed with the desire to show her the risks involved with playing this foolish game of trying to tempt him. She was playing with fire.

So, the brides-to-be thought they could change his mind about marriage? He had half expected this . . . this turn of attention from his brother to himself. He suspected the silly chits would get it into their heads that one of them could change his mind. But not her. Not Madelyn. Oh, he wasn't worried about the other women. He knew without a doubt none of them would ever be able to sway his mind. Their manners were faultless, their form always the epitome of social grace.

Perfectly forgettable.

He wasn't so sure about Miss Haywood. The pang of her deceit rankled his spirit. He had believed her. He had believed she didn't want anything at all to do with his bride hunt.

So then why do you keep her here?

The answer came easily, though it was no less of a shock. He kept her here for selfish reasons. Hell, he had to give up the pretense that he kept Miss Haywood under his roof because he thought he could alter her opinion of his brother, that maybe she'd begin to find Tristan appealing, that maybe Tristan would choose her. All of those reasons were glaringly false. In fact, if his brother did choose her, and if the aggravating woman accepted, he just might go mad.

He had kept her here for himself. To see what she did next, said next, wore next; to see what new feeling, new insight, her smile inspired within himself. It was suddenly apparent that somehow he had allowed her to break some unseen barrier within him.

And her only weapon was her sincerity. If she was part of this ruse, if she thought to trick him, it meant all his impressions of her were based on a lie. He didn't want to believe it, but it appeared to be true.

Tomorrow, Tristan had scheduled a ride to the falls on the outskirts of the Wolverest estate. Perhaps there he could lure her away from the others and persuade her into a confession. Yes, that could work. Perhaps in the light of a new day, the situation would untangle itself.

Chapter 12

⟨⟨◦◦⟩⟩

T hey were loaded in a wagon like sheep at the market.

"The terrain is simply too steep," Lord Tristan was explaining, handing Belinda Fairbourne up into the waiting wagon laden with blankets and pillows of every size. He waited until she settled her skirts, then strode over to collect her sister and guide her up the steps placed at the open end of the wagon by the footman.

"What valleys we will cross," he continued, "are strewn with ruts and rocks. Too dangerous, I'm afraid. Can't have any of my precious spring blossoms thrown from your mounts."

Madelyn grumbled. "More likely, his concern is for his horse's welfare alone," she muttered under her breath. Standing with arms crossed over her chest in a mutinied manner, her gray wool cloak whipped and flapped in the brisk wind. Her wide-brimmed bonnet was secured to her head with numerous pins and a band of yellow ribbon tied tight under her chin, but the breeze still threatened to lift it off her head.

Charlotte stood next to her, spectacle-free and apparently sinking in the mud from the previous evening's downpour. And sinking fast. Her friend was at least a foot shorter.

Madelyn looked down at Charlotte's feet with avid concern. Only there wasn't any mud, just gravel. A niggling suspicion surfaced in her mind. "Charlotte Greene," Madelyn admonished. "Are you slouching?"

Charlotte only gave her a side glance, hesitant to break her attention from Lord Tristan. "Ah . . . do I *look* like I'm slouching?"

"I . . . I suppose not." A frown wrinkled her brow. "That is, if one isn't aware of your true stature."

"Good," Charlotte mumbled out of the corner of her mouth. "Because I am."

Madelyn's jaw dropped. "Whatever for?"

"Shh, Maddie," Charlotte pleaded.

Relaxing her defensive stance, Madelyn stared down at her friend with a sense of wonder and growing amusement. "Let me guess," she whispered. "Lord of Perfection doesn't like tall women."

Charlotte nodded solemnly, trembling a touch from the effort it took to hold herself with bent knees for an extended period of time. "Tell me this . . . do you see Miss Laura Ellis here?"

Madelyn glanced about. The long-limbed blonde was nowhere to be seen. "Don't tell me he got rid of her too?"

"As a matter of fact he did. She left this morning during breakfast . . . in a fit of tears."

"But why would she leave?" Madelyn asked, knowing the woman had set her bull's-eye mark on Gabriel's heart instead.

"You might have too if he told you that your skirts were so long that he fancied he could use the material to drape one of the towering columns in the ballroom."

"Oh dear," Madelyn exclaimed, regretting now that she had arrived at the breakfast table after just about everyone had finished.

"It didn't end there. He went on to say that he'd prefer to have a bride whose feet wouldn't hang off the end of the bed."

Madelyn's mouth dropped open again.

"She was mortified," Charlotte continued in a whisper. "Called him a libertine and dumped an entire pitcher of cold milk from the side table onto his lap."

"Good Lord. What did he do?"

"Well," Charlotte said, blinking, "jumped up, of course. I couldn't quite make out the look on his face—no spectacles, you know—but I think . . . I think he was laughing."

"No doubt the coxcomb thought he was being droll."

"I'm not certain. It was sort of . . . oh . . . I shouldn't say."

"Go on," Madelyn urged. "He's almost done handing up Harriet." She looked over her shoulder and spied three riders approaching through a clinging cloud of mist on the crest of a hill. The party looked to include Gabriel, Lord Fairbourne, and Lord Rothbury. This jaunt to the falls seemed less appealing with every passing second. Her heart lurched as Gabriel touched the rim of his beaver topper in apparent greeting to her, though the affable gesture was outshadowed by his scowl.

The memory of their kiss in the dark corridor spurred a shiver of awareness to skip down her spine. She cleared her throat, suddenly burdened with the predicament of how one was supposed to behave in the light of a new day following such a scandalous encounter. She'd kissed him, for heaven's sake! Not that he was an unwilling participant, but still, never in her life would she have dreamed that she would be found in this situation. Perhaps pretending nothing happened at all was the easiest approach, if not the most cowardly.

"Do tell me what you had meant," Madelyn pressed, pretending she hadn't noticed the duke at all.

"Well, it isn't at all very cordial of me to say, but . . . Julienne Campbell constantly proclaimed she was most definitely the greatest beauty in all of England, and Laura Ellis often reminded all of us that men preferred long, sleek limbs. So, Lord Tristan's remarks almost felt . . . " She shrugged. "I don't know. I'll just say their reactions to his criticisms were interesting."

Madelyn shook her head in disapproval. "He certainly isn't a gentleman. Surely you now see how low the man can stoop, how callous and insensitive? Again, I beg you to see his true character, Lottie.

Why set your cap for a man so well equipped to inflict pain?"

But her query went unanswered as the man in question settled his gaze on her friend, crooking his finger at her while the breeze ruffled his dark auburn locks. "You're next, Miss Greene," he said.

Madelyn stayed her with a gentle nudge of her elbow. "About the slouching," she said quickly. "You're forgetting a most important detail."

"And that would be . . . "

"You, dear, are as short as I am."

Charlotte took a deep breath, apparently contemplating the benefits—if there were any—of continuing to pretend to be something she was not. She nodded her reluctant agreement and cast Madelyn a small thankful smile. "I have been silly, haven't I?" Bending forward, she feigned dusting off her skirts, straightened to her full height, then flounced over to a patient Lord Tristan, who made a great show of handing her up the steps and into the wagon.

"I say, Miss Greene," he whispered into Charlotte's ear, and Madelyn strained to hear his softly spoken words over the twitter of the other girls in the wagon. "After dinner this evening, would you care to accompany me to my private library?" His blue gaze, falsely innocent in appearance, dipped to Charlotte's mouth as he waited patiently for her response. "I'm afraid disappointment haunts me ever since we missed our chance after the musicale the other evening."

The smooth wretch! Madelyn's eyes narrowed as she itched to march over and yank him away from her fragile friend by the tops of his ears. Alas, such a display would surely mark her as a madwoman, not to mention prove to the pompous scoundrel just what her mission was—to keep Charlotte safe from his lecherous advances. And then he'd probably want Charlotte all the more.

Snorts from the mighty horse hitched up to the wagon as the beast shook its heavy head and jangled the harness barred Madelyn from hearing Charlotte's reply.

Frustrated, Madelyn pressed her lips together tightly and looked over her shoulder. She nearly started in surprise when she found the duke staring down at her from atop his shiny black mount.

To her mortification, Gabriel nudged his horse closer to her, and after dismounting in one fluid movement, surprised her further by taking her left arm and threading it with his right. With a rushed, almost angry pace, he guided her to the wagon. She had no choice but to go along—it was either that or let him drag her.

"You're too kind," she remarked with a touch of sarcasm, nearly tripping on a stone. Only the unflinching anchor of his arm kept her from falling face first into the gravel drive. Was this how he treated a woman he'd kissed passionately only the day before? Perhaps he wasn't marrying because of the simple fact that no one would have him. He possessed all the charm and gentleness of a wild boar startled from a nap. "You're creating quite the stir by your attendance on me," she said, noting Bernadette's pout, Belinda's gaping, affronted mouth, and Harriet's squinty-eyed glare. "Pray, I wonder why you singled me out?"

"As do I," he said dryly.

His casual remark stung. "What makes you think I prefer your escort to that of your brother's?"

He looked down at her, raising a dubious brow. "Feeling guilty already? You'll not sway my opinion now."

They reached the steps placed by the wagon, stopping abruptly. Madelyn studied his gaze with confusion. She'd be damned if he thought she should feel guilt over protecting her friend. Was this the sort of confession he wanted? Was this the "dangerous game" of which he spoke?

He smiled down at her and she nearly shrank back. Gone was the half-adoring, half-captivated predatory gleam that he managed to fix on her since their first meeting. In its place sparked something altogether different, a curious mix of emotions. In his sparkling blue depths she spied a dash of discontent, a restrained resentment, and a darkly sensuous promise. Somehow she knew, without a doubt, that had she been alone with him at this moment, her virtue would be sorely threatened.

Madelyn pulled her arm from his, despising the shiver rippling through her. Standing between both Devine brothers was a disconcerting sensation. Their tall forms and solid, board chests deftly blocked the wind. And Gabriel's body heat seemed to sear through the fabric of her cloak.

Through some unspoken language, Lord Tristan only offered her a crooked grin, then strode to his mount—his actions allowing his elder brother the opportunity to guide her.

Heat permeated through Gabriel's gloved hand to her own as he took her hand in his and led her up the steps. The sensation was not a new one, and she foolishly thought that was all of his touch she would have to endure, and then he placed his other hand at the small of her back. She kept her head down, scooted next to Charlotte—the pointed stares of Harriet and the twins burning holes in her already flushed face.

"Once Miss Haywood is settled, we'll be off," Lord Tristan exclaimed, mounting his horse. He acknowledged the other men choosing to accompany them, then turned to his flock in the wagon with a wide grin. "I apologize for the cramped quarters, my fair creatures. But the view, I promise, is worth the jostled ride."

Wedging herself between two overstuffed faded red pillows, Madelyn tried to relax. If these were the same falls she visited as a child, there were certainly more ways to get there than in a padded wagon through the mud.

The footman put the step under his seat in the front of the wagon and hopped aboard. As the wagon lurched forward, Madelyn turned to watch Gabriel hoist himself atop his horse with an easy swoop, his movements sinuous, mesmerizing. Taking up the reins, he urged his mount into a gallop, slowing his pace once he pulled far enough ahead, taking the lead with an air of confidence. Tall in the saddle, his elegant riding clothes were tailored to his sleek-muscled form with strict precision. His long black cape whipped behind him, exposing his chocolate-colored riding breeches, which fit snuggly, hugging his thighs and displaying the flexing muscles rippling beneath.

Her admiring gaze raked his strong, long form down to his black riding boots, almost as shiny as his mount's coat, and back again to his thighs. His waist was trim, his stomach flat, and her hungry gaze didn't miss the broad expanse of his back, nor the inch or two of tousled black locks resting on his shoulders, his fine—if slightly bristled—jawline . . .

Madelyn's breath caught in her throat as her gaze locked with Gabriel's. With a knowing grin, he regarded her from over his shoulder, his heated stare letting her know he had witnessed her slow perusal of his body. In response, the prickly hot flush of a blush bloomed like wildfire across her face, spreading to her neck. She swallowed hard as she contemplated the benefits of burrowing into the wealth of blankets heaped in the wagon.

However, she was saved from further mortification when another rider spurred his mount forward, blocking her view. Rothbury. He smiled at her like a tawny lion, his dark gold locks peeking around the rim of his top hat in a deceptively boyish manner. All of a sudden she fancied she knew exactly how a plump hare felt if surprised by a blood-starved carnivore. He tipped his hat and offered her a slow, conspiring wink, which she suspected had less to do with a rakish, perfunctory greeting and everything to do with the pleasure he found in unsettling her nerves.

"'Tis a good thing I consumed only a slice of dry toast this morning," Madelyn replied over the rumbling of the jostled wagon. "We've been tossed around so much, had I ate more I'd have surely cast it up long ago."

Charlotte laughed, holding onto her bonnet. "It's kind of fun. I almost feel like a little girl," she said, then let out a squeal along with all the other occupants. The wagon pitched sharply to the right, nearly dumping them all in a stream of mud left behind by the swollen river. It looked to have receded only an hour or so before.

Madelyn buried her face in her hands. "This is absurd." Peeking through her gloved fingers, she spotted Lord Tristan riding alongside them, on the dry side, of course. He wore a suspiciously sheepish grin and covered a laugh with a well-timed cough.

"He's done this on purpose. Charlotte, don't you see? The insufferable man has taken it upon himself to humiliate us for his amusement."

"I want to go home," Bernadette whined from the other side of the wagon, her yellow bonnet sitting at an odd angle atop her head.

"What I want," Belinda remarked from next to her sister, "is to know why His Grace helped Maddie into the wagon."

"Yes," Harriet agreed, crossing her arms.

Madelyn kept her gaze averted, choosing to ignore

their taunts. A few moments later the wagon slowed its pace and the ground, thankfully, smoothed.

To Madelyn's delight, their rocky trail brought them surprisingly close to the beautiful village she had resided in as a child. After nearly an hour of traversing steep hillsides only to dip into deep valleys and back up again, their party finally rode high above the tree-lined town of her birth, nestled within an expansive moor. She spotted the old hostel, where travelers were promised a hearty meal and ample rest within the gray stone structure, and beyond that Mr. Walden's farm, his ponies grazing in the field. The sight of the welcoming village brought a pang of remembrance to her heart. The last time she was here, she was an eight-year-old imp, often muddy, always happy, and never far behind her mother's skirts.

Just as they passed a tumbled-down abbey, the curious sound of a bubbling stream and the slosh of falling water enchanted the air around them. The horses were tethered to an old post near a copse of trees forming a canopy overhead.

One by one each of the ladies were brought down from the wagon. Madelyn teetered a bit, her eyes feeling a bit like loose marbles rolling about her head. Lord Tristan led the way into the woods, first passing up a fidgeting Charlotte to ask Harriet if he might be allowed to escort her over the bridge crossing the river. Madelyn inwardly cringed. From her friend's expression and hasty step forward, it was painfully obvious Charlotte thought Tristan had asked her. She stood wringing her hands, her expression flushed and uncomfortable. Madelyn itched to go to her, but a meandering Lord Fairbourne, a daughter on each arm, stalled her progress.

A warm hand touched her arm, and she looked back to see Lord Rothbury regarding her much like a panting lion.

"Miss Haywood," he said, his finger making a little circle on the sensitive skin on the inside of her arm. Reflexively, she snatched her arm away. The sensation might have been distracting, not to mention troubling, had her mind been able to focus on anything other than getting to Charlotte. "If you would allow me . . . " And without waiting for an answer he took her hand and placed it on his sleeve.

The Fairbournes finally stepped to the side, choosing to admire the stream lapping at the sandy bank instead of crossing the bridge stretching across the tumbling, crashing river. And then she finally caught a glimpse of Charlotte, her face flushed, only not with embarrassment, but with laughter as Gabriel mumbled and pointed to the great wall of rock at the north end of the falls.

"He came to her rescue," Madelyn whispered.

"Who, sweetmeat?" Rothbury asked.

Sweetmeat? She turned to the earl, a brow raised.

"What's the matter? You don't like being referred to as an edible treat?"

She could do nothing but shake her head.

"Well, it did snare your attention from that tedious prig, anyway," he said casually as they crossed the bridge.

The last thing she wanted to do was converse

with Rothbury—he might take it as encouragement on her part—but the disdain she identified in his reproach sparked her curiosity. "You don't like Gabri—His Grace?"

He shrugged. "Just bores me, 'tis all. That, and the fact when I asked permission to court his sister, he stalwartly refused."

"Surely you cannot fault him for responding negatively. You asked a question. It would be presumptuous of you to believe you should not be denied. As her guardian, he has every right to govern those who seek her company."

"Miss Haywood," he said forcefully. "He threw me out of the house by the scruff of my neck."

The animated remark on his otherwise serious face influenced a chirp of a giggle from Madelyn.

"It's not at all funny," Rothbury said, wounded. "My neck was sore for a week." He rubbed his aforementioned body part for emphasis. "Not to mention the effects his boorish reaction had on my pride."

"I'm sorry, my lord," she managed through her wobbly grin.

Rothbury smiled suddenly, instantly putting Madelyn on her guard. "See, sweetmeat? I make you laugh. What say you and I give it another go?"

The thought of being courted by Rothbury made her stomach tighten into a stubborn knot. If that was what he meant by "giving it another go" . . . She shook her head, unable to suppress her smile at his unwavering tenacity. "Let us instead admire the scenery surrounding us, my lord. I have not seen such a beautiful sight since I was a wee one. "

He sighed, too dramatically for it to be genuine. "You've ice in you veins, you know."

Because of the recent steady rains, the river was a torrent of water, rushing over rock slabs of incredible proportions. The swirling, frothy water tumbled down the ledges like giant, flooded steps with a roar of sound that muted their party's spoken observations. Farther down, the rushing of the falls eventually settled to a placid stream as the river widened at the base, trees reaching over the water like the sheltering arms of a parent soothing a wound-up child.

It was there that their group dispersed. Some poked about the trees, exploring their naked, exposed roots, which twisted and crawled about the ground. Others, mostly the men, gathered farther down to talk of fish and game. Madelyn stayed close to the water's edge, squatting as she hunted the ground for bits of flat rocks to skip across the water. Despite its impropriety, she had taken off one of her gloves so as not to soil it as she picked through the sandy pebbles on the bank. Besides, everyone else seemed preoccupied. There were no society matrons patrolling the area, ready to box her ears for removing a glove.

The crunch of gravel caught her attention. Without standing, she pivoted on her heels and found herself staring at Gabriel's muscular thighs as he squatted next to her. Blinking, she raised her head, meeting his blue stare, which sparkled with a light of their own as the water reflected within them.

She watched the play of muscles in his throat as he spoke. "These should do," he said.

She looked down, noting he held three smooth, flat stones of various size and shape. "Thank you." She reached into his palm to take them, noting too late he had removed his glove as well. Their bare skin touched and a zing of sensation skittered through her. Tenderly, he captured her hand in his by curling his long, bare fingers over hers.

"You have to dig for them, as the children from the village come here often and find the best stones," he said.

She nodded. "I know. I used to be one of those children."

This seemed to intrigue him and he arched one coal black eyebrow. "Born and bred in Yorkshire? Then you're made of hardy stuff. You lived in the village?"

She smiled with pride. "I lived at Willowbrooke Cottage."

"I know that place," he murmured. "'Tis a beautiful structure. I used to pass it while taking my riding lessons as a lad. Did you live there long?"

"Until I was eight. When my mother became sick, my father moved all of us to London to be closer to her physicians."

"From your expression, I can see they were useless," he said softly.

Madelyn swallowed a tickle in the back of her throat. "They said she was born with a weak heart and it was a miracle she had lived as long as she had. They confined her to bed, urged her to rest, and informed us never to distress her. When her strength was finally depleted and she left us, I yearned to return to Yorkshire."

Gabriel nodded. "To come home."

"Yes," Madelyn said, smiling at his perceptiveness. "There was nothing for me in London. Only the painful memories of my mother slipping away." She took a deep breath, steadying her emotions. "But by then Father had become entranced by the delights city life could offer him and I never saw home again."

He released his gentle hold on her hand, only to lift it and press his mouth on her knuckles for a soft, lingering kiss. A delightful shiver ran through her. How many times he had kissed the air above her hand, and now, finally, made contact.

"You are here now," he murmured. His tender gesture did not shock her, nor did the sympathetic understanding she saw in his gaze move her to retreat into a protective shell. Rather, she found herself tempted to share her entire past with him.

She sighed, reluctant to surrender to the temptation. "Yes, here I am again," she said with a small smile. "And if I get my way, I'll get to stay." That is, if Priscilla decided she was trying to snag the duke. And at the moment, Madelyn wasn't feeling very confident about that.

"Your way?" Gabriel asked, both of his dark brows raised. "Miss Haywood, explain what you mean."

"W-Well . . . " she stammered, calling herself a blithering idiot. She had become so relaxed, talking to him felt so easy, so natural, she'd forgotten *he* was a part of Priscilla's twisted plan. "Er . . . you see, the cottage is now owned by my stepmother's family, and I—" She broke off, suddenly incapable of digging her foot out of her mouth.

"We should talk about what happened last night, in the corridor," Gabriel said abruptly.

Madelyn lifted a shoulder. "We don't have to," she replied, hoping he wasn't going to spout some polite apology. She had thought that was what she wanted, but now she gathered it would make her feel worse—that she was the only one who felt the pull in their wave of passion. Her heart skipped a beat then two while she stared into his tan, handsome face, the wind tousling his black, wavy curls making him all the more attractive.

One side of his mouth lifted in a sardonic smirk, reminiscent of his younger brother. "Despite my efforts at self-control, it seems around you I cannot help myself."

"I cannot believe that," she parried softly.

"You had better," he drawled, letting the stones he found drop into her open palm. "Because if you do not, if you continue to tempt me, you need to know there will come a time when I will not be able to stop myself. You are no longer safe with me."

"Women like me do not tempt men like you," she spat.

"There aren't many women like you," he growled. "In fact, I've never met anyone like you in my entire life."

"I don't believe you," she said automatically, though she had to admit her argument was losing its strength. She could no longer ignore nor discount the heat building between them—no matter how implausible.

He took a deep breath, exhaling slowly. "To disbelieve me at this point would be putting your virtue at a grave risk."

The sounds of the falls and birds and wind evaporated from her mind. There was only her and Gabriel. His steady, studying gaze dropped to her lips, and she swallowed, aroused and oddly undisturbed by his warning.

"If we were alone," she said, staring at his mouth as well, "would you kiss me?"

"Miss Haywood, if we were alone, I would not hesitate to lay down my cape and take you right here on this bank. If you continue to play your part in this infernal game—"

The comment halted her blush and took her aback. "A game? There you go again with this 'game.' What is your meaning, sir?"

His jaw tightened, a muscle working in his cheek. "Do not pretend to misunderstand me."

"Misunderstand you? I cannot even begin to comprehend the words coming out of your mouth. You've been speaking in riddles ever since you pinned me against the wall."

"Pinned you?" He gave a short laugh. "You were willing and ready."

A short, exasperated exhalation left her mouth.

"Besides," he added, "if you will recall, I told you to return to the safety of the others straight from the beginning. You could have left."

"And you could have kept your lips to yourself, sir."

"And you could have kept your tongue inside your own mouth, madam."

She gasped loudly, her blush so fierce she imagined she glowed. "And you could have kept your . . . your . . . "

"My what?" Gabriel taunted, his eyes taking on a sultry gleam sizzling into her soul. "This argument hasn't anything to do with what body part one put in whom, is it?"

"Your Grace," came Bernadette's whine from behind them. "I cannot find any good stones either."

Gabriel and Madelyn stood abruptly, like guilty adolescents, and turned away from each other. She directed her attention to the stream, and he to Bernadette's delicate beauty.

Gabriel didn't even try to smile. He scanned the path along the stream, looking for Tristan, and finally spied him picking wildflowers, handing them alternately to Miss Greene and Miss Beauchamp. Without his help, the young pup managed to find the two women in this bride hunt who still truly wanted him. Perhaps, Gabriel mused, Tristan's instincts were stronger than he had originally imagined.

His gaze swung back to Bernadette. "Might I suggest you inquire after Miss Haywood's assistance?"

"Oh no," she stressed, drawing out the words dramatically. "A gentleman could not expect a lady to soil her gloves. Not even Miss Haywood."

Out of the corner of his eye, Gabriel watched Miss Haywood discreetly dust her finger on her skirts, then quickly slip on her glove.

Her subtle attempt at propriety provoked his grin, but he instantly regretted it, as Miss Fairbourne assumed it was directed toward herself. She batted her lashes, tilting her head to the side in supplication.

Wearily, he sighed. "All right, Miss Fairbourne, let's see what we can find." As he bent toward the ground, he could have sworn he heard Miss Haywood laugh softly.

He had found two stones when a lace handkerchief floated in front of his face, landing on the toe of his boot.

"Oops," Belinda Fairbourne said.

He should have known her sister would soon follow. Picking up the heavily perfumed square with his thumb and index finger, he stood, holding it in the air between them. "Dropped something?"

"*Mais oui,*" the younger twin agreed silkily. "Seeing as you so gallantly retrieved it, why don't you keep it? Consider it a memento of *moi.*"

Now he was sure he heard Miss Haywood laugh. With flicks of her wrist she sent the three stones he had given her skipping across the slow moving stream in quick succession. Before she walked away, she tossed him a secret smile from over her shoulder.

He looked down at the handkerchief, shaking his head slowly. "Thank you, Miss Fairbourne, but I'm afraid in accepting it, my brother might become enraged with jealousy." He returned it to her hand,

AT THE BRIDE HUNT BALL   219

and she purposely brushed her thumb across his knuckles.

"And what sparks your jealousy?" she whispered.

"Belinda! His Grace was helping *me*," Bernadette cried.

"Why would he want to help *you* when talking to *me* is far more appealing?" Belinda softened the rebuke with a giggle and winked at Gabriel.

And so it began. Discretion might have been in the Fairbourne sisters' original plan, but the palpable sense of competition between them propelled them to desperate heights.

By the time they were all halfway back to Wolverest, Madelyn had her fill of watching Gabriel bandied about in a Fairbourne-orchestrated tug-of-war. But she did find the sisters' diminishing lack of decorum and Gabriel's growing discomfort while he tried to maintain his patience and polite indifference humorous. She could have let Charlotte in on her secret knowledge, telling her that the twins no longer wanted Tristan, but feared that would only encourage her friend and set her up for eventual disappointment and pain.

Their party was a mere mile away from the castle when the skies suddenly clouded over and a light drizzle began to fall. Gentle, distant thunder rumbled in the distance. In reaction to the rain, the driver urged the plowhorse to a faster pace.

And then it happened.

A freak spear of lightning cracked like the wicked snap of a whip directly in front of the wagon. The mare reared up and jerked into a frenzied run, throwing the driver and an unsuspecting Bernadette Fairbourne from the wagon. With a death grip on Charlotte, Madelyn looked back, noting that the driver managed to quickly return to his feet. He ran after the wagon, waving his hat and shouting. Miss Fairbourne remained on her back, her feet in the air, reminding Madelyn of the dead mouse she spied by the stable earlier that morning on her way to the wagon.

The men went into immediate action. Rothbury and Tristan rode ahead, desperately trying to herd the startled beast from crashing into a nearby wooded area. Fairbourne stayed behind, seeing to his daughter, who was now attempting to stand.

Losing his hat to the wind, Gabriel stood in his stirrups, his black cape whipping behind him like a pirate flag as he urged his mount alongside the wagon. He rode dangerously close to the frightened horse, leaning forward in order to grasp the reins bouncing along the startled mare's back.

Before the duke could grasp them, however, the wagon crested a small rise, and the entire contraption hopped up into the air, then came crashing down with a slam, jolting Madelyn free from Charlotte and sending her over the edge. Frantically, she grasped at a blanket and held tight, her feet furrowing along in the mud as the wagon plowed onward, dragging her with it. She cried out, her right foot popping up as it connected with a rock. Her grip slipped and she flew backward, landing in the cushy mud, flat on her back.

In the distance, the rumble of the wagon lessened as Gabriel regained control. With her bonnet sitting cockeyed on her head, Madelyn remained still, helplessly molded into the mud, stretched out in a giant X.

She would have laughed uproariously if not for the shooting shards of pain centering from her ankle. Gingerly, she attempted to lift her head.

"Wait!" Gabriel shouted, running to her side and coming to a sliding stop on his knees. His broad chest rose and fell as he fought to control his breath. "Don't move yet."

To her surprise, he proceeded to expertly pat down and inspect her entire body; the tips of her fingers, her wrists, down her arms, shoulders, and collarbone.

"Tell me if anything hurts." He smoothed her every rib, working from the back to the front, utterly oblivious to the effect his light touch had on her body.

The light drizzle and, she suspected, sweat from their ordeal, dampened Gabriel's obsidian hair, leaving wispy locks to frame his face and feather across his neck.

"God damn fool!" He looked up from his work and centered his azure glare across the lawn at Tristan, who stood consoling Charlotte, Belinda, and Harriet. The footman tended to the horse along with Rothbury. "He should have listened to me and canceled this blasted trip to the falls," Gabriel ranted, mussing up his hair further with a frustrated sweep. "Bloody hell, woman, you fell hard."

Her breath caught as his warm hands rolled over her hips and gently pressed her leg bones and knees. A voice inside her head told her she should have told him by now it was only her right ankle that hurt, but some sinfully delicious part of her knew he would then stop his glorious torment on her flesh.

"I—Is Bernadette all right?" she asked.

He nodded, looking up at the girl and her father briefly. "Got the wind knocked out of her is all, I suspect," he muttered as he inched his way down her calves. "Her father's walking her back to the castle as we speak."

"Oh," she managed, hoping her response didn't sound like a moan—for it did to her ears. Now completely at his mercy for want of his touch, she didn't even blink when he removed her boots.

Her sharp intake of breath when he reached her right ankle stopped him cold. "Your ankle," he said, finally meeting her gaze. "It pains you?"

She nodded. "When I was falling out of the wagon, I whacked it on a rock."

He cringed in sympathy, then assessed it, gently turning her foot this way and that. "No pain here?"

She shook her head. "Only when you—" She gasped as his fingers gently brushed against the sensitive skin on the inside of her ankle.

"I'm sorry," he said, his damp brow scrunching together. "I think it's only bruised. I'll send for the physician once we return. Here, just in case." Lifting his chin, his nimble fingers loosened and untied his cravat. He unwound it from around his neck and proceeded to wrap her foot and ankle.

The fine linen felt warm, almost hot to her cool, stocking-enclosed flesh. Her attention was immediately drawn to the golden skin of his naked throat. She gulped as his warm, masculine scent reached her, and a sudden longing rose up within her to be kissed by him, held by him, or to be the recipient of any act, really, that would involve this man being closer to her.

"I'm afraid you'll have to help me stand. You see," she said, grimacing, "I believe I'm suctioned to the earth."

She was rewarded with his slow grin. He spared her a quick glance, a flash of blue, then continued to busily wind his cravat around her ankle. His long, tan fingers touched her gently and she found herself longing to feel his deft fingers along her calves again.

"Only you, love," he said softly. "Only my lovely Miss Haywood would find humor in this situation." The faint wail of Bernadette compounded his comment.

When he finished, he reached out, slowly pulling her to a sitting position, then helped her bring in her legs.

"Are you certain nothing else pains you?"

She nodded, wondering how in the world she would hobble back to the castle. They were only about five hundred feet away now, but she fretted that she'd have to limp all the way there. And as far as she was concerned, she'd never ride in a wagon again, calm horse or not.

"I will carry you back," he stated matter-of-factly,

as if reading her thoughts. "And might I say, you have very cute feet by the way."

"Ah, thank you. Oh!" He lifted her effortlessly in his arms, his hard, unyielding body instantly warming her. "I don't think this is a good idea. I'll ruin your fine clothes."

He shrugged, which jostled her. "Ruin me, then."

She quieted, contemplating his gentle ministrations and the protective, almost loving way he held her to his chest. Unable to stop herself, she rested her cheek against his breast, giving in to the comfy sensation of being taken care of by the man she had thought was an insensitive, pretentious bore.

"As soon as we reach Wolverest, I'll send for the physician. Baths will be readied for you both, of course. And then. . . " His voice trailed off, and she lifted her head to meet his gaze, but he was staring, no, scowling ahead. She felt his muscles stiffen and she suddenly likened her position to that of clinging to a brick wall.

"And then . . . " she prompted.

"And then I'm sending you home."

Chapter 13

Pulling the thick, ivory coverlet up to her nose, Madelyn sank deeper into the blankets, suddenly overcome with a need to regain some unreachable level of warmth that at the moment evaded her no matter how many blankets were stacked upon her bed.

Priscilla paced the room, her fists planted on her slim hips, her face set in stern displeasure. "Eliminated! How dare he!"

Delicately, Madelyn cleared her throat. "I believe what the duke said yesterday was that he was sending me home. Now, if you remember," she started with care, "you had promised I could return to Willowbrooke if I had at least tried—"

"Sending you home! Why? What did you do now?"

Madelyn had no answer for that. According to Gabriel, she owed him a confession for her part in some sort of game he claimed was far too dangerous for her to play. If he was talking about her attempts to save Charlotte from Lord Tristan's clutches, then he had a long wait. Forever, really—she would never apologize for protecting her friend.

"I'm not sure why," Madelyn offered finally. "But it is done, his decision is made."

"Nonsense" Priscilla exclaimed, tapping the point of her finger on her chin. "I wonder . . . could his abrupt dismissal have anything to do with Lady Eugenia's arrival?"

Madelyn pushed herself up to a sitting position, tucking the covers under her arms. "Who is Lady Eugenia?"

Priscilla sighed impatiently. "How could you not know? She happens to be the old duke's unmarried sister. Her superior opinion is sought throughout good society. One word from her and even . . . and even *you* would be welcomed at Almack's again."

Well, that statement certainly spoke volumes about the woman's influence, Madelyn thought. Somehow, she knew she'd never again see the inside of that King Street assembly room after the Unfortunate Punch Bowl Incident.

"So you believe he's sending me home for fear I'll disgrace myself further?"

"Perhaps, perhaps," Priscilla muttered, stopping just before the connecting dressing room door. "We must sway his mind. Find a way . . . " And with that, she strolled out of the room, deep in manipulative thought.

Exhaling with relief, Madelyn silently sent the Lord her thanks as her stepmother left. It was awful enough that she had been ordered not to leave her room since returning from the falls yesterday. Making matters worse was having to endure her stepmother's incessant ranting—and in front of the maid, who desperately tried to appear as if she hadn't been listening.

Though she and Bernadette were seen again by the physician hours ago—Miss Fairbourne given a clean bill of health, Madelyn given orders to rest her bruised ankle as much as possible to promote quicker healing—Gabriel refused to allow her out of bed, much less out of her room. He stationed Jenny in her chamber like a prison guard, and the bored girl sat flipping through botanical volumes, looking at the pictures. Every once in a while she'd send Madelyn a sympathetic smile and quietly ask her if she needed anything.

What she needed, Madelyn mused, was a brain. If she had one of those, she'd know who was inconveniencing her when she had first arrived, she'd know what sort of confession Gabriel kept on about, and she'd understand why he kept her here when it was so painfully obvious she had no interest in Lord Tristan. And if her apparently pea-sized mind could figure those things out, she guessed she'd have figured out why Gabriel had chosen to send her away . . . and why his abrupt dismissal pained her to the quick.

At least, she knew the answer to that last one— her part in it, anyway. Guarded and tucked away in her chamber like a guest turned thief, she had plenty of time to think about her feelings. And she was most assuredly falling in love with him. How perfectly horrid.

From the moment she first stumbled onto his property, Gabriel acknowledged her social missteps and pressed her to move on, not to hide, not to run, which was her natural inclination. He never pretended she was perfect nor did he patronize her with insincere flattery to placate her often wounded spirit. Instead, he'd made her feel beautiful and desired and worthy. Unintentionally, for sure, he even made her feel a bit adored, and she couldn't help but adore him as well. It was a feeling she hadn't experienced since she was a little girl shining in the glow of her mother's love.

And now he was sending her away.

She needed to stay. Not for her own selfish reasons, but because Lord Tristan was so very obviously giving Charlotte the impression he would choose her to be his bride. And because she believed the fickle man couldn't be trusted to make a lasting decision as far as she could spit. Well, if she were the sort of woman who spat, anyway.

There was a swift knock on her door and a maid entered, announcing the presence of Lady Rosalind. She then curtsied off to the side, signaling to Jenny that she was to be dismissed.

Rosalind entered, a smile on her lips and a worry in her frown. "My dear Madelyn," she exclaimed as she crossed the room to sit on the edge of her bed. "I heard about your fall. Simply dreadful of Tristan." She shook her head in disapproval.

Madelyn managed a wry smile. "Yes, I agree. I fear your youngest brother's sense of amusement satisfies only him."

"Quite. There's no hope for him, I'm afraid," Rosalind replied. "Were you terribly hurt?"

"No, a bruised ankle, 'tis all."

Rosalind's brow rose in apparent astonishment. "That's all? Forgive me, Madelyn, I don't mean to understate the extent of your injuries," she said mildly, "but my eldest brother informed me that you were confined to your bed and not to be disturbed by anyone. And I've been wanting to speak with you. Our aunt arrived late yesterday. Are you well enough for an introduction?"

Perhaps Priscilla had been correct in her assumption that Gabriel didn't want her in the presence of Lady Eugenia, Madelyn mused. "I'm all right, I think," she replied. "And Miss Fairbourne is well enough, I believe."

Rosalind nodded, her exotic eyes taking on a tinge of curiosity. "Tell me, dear . . . is it true Gabriel carried you inside?"

"Yes," Madelyn answered with a shrug.

"I have a confession to make." With a quick look over her shoulder at the door, Rosalind continued in a whisper, "The other day . . . I saw you two waltzing in the ballroom."

Madelyn felt a guilty blush creep across her cheeks.

"I have to say," Rosalind went on, her gaze warming on Madelyn, "I was shocked."

"It was all perfectly innocent," Madelyn rushed out. "I hadn't expected him to follow me there. It was his suggestion and I—"

"Madelyn, my brother doesn't dance."

Rosalind's statement halted her hurried thoughts. "That cannot be true. He handled the steps quite expertly."

"Well, you see, I didn't say he couldn't dance, but rather that he doesn't," Rosalind replied, a knowing look in her round blue eyes. "He feels it is a waste of time and energy. I asked him once if he scowls so horridly in order to scare away his female acquaintances from thinking they might coerce him into allowing them to pencil his name on their dance cards."

"And what did he say?"

"He said something about never finding a woman that was worth spinning around the room like a child's top."

"Perhaps he made an exception," Madelyn mumbled, not sure what to make of the information Rosalind presented. "I had just told him how positively ghastly I am—I was—at waltzing."

"That may be so, but my brother's been behaving differently ever since you've arrived at Wolverest. Not only does he not dance, Madelyn, he hardly ever talks without someone provoking it, he seldom smiles, and almost never laughs. And he does all these things with you." Rosalind smiled, patting Madelyn's hand. "Oh dear, you've turned pink again." She sighed. "I guess what I'm trying to say is . . . I'm so very happy you're here."

Obviously, Rosalind didn't know her brother had decided to send her away.

"Now, wipe that shaken look off your face and

tell me all about where you used to live. Gabriel said you lived not too far from Wolverest . . . "

With no more talk of the duke, the women fell into easy conversation. Mostly about Madelyn's love of Willowbrooke and how she came to cut and sketch silhouettes to amuse her bedridden mother.

Just as Madelyn felt herself relax, Gabriel swept inside the room, and the atmosphere changed in an instant. The air felt charged and the room seemingly shrank.

"Miss Haywood." He bowed. "Rosalind."

His sister stood, her brows quirking together. "Did you know I was here?"

"Of course," he replied, walking into the room with slow, deliberate steps. He stopped at the foot of Madelyn's bed.

"Well, I should hope so," Rosalind said. She waggled her finger in his direction. "You cannot visit a single lady in her bedchamber. Even under the most dire situations. A chaperone must be present. Gabriel! She's not even dressed!"

Ignoring his sister, he nodded slowly, his hard eyes never breaking contact with Madelyn. All of a sudden, Madelyn felt overheated, suffocated by the thick blankets that only minutes ago had afforded her little warmth. Oh, but she needed them now, for modesty alone. The heat in Gabriel's eyes scorched her from the inside out. There was no doubt in her mind that if Rosalind excused herself from their company, Gabriel would be joining her in the bed. She eyed his tall form, finding herself shockingly curious of how his weight would feel atop her.

He was dressed entirely in black except for his linen shirt and loosely tied cravat. The tops of his polished boots were turned down, and he stood proud and angry, spearing her with his blue-flamed stare. He took a step closer and a black bang fell down over one eye, making him look just as he had in his garden during the approaching storm.

Gabriel realized, with a stab of lust, that it was a mistake to have come to her chamber. He watched her squirm under the covers with wolfish delight, his body ever alert to Madelyn's delicate scent, which permeated his senses.

With the ivory blankets heaped around her, and her white dressing gown buttoned up to nearly her chin, he thought she rather looked like a bloodred rose petal amid a cloud as all her glorious dark cherry locks framed her flushed face. It was obvious his unwavering admiration was making her uncomfortable, and he didn't give a damn.

"Well," Rosalind cheerfully injected into the quiet room, her hands on her hips. "I for one am glad to find Miss Haywood in such good shape, considering yesterday afternoon's disastrous conclusion."

Silence.

"And I . . . " Rosalind's words faded as she looked to Gabriel, then Madelyn, and back again. "So," she said a bit loudly. "Shall we talk of the dinner menu, then?"

"There's no need," Gabriel intoned. "Miss Haywood is staying in her room." Indeed, she was safer locked in her room than being anywhere near him. The woman ignited a yearning inside him that fairly burned him with pain. That, and the anger he felt at her little ruse, brought his state of arousal to a fever pitch. Right now all he wanted to do was show her how foolish it was to attempt to trick him.

"Not going to dinner?" Rosalind strolled around the bed, apparently aiming for Gabriel. "Don't be silly. Her ankle's only bruised." Reaching him, she linked her arm with his and tried tugging him away from the foot of the bed. He remained motionless.

While smiling innocently up at him, his sister muttered through her teeth so she wouldn't be overheard. "Stop it. You look like you're going to eat her alive."

"What a tempting suggestion. I just might."

She kicked him in the shin. He didn't even flinch.

Rosalind turned her smile to Madelyn. "Do tell me you're coming to dinner?"

"I don't think that is possible," she replied. "His Grace informed me that I am to stay abed until I am well enough for travel."

"Stay abed? Nonsense! You said you were feeling better already. You are coming, and I will hear no more on the subject." Rosalind turned, heading for the door with the false belief Gabriel was following her out. "Our aunt Eugenia will be joining us. I know she's reputed to be fussy and disagreeable, but you needn't worry. You'll be seated clear across the table from her, and if I know my aunt well enough, she'll be too busy complaining about the state of the venison to offer more than a cursory glance in your direction."

Gabriel cleared his throat. "What you have not realized, Rosalind, is that Miss Haywood is leaving tomorrow." She had better, or else they would both find themselves in a situation where neither of them would be able to walk away.

Rosalind stopped just outside the door. "Leaving? Why?"

"It seems she no longer wishes to participate in the bride-hunt," Gabriel offered, unwilling as he was to expound on his real reasons in front of his sister.

"Well, who could blame her?" came Rosalind's reply. "Tristan's a complete scoundrel. He has been everything but a gentleman." She turned to Miss Haywood, her gaze both pleading and hopeful. "Do you wish to stay? As *my* guest, that is?"

Ah, hell. He should have known his sister would grasp this approach. With growing discomfort, Gabriel watched Miss Haywood nibble on her bottom lip, her eyes centering on the middle of his chest. Indecision washed over her features as he struggled to remain still and not scoot his sister out the door so he could prove to Miss Haywood, once and for all, how close he was to losing his self-control. He didn't know himself anymore, this man who lusted after this one woman day after day, tormented with dreams of her lush body straddling his hips, of her hair long and loose about her naked shoulders, of her gasp when he pulled her down, entering her and making her his forever.

"Oh, come now, Madelyn," Rosalind urged, "please say you'll stay as my guest."

Gabriel couldn't keep a low growl from emerging from his throat. "That wouldn't be wise."

"And why not?" Rosalind asked.

He didn't have a ready answer, a plausible reason to refuse his sister's request. Well, he did, but he knew it was nothing he should express aloud. "It would not be wise for the simple fact Miss Haywood is unwell. You should take it into consideration she might accept your invitation simply out of politeness."

"Thank you, Rosalind," Miss Haywood said, her tone mild. "I accept your invitation. And I am well enough to come to dinner, I suppose." She threw a pointed glance at Gabriel, which gave him the funny feeling she was challenging him for some reason or another.

Rosalind clapped her hands together lightly. "Good. Good," she chirped. "Then I—then we—should leave you to your rest until then."

Miss Haywood nodded with a smile, then preoccupied herself with straightening the wrinkles out of the blanket covering her legs. She was obviously trying to avoid his gaze.

Gabriel waited until Rosalind stepped out and into the hall. Then, with slow steps, he approached the side of her bed. Bending low, his eyes closed briefly as her alluring scent washed over him. His lips brushed the edge of her earlobe. She held herself still, but he did not miss the way she tilted her head to the opposite side ever so slightly, as if silently offering her ear, neck, skin, to his exploration.

"I will await your presence," he whispered, letting his breath stir the tiny hairs curling near her ear. "Oh, and Miss Haywood . . . "

"Hmm?" came her languid reply.

"Be sure to allow your stepmother to choose your gown."

Let the man squirm, Madelyn thought while reaching inside the depths of the deep armoire in her bedchamber an hour later. Let him worry I'll embarrass them all during dinner with my social ineptitude. It would suit him well for his arrogance.

"Ah-ha! There you are," Madelyn exclaimed as she grasped the edge of a lace shawl, pulling it free from under a pile of fresh bed linens. Unfolding it, she examined it, front and back, for cleanliness. "Fancy that," she said, shaking her head in wonder. "You missed one, stepmother."

Confronted with her obvious lack of enthusiasm for Priscilla's original plan to snag the duke, Madelyn found herself bullied into wearing her stepmother's new, dark green velvet gown. It appeared Gabriel's request would be fulfilled. The soft fabric hugged every curve, dip, and swell of her body. She had to suck in her stomach, which made it hard to breathe, for the luxurious garment allowed no room for even the slightest flaw in form. Her breasts were, naturally, pushed up and together, for the gown

had been fitted for her more slender-in-the-bosom
stepmother.

Madelyn had glanced down at the deep crevice
formed between her breasts and wondered how
anyone would be able to talk to her during dinner
with a straight face—it was even distracting to her
own eyes. She'd sought to remedy the situation with
a shawl, only to find there weren't any, or there were
but someone—likely Priscilla—had stained them
all with rouge.

Even Charlotte could offer little help, as the only
shawl she owned that was fit to wear to dinner
had been ruined that morning on the ride to the
falls.

So Madelyn had stayed behind, vowing to find
something, anything short of a window hanging,
to drape over herself, covering her bare shoulder
blades and shielding her ample bosom.

Settling the somewhat dated lace shawl about her,
she quit her room, heading to the drawing room to
join the other guests awaiting both an introduction
to Lady Eugenia and the dinner bell.

Parts of Wolverest Castle were full of light and
contemporary comforts such as smooth Italian
marble, Aubusson rugs, and ample, cozy fireplaces.
But still other parts, sections of ancient living spaces
yet untouched by restoration, were drafty and damp
and full of troubling darkness.

Madelyn thought about this as she descended
the steps into the main hall. At the base she passed
an arched alcove steeped in fathomless shadows.

Squinting, it was impossible to discern if it was only a niche in the wall or an endless corridor.

A rustling of fabric coupled with a familiar whine caused her to come to an abrupt stop just behind a column. Behind her, to the left, the dark alcove with its worrisome presence could not be ignored.

"Where did he go? He was here, just."

"Shush, Bernadette! I'm not blind. I saw him step around the corner."

"Couldn't have, you big ninny," her sister Belinda continued in a loud whisper. "I've just looked down that hall for the second time. He's disappeared."

"Oh no," Bernadette whined dejectedly. "And we were to catch him."

"We're not giving up yet."

"Perhaps Madelyn has managed to occupy him again," Bernadette complained. "Did you see the way she hoarded his attention at the stream? I dare say, she was overcome with jealousy once we stepped in."

"With everyone else waiting in the drawing room, His Grace is bound to come this way again."

"I fear he saw us. Perhaps he deliberately went into hiding."

"Are you joking?" Belinda asked, their voices moving away from Madelyn. "What man in his right mind would pass up a chance to be alone with either of us?"

At Bernadette's crooned agreement, Madelyn ventured a peek from her hiding spot. A shiver of awareness, a sense of being observed from behind, invaded her thoughts, but she ignored it as she watched the twins saunter away.

Her uneasiness wouldn't abate, however, so she dared a glance over her shoulder into the darkness. And there came the slightest, nearly imperceptible scraping sound of the slide of a boot.

Her breath caught and she swallowed, her heart hammering inside her breast. The hairs on her arms stood on end and the muscles in her legs tightened as the urge to flee took hold. Just when she thought to run, the echoing sounds of the approaching Fairbourne girls drifted to her. Madelyn took one small step forward. Avoiding the twins or not, she had to get away from that alcove.

A large, smooth, warm hand clamped over her mouth, effectively covering the lower half of her face, and she was pulled backward against the solid form of a man. She struggled against him, too scared to scream as he snaked an arm as giving as granite around her middle and dragged her back into the inky darkness from whence he had come.

In the tussle, half of her shawl fell away and the exposed part of her back rubbed against the soft folds of a man's cravat and the unyielding heat of his broad chest. The warmth was matched in his skin as he bent his head, pressing his cheek to the side of her head.

"Don't . . . say . . . a word," he whispered hotly into her ear.

Gabriel.

Madelyn stilled, slumping against him, a whimper of relief coming from the back of her throat.

"Quiet," came his whispered commanded. "Do you understand?"

She nodded slowly, his big hand yet covering her mouth. Her body started thrumming with familiar heat and she had a difficult time concentrating on *not* burrowing into his embrace.

"Good," he growled into her ear, holding her tightly against him. "You've been warned. Now that I've got you in my arms, you're not getting away."

Chapter 14

B elinda and Bernadette continued to poke about the hall with youthful exuberance, apparently hoping the duke would come their way in the near future and they'd have him all for themselves. By chance alone they steered clear of the shadowed alcove where, unbeknownst to them, Madelyn battled the urge to flee against the impulse to surrender her soul.

Gradually, Gabriel uncovered Madelyn's mouth, his hand sliding with deliberate slowness over her jaw and down her neck. She swallowed convulsively, her breaths coming in quick, short bursts as his long fingers smoothed a path along her collarbone. Reaching her shoulder, his fingertips slipped under her shawl to shove the rest of it off and onto the floor.

"Must you always leap at me from the shadows?" she asked. Shivers scattered across her skin.

"If you didn't look so damn tempting, I might be able to restrain myself."

Tempting? Part of her thought he was being ridiculous, part of her rejoiced at the words. She yearned for his touch . . . at least in this moment.

Yes, he could hurt her, use her and toss her aside, yet the reward he inadvertently offered her each time he looked into her eyes outweighed the risk. Like an obsession, she had become addicted to the rush of excitement she felt in Gabriel's company. And as much as she wanted to pretend differently, she had to admit, at least to herself, that she anticipated his company, his attention, each and every day since the day she fell into his pond.

His hand swept from her shoulder to the center of her chest, resting flat against her skin. She knew he could feel the wild beat of her heart against his palm for she could feel his own thumping against her back.

"Nervous? Excited?" Gabriel breathed the words. "Or scared?"

"Yes," she whispered.

His soft chuckle was buried in her hair. "How do you do it?"

"Do what?"

"Infuriate and fascinate me at the same time." He swept his slightly bristled chin on the back of her neck. "You drive me wild, Madelyn," he said against her skin. "You feel it too, do you not?"

Her agreement came out as a soft sigh. She closed her eyes.

His lips brushed the top of her ear. "Now do you see the danger, the risk, in your ruse?"

"What *r-ruse*?" she asked, and was tugged roughly against him in response. Her breath seemed to be trapped inside her chest. "Do you mean . . . do you mean Charlotte and your brother?

Because if you do, you should know now I shall continue my endeavor to protect my friend from heartless, inconsiderate libertines until she finds herself safely joined in matrimony to a deserving, agreeable man who—"

His hand clamped over her mouth again.

"As well as I would love to hear what comes out of your mouth next," he breathed softly into her ear, causing her legs to feel wobbly, "I should like to go unnoticed at present."

She mumbled "I'm sorry" against his hand, and he uncovered her mouth once again. "Are you hiding?" she asked breathlessly.

"Mm-hmm," came his lazy reply, his lips now pressed to her temple. "Idiotic chits have been pestering me ever since I left your chamber. It's damn annoying, but I think they're giving up."

The thought that this strong, intelligent grown man was hiding from a pair of young women was ridiculous. She would have giggled if not for the heady distraction of his breath in her ear, his warm masculine scent washing over her. Plastered as she was to the front of his body, with his left arm latched around her waist, she could feel the hardness of his thighs pressing into her own and the rise and fall of his heated chest against her back. "I'm finding it exceedingly hard to concentrate, given our proximity," came her hushed entreaty.

"Good. So am I."

Yet he didn't budge an inch. "I should like to tell you . . . I know the reason for their pursuit," she managed. "Do you?"

She felt his nod. "Oh yes," he drawled, his voice a low purr. "They want the same thing as you."

"They do?" Her brows pulled together, then immediately relaxed as he grazed her earlobe with his teeth.

"They think to change my mind about marriage. Bloody slow-witted creatures are wasting their time with this foolish game. Besides," he breathed, dropping a kiss on her neck, "I prefer the way you play."

"Me?" She blinked, and then suddenly everything he had said about "a confession" made sense. He thought she was scheming along with the Fairbourne girls. That had to be it. But what in the world would give him that idea? She tilted her head back to look at him even though she couldn't see him in the dark. "But I'm not—"

He caught her lips, kissing her with such need, such ferocious passion, she was at once grateful for the anchor of his arm at her waist, for she would have surely sunk to the floor. His kiss was of complete possession. All at once intoxicating and startling. She wanted to match his fierce passion, but her inexperience wouldn't allow it. His mouth moved hungrily over hers, taking, giving, tasting, until she was overcome with the need to seek something more.

And then his tongue penetrated her mouth and all logical thought crumbled away. With deep sweeps of his tongue, he explored her warmth, making her shudder with pleasure. With a hushed whimper, she tried twisting in his hold to face him more fully, but he held fast. Her arms felt useless to her in their position, so she grabbed onto his forearm. His muscles were taut under her fingers.

Gabriel kept one hand safely molded to her hip and the other at her waist. He itched to cup her breasts, squeeze her, caress every inch of her skin. But he wouldn't allow himself. He suspected he wouldn't be able to stop.

She tasted so good and felt so right. Never before had he experienced this level of passion, this intense immersion of feeling. He wanted her, all of her, her heart, her mind, her soul, and especially her body. Right now. In this corridor or on the floor or up against the wall, he didn't care. But he didn't dare either. Not with those blasted twins scampering about, not with the guests awaiting his presence at dinner, not with an innocent woman who had no idea of the jeopardy she was in. Dragging his mouth away from hers, his body trembled with the intensity of his restraint.

With a soft whine, she followed his mouth, seeking more. She arched against him and it drove him wild. "No, Madelyn." He pressed a finger to her lips; she took it into her mouth and touched it with the tip of her tongue. "Oh God, you have no idea," he said with a groan.

"Then tell me," she whispered. "You keep stopping. I realize I'm an innocent, but even a person with a modicum of intellect knows there's more. You kiss me, but nothing else." She shrugged. "I displease you."

Her ridiculous statement ignited the hunger

buried inside him. Clamping his hands on her hips, he jerked her backside against his hard arousal. "Does this feel like displeasure?"

Surprising him, her hips moved against his and he almost moaned.

"Night after night, I struggle to fall sleep, stay asleep, my mind, my body, craving you, only you." He spoke while grinding his hips slowly and fully into hers, and she continued to amaze him by matching his movements. "I wake every morning rock hard, the only remedy a frigid bath, and then I see you, smell you. It's torture just knowing you sleep under my roof." Reaching up, he grasped the front of her bodice and tugged it down, her breasts tumbling free. "Your gowns, you nearly fall out of them. Like a trained gentleman, I pretend to ignore, but all the while it drives me insane." With both hands, he cupped the weight of each breast, kneading them, and circling each nipple until a small moan erupted from the back of her throat and she sunk more fully against the support of his chest.

Madelyn's head lolled back on his shoulder, waves of pleasure undulating through her, her body surrendering to his touch. Then, while Gabriel still teased one of her breasts, his other hand grabbed a handful of her skirts, burrowing underneath, searching. At last he made contact, grabbing her knee and squeezing, then sculpting his large, hot hand along the soft skin of her inner thigh, his fingers slipping under the garter that held up her stocking. Instead of clenching her thighs together, they fell open of their own accord. The muscles in her legs trembled with a strange need as his hand stopped, his fingers an inch away from her damp center. Just when she thought he would not dare, his hand cupped her there, and her breath caught in her throat.

"You were warned," he whispered, slipping one of his fingers into her wetness, "to stay away from me, to cease tempting me." He rocked his hips into her, all the while moving his finger in and out, in and out, matching the pace. The shock of his intrusion both thrilled and stunned her. A breathy moan rushed past her lips and she shuddered with pleasure, matching the rhythm he set by rolling her hips.

He rained a series of soft kisses along the column of her neck, his slick fingers moving relentlessly. "Do you see now, lovely one, why I kept my hands off you when I kissed you, only daring to touch your face?"

She could only shake her head, so caught up was she in the waves of sensation teasing at her body, prodding her toward some unseen horizon.

"I knew down to my core when I touched you, once would never be enough." He probed deeper, his thumb flicking a splendidly sensitive nub of flesh in between her folds. He gave her neck a little nip. "This," he growled, "is just the beginning of all I plan to do to you."

Raising one hand, Madelyn reached back, threading her fingers through his tousled hair. With steady strokes of one hand, his fingers persisted in coaxing her onward, while his other hand grasped at her breast. He commanded over her as he worked his magic, manipulating her body as if she were an exotic musical instrument. Myriad sensations coiled within her, and her heart fluttered inside her chest.

"It's there, Madelyn," he breathed into her ear. "Give in, just give in to it . . . "

Her movements becoming frantic, a thousand sparks seemed to rain over her in an undulating sea of frightening pleasure. Her head fell back against his shoulder and she gasped, about to cry out his name, but he silenced it by catching her mouth with his for a deep, thorough kiss that seemed to go on forever. Ever so gradually her heartbeat slowed, though it still beat heavy and strong, and she became vaguely aware of what had just happened. It was as if she was half asleep, so foggy were her thoughts.

And then with an abruptness that nearly made her stumble, he released her and stepped back. Trembling, she turned to face him, to see if he was scowling, smiling, or if desire yet smoldered in his eyes, but he was only a large shadow in the dark.

Gently now, he adjusted her bodice and patted down her skirts like a dutiful lady's maid. Bending low, he picked up her shawl, shook it out, then placed it upon her shoulders.

The ability to speak, it seemed, had left her. Her thoughts tossed about her head in a turbulent tempest of emotions.

Gabriel had introduced her to sensations she hadn't known existed until a few minutes ago. Part of her wanted to cry now that he'd stopped. She wanted more of him, of his touch. And he said that was the beginning? Good Lord, she should be glad he had stopped, she thought, for she would have certainly given herself to him completely. Only then she would be well and truly compromised. But Gabriel wouldn't marry her. And even if he would, could she force her perfectly unsuitable personality into the mold of a perfectly proper duchess? No. She could not. She was unfit to be a duchess, and Gabriel had told her so on her first day at Wolverest.

In allowing him to take liberties with her body, no matter how well she enjoyed it, she was setting herself up for the same blend of pain she had been protecting Charlotte from so adamantly.

The heartache that comes from loving someone who only sees your faults.

The dinner bell sounded in the distance. Gabriel leaned out of their hiding spot, took a quick look around, and then, holding her gloved hand, guided her out of the darkness and into the wide, candlelit hall.

"They're gone," he replied, referring to the twins. He turned to face her, his brilliant blue eyes piercing her to the spot. Holding her face tenderly with one of his hands, he kissed the bridge of her nose, the apple of both cheeks, then pressed his lips briefly to hers.

"You deserve better than a ravishment in an

alcove," he said, adjusting a curl or two atop her head.

Finally, in the gentle light, she took in his appearance. Still dressed in black dinner clothes, he looked impeccably put together except for a slight tousling of his hair where she imagined her fingers had run through it. She, on the other hand, felt decidedly rumpled. Like she had worn her gown to sleep, simply rolled out of bed and come straight down to dinner.

"We'll be late," she replied. "You're to escort your aunt. Undoubtedly, everyone is waiting for you."

"Let them wait," he said, kissing her again. She stood on her tiptoes, trying to deepen the kiss, but he didn't allow it and pulled his mouth away from hers with a groan.

"Gabriel," she said, placing a hand on his sleeve. "You should know, though I overheard the Fairbournes talking about you, I was not involved with their conversation, their plot. I've never thought to try and change your mind."

His azure gaze was steady, though doubt lingered in the depths. "Are you trying to tell me that your presence here, Madelyn, is solely based on winning the affections of my brother?"

"No," she said, suddenly realizing he had been using her first name since pulling her into the alcove. "I have no interest in your brother."

"Then are you saying you're here simply to forestall gossip and social censure for refusing my invitation?"

He seemed to be crossing off items on a list existing only in his mind. "No," she replied, feeling over-heated as he weeded toward the truth. She had no way of knowing how he'd react to it. Anger. Laughter. Or worse, pity.

He straightened to his full height. "Then it is to protect your friend from my brother," he stated. "I can only admire your devotion, no matter your efforts will prove useless. If he should choose her to be his bride and she accepts, there's little you could do to stop them."

"That is not all," she said, ignoring his taunt, though she thought it fortuitous. "My stepmother, she thinks I . . . that is, she thought I . . . " Madelyn looked to the ground, making a tiny circular motion with the tip of her green satin slipper. Taking a deep breath, she raised her chin and looked him square in the eye. "She thought I could tempt you into wanting to marry me."

With a serious expression, he nodded slowly, his intense gaze so direct, she knew her face was redder than her hair. Of course, he said nothing, making her feel quite like she'd just told him the beginning of a joke and he waited tolerantly for the rest of it.

She cleared her throat. "I never said I would go along with it, you see, and even tried to explain how impossible, how very imprudent, her idea was."

The dinner bell sounded again and she rushed her words, trying to get everything out in the open. "But she couldn't be swayed in her opinion. When she married my father—"

"Madelyn," he interrupted, only she kept on talking.

"—he sold her family Willowbrooke. The only home I've ever known. Upon my father's death, he asked her to return me home, having finally realized how important that connection was to me—"

"Madelyn," he said softly. "Your stepmother's assumption was correct."

And then she did shut her mouth, her lips felt pasted together. In fact, the only thing that seemed to be working was her blinking eyes and her legs. She remained in such a state all the way to the drawing room, all through a hurried introduction to his aunt Eugenia and all the while she was escorted to dinner.

Did he mean to say she was tempting him into marriage? Because that was what it seemed. And was that good? She suspected the answer was no, it was not. He expected flawlessness, in manner, in dress, in speech. And she was full of imperfections. She must have misunderstood.

She needed to be alone, to think, to iron out her jumbled thoughts. Being surrounded by people, some she knew, some she didn't, only filled her with frustration. As she smiled and nodded her head politely at an acquaintance who said something to her from across the table, a sudden annoyance took hold. She sighed, hoping dinner would be quick and uneventful. Instead of retiring to the drawing room afterward for tea and card games, she'd plead a headache and return to her room. Yes, that was a splendid idea.

* * *

By some error in the order of precedence, Lord Rothbury was seated next to Madelyn. While she tried to feign a cool collectedness she did not quite feel, the earl stared at her in abject silence, sparking in her a rare and haughty irritation.

A footman placed a bowl of pheasant soup before her. With her hands folded in her lap, Madelyn turned to face Rothbury, struggling to ignore the blur of Gabriel in her peripheral vision at the head of the long table, his sour-faced aunt at his right.

"Pray sir, why do you stare?"

"My, my," Rothbury drawled. "You are positively flushed."

"It is warm in here," she pointed out, her tone short.

"And your hair," he said, his amber-flecked eyes alighting upon the top of her head, "mussed, for sure."

Her mouth tightened and she picked up her spoon. "That's the trouble with hair given to curl."

"And what is that?" Rothbury asked, studying her neck.

"What is what?" she bit out, bringing up a hand to self-consciously rub where he looked.

"Red marks . . . " He nodded, apparently agreeing with himself. "Definitely some sort of chafing, like a man had rubbed his jaw—"

"'Tis nerves, I imagine. Just nerves."

"And your lips, my dear . . . " He bent low and whispered, "Swollen and throbbing, I wager."

"Next, you'll be telling me 'what big eyes I have.'"

He chuckled softly. "No," he said, shaking his tawny head. "Though you do. But I will say, you look as if you had just—"

"Please, my lord," she warned, pausing in the act of lifting her spoon to her mouth. "I'm starved, really, and your conversation is . . . delaying the appeasement of my hunger."

"By all means," he said with a turning sweep of his hand. "I prefer to make it a habit to indulge females who are in possession of hearty appetites."

She nodded, distractedly, and finished her soup.

By the time the third course was served, Madelyn was finding it steadily harder to avoid conversation by shoveling food between her lips. She wasn't very hungry, and if she sipped any more wine, would render herself unconscious well before the footman brought dessert.

Truthfully, she was feeling quite proud of herself at the moment. She'd managed to studiously evade speaking with Rothbury for quite some time now, and she'd never looked at Gabriel at all. Well, just once. All right, three times. But thank God he didn't make eye contact with her. She didn't think she could handle that. Instead, he had been busy shooting questionable glares at Lord Rothbury.

Murmurs of separate conversations rumbled about the table, but Madelyn was oblivious to them all save one. On the other side of Rothbury sat Charlotte, and next to her, Tristan. Each time Gabriel's brother bent low to whisper into Charlotte's ear, Madelyn leaned toward Rothbury in order to hear.

"Miss Haywood," Rothbury said, turning to her, a square of roast beef on his fork. "Are you attempting to flirt with me or are you trying to overhear the conversation to my left?"

She took a gulp of her wine. Sighing, she looked into the earl's handsome face. His eyes swam a bit and she knew the wine must have gone to her head. "Eavesdropping, I'm afraid," she admitted.

He shook his head. "That's too bad. I was hopeful for the former."

She hiccuped. "Pray, might you tell me . . . exactly what it is they're saying?"

"Why, you naughty girl," he drawled with a smile. "I'd rather take advantage of you in your present state. However, as Wolverest over there would surely run his dinner knife through my heart if I tried, yes, I do believe I can help you."

She chased a pea around her plate with her fork as she waited for Rothbury to finish listening to Lord Tristan's and Charlotte's whispers. He was quite the expert eavesdropper, she thought, popping the pea in her mouth. His looks never betrayed his real intentions and he even managed to hold a casual conversation with another earl seated across from him. After several minutes she became restless and even began to worry that he'd forgotten what he was supposed to be doing.

Finally, he turned back to her.

"After dinner," he whispered. "His library. Something about a book of rare orchids. And she's to wear only her bonnet, spectacles, and stockings."

"Oh no," she said in astonishment.

"Wait. I added that last bit. Small fantasy of mine."

"Oh! That scoundrel! I have to stop them. Stop him." She went to take another sip of wine, but the glass was empty. Almost instantly a footman appeared, taking her glass and replacing it with a full one. She reached for it, but Rothbury got to it first and placed it out of her reach.

"Certainly, *I* would never be caught spoiling a romantic tryst. However, you cannot traipse about saving virgins with your nose buried in a rug."

"Yesh, of course. You're right." She went to stand, but he stayed her by pressing his hand to her forearm.

"At least wait until after dinner," he suggested.

Settling back down, she shook her head to clear it as the room appeared to slant.

"Miss Haywood," Lady Eugenia called out from down the long table. "It has been brought to my attention that your mother was an American."

The whispers and mumbles of exchanges from the other guests faded to silence.

At the mention of her mother, Madelyn straightened in her chair. "Yes, she was. A Bostonian."

Lady Eugenia smiled like she'd just figured out the last piece of a puzzle. She leaned back in her chair, clasping her plum-colored linen napkin between her hands in a self-congratulatory gesture. "This explains so much about your nature, child."

"Aunt," Gabriel said, a warning in his voice.

All around them a bevy of footmen worked to remove the entree plates and replace them with dishes of raspberry cream. They worked silently, diligently, paying no heed to the tension rising in the room like a foul stench.

Madelyn found herself regretting the amount of wine she had consumed. Sober, she would have been able to mask her emotions. As it was, she suspected she was an open book. "And what, exactly, is in my manner that my parentage explains, my lady?" she asked, her hands starting to tremble.

"Why, your inclination for clumsiness. Not to mention your comportment. I always say one can spot an American simply by the way they walk . . . "

"Aunt," came Gabriel's stony warning once again.

"There's always some sort of movement going on," she continued with a smile, "a gangly, loose-limbed sort of gallop. However, I believe with a firm instructor, of course, those tendencies could be ironed out of existence."

Rosalind cleared her throat from across her aunt. "Did I tell you, Aunt, about our outing tomorrow? If the weather permits, I thought the women should like a stroll in—"

"And of course there is the way you talk," his aunt continued. "So loud. One of my friends, a patroness at Almack's, told me that she never had to ask you to repeat yourself. You are definitely not given to mumble, dear."

"Aunt Eugenia," Gabriel growled through his teeth.

Madelyn looked down, half noticing that Lord Rothbury had now pushed a full glass of wine within her reach, apparently for her benefit. She didn't partake, however, knowing, as tipsy as she was, no amount of wine would lessen her mortification at being singled out for ridicule.

"But I see now why my nephew decided to allow your name to remain on the list," Lady Eugenia said, dipping her spoon into the dessert set before her. "It is no great secret my youngest nephew enjoys a good jo—"

"That's enough!" Gabriel slammed his fist upon the table, causing a clattering shake. A heavy silence filled the room as all eyes swung alternately from the duke to his aunt. "I will not have . . . one of my guests slighted at my table, in my house, by my aunt, no less."

One of his guests. Madelyn swallowed, fighting back a surprising twinge of pain. Was that all she was to him? Suddenly, what happened in the alcove before dinner became a shameful memory.

Lady Eugenia's face pulled into an expression one would make if they had just tasted something quite bitter. Madelyn imagined it was the sting of disapproval from her oldest nephew.

"Miss Haywood was invited for her unique qualities," Rosalind said loudly, giving Madelyn the barest of glances as she spoke. "She's an accomplished silhouettist. And more importantly, I quite like her."

Lord Fairbourne chuckled jovially, giving Madelyn an encouraging fatherlike wink, which surprised her. "She's certainly not a dull one. Pluck to the backbone, those Americans. A more optimistic bunch I've never known." He raised his glass to her and took a drink.

All around her conversations began anew. They started as a low rumble, until the guests seated at the table twittered, grumbled, laughed, and simply chatted away as if nothing out of the ordinary had just happened. Not being the center of attention any longer, Madelyn exhaled, grateful for their diversion but still pained by Gabriel's indifferent address.

Her conscience nagged at her. What was he supposed to call her? His lover? The woman of his heart? The tart in the hallway? Smiling wryly, she shook her head. She had no right to berate his words. She had never given him leave to call her Madelyn, though he did on occasion. And to address her in such an informal manner would have induced a wildfire of gossip. At the very least he could have said "Miss Haywood." A shaky sigh rushed past her lips.

"Are you all right?" Rothbury asked.

"Yes, I'm fine." Perhaps she was being too sensitive.

Dinner ended with no further hitches. The ladies began to rise—the gentlemen standing dutifully—to wander back to the drawing room for tea and more chattering.

Madelyn looked over to Priscilla, who had been

very pleased earlier to see that she arrived late to the drawing room on the arm of the duke, no less. Presently, she caught Madelyn's attention and gestured discreetly with a nod of her head toward the end of the table where Gabriel stood.

Turning, Madelyn's gaze was instantly locked with Gabriel's. His stare was possessive and intense, and she shivered as his eyes burned into hers.

An accompanying heat suffused her entire body, coaxing to the forefront of her mind the memory of his kiss, of his hands roving over her skin, of the wicked delight he created. She closed her eyes against the recollection. When she opened them a second later, he gave her a slow smile and a nod. She had that strange feeling again, like he could read her thoughts and was silently promising her from across the room that he meant to have her.

Swallowing hard, she looked away, pretending to be interested in the conversation to her right. She must push all thoughts of Gabriel out of her mind, she told herself. He might want her, and she might want him, but there was an infinitely more important task at hand.

Lord Tristan meant to seduce her friend within the next hour, and she meant to stop him.

Next to her, Rothbury stepped away from the table. Charlotte's and Tristan's seats were empty.

Madelyn looked about the room, but the pair had vanished. His library. He was taking her to his library under the pretense of showing her a book.

Rising herself now, she excused herself from the room without hesitation. Though she was aware of the whereabouts of the private wing of the castle from the tour, she had no idea where Lord Tristan's rooms were. She took a deep breath and assured herself that snooping around was her specialty.

Chapter 15

It was harder than she thought.

In fact, it was turning out to be impossible. She had been searching for Charlotte and Lord Tristan for nearly an hour now, and all she found were locked doors and dead ends. Surely if his lordship was a fast mover, her friend could have already been seduced, thinking a marriage proposal at the ball would be Lord Tristan's next move.

A sharp jab of pain sliced at Madelyn's ankle, reminding her of her recent injury. She paused until it abated, then heaved a frustrated sigh and turned down yet another corridor. It looked—aggravatingly—just like all the others she'd been down. With her luck, she was running in circles. However, she knew she had only herself to blame for her befuddled mind. After all, she had imbibed too much wine at dinner.

Most of the corridors in the private wing of the castle were blanketed in shadows. She adjusted her grip on her candle holder, thankful she had thought to bring it with her. The hall she was currently searching was long and dark, lined on both sides with doors. Quietly, she tried opening them, but to no avail. They were all locked.

As she continued down the hall, she thought of Gabriel and whether any of the doors opened to his private chambers. Never in a hundred years could she have imagined the passion she felt under his influence. He felt it too. He had told her so. It was maddening and exciting and wonderful . . . and it must not ever happen again. Just who was she becoming? A woman of such loose morals she daydreamed about a man who ignited her with immeasurable pleasure and anticipated when or if he would do it again?

She tried pushing Gabriel out of her thoughts and focusing on her mission. Looking ahead, she squinted into the shadows. Her slippers padded softly on the rug and her pace quickened as the small, flickering light she carried revealed a bend in the corridor up ahead . . . a bend instead of a sharp corner. She had never been down this way before.

"I must be in one of the towers," she whispered to herself.

Reaching the end, she rounded the curve and promptly stumbled atop a set of winding stairs. Her lamp went clattering to the stone steps along with her, the flame extinguishing in an instant. She took a deep breath, her eyes filling with tears, for the unexpected spill jarred her sensitive ankle. Covered now in a blanket of darkness, she held herself still to allow her eyes to adjust, and her aching body as well. She murmured a prayer of thanks that she had fallen *atop* ascending stairs instead of crashing *down* descending ones. In this huge castle, no one would have found her body until the next century. She might very well have become a part of a tour.

After a few moments she noticed a faint, bluish light beckoning at the top of the stairs. The sound of rain pelting sporadically against a windowpane drifted to her, leading her to assume that the light came from a window. Grabbing her now useless lamp, she rose from her sprawled position with a wince, then ascended the steep, narrow steps. Cool, rain-scented drafts wafted in the air.

The top came sooner than she'd thought it would, opening to a small room. Two narrow windows were on her left, and a heavy oak door flanked with unlit sconces stood across from her. She peered out the window, which overlooked a private garden from high above. The full moon shone brightly, sitting bravely in the night sky as a swath of black clouds raced across the wide velvety expanse, as if to swallow it whole. Fat raindrops tapped hard and irregularly against the panes of glass, promising an imminent downpour.

Madelyn took a deep breath. She was getting closer, she could feel it. With nothing but a pit of darkness awaiting her at the bottom of the stairs, she decided to press forward instead. She lifted the heavy iron ring handle of the door and pulled. Nothing. Placing her useless candle holder on a ledge, she grasped the door handle with both hands and pulled with all her strength. There was a crack and a moan, and the heavy door relented, opening to the outside. Damp, cold air penetrated her green velvet skirts, chilling her skin.

A narrow footbridge stretched before her, connecting to an adjacent tower. Madelyn looked about, noting how still the air seemed, although the clouds rushed across the sky. It was as if the night was waiting for something, for someone. She stepped out and then jumped when the heavy door slammed shut behind her.

"Oh-no-oh-no," she muttered, spinning around with the intention of opening the door . . . only there wasn't a handle on the outside. Groaning, she slumped a shoulder against it. "Brilliant. Just brilliant. It cannot possibly get any worse."

And then the rain came down in sheets.

He could smell her. It was either that, Gabriel mused, or he was going mad. Having dismissed his valet before coming up, he had chosen to retire early, hoping sleep might offer him sanctuary from his most ardent desire. Apparently, he was wrong— for at the moment it appeared he was imagining he could smell her delicate perfume in every blasted corridor of the private wing of the castle.

With sharp tugs, he undid his cravat as he strode down the corridor leading to his private chambers. He supposed that perhaps it was *he* who smelled like her. After all, she had been in his arms, writhing in ecstasy, not more than a couple of hours ago. Yes, that must be it. He reminded himself that all through dinner he kept catching a trace of her scent around him. It had made him distracted, aroused, and impatient. Thoughts of her lush body, her moans of pleasure, played in his mind while they dined. She had been exquisite. Better than he imagined. And he should never, ever do it again.

His nostrils flared. There it was again.

His steps slowed as the unmistakable scent of rose and mint continued to tickle at his senses. Senses that had been at a steady attention—just like another part of him—since the day Madelyn walked—or was it stumbled?—into his life. The clumsy, adorable, accident-prone vixen had wiggled her way into his thoughts and, he suspected, his heart.

He shook his head, trying to dispel the enticing aroma in the hall, and entered his chamber. What a folly it was that she had agreed to stay at Wolverest. The ball was in two more days. Which meant two more days of surviving the delicious torture of being in the presence of Madelyn. He kicked off his boots, setting them aside for polishing.

Throwing his cravat over the back of a red wing-back chair, Gabriel stood before the hearth, a roaring fire crackling in the grate left for him by a servant. He removed his coat and waistcoat and placed them on the seat of the chair.

Tense. Everything about him felt rigid. His muscles, his mind, his cock. Without a doubt the only remedy was to make her his. All of her and in every way. He would be bound to her and there would be no turning back. Could he do that? Of course he could; he was the Duke of Wolverest, he could do whatever he wanted.

He looked into the fire while divesting himself of his linen shirt, breeches, and drawers. They joined the heap on the chair and he was finally naked. And starkly aware of his state of arousal.

A frustrated groan rumbled forth and he swept a hand through his dark locks. He looked across his room, spying the washstand next to the window that overlooked the flower garden down below. A sudden surge of rain beat against the pane of glass in drumming waves pushed by the wind.

"Dreadful weather," he mumbled, shuffling toward the window. Perhaps he should ring for a bath and submerge himself in the frigid depths again. It seemed to be the only thing that worked, albeit temporarily.

Deciding instead to pour the cold water in the pitcher over his head, he flung his wet head back and blotted the rivulets of water streaking down his face, neck, arms, and chest with a wide towel. Just as he was opening his eyes, a shadow raced between the battlements outside.

He blinked, thinking he'd imagined it, and promptly shrugged the notion off. Hanging the damp towel on the rod connected to the washstand, he strode for his bed knowing sleep would again evade him.

There was nothing like being blasted with a blanket of icy rain to completely dispel any lingering effects of spirit indulgence.

Wetter and colder than she had ever been in her

life, Madelyn dashed across the battlements, heading for the adjacent tower and the door she spied there.

"Please-be-open-please-be-open," she chanted while descending the few, short steps hugging the tower. At the bottom she nearly shouted for joy when she saw a handle. She grabbed it with both hands and pulled the door open. A sigh of relief rushed past her trembling lips.

She peered into the room. It was lavishly decorated in shades of dark blue and beige—everything, the silk-covered walls, the plush rugs, and the paintings. To the left on a dais sat a large, rumpled bed, a tall canopy of blue velvet hanging overhead. On her right was an ornate wardrobe, washstand, and side table. The room radiated masculinity and gave the appearance of belonging to someone of great importance. But whoever it was, they appeared to be absent. At least for now.

At the far end were a pair of scarlet wing-back chairs sitting before a cheery fire, which beckoned her to enter and warm herself. But she would not take the risk, no matter how badly she wanted to. The occupant of the room could return at any moment. And that person could be Lord Tristan.

She dashed across the room, heading toward the door. First, she would see if it led to the hall. If it did, she would hide there, hoping to see who entered . . . and if they were alone.

A shiver skittered down her spine—not wholly unlike the ones she got around Gabriel—and she blamed it on her current state. She reached for the brass handle. The door opened a crack, then slammed back shut. Slowly, her gaze lifted to a spot on the door just above her head.

A man's hand—Gabriel's hand—splayed against the wood, keeping it shut . . . and her from leaving the room.

"Though I have never been one to be impressed by the new trend of wetting one's chemise," Gabriel drawled, his animal heat engulfing her, "I find I am rendered speechless by your interpretation. Although, I do believe you have outdone yourself."

She spun around and quite forgot to breathe.

His ink-black hair was wet . . . and he was completely naked. And completely aroused. And smiling wickedly.

Madelyn blinked like a madwoman in order to keep herself from looking down. "You—You—" she stammered.

"Me—Me," he mocked lightly, a smile in his voice.

She threw a hand over her eyes. "You're naked," she announced.

"Yes."

"I mean, all over," she said, making an up and down gesture with her free hand.

"That is what naked means," he said.

She stole a peek between her fingers, her eyes alighting on the broad expanse of his muscled chest, his flat stomach, his belly button ringed with black hair trailing downward, pointing to . . . "Good Lord in heaven."

"Madelyn," he called softly. "What are you doing in my chamber?"

"Miss Haywood," she corrected weakly, with her hand still covering her eyes. There was something glaringly intimate about a naked Gabriel using her given name. "I was looking for someone and became lost."

"Oh?" came his husky reply. "Was it me?"

"Of course not!"

"You should be abed, Madelyn, or at the very least sitting in the drawing room with the others. Your ankle cannot have healed so quickly."

She ignored his statement and the dull ache that yet throbbed from her fall. "Mr. Devine," she started, totally out of sorts. "No, I mean Gabr— No, I mean, Your Grace, hasn't—"

"Gabriel," he supplied.

"Hasn't anyone ever told you that it's dreadfully improper to stand before a lady without your clothes on?"

She felt him lean toward her, his hand still pressed against the door at her back. He smelled faintly of wine and soap and warmth. And she was so very cold.

"Madelyn," he said, using his other hand to try and pry her hand from her eyes, "hasn't anyone ever told you how scandalous it is to visit a man's bedroom, a man who so profusely has told you how very much he would like you in his bed?"

Though her lips were eager to form words, nothing came forth. She allowed him to remove her hand from her face, but she still kept her eyes closed.

"You need to take your clothes off," he said. "You are soaking wet and trembling with cold. Come by the fire."

As if to underscore his statement, a shiver quaked through her body. If she stayed—and some naughty part of her wanted to desperately—she knew what could happen.

"I should leave," she said, but her voice didn't sound convincing even to her own ears. Lord, but she was cold.

He stepped away for a moment and her body betrayed her by leaning forward into empty space. Then he smoothed his warm hand over one of hers. "If you leave," he drawled, "I would only follow you and bring you back. Come. Keep your eyes closed if you like." And with that he guided her across the room.

She knew she stood before the fire when light danced behind her eyelids and heat washed over her in flickering waves.

"You should tell me what brought you here," he said, removing her wet shawl.

"Perhaps . . . if you put something on I could open my eyes."

"If it would make you more comfortable."

She nodded, shakily.

There was a swishing sound, like that of fabric over bare skin. "You may open your eyes now, Madelyn."

She did, then gasped. Oh, he put something on all right. Just his breeches. Shirtless and barefoot, he stood proudly before her like a beautiful, potent Adonis, his black locks tousled around his face, his piercing blue eyes undressing her soul.

"You are very casual about your attire," she mentioned with a shrug. "Are you always this informal with females?"

In answer he gave his head a slow shake and offered her a lopsided smile.

His skin looked golden in the firelight, and her gaze, again, was drawn to the tantalizing trail of hair disappearing down the front of his breeches.

"Madelyn—"

"Miss Haywood," she corrected again. He had the most beautiful mouth she'd ever seen on a man. When he smiled at her, she felt dizzy and muddled. Lord, she wanted him to kiss her.

"You're dripping all over the rug," he said, his eyes crinkling at the corners.

"I'm sorry," she mumbled, watching him cross the room to fetch a plump white towel from a table.

"You'll catch cold. Allow me to at least offer you a towel." He handed it to her, letting his fingers skim over her knuckles. "I see you're no longer wearing your gloves," he said, turning her hand over to inspect her palms. The pad of his thumb brushed her skin.

She shook her head, biting her lip at his excruciating gentleness. The towel fell to the floor from her loose grasp.

"Good. I see no sign of damage from your fall on the stepping-stones at Devine Mansion." He brought her open palm to his lips and kissed it, then did the same to her other hand.

Despite her cold, sodden clothes, Madelyn suddenly felt overheated. In a few more days she'd leave Wolverest Castle and probably never see Gabriel again. She didn't want her last memory of him to be of their encounter in the alcove. As beautiful as that was, the fool inside her wanted more.

Her gaze lingered on his strong, smooth, bare chest. "Gabriel, please. I need you to kiss me," she pleaded, her voice barely audible.

His head snapped up at her words. Gone was his cool expression, his crooked grin. He stared down at her with such heat, she forgot to breathe for the second time since breaking into his room.

Slowly, he shook his head. "That, madam, I cannot do." He released her hand and it fell to her side. "Ask me for money, for jewelry, bloody hell, ask me for anything but a kiss. Let me indulge your every whim . . . but a single kiss at this point would be acute torture."

"Then make love to me." Her heavy words seemed to ring out in the room. They even surprised her. "I don't expect anything in return. Just love me."

Silence hung heavy between them. She had meant to say "make love to me" again, but it seemed her heart spoke louder than her mind.

Gabriel straightened and she became aware of a muscle ticking in his cheek. "Do you realize what you ask?"

"I do," she said firmly.

She watched his throat work as he swallowed. "Do you realize the consequences? Do you realize what that means?"

She nodded, unwilling to think of how she'd feel about her decision in the morning. He took a step toward her, then looked deeply into her eyes. Thoughts, unspoken but understood, passed between them.

"I will not change my mind," she said.

And still he hesitated. She had the impression he was giving her ample time to renege on her offer.

She lifted her chin as the pad of his thumb smoothed slowly over her bottom lip. "Your emotions, your very thoughts, are all here for me to see in your eyes," he said. "I was a fool to think you had a hand in the Fairbournes' game."

He took a long, deep breath, then circled her, stopping once he was behind her. "I hate to admit this," he said, unfastening the row of buttons down her back, "but I haven't the strength to tell you no, and I imagine it will always be so."

A delightful shiver coursed through her as he pressed a kiss between her shoulder blades. "This gown . . . is your stepmother's, I presume." His breath tickled the fine hairs on the back of her neck as he moved in closer.

Nodding, she cleared her throat to speak. "I like it, really. Only it doesn't quite fit." And then her thoughts were put on hold as he peeled the soaked green velvet down to her waist. Her cool skin was instantly warmed—from the heat of the fire and the anticipation of his touch.

"You look lovely, though I suppose I would find you utterly delectable had you worn a coarse sack."

"Lovely? Well, I don't know about that."

"I do." And he did. From the moment he spied her in his garden, Gabriel had imagined her in every stage of dress or undress. Wet or dry. Mud-dotted or fresh from a bath. Draped in the finest red silk or naked, glistening with perspiration from a rather wild bout of their lovemaking. Any and every way, he had envisioned it all.

"The faster we get you out of these clothes," he said, slipping his fingers under the straps of her chemise, "the faster I can warm you."

She covered her chest with her arms. Being ravished by Gabriel in a dark alcove was one thing, but baring herself in the full light of a roaring fire was quite another. As cold as she was, she grasped at her chilly, wet gown and pulled it back up, clutching it to her chest.

"Madelyn, do you want me to stop?"

"No, it's just that . . . well, it's so bright in here."

With his hands on her shoulders he turned her to face him. Desire and tenderness in his eyes, he said softly, "I still can't believe it, but it has occurred to me that you have absolutely no idea of just how beautiful you truly are." And that facet of her personality only made her all the more exquisite. He waited for her to drop her gown. When she did, kicking her slippers off in the process, he took her hands in his, then placed them on his bare chest.

Sinewy muscle fairly rippled beneath her fingertips as she smoothed her hands over his sculpted shoulders, his arms, and the heated skin of his chest. When she reached the flat plane of his stomach, his skin tightened in response. She circled the oval of his navel with the tip of her finger.

His breath hitched and she looked up to see his face. His eyes were closed and he swallowed convulsively. Standing there in her damp chemise, some sort of switch flicked on inside of Madelyn. Suddenly she felt powerful—that she could evoke this sort of reaction from a man like him. And that power made her bold.

Dipping her fingertips into the waist of his breeches, she pulled him toward her. With a glimmer of desire in his hooded gaze, he immediately came to her. Molding one of his hands on the back of her head, he captured her mouth for a searing, open-mouthed kiss. It was not gentle. It was not sweet. It was all-consuming and masterful. Hot and fast-paced. Over and over his mouth slanted across hers, giving and taking, coaxing and devouring.

Holding her soft body tight against him, his free hand pressed to her lower back, then lower still, rounding over the curve of her bottom. When her lips parted on a whimper, he sunk his tongue into the warm depths of her mouth, stroking her silky sweetness. She responded with tender eagerness, making him shudder with pleasure.

Gabriel's heart slammed inside his chest. Never in his life had he felt such complete lack of self-control. The strength of his ardor stunned the hell out of him.

Her light floral fragrance was intoxicating. She

felt so right, so soft in his arms. Her fragile entreaty, to make love to her, to love her . . . hell, he wasn't sure he deserved the precious gift she was offering him.

Madelyn moaned into his mouth, and he answered it with one of his own. Slipping his fingers into the front of her chemise, he meant only to push the thin silk garment down, but it ripped under his large hands so he finished it off, tossing it to the floor. Next, he rid himself of his breeches and nudged them aside to join the puddle of green velvet. Her hands smoothed over his back, urging him closer. His hot, hard arousal pressed into her soft belly.

An escalating surge of sensation pulsed through Madelyn. His strong hands were everywhere. Caressing her back, in her hair, knocking hairpins soundlessly to the rug. Her sodden burgundy locks fell around her shoulders, leaving damp trails along her back and shoulders, but she paid no attention to it. In fact, the feeling only intensified the glory of being naked in Gabriel's arms.

Sighing softly, her head dropped back as he cupped one of her breasts, kissing and nipping the swell of her bosom.

With his lips still hot upon her, he murmured, "Mmm. You're simply delicious."

Closing her eyes, she could only nod jerkily, though his words thrilled her.

He pulled the hardened nipple into his mouth with a lazy swirl of his tongue. She gasped as a tumult of delight coursed from his point of contact down to the damp center between her thighs.

Wearing only her silk stockings and garters, he stroked one of her thighs, urging her leg to ride high on his hip. Then he slipped a hand between their bodies, rubbing between her feminine folds with gentle, long sweeps of his fingers. His movements coaxed an impatient whimper from Madelyn. "And I cannot wait to taste you here," he whispered thickly.

He smiled at her gasp. He couldn't help it. Never before had he felt such bliss. Having Madelyn in his arms was heaven. This beautiful, unpretentious, tender-hearted woman.

He eased her leg down and together they sank to the rug before the fire. On their knees before each other, Gabriel cupped her breasts, making circles around her nipples with his thumbs.

"Gabriel, please," she breathed, as delicious shivers sparked through her.

Dipping his head, he nibbled on her earlobe, then the side of her neck, before moving downward to nuzzle her breasts. Only when she quivered with need did he take one pebbled nipple into his mouth. With a groan, Madelyn threaded her fingers through his silky hair, holding him there. He suckled at one breast while tugging on the nipple of the other. With a groan of his own, he relished every little sound of pleasure she made.

When her hips began to writhe with need, he eased her onto her back, spreading her hair like a halo around her. Grasping her hands in his, he lifted them above her head, pressing them into the soft plush of the beige and blue rug while he caught her mouth for more of his kiss. He kept his weight off her by settling half his body to the side of her.

Madelyn tried to lift her hands from under his, and he instantly released his hold.

"I want to touch you," she said, reaching down with one hand to tentatively run her fingertips up his arousal.

His breath came in quick bursts.

She pulled away, a worried frown marring her brow. "What did I do wrong?"

Chuckling softly, he exhaled then scattered kisses along her jaw and the underside of her chin. "Too good," he murmured, sinking lower to paint a trail of kisses down her neck.

She rubbed his broad back as he continued downward, nuzzling her breasts, his hot tongue alternately teasing, flicking each hard nipple. She moaned, and he answered with reassuring sounds of his own though they were muffled by her dewy flesh upon his lips.

His warm hands expertly molded, sculpted, and smoothed all of her, leaving every inch of her flesh branded by his touch. With one hand threaded through her hair, he reached down across the curve of her stomach and rubbed a long finger in between her moist folds in a slow, relentless rhythm, her hips moving eagerly along with him.

Gabriel knew he wouldn't last much longer if he didn't speed things up, but he wanted this to be perfect for her. He needed to be patient, to cherish each and every moment of this heavenly surrender. Hers and his.

"Gabriel." She bit her lip on a moan. Instinctively, Madelyn spread her thighs a touch wider. "I feel . . . impatient. I need something."

Repositioning himself, Gabriel took hold of his arousal, rubbing the tip against the opening of her sex. He smiled wickedly at her gasp of delight.

"Is this want you need?"

She nodded. "Mmm-hmm."

He positioned himself and entered her a scant inch while he captured her moan with his mouth for an erotic, teasing kiss. His intent was to go slow, but impatient Madelyn instinctively hiked her legs up high around his waist and pressed his taut buttocks with her heels in a gesture of urgency.

Gabriel unraveled. He plunged into her with a deep thrust, then paused to allow her to adjust to his intrusion. He didn't have to wait long. Trembling with the strain of holding himself still when all he wanted to do was slide within her liquid heat until they both crested and then crumbled with their climax, he released her mouth and stared into her eyes. She was panting, her face flushed with desire and . . . worry?

"What is it?" Gabriel whispered, panting himself. "What's wrong?"

She nibbled her bottom lip, which was swollen and rosy from his kiss. "Was that it? Are we done?"

The muscles in his face instantly softened. He smiled and shook his head. "No," he said, making small circles on her temples with the pads of his thumbs.

She relaxed beneath him. "Oh, good."

He kissed her lips. "Did I hurt you?"

"A little," she answered, "but I think it's gone. Move a bit, let's see."

He complied, his jaw rigid with intense restraint.

The burn slowly faded and Madelyn moaned as a pleasurable sensation took hold. One that yearned for Gabriel to move again. The feel of his weight atop her was bliss. She looked into his blue gaze, eyes that shimmered with light and desire, and rejoiced in the pleasure of having Gabriel buried deep inside her. What a delightfully decadent picture they presented, this beautiful, dark-haired, lean-muscled man covering her much softer body with his own. Her legs wrapped about his waist in tender submission, their skin glowing in the firelight.

He traced a path across her lips with his tongue, then nipped playfully at her neck until Madelyn started to squirm underneath him. Slowly, he withdrew and held back, only to plunge deep inside her again. She gasped his name, digging her fingers into his hips.

And he repeated this decadent torment, over and over, withdrawing almost all of his length, then rocking into her once again. She found his pace maddening, the pleasure frighteningly wonderful.

" . . . so good, so perfect," he murmured on a groan. He sought her mouth and slanted his across her lips, dipping his tongue in deep sweeps. She moaned sweetly into his mouth, and he couldn't take it any longer.

Again and again he drove into her, their bodies working together in an unrelenting, ancient rhythm, her thighs holding him tightly to her.

Pleasure overwhelmed Madelyn until she was moaning in ecstasy. And then a startling wave of unimaginable bliss crashed over her again and again, and she cried out his name. Perspiring with muscles straining, Gabriel worked over her, stretching out the extent of her climax into a dizzying length.

Gabriel whispered her name and finished with one deep thrust, spilling his seed in her with a low groan. And there they stayed, bodies trembling with exertion as they both fought to catch their breath.

A long moment later he slid away from her, urging her to her side. He then cuddled behind her so she could take full advantage of the warmth from the hearth.

"You want me to believe you're being kind by allowing me full access to the heat of the fire," she said, delighting in the shivers running through her as Gabriel dropped kisses on the back of her neck. "But the truth is," she giggled, "you're just as over-heated as I. Your kind gesture is steeped in cruelty, sir."

He chuckled softly, nuzzling her ear.

"That was wonderful, Gabriel," she whispered.

"Better than waltzing?"

She laughed. "Much better. Why?"

"Because I sensed a hesitation in your statement."

"Well, it's just that . . . I feel I didn't participate very much. You gave me so much pleasure, but I don't know how to do the same for you."

"Believe me," he said dropping a kiss on her shoulder, "had you pleasured me any more, I would have surely died."

"Oh," she said softly. "Really?"

"Quite." Gently, he rubbed his bristled jaw between her shoulder blades, and she sighed. "You left right after dinner," he murmured. "Why?"

"Oh sweet Lord! Charlotte! I'd forgotten." Madelyn went to jump to her feet, but Gabriel clamped a hand on her hip to halt her.

"What have you forgotten?"

"Lord Rothbury told me your brother was making plans with my friend to meet in secret."

"Ah, so that's why you were talking to that partridge."

"Partridge?" She shook her head. "Gabriel, I must go. I must stop them."

"Do you mean to say you never found his private library?" When she flipped to her back in an effort to wriggle from his hold, he threw one long, muscled leg over hers.

"No. 'Twas how I managed to get locked out on the battle—" Her eyes narrowed. "How did you know they were to meet in his library?"

"Because that's where I found them. I watched them leave, followed them, then . . . influenced Tristan to reconsider his objective."

"You did?"

He nodded, brushing his lips on her shoulder, and she shivered. She turned back over to face the fire, a smile playing on her lips. And she believed him.

"Thank you," she murmured quietly.

"Mmm-hmm," he mumbled, holding her close. "Right now, I imagine a very bored Miss Greene sits alongside her dozing mother."

And wondering where in the world I went off to, Madelyn mused with a mixture of regret and panic. Somehow, she managed to push the feeling away. Right now she wanted to revel in the afterglow of the glorious moment she had shared with Gabriel, for she knew that tomorrow it would seem less like a wonderful merging of souls and more like one big fat mistake.

Steady rain pelted the windowpanes overlooking the gardens. Sighing with a forced contentment, she closed her eyes. Lulled by the coziness of the fire, the softness of the rug beneath her and the hard-muscled male behind her with his arm draped protectively over her waist, Madelyn fell into a deep sleep.

She dreamed of being enveloped within a sea of warmth where masculine fingers traced tantalizing trails along her spine and over the curve of her hip. She dreamed of being draped with heavy blankets and lifted against a wall of strength, muscular arms tenderly keeping her close and safe. Finally, she dreamed of being placed upon a bed of ivory, and shivered at the abrupt absence of the heated presence she had clung to moments ago. A frown knitted her brow and she yearned for its return, even while she slipped further into the depths of slumber.

Bending low, Gabriel kissed away the wrinkle on Madelyn's forehead.

"Definitely a deep sleeper," he whispered as he pulled her covers up to her chin.

Returning to his chamber after a discreet inspection of his guests whereabouts, he didn't hesitate getting Madelyn back to her room. Luckily, Lady Haywood was deep into a game of whist, too distracted to notice how long Madelyn had been gone. Only Charlotte looked a bit out of sorts at her friend's continued absence. And so Gabriel had pulled one of his linen shirts over Madelyn's head, wrapped her with a heavy silk blanket, and carried her to her room using less traveled corridors.

The rain had stopped and the moon shone brightly in the night sky. A soft light fell upon Madelyn's features, and Gabriel found himself fighting the urge to join her in bed. In her presence he felt a sense of comfort, of completion, and only his cold, lonely bed awaited him.

With a sigh, she rolled to her side, facing him, and he couldn't help but smile. Oh, how he wanted to be in this room when she awoke. To hold her, to love her again. He certainly hoped she had the good sense to shield her attire from the maid and whoever else happened to see her before she dressed in the morning.

Sitting on the edge of her bed, he bent over her slumbering form and kissed the bridge of her nose, the apples of both her cheeks, and finally the corner of her lip where a lone freckle dotted her skin. What the hell had he been thinking? He loved freckles.

Rising, Gabriel shrugged as the burden of worry pricked at his thoughts. So much could go wrong before he could set the situation right. Someone could have spotted him with Madelyn in his arms, or now as he left her room. And how in the world would Madelyn explain the condition of her gown and torn chemise? Hell, he'd throw the latter in the fire as soon as he returned to his room, and as for the gown . . . He'd have a talk with the maid and see what could be done.

With reluctant steps he headed out of her chamber. It didn't matter if a sea of gossip flooded the castle walls at sunrise. So be it. A surge of possessiveness thrummed through him. Madelyn was his. And he would make her so in every way imaginable.

For on the morrow he would ask the imperfect Madelyn to be his perfect bride.

Chapter 16

The next morning, there came a knock on Madelyn's bedchamber door. Frowning, she rose from the satinwood dressing table and crossed the room.

Dressed in a pale pink calico walking dress with a white overskirt embroidered with tiny pink flowers, she looked the part of a lighthearted, virtuous young lady. A contradiction, for sure. In the light of day, she felt consumed by her shameful abandon of the night before.

Passing a tall cheval mirror, she frowned at herself. "You are a wanton woman," she muttered in distaste.

What had she been thinking? Her conscience screamed that it was all painfully clear. Quite simply, her practical mind had succumbed to the desires of her heart. And now—she swallowed against the ache in her throat—now she was an empty shell of woman hopelessly in love with a man who would never return her affections, never make her his bride.

But he could make her his mistress. If fact, she

had every expectation he would make her an offer. And, of course, she would refuse.

She sighed, grabbing the cool brass of the door handle. There was no sense regretting the past. She had made her decision and would have to find comfort in the memory of their one night of passion. She would never allow him to touch her again.

She pulled the door open and only had enough time for a second of recognition and a small gasp before Gabriel seized her. He crushed her to him, cradling the back of her head with his free hand. The smell of soap and warm male enveloped her as his lips slanted over hers in a tender onslaught. At her lower back, his other hand pressed her to his tall, muscular form, all her misgivings of the night before disintegrating in the ferociousness of his enthusiasm.

She lifted her heavy arms, wrapping them around his lean waist. When his tongue slipped inside her mouth with lazy swirls and dips, a familiar languorous heat rushed through her limbs, pooling between her legs. His strong hand at her back slid down, cupping her backside and pressing her into his arousal. A profound craving, half pain and half pleasure, ached within her traitorous body.

And then he ended the kiss, leaving her feeling empty. She smothered an unladylike whine of frustration.

He pressed his nose to hers and smiled. "Good morning, my angel."

"Good—Good morning," she stammered.

He kissed her nose and took a step back to look at her. "My," he said, his gaze feasting on her. "Wearing one of your own frocks? You look absolutely breathtaking. However, I find I quite prefer you naked."

"Shh!" She swatted at his broad chest. "Someone will hear you." Peeking around his shoulder, she glanced up and down the hall. "Or see you."

"And so what if they do? Let them."

"Are you insane?"

His azure gaze narrowed on her as she blinked up at him in astonishment. "Something tells me that you regret what happened last night."

Her face flamed with a blush. "Whatever are you doing here?"

"Ah," he said, nodding like he'd made up his mind. "You do regret it."

That wasn't necessarily true; it was more complex. But she wasn't about to discuss this with him in her bedchamber where anyone could come down the hall and see them together at any moment. Depending who that was and just what it was they witnessed, Gabriel could be forced to do the honorable thing and make an offer for her hand in holy matrimony. And a marriage based on obligation alone was something she could not handle.

Madelyn pushed against the wall of his chest, urging Gabriel out into the hall. Mercifully, he relented to her puny shoves, for if he truly didn't care to move, she knew there was no way she'd ever manage to scoot him even an inch.

Careful not to make a sound, she closed her chamber door behind her. "This is neither the time nor the place to discuss such things," she said, hating the fact her words sounded as stern as the mewl of a kitten.

"Tell me," he whispered, curling a lock of hair around his finger that had escaped her coiffure, "did anyone see you in my shirt?" He kissed the curl.

Shivers scattered across her skin. Then he bent his head down to her collarbone to drop three kisses there. "No," she breathed when his teeth tugged on the lace trim of her bodice.

It was partially true. She had managed to stuff it in the back of her armoire before Jenny came to help her with her bath. Jenny subsequently found it while gathering the soiled shawls for cleaning. Her eyes nearly bugged out of her head, but she kept her silence and finished helping Madelyn dress. Only once did Jenny dare ask a question. She wanted to know where the green velvet gown had gone. Madelyn had no answer, and the maid didn't press.

"Come," Gabriel whispered against her throat. "I want to show you something."

"I think I've already seen it." And oh, how she secretly wanted to see it again.

She felt his smile against her skin. "It's not what you think."

Good Lord, if he only knew what she thought. His warmth and the scent of him, the play of his lips upon her skin, the way his teeth were now nipping at her earlobe . . . all she could think about was how much she wanted to be naked and writhing in ecstasy beneath him once again.

"Whatever it is you desire to show me will have to wait," she replied, slipping her fingers into his silky black hair.

"Why?" he growled.

"Because we are all to meet at the parterre in a half hour for a stroll and then tea. My stepmother and the Greenes will be coming to collect me."

He pulled away from her, heat and desire apparent in his heavy-lidded gaze. "I'll have you back before they come looking."

With that, he linked her arm with his, guiding her down the corridor.

And like a weak-willed ninny, she went along without a fight.

When they passed the servant staircase, Madelyn turned to look at him. Her tone wary and careful, she asked, "Are we not to use those? For discretion?"

He shook his head once and a thick lock tumbled down, covering one eye like a patch. His jaw was lightly covered with bristles today, making her itch for the feel of his scratchy cheeks on her bare skin. Tall and lean-muscled, he looked the elegant gentleman this morning in his fine clothes. And, oh, how she wanted him to be rid of them, to see him again in all his naked glory. With secret appreciation, her eyes flicked over the cut of his black frock coat, which was tailored to fit him to perfection, displaying the broad expanse of his chest and shoulders. She smothered a wistful sigh.

Sooner than she thought, they were standing before a wide mahogany-paneled door. Madelyn exhaled, the muscles in her shoulders relaxing. Surprisingly, they had encountered nary another guest, only an upstairs maid who kept her eyes downcast. However, Madelyn wasn't hopeful. Considering how fast news of her wasp sting had traveled, she expected all of Yorkshire to know she had been spotted alone with the duke by the end of the day.

Gabriel inserted a long key into the lock and the door clicked open. He pushed it wide, gesturing with his other hand for her to proceed inside the long, shadowed room. She stepped past him, a shock of awareness running through her as his body heat pervaded through her frock.

The harsh afternoon sunlight was blocked by heavy brocade drapes hanging on the tall, mullioned windows on the right. Still, a faint, weak light filtered into the room, allowing Madelyn to examine the wall of portraits to the left. Gabriel had taken her to see the private art gallery.

She turned to smile at him. He returned her grin with one of his own, though his held a decidedly sensual promise. "My butler found his key," he drawled.

"I see," she said turning to peruse a portrait of a young girl in a frilly white dress sitting at a pianoforte. Her hands were placed delicately upon the keys, her short black locks curling around her shoulders.

"My mother at age five," he said.

"She's absolutely beautiful. You all look just like her," Madelyn said softly.

"Do you look like your mother?"

She gave an unsure gesture that was half nod, half shrug. "I suppose. I lost her so young and now my memory is fading. Someday I fear I will not be able to recall her likeness at all."

"Have you no portraits?"

"I have a pencil sketch I did when I was seven and another I did from memory when I was twelve. Needless to say, I wasn't an artistic prodigy. I'm much better at silhouettes."

"Have you no miniatures? Nothing?"

She smiled sadly at him. "Not with me, unfortunately. They're all at Willowbrooke Cottage, I'm afraid. Or, they all *were* at Willowbrooke." From behind her eyes Madelyn felt the familiar sting of tears that always came when she thought of her mother and how much she longed to see her face, her warm eyes always shining with tenderness and love.

"You must miss her terribly," he said, effectively reading her thoughts. Or rather, she imagined it was all there to be seen on her face.

"Yes. Yes I do," she said, swallowing the ache in her throat. "A mother's love is irreplaceable."

Madelyn moved to observe a painting of a giggling little baby, his blue eyes and broad, toothless smile portrayed with such clarity, she thought she just might hear a laugh come from the portrait. She squinted to read the gold label at the base of the frame. Expectedly, it read: BABY GABRIEL.

"Will not the baroness allow you to return and retrieve your mother's things?" Gabriel asked, his deep voice vibrating through the room, through her.

"No," she answered flatly. "The cottage was sold to her family before my father's death. And they are not the sort of people who would see beyond their needs and wants to acknowledge that I might long to return there and recover her possessions, my things even, portraits and so on."

"So you haven't returned since your father had you all moved to London when you were eight?"

She nodded.

"Your things could still be there, tucked away in the attic or thrown in a shed," he offered.

"I doubt it," she said, shaking her head forlornly. "But I was willing to hope." Her comment was met with silence, and Madelyn wondered at his thoughts. She stopped before a large portrait of a beautiful, dark-haired woman with familiar icy blue eyes. The woman smiled serenely with a plump baby on her lap, her thumb trapped within his pudgy fist. On her right crouched a young girl equal in her mother's beauty, her rosebud lips almost pursed in a pout. On the other side of the seated mother stood a handsome boy of about ten, his chin raised to a challenging angle, his blue eyes flashing with the promise of future arrogance. Gabriel. He had to be the boy standing in the picture.

Breaking out in a wide grin, Madelyn turned to look at the duke. He stood in the shadows, his broad shoulders pressed against the closed doors.

He stared at her intently, and she pretended his desire-filled expression was a figment of her imagination.

Her mind listened, but her body warmed in response.

She gestured to the portrait with a nod of her head. "So serious for such a young lad?"

He nodded slowly, his eyes never leaving her face.

A rush of anticipation flowed through her. The thought that he brought her here for other, more sinful reasons toyed with her conscience. She shouldn't want him to desire her again, but she did. And she desired him, his touch, and just his company as well.

"I never smiled much." His voice was a low purr in the shadows.

"Don't be silly," she replied, taking a step closer to the next portrait—and farther away from him. "You smile all the time."

"At you," he conceded, "with you, because of you."

For a brief moment her eyes met his, but she soon blushed and looked away. She took another step to peruse a painting of a dour-faced young miss, her stern expression making her appear older than she was. Lady Eugenia in her youth, no doubt.

The next portrait had Madelyn instantly intrigued. It looked to be of his mother, albeit at an older stage in her life. Terribly thin, the duchess smiled, though the sharp beauty so dominant in the other likenesses of her was now nowhere to be seen. In its place sat a deep sadness that his mother couldn't seem to hide. Madelyn turned, her unspoken question stalled upon her lips.

When Gabriel spoke next, his words were soft, but hard-edged. "She mourned her marriage." He sighed, long and heavy, like a burden sitting on his shoulders temporarily lifted.

Patiently, Madelyn waited for him to continue.

"Originally, my father stood behind her in that picture, though he wasn't present for the sitting. After he passed away, she had him painted out, as he was never truly there in the first place. And my meaning is literal and figurative. Their union wasn't a love match, as it usually isn't in such cases." He paused and shook his head slowly. "However, my mother grew to feel very deeply for my father. He never returned the sentiment, but that didn't stop her from grasping at an exhausted hope that one day he would."

"Your father never showed her affection?"

"Indeed not. He had many lovers." He shook his head in disdain. "I was away at school so often that I don't believe even *I* grasped the extent of my mother's depression until I came home from Eton on holiday one year and found she'd grown sickly pale, lost considerable weight, and only came to life in front of her children."

Sadness welled inside Madelyn. "It must have brought you great pain to see her so." Her eyes flicked over the portrait once more, then back to

Gabriel. His wore a guarded expression, but she detected sorrow there as well. "I must ask . . . why would you have such a likeness of your mother displayed if it brings you pain? Why not simply take it down and allow only those portraits of when she was content?"

"Find it maudlin if you like, but put simply, it stays because it is a reminder to me of the unquestionable power of love . . . and the destructive consequences when that love goes unreturned." He sighed, shifting his shoulders against the door. "I made a vow when I was fifteen to never inflict that sort of pain nor bear it. I thought all I had to do was keep my heart from becoming engaged." His eyes took on a darkly intense nature, as if his body and mind were homing in on her. "Only recently has it occurred to me, however, how incredibly futile that endeavor would turn out to be. Besides, I do not have it in me to be like my father."

"Where are the portraits of him?" she asked, the abruptness of his mood change making her a touch nervous. Perhaps it wasn't a mood change after all, she thought. Perhaps her perusal of the portraits and her following questions merely distracted him, albeit temporarily, from his true intentions.

"There are very few," he said. "Most are in the corridor leading to my private office." He pushed off from the door. Turning briefly, he locked them in. "My father wasn't fond of his likeness painted."

"Oh? Why so?"

He shrugged and angled toward her. "He was never happy with the finished product. Claimed the artist portrayed him unflatteringly or some other such nonsense."

Madelyn cast a sidelong glance at Gabriel, figuring that must be where he had inherited his innate sense of fastidiousness. She took another step and nearly tripped over the leg of a cushioned chair. She skirted around it, thinking the piece of furniture might prove beneficial in keeping him at bay.

With slow, exaggerated steps, he reached the chair, then surprised her by sitting in it instead of advancing on her. When he stretched his long legs out before him, Madelyn stole a glance at his sleek, muscled thighs sheathed in snug black breeches. She thought of the intoxicating feel of having that strong, virile body press against her own.

"He was a perfectionist . . . " Gabriel's voice trailed away, pulling her attention from her sinful musings.

Clearly, he was planning to carry on with their conversation but had stopped once he spied the desire so apparent in her eyes.

He pulled his legs in, bracing his hands on the arms of the chair. "Come here, Madelyn."

How much closer could she get to him? If she took a step to the right, she'd bump into his thigh.

That was what he wanted, apparently, because he grabbed her by the hips and pulled her swiftly down onto his lap. The abrupt hardness of his thighs against her soft bottom evoked a small squeak from her. She looked to his smooth mouth, then to his hooded blue eyes, knowing the naked hunger apparent there matched her own.

He leaned in close, their breath mingling. "Kiss me," he whispered.

And she was helpless but to obey his gentle command. Leaning into his warm chest, she brushed her lips across his. He kept still, his eyes open a mere slit, watching her.

Impatient with his lackluster response, she pressed her lips to his again, her palms splayed on his broad chest. Shyly, she ran her tongue across his bottom lip. His nearly imperceptible intake of breath told her he was not immune to her touch.

"More," came his gruff command.

Closing her eyes, she kissed him again, deeper, slipping her tongue into his warm mouth to stroke his. He groaned. One of his hands slowly smoothed over her thigh, then up her bodice to cup her breast. A thousands sparks of delight shimmered through her as he rubbed his thumb over the hardened tip. She squirmed deeper into the unforgiving cradle of his lap, desperate for him to kiss her back more fully.

And then Gabriel took over, kissing her with the ferocity of a thirst-starved man. He sank his tongue into her mouth, tasting her, showing her with his kiss that she was his and always would be. A low ache welled between her thighs and she tightened her muscles in response. She whimpered in yearning, and he answered her with a groan of his own. The play of his hands became steadily more demanding, roving over her bottom, her back, molding to the back of her head as he devoured her mouth. Shivers raced across her skin as her heart thundered in her ears.

Gabriel felt completely out of control. He had to have her. Now and forever. If she would deny him, he thought he'd explode. With rough urgency, he tugged at her bodice until her breasts spilled free, then broke their kiss to nuzzle and nip her neck.

"'Tis a lovely gown," he said, his hand sculpting up her back, over her shoulders, then down the arms that clutched at him. "Awful of me to wrinkle it, don't you think?"

Her head lolled back as his lips wandered lower still. "My—My stepmother hates it. Told me—" she gasped as he flicked his tongue over her nipple. "—that I looked plump."

"Wrong," he murmured, then suckled at one breast, then the other. "You are perfection."

Madelyn felt as if she was melting in his arms, her body trembling with need. At Gabriel's urging, she didn't hesitate to change her position in order to straddle him in the chair. He helped and pushed her skirts to her waist.

Cupping her bottom, his mouth seared onto hers for another wet, hot wanton kiss. Madelyn knew it was wrong of her, but in that moment she felt something break free in her soul. In that instant, with his lips slanting across hers, hunting for her surrender, she gave her heart over to him completely.

Relishing the feel of having Madelyn's supple,

lush body draped around his, Gabriel smoothed his large hands over her stocking-enclosed knees, then splayed them over her bare legs. He smiled against her mouth when she mewled with pleasure as he made small circles with his thumbs on the soft flesh of the inside of her upper thighs.

Madelyn clutched at his shoulders, her fingers curling into the woolen fabric of his coat as his dark head moved downward, leaving a molten trail of heat down the curve of her throat. Threading her fingers through his silky black locks, she gasped as he returned his attentions to her breasts. Relentlessly, he kissed and licked her, all the while holding her to him with his hands at her lower back. Dampness spread between them and she rocked against the hardness of his arousal.

"Unbutton my breeches," he said hotly against her neck.

Hurriedly she complied. With a great deal of fumbling, he was freed.

"See what you do to me?" he asked, lifting her hips effortlessly.

Instinctively, Madelyn guided his arousal to her. "We're going to. . . like this?"

"Indeed," he growled against her throat. "I plan to show you every single way even if it kills me."

He reached between their bodies and stroked at the sensitive nubbin of flesh hidden in her folds until she was fairly vibrating with need. When her breaths came faster and her moans sounded near frantic, Gabriel impaled her with one smooth upward thrust of his hips.

Her mouth opened on a moan and he caught it
for a soul-reaching kiss. Panting with desire in between kisses, he hesitated, wanting her to adjust to
the feel of him and allow himself to gather some
much needed strength so as not to succumb to his
release in the next damn second. He thought of her
pleasure first and foremost. Without it, his meant
nothing, was nothing.

To his surprise it was Madelyn who began to rock
against him first. She clutched at his head, and he
curled downward, to nuzzle her breasts.

Waves of glorious sensation pooled within Madelyn. A swell of pleasure so intoxicating poured
through her, she imagined she could do this forever
and ever.

It was sweet torture, but Gabriel allowed her to
set the rhythm, gentle and achingly sweet. When
her breathing quickened and she began to tremble
atop him, he couldn't hold back any longer.

Holding her to him with his large hands clamped
to her waist, he reared his hips upward in fluid
surges. She bucked against him with an uninhibited pace that took his breath away. She cried out his
name the same time he groaned hers, and together
they shuddered with the power of their release.

As she quavered atop him, he kissed her cheeks
tenderly, then pressed a soft kiss upon her lips.
Madelyn feared her heartbeat would never return
to a more sedate pace. Gabriel's chest rose and fell
powerfully against hers. Astonishingly, she craved
the feel of his hard, naked chest against her skin and
realized she wanted him again.

Unbeknownst to her, Gabriel felt the same way. And he would have her again, that he knew, but first he had an infinitely more important task at hand.

"I need to ask you something," he whispered long moments later while he fixed her bodice.

Madelyn swung her leg down, readjusting her position so she sat upon his hard lap instead of astride him. She'd have stood if not for her shaky legs.

She gazed up at him, observing a flicker of doubt, of hesitation, in his eyes. An immediate sense of foreboding bloomed in her mind. She blinked away a sudden surge of panic. Here it comes, she thought.

Gabriel couldn't ask her to be his bride. She was "glaringly unfit." Indeed, those were his very words to her in the orangery. No, she couldn't be his duchess. But there was nothing stopping him from asking her to be his mistress.

Yet she knew she couldn't blame him for thinking to ask her such a thing. She had slept with him. Twice.

Her recent behavior was so out of character, so unlike herself, so wild and without thought of the consequences, she rather thought this love business wasn't all it was cracked up to be. Who would seek something that made one behave impulsively, where reason and good, sound judgment were thrown out the window in order to drown in all-encompassing passion?

She slid off of his lap though his tense hands tried to keep her there. Standing shakily, she brushed at her skirts, trying to ignore the ache of a restrained sob in her throat.

She wanted to snip this moment in time and save it before it was ruined—before *he* ruined it. Their lovemaking was beautiful and precious, and if Gabriel spoke those hurtful words, she knew she wouldn't be able to bear it. She could take a thousand veiled insults from her aunt, could endure a scathing mile-long list of her shortcomings from her stepmother, but she could not suffer the pain of Gabriel asking her to be his lover, and only his lover. To have it implied by the man she loved that she was good enough to tup but not to marry. Why oh why did she have to go and fall in love with the man?

Sitting up, perspiration from their recent, primal lovemaking still dotting his brow, Gabriel reached for her, but Madelyn stepped back.

She swept at a coil of hair that had escaped from her once elaborate topknot. "Whatever it is you have to ask me, it shall have to wait," she said, trotting toward the door.

"It cannot wait," Gabriel intoned. A quirk in his brow told her he was confused by her sudden change in behavior.

Her breaths came faster as she fretted that he would simply blurt out the words. "I've been gone too long, I must go," she blurted. "We shouldn't have done this again. It was a mistake." Rattling the door handle, she belatedly remembered that he had locked them in with a key.

He was there a moment later, apparently after refastening his breeches. Slipping the key into the lock, he looked down at her, his expression both perplexed and concerned. "A mistake. What is it you are afraid of, Madelyn?" he whispered, opening the door. His hand rested on the doorjamb, blocking her retreat.

"You," she replied, then slipped underneath his arm and ran down the corridor without turning back.

Chapter 17

〰️〰️

"**H**is gaze has been fastened on you since the moment we stepped out into the garden," Charlotte whispered as they angled their way through the course of Wolverest's intricate parterre, the low box hedges barely knee-high.

"You must be imagining things," Madelyn answered with a shrug. She hoped that she was giving the appearance of deeply concentrating on the miniature maze before her. With something akin to desperation, she worked to make certain their path never crossed Gabriel's. And what a Herculean feat that was turning out to be.

Escorting no one through the geometric patterns, the duke kept his pace slow, his hands clasped behind his back. Indeed, Charlotte was correct. With prowl-like concentration, he kept his steady gaze on Madelyn's every move.

Oblivious to their cat and mouse game, the other guests milled about whispering, giggling, and generally enjoying an innocent stroll about the interlocking paths. Madelyn envied their ignorance. Her body flushed anew with prickling heat as Gabriel's unflinching gaze raked her with stark intensity. She didn't need to be told he was looking at her. She could feel it.

The coward in her wanted to run and hide, or at the very least avoid his gaze, but Gabriel wouldn't let her. And if he didn't stop it, everyone else was going to notice as well.

Unable to stop herself, she looked over to him. Their gazes caught and held. Her breath stopped for a long moment, then came out in a low whoosh. Good Lord, he was beautiful. His skin appeared sun-kissed, his ink-black hair tousled and glossy in the warm sunlight. Tousled, no doubt, by her own hands in the art gallery. His intense, sparkling blue gaze made her feel drawn to him, like he was silently beckoning her to come to him and she was helpless but to obey. However, she made no move to fulfill his unspoken command and simply carried on her stroll with Charlotte. Only, she couldn't seem to tear her eyes away from him. She felt trapped within his gaze.

And though she wasn't quite sure why Gabriel yet stared at her, she was certain of why she was compelled to gaze at him. She loved him.

She loved him, and that very thing was propelling her to avoid him and his "question."

She swallowed, thinking he'd look away at any moment, but he never did. His booted feet unerringly wound around the intertwined paths. Never once did his step hesitate—

"Oh!" Arms flailing, Madelyn tripped over a low, ankle-high hedge, catching herself by hugging the small tree at the center of the boxed section. Charlotte retrieved her. Together they stepped back onto the graveled path.

"Heavens, Maddie!" Charlotte swatted at Madelyn's skirts, taking care to see if she had snagged her gown. "Are you all right?"

"Y-Yes. I'm fine," Madelyn assured her friend. Her eyes flicked to Gabriel in order to see how he took her spill. Secretly, she hoped he'd found her clumsiness humorous so she could be mad at him, but he only raised one dark eyebrow.

Charlotte gave Madelyn a little nudge with her elbow. "Do you know what I think?"

Madelyn linked her arm with hers. "Hmm?"

"I think his steamy looks and your shy glances have something to do with where you went off to after dinner last evening *and* where you were when we came looking for you just before we were due to the parterre."

Madelyn cringed. She wanted to confide in Charlotte. Just not now. Not here.

"Could we turn up ahead, dear?" Madelyn asked, noticing Gabriel was heading toward them.

"All right," Charlotte muttered, her tone holding a trace of suspicion. "Say . . . are you trying to avoid His Grace?"

"Ah . . . yes, quite frankly," Madelyn replied. "Can we speed up, please?"

"Of course." Charlotte looked over her shoulder, as the duke was certainly behind them now. She turned back. "Are you sure this is what you want to do? I think he knows what you're doing, and he doesn't appear to be happy about it either."

"I don't care," Madelyn said lightly, with a tight, fake smile. "Keep moving."

"I think you do. Or you should. He looks like he wants to . . . to kiss you. Or toss you to the ground. Perhaps both." Charlotte took another quick look over her shoulder. "He has turned."

"Good." But her relief was short-lived for he turned directly onto an interlocking path to their right. Bumping into Gabriel was imminent.

Well, she could turn back and make her way through the section of the maze she'd already been through. Though she imagined she'd need to jump the hedges like a thoroughbred to avoid him gaining on her. Madelyn sighed. That probably wouldn't work and she'd look like a loon. Besides, she couldn't avoid him forever.

As he approached them, the friends came to a halt, but Gabriel only slowed. Trying to ignore the way her body thrummed at his nearness, Madelyn found a peculiar interest in the stones on the path.

"Miss Greene," he said in greeting.

Charlotte gave a quick curtsy. "Your Grace."

And then, just as he passed them, he brushed his arm playfully against Madelyn's but said not a word to her.

Unable to stop herself, her mouth gaped open at his coolness. She wanted to lash out at him, but reminded herself she was the one who had been studiously trying to sidestep him. Apparently, he knew that and was letting her know he didn't care for it one bit.

Now it was her turn to glance over her shoulder at him. To her surprise, he was looking back at her as well—as if expecting her reaction. "Miss Haywood," he drawled with a lopsided grin.

"Your Grace," she bit out, her eyes narrowing.

He stopped and turned, giving her form a thorough sweep. "You're looking fine this morning," he fairly purred.

"Likewise," she said stiffly.

He inclined his head politely. "You've a glow about you today. A glistening effervescence, if you will."

"Oh?"

"Quite enchanting, really," he intoned. "Whatever it was you did this morning that put such a healthy glow upon your skin, you must do it again and again."

She flushed crimson. "Never."

"Come now, Miss Haywood," he drawled. "Was it that bad?"

"On the contrary, it was magnificent. So much, in fact, that I fear to do it again might cleave my heart in two."

"Perhaps your heart is not in as much danger as you perceive."

"I have my reservations," she said in a clipped tone. With that, she whipped back around and continued on with Charlotte. What a scoundrel! Adorable, but a scoundrel no less. She gave herself a mental shake.

"So tell me," she said to her friend, "the ball is in one more day. Has Lord—"

"What in the world was that all about?" Charlotte asked, her eyes round with astonishment.

"What?" Madelyn blinked innocently.

"Don't you dare feign indifference with me," Charlotte chided. "I know flirting, and that was flirting. And what the devil were you two talking about anyway?"

"Shh, someone will hear you."

"Fine. But you'll not keep your secrets from me forever. Promise?"

"Promise," Madelyn dutifully replied, though Charlotte looked on with disbelief. "Now tell me, has Lord Tristan given any sort of clue as to who he'll pick to be his bride?"

Charlotte bit her lip. "Though he has not named anyone . . . he did tell me during dinner that he quite liked my eyes . . . "

Oh dear.

" . . . and that if he were my beloved, he should think he'd never tire of my company," Charlotte finished with a small smile.

Madelyn looked to where Lord Tristan ambled through the path, Harriet Beauchamp's arm threaded with his.

"If I were you, dear Lottie, I wouldn't put much credence in his adulations. Though you do have fine eyes and I do so love your company."

"I know I shouldn't believe him," Charlotte said as they neared the exit of the parterre. "It's just that . . . there's something about the way he looks at me sometimes. It's as if he . . . likes me."

"Believe me," Madelyn intoned, "I think it's a trait Devine males are born with, and we shouldn't flatter ourselves thinking we are the soul recipients of their adoring stares."

Madelyn's heart jumped into her throat as she looked ahead and saw that Gabriel waited at the end of the maze.

He seemed to be waiting for something.

She hoped to God it wasn't for her.

To their left was a towering castle wall covered with ivy, and to their right an alluring pergola, the sides and arches of its trellis heavy with honeysuckle vines yet to bloom. Madelyn pursed her lips in thought. It would seem the only option was to walk past Gabriel. Either that, she mused with a cringe, or burst through the latticework and constricting vines of the pergola.

She frowned as she approached, thinking foolishly that her expression of irritation might dissuade him.

He waited for Charlotte to pass and be intercepted by his brother before blocking Madelyn's path. She glanced down as he took her arm and linked it with his own.

"If you fail to come with me now," he said, his steely tone causing a ripple of warning to run through her, "then I shall have no choice but to drag you off like a savage."

Taking a deep breath, she looked into his cool blue eyes and knew without a doubt that he wasn't bluffing. He'd do it.

Relinquishing, she gave him a small nod and permitted him to guide her away from the others who were exiting the maze and wandering off to take tea underneath a towering willow tree. If anyone saw them go off alone together, no one said a word. Yet.

His arm unrelenting against hers, Gabriel ushered Madelyn inside the privacy of the pergola. The honeysuckle vines choked the long tunnel of latticework on both sides and above their heads, letting in only a wink of sunlight here and there.

A lump grew in Madelyn's throat. It was a perfectly romantic setting, enclosed as they were outdoors. Birds twittered merrily on the outside of the pergola, while the faint humming of bees said they were heartily impatient for the blooms to open. Yes, a perfectly lovely day, no threat of rain, plenty of sunshine, just the sort of day one would remember with fondness in the upcoming winter months.

She shifted her foot in the gravel of the path, making a circle with her toe while Gabriel fumbled in his jacket for something or other.

Oh, for goodness sake, Gabriel, just ask me and break my heart already.

The air was cool against her skin, and she longed to be enveloped in the heat she'd find in his embrace. He wouldn't deny her, she knew, but pushed the urge away. She straightened her spine, determined to mask her feelings behind a cool facade. Yes, this might be an ideal spot for a marriage proposal. But it was a perfectly horrid spot for a broken heart. Which is what she'd have as soon as Gabriel found whatever he was looking for and opened his mouth to speak.

To her surprise, he pulled her lace glove off her left hand with one smooth tug. She didn't even have time for a gasp. Bending over her hand, he kissed her knuckles, then the backs of her fingers.

For whatever reason, Madelyn was instantly reminded of that evening in his garden when Gabriel had knelt before her, offering to assess the injury to her bruised knees.

He cleared his throat. Blinking up at him, she frowned at his expression. He looked nervous. There was tick in his cheek and a dash of uncertainty flashed in his crystal blue eyes. And in that instant, she thought that he looked more like a boy than a man. She stared at him in wonder as a lock of ink-black hair shifted then coiled over one eye. In a gesture of irritation, he raked his hand through his hair in order to get it out of the way, but it only fell back.

"Madelyn . . . "

Here it comes, she mused with something akin to panic. How would she tell him no? What should she say so as not to insult him, even though his question would insult her? Why in the world should she care? Should she smile politely? Cry? Oh, she had no doubt about that, she'd definitely weep like a teething babe. But hopefully in the privacy of her bedchamber.

"Madelyn, would you . . . " He cleared his throat again. " . . . would you be my bride?"

Stunned, she could only blink at the square cut diamond ring he revealed in his open palm. The facets picked up a stray wink of sunlight and it glimmered with sparkling reflections.

"I hope you like it," he said. "It was my mother's and her mother's before her. An heirloom."

"B-Bride?" Madelyn swayed where she stood.

"Say something," he implored, a nervous laugh in his command.

"Bride?"

He stood, then smiled, all lopsided, and her insides melted. "Say something else."

"I was wrong," she replied softly, still wondrously baffled. "I—I thought you were going to ask me to be your mistress." She didn't think it was possible, but her heart sped up even faster. It felt as if it would burst out of her chest.

Gabriel shook his head and smiled down at her in that adoring fashion now so familiar to her—like he thought her the dearest, most lovable creature on earth. "Why?" he asked, caressing her cheek with the back of his fingers.

When she didn't answer, he first closed his eyes, then slowly opened them, giving her the impression that he'd come to his own conclusion and didn't like it. "You thought I'd take your virginity without thinking to take a vow? You thought it was only lust that spurred my notice of you?"

Her mouth could only open and shut. His words bewildered her.

"Sweet Jesus," he said, running a hand through his hair. "If that was all it was, I could have bedded anyone to slake my desires."

"I—I thought I was merely convenient."

"You thought wrong," he replied sternly. He shook his head in bemusement. "My mistress? Do you not think you deserve more? I want to share my life with you, Madelyn, by my side, not just in my bed." He brought her hand up to his mouth and kissed her fingertips. "Be my wife."

Her eyes welled with tears and her voice did an odd little cracking sound when she said, "But I'll make you a horrible duchess."

He nodded, smiling. "I've thought of that, of course, and it's nothing we cannot fix."

Her trembling lips stilled. Inside, somewhere around her heart, something deflated. "Fix?" she squeaked out.

"The first thing we'll do, of course, is have you measured for some new gowns. Since I'm not accustomed to the peculiarities of ladies' fashion, we can leave that up to Rosalind, of course."

His every word was a crumbling brick, and her fragile, newfound joy came tumbling down. "Of course," she spat.

"And we'll have an instructor brought in to—"

"Instruct me in the proper comportment and manner befitting my new, elevated station?"

"Quite," he said, eyeing her warily as she

withdrew her hand from his hold. "Charming as I find you, we cannot have the new Duchess of Wolverest falling into lily ponds across the countryside . . . "

For a mere second she thought he might be teasing her. His words sounded so ridiculous to her ears, but he went on and on, shattering her heart into pieces.

" . . . the way I look at it, we'll have you ready for your first introduction into society as a duchess no later then next Season."

"My, your sanguinity is flattering," she replied, not bothering to hide her sarcasm.

It was not missed by him. "Madelyn, you cannot pretend that you would blend in without a hitch in this superior level of society."

"Perhaps I don't want to 'blend in,'" she ground out, hating the way her voice shook.

His jaw tightened. "You cannot fault me for wanting you to feel comfortable in your new surroundings. I was raised amongst these people. The *ton* will not find your clumsy manner charming or your penchant for saying and doing just what you feel as refreshing as I do. They'll pick you apart. Find every fault until you are bared, defenseless under their unsympathetic gazes."

Gritting her teeth, she snatched her glove from his hand. "I don't care what *they* think," she said through her teeth. "And I will *not* marry you. So you can cease all your concerns right this instant, Gabriel."

"You are being impractical," he snapped.

"You want to fix me. Make me better." She tugged her glove back on with short jerks. She was trembling with hurt, with anger, she couldn't even calm herself enough to speak.

The tears that had gathered in her eyes threatened to spill. She turned abruptly and headed for the end of the pergola opposite to where the others were still gathered for tea. The steady crunch of gravel coming from behind her, however, told her that Gabriel was following her step for step.

"Madelyn," he called out. "Where are you going?"

"To my chamber and then home . . . or at least back to London anyway."

"You're only running and hiding again," he said gravely. "See reason, and be with me, Madelyn."

"I will not," she stated flatly, not bothering to turn around. "I cannot."

And with that Gabriel's footsteps stalled. She kept walking, feeling his gaze upon her retreating back. Must she ever be acutely aware of his notice, of his presence? Not being able to stand it any longer, she hitched up her skirts and broke into a run.

Tears spilling down her face, she thought of all the years and all the borrowed frocks that Priscilla had scrunched her into, trying to force her body to be slim and straight. She thought of all the soirees where she was ordered to say as little possible so as not to embarrass her stepmother by uttering a less than witty phrase. She thought of all the times she longed to dance, but hid by the wall with Charlotte, fearful of a misstep and of disappointing her stepmother once again.

And she thought of all the times she reached for acceptance and came away with empty hands.

Chapter 18

A wide, shallow puddle sheltered from the sun by a towering yew hedge blocked Madelyn's path. Without hesitation she sloshed through the puddle, thinking only of gaining the sanctuary of her guest bedchamber. Rounding the corner, she slammed into the solid wall of a man's chest.

She nearly bounced backward from the force of the contact. He barely moved, only reaching out to catch at her back, steadying her and keeping her from falling down.

"My lord," Madelyn said, blinking up in surprise at Rothbury's golden gaze. "I didn't see you."

"I imagine you couldn't. Not while clipping along at such a fast pace as you were."

"If you'll excuse me," she said hurriedly, not wanting the earl to notice she had been crying. Too late, his relaxed, slightly amused expression changed into hardened male concern.

"Something has happened. What is it?"

"Nothing. I'm fine," she replied with a smile, though his countenance wobbled through the sheen of her tears.

Rothbury pulled an embroidered handkerchief from his pocket. She took it and blew her nose. After she'd finished and folded it, Madelyn went to hand it back to him, but he declined, shaking his head and looking at the square of linen as if it contained the plague.

He sized her up with a sweep of his exacting gaze. "Well, now that you've . . . cleared yourself up, tell me what I can do to help."

She gave a sad little laugh. "You cannot help, sir."

"Does this have anything to do with that aloof duke that refuses to allow me to court his sister?"

She nodded then hiccupped.

"Bloody hell," he said on a sigh. "You're in love with him, aren't you?"

She shrugged, not willing to delve into her personal feelings with the man who proposed to her last year only to offer her an invitation to his bed at her refusal.

"Dash it all, thought I still had a chance." He shook his head grimly. "Stubborn fool, is what he is," Rothbury muttered while straightening her bonnet ribbon under her quavering chin. "Doesn't appreciate your spirit, your spontaneity, I imagine. Well, don't you worry, my dear."

She paused in the act of wiping her cheeks with the back of her hands. "What do you mean 'do not worry'?"

"All the old wolf needs is a little push in the right direction," Rothbury offered with a sly grin and a wink.

"I do not know what you mean and I do not think you should become involved, my lord." She stepped past him. "But thank you," she said over her shoulder. "Good day."

"Good day," he returned, a calculating note in his voice. "And don't fret, sweetmeat. If I play my cards right, you'll have him begging for your hand in marriage by tomorrow evening."

"Don't count on it," she muttered, knowing well enough that the earl couldn't hear her reply.

Suddenly weary, Madelyn shook her head. No, she could never marry Gabriel. She would only disappoint him and frustrate herself. Contrary to how everyone else seemed to feel about her, she liked herself just as she was. She'd dance a jig on a slippery rooftop before she'd alter herself to fit someone's ideal. Even for the man she loved.

Twenty minutes later Madelyn sat on the edge of her bed in the guest wing of the castle. With a heavy sigh, she stared at the few gowns she had folded to be packed away for travel, though she knew she couldn't depart Wolverest just yet. Not with the ball tomorrow evening. She would never leave Charlotte to fend for herself now.

The door to her bedchamber creaked then, and she knew someone had entered unannounced. Looking up, she saw her stepmother in the doorway, arms crossed over her narrow chest, her thin lips turned down at the corners like those of a condescending monarch.

"You've been crying," Priscilla said sharply, stepping into the room.

Madelyn pressed her hands to her hot cheeks. Although she hadn't shed a tear for nearly ten minutes, she knew that her face must show the signs of recent crying.

"I'll come straight to the point," Priscilla said, coming to a halt before her. "What, exactly, has transpired? And do not bother being obtuse—I saw the two of you go off alone and now I find you here, weeping like a babe."

There was no sense contradicting her, but Priscilla had never been the sort of person she could confide in. Her stepmother had always dismissed her concerns and wishes as if she were no more significant than a pesky fly. So she sat there and stared at her lap.

"You'll tell me what's happened and you'll tell me now," Priscilla snapped.

"He proposed," Madelyn said in a small voice, dreading her stepmother's reaction to her news.

"Proposed! Dear Lord! Madelyn, I had always hoped, dreamed even." Priscilla clutched her arms around herself and twirled in a circle. "And it is better than I ever imagined. A duke! Oh, I shall want for nothing more!"

"I refused," Madelyn replied, her voice barely above a whisper.

Priscilla froze at her words. "What? Y-You *refused*?"

But Madelyn did not explain. How could someone like her stepmother ever understand why she couldn't marry Gabriel?

"You *are* completely mad," Priscilla stated, eyes wide with disbelief and anger.

"I am not mad," Madelyn managed calmly. "I simply desire to marry a man who loves me just the way I am."

"Just the way you are!" Priscilla laughed bitterly. "Who could love a table with uneven legs, a deck of cards that counts short, a book missing its last page."

Madelyn swallowed the lump forming in her throat. She knew that defending herself would only lead to more scathing laughter.

Priscilla shook her head in disapproval. "What a waste. What a damn shameful creature." She looked away from her, wringing her hands together in thought. "All right, then," she said after taking a deep breath. "I think we still have time. Surely, he could be cajoled into thinking you were simply being coy. Perhaps I could persuade him into asking again."

"No."

It was such a simple word to be thrown between them, but Madelyn said it with such resolute power, Priscilla reared back as if slapped. However, true to form, the baroness bounced back in mere seconds, rounding on Madelyn until her nose was a scant inch from her own. "When I first met you, all weepy and mumbling over the loss of your mother, I saw potential. I knew *you* could be an asset to *me*. Imagine my disappointment when I discovered you to be an ungrateful miss with an inclination for ungainliness, and now abject stupidity! This opportunity fell into our lap and you let it be all for naught!"

Suddenly, Madelyn felt like a little girl again. She bit her lip as uncertainty took over.

Losing her mother at eight years of age left a fathomless hole in her heart. When her father remarried after a year of mourning, she had sought unconditional acceptance and love from a new stepmother whose coldness seared her to the quick. It only took two months for her to realize she'd never please the oft-dissatisfied woman. But that didn't make the pain go away, nor shrink the size of the hole left behind from her mother.

"Did you ever love me?" Madelyn blurted out the question.

Taking a step back, Priscilla's eyes narrowed as she contemplated the question. When she spoke, her words were cool and delivered with stinging satisfaction. "I didn't even love your father."

The sob aching in Madelyn's chest died on a wave of indignation. "Then why did you take me in? The burden wasn't yours. You didn't have to be my guardian."

Priscilla shrugged. "Your father's will stipulated that if I raised you, fed you, and clothed you until you reached the age of twenty-one or were married, whichever came first, I would receive three thousand pounds more a year. So naturally . . . "

"Naturally," Madelyn said, baffled by her stepmother's bluntness.

"And I suppose now is as good time as any to tell you about Willowbrooke," Priscilla continued with a smug lift of her chin.

"Yes, about the cottage . . . " Madelyn sat straighter. "As it would be safe to assume you'll not allow me to reside there any longer since I failed your marriage mission, I should like to take a ride there before we head back to London."

Priscilla threw her a scornful glare from over her shoulder as she turned and headed out of the room. "There's no need."

"I do realize your family most probably cleared the home out when it fell into your hands," Madelyn said, "but I'd like to take a look for myself. I trust Mr. and Mrs. White are still the caretakers."

Reaching the door, Priscilla gave a careless shrug. "I've absolutely no idea. You see, I just happened to sell the dratted thing this very morning."

Madelyn bolted to her feet. "You what?"

"Sold it, dear." Priscilla smiled tightly.

Shaking with fury now, Madelyn's fists tightened at her sides. "You're lying."

"No, child." Priscilla shook her head in mock sympathy. "It seems there was a lot of interest in that unoccupied crumbling heap. With Mr. Ashton's help, it was snapped up this very morning for thrice its value."

And with that, Lady Haywood swirled out of the room, nose tilted in the air, leaving Madelyn to shake violently as the strain of the events of the past hour threatened to topple her and render her a pitiful puddle of tears.

Chapter 19

The Bride Hunt Ball

"**S**o tell me," Charlotte murmured from behind her glass of lemonade, "can you tell I stuffed padding into my bodice?"

Mid-swallow, Madelyn sputtered and coughed. They stood at the refreshment table, the twirling, weaving couples of a quadrille at their backs. Dabbing her mouth with the corner of a linen napkin, she finished clearing her throat while giving an appreciative nod as a passing gentleman patted her gently between the shoulder blades.

"I'm fine now, thank you," she rasped. She waited until the man and his lady threaded into their place in the dance before turning back to Charlotte.

"Well," her friend prodded. "Can you tell?"

Madelyn gave the enormous yet overstuffed ballroom one quick assessing sweep of her gaze to make certain no one was paying close attention to them, then quickly reviewed the state of Charlotte's bodice. "Ah . . . no, not really. But only if the one standing before you is your exact height—as I am, dear. Should anyone be taller than you and in possession of a keen eye . . . say someone like Lord Tristan, then all he'd have to do is look to your unnaturally ample bosom to discern the wads of silk stuffed inside."

"Oh," Charlotte replied, her voice small. Looking down at herself, she brushed imaginary wrinkles out of her pale pink skirts. And then with a tiny shake of her head, her spirit became buoyant once again. "I guess I shall have to go to the retiring room to fix it, as I have promised the next dance to Lord Tristan."

Madelyn couldn't help but smile. This evening, Charlotte was bursting with a blend of enthusiasm akin to that of a bride on the eve of her wedding day. How it would pain her to see her friend's mood crushed if Tristan should break her heart.

He was to pick his bride at midnight, presenting her with a hothouse bouquet of red roses. Madelyn gritted her teeth. It had to be nearly midnight now. And she had a sinking feeling the woman his lordship would chose would be Harriet Beauchamp. Madelyn had expressed her suspicions to Charlotte just that evening while they dressed for the ball, but her friend's hopes remained ever resilient.

At least she was here for Charlotte should her friend need a shoulder to cry on or a patient listener to hear her woes. It was all she could do to repay Charlotte for listening to her drone on and on about Gabriel last night.

In truth, Madelyn hadn't wanted to attend the ball. She'd have much preferred to hide away in her assigned room until it was time for them to depart for London. But Charlotte needed her, and she wouldn't dream of not being here for her friend. She reminded herself that it was one of the very reasons she decided to come to Wolverest in the first place.

So Madelyn continued to sip her lemonade—though her throat yet burned from swallowing the wrong way—and took delicate care to look about the room without appearing to be desperately searching for a glimpse of Gabriel.

At the top of the room sat the orchestra. Great swaths of flowing ivory hung from the ceiling, partially surrounding the ensemble and giving the room an ethereal beauty. Amplifying this ambience was the wall of French doors, which were all left wide open. The wafts of cool air billowed the fabric around the orchestra and made the hundreds of beeswax sconces flicker and nearly wink out, only to surge with new life once the breeze settled down once again.

He was here; she could feel it. Goose pimples ran down her arms and she shivered, thinking of the heat that would bloom within her just from one glance from Gabriel.

"By the way," Charlotte said, breaking through Madelyn's pondering, "do you realize we've been in this ballroom for nearly three hours and haven't seen a glimpse of your duke?"

Madelyn bent to place her empty glass on the refreshment table. "He's not *my* duke, Lottie. And please lower your voice," she gently pleaded. "Just because *you* can't *see* anyone's faces, doesn't mean *they* can't *hear* you. You should've worn your spectacles. I'm worried you'll trip."

Charlotte shrugged. "I shall employ extra care and promise to . . . "

As Charlotte's voice trailed off, Madelyn looked up to see her friend in the midst of a hard squint just off her right shoulder.

"What is it?" Madelyn asked, without turning in that direction. "Or rather, who is it?"

"I'm not sure. It's undeniably a man. Tall, a definite swagger, and he's coming straight this way."

Could it be Gabriel? Madelyn had barely enough time to contemplate if it was hope she was feeling or dread, when she felt the unmistakable sensation of a virile, warm male standing behind her.

She spun around and found herself staring up into the amber-flecked eyes of Lord Rothbury. Her shoulders visibly slumped.

"Well, now. Was that with relief," the earl drawled, stepping between the ladies, "or disappointment that it is *I* who now stands before you?"

Madelyn's mouth opened, then shut. She had no idea what to say that wouldn't insult him or give herself away.

Thankfully, he grinned and gave his head a slight shake, silently letting her know he wasn't expecting an answer. He turned to Charlotte.

"Miss Greene," he replied, bending over her

gloved hand in greeting. "Might I say how lovely—"
And then he stopped, his polite smile frozen as his
sharp gaze centered, blinked, and then refocused
on Charlotte's bodice. Slowly, he rose up to his full
height. He cleared his throat. "Ah . . . er . . . your
loveliness is quite . . . bountiful this evening," he
replied, though his lips twitched with concealed
amusement.

"Why, thank you," Charlotte murmured distractedly, dipping into a quick curtsy. Her eyes weren't
on him, but squinting at some point behind him.
The lengthy quadrille was finally coming to an end,
Madelyn surmised, and Charlotte would need to go
off and fix her gown before Tristan came to claim
his dance.

"If you'll excuse me. There's something important I must attend to without delay," she said, smiling pointedly at Madelyn. "My lord."

"Of course," Rothbury murmured.

Charlotte dipped into a shallow curtsy once
again, and Rothbury bowed. And then she was
gone, heading in the direction of the ladies' retiring room, which, much to Madelyn's dismay, left her
completely alone with the sinful earl.

With one winged brow raised, he followed her
friend's departure until she could no longer be seen.
"It'll be a miracle if she manages to make it across the
ballroom and back without slamming into a marble
column." He turned his unshakable predatory gaze
back to Madelyn. When he spoke, his voice dripped
with a curious deception. "I've set in motion a plan
to aid you in your quest."

Madelyn's brow furrowed. "Pray, do not talk in riddles. I must attend to Miss Greene. What quest?"

"For the duke."

Her heart sank and she hoped her emotions couldn't be read in her eyes. "I do not have a *quest* for the duke."

"Ah, but you do," he drawled. "Only, I've changed my mind."

Her irritation mounting, Madelyn nearly growled. She had no idea why, but this man always had this effect on her. "Changed your mind about what?"

"Telling you."

"Normally, I would express my disappointment," she said through a tight smile, "but as I have no idea as to what on earth you're talking about, I shall simply have to be patient."

"Good. Let us be off, then," he said, taking her hand and placing it on his arm. When she tried pulling free, he pressed his hand atop hers, trapping her. She'd have to yank hard to loose herself from his hold now, and that would draw unwanted attention.

"I'm wondering if you'll take a turn about the room with me, Miss Haywood," he said, not waiting for her reply. "I imagine these doors will lead us directly to the rose garden. And I do so love a stroll in a garden at midnight, don't you?"

Her heart started thundering in her ears. She didn't know what the earl was up to, but her body responded as if he'd just told her she was going to debtor's prison.

"What are you doing?" Madelyn asked, her voice husky with fear.

"Making you a duchess."

Taller than just about everyone in the ballroom, Gabriel stood with his back to the open French doors, the cool air wafting across his back and matching his mood. Studiously, he stared at Madelyn as she conversed with Miss Greene. Madelyn was looking for him. He knew it. Oh, she did a fairly good job of feigning an interest in Rosalind's decorations, but he didn't miss how her eyes skimmed through the crowd every now and then.

Bloody hell, she looked amazing. Her ball gown was of light blue satin with an embroidered band of white at her hem that matched the silk band under her breasts, which of course drew his appreciative attention. Her dark red locks were swept into an intricate coiffure, with dark cherry tendrils curling on the top and cascading down the back of her head. He flexed his hand. Damn, how he longed for the silky feel of her hair in his hands, across his bare chest.

But then he realized it didn't matter what she wore this night, or any evening, for that matter. He wanted her whether every damn curl sat in place or if it all came tumbling down. Actually, he preferred her imperfect, spontaneous, giggling and outspoken. That was the very reason he fell in love with her in the first place. And he was a stupid ass for making her believe he'd want to change her once they married.

"Ah-hem."

Someone cleared their throat to his left.

"Ah-hem!"

His nostrils flared as the pungent odor of sour wine drifted over to him. He heard a sound. A funny sort of sound like that of a belch in someone's throat. He blinked as an unsteady woman shuffled her way in front of him, the ostrich plume in her turban effectively blocking his view of Madelyn.

He scowled. "Lady Beauchamp."

She gave him a wobbly smile. In her drunken mind's eye, Gabriel imagined she thought it a particularly charming one.

"Your Grace." She held out her hand, and he had no choice but to bend over it like the gentleman he was brought up to be.

She started to curtsy at the same time but was so unsteady that Gabriel supported her by her elbow so she wouldn't fall down.

"I've come to congratulate you," she exclaimed, opening her fan and waving it rapidly in front of her face.

"And that would be for . . . "

"The upcoming nuptials, you silly man."

"Ah," Gabriel said, taking a step backward. Lord, her breath was foul. "And I thank you on Tristan's behalf."

"No, no, no," she said, punctuating each word with a swat at his chest. "I've heard it on confidence, no. With confidence. No, that's not what I mean to say." She hiccupped. "What was I saying anyway, good man?"

"Nuptials," Gabriel supplied.

"Oh yes." She smiled. "My, you're a handsome fellow. Were I twenty years younger, I'd fancy you for myself. Got the look of pirate in you." She winked. "All devilish good looks and a swagger to boot. Too bad you're always scowling."

"Lady Beauchamp, please," he implored, his deep tenor barely above a growl.

"Oh, all right, then. What good could come from rousing your ire?" She paused, wetting her lips as if savoring the juicy tidbit of gossip she was about to relate. "I've heard it on good authority that Lord Rothbury and Miss Haywood are to be wed. Engaged this very afternoon. Can you believe it?"

For a second it felt as if his heart had stopped beating. But then Gabriel's brow furrowed deeper, if that was at all possible. He had followed this woman's direction once before, when he was told a guest wandered in the darkened corridor, and look what a misunderstanding that turned out to be. Besides, it was obvious that the woman had fairly marinated herself in an abundance of spirits.

"You must be mistaken, Viscountess," he said.

"Oh no," she said, looking appalled at the very idea. "I heard it from the earl's very lips. To think that Miss Haywood snared herself an earl. Well, grasp him and hold on for dear life, is what the girl should do. It's not every day someone with her lowly connections should marry so well."

Gabriel crossed his arms over his chest and raised a winged brow. "Let us not forget, madam, Miss Haywood is your niece."

With some satisfaction, Gabriel watched Lady Beauchamp blink in apparent astonishment, realizing she had just insulted herself. If she weren't inebriated, the woman would have surely caught her error in judgment before it spilled from her lips.

"Again, I believe you are mistaken," he cut in when it looked as if she might expire on the spot.

She blinked and shook her head as if to clear it. "If you don't believe me, young man, just take a look at them." Stepping aside, she waved her fan in Madelyn's direction.

Lo and behold there strode Rothbury, his arm linked with Madelyn's as they strolled toward the open doors farthest away from where Gabriel stood. No doubt the earl's intentions were to lure Madelyn out into the garden for a mauling.

"Look at him!" Lady Beauchamp beamed. "Has he not the very appearance of a man in love?"

As the words tumbled from the viscountess's mouth, Rothbury leaned down and pressed two lingering kisses on Madelyn's gloved knuckles. And then . . . Madelyn smiled . . . or was that a grimace? He couldn't tell from this far away, and neither was he ready to make an opinion on the matter of her alleged engagement. But he planned to find out right now.

All the muscles in Gabriel's body tightened, especially his forearms and fists, and he fought to restrain himself from lunging across the ballroom and shoving aside anyone who got in his way.

"If you'll excuse me, madam," he muttered. Not waiting for her consent, he shouldered his way through the crush of guests.

"If you kiss my hand again, I will bite your arm," Madelyn said through a fake smile.

"My, my. Usually a statement such as that would have quite the effect on me, sweetmeat. However," the earl's grin deepened, "I find your ill mood makes me question why I even thought to help you in the first place."

"Let me assure you, I don't need nor want your particular style of assistance." Catching him off guard, Madelyn managed to pull free from the tight hold he had of her fingers. "Just what are you hoping to do anyway?"

"Inspire a tempest of jealousy."

"In who?"

"The duke."

She sighed in exasperation. "Whyever would you want to do that?"

"You might think it little of me, but I don't like the fellow. I want his sister, and he is determined to keep her from me. Torturing him a bit, dangling what it is *he* wants, *who* it is he wants, just above his reach brings me great pleasure. An eye for an eye, so to speak." His sharp gaze flicked off her face and into the crowd for a fleeting moment. "And look, apparently he hasn't an ounce of willpower, for here he is right now."

Madelyn had barely enough time to place a mask

of indifference on her features before Gabriel came to an abrupt halt before her. She looked up at him, but he only had a scowl for Rothbury.

To the earl's credit, he held Gabriel's stare without flinching. If she were Rothbury, Madelyn mused, she'd have turned tail and fled into the night. Gabriel's expression was that intense.

At the top of the room, the orchestra played a series of harmonized notes to signal the commencement of a waltz. In reaction, Madelyn glanced about the room and found Charlotte being led to the dancing area on Lord Tristan's arm. From the look of it, she hadn't found the retiring room and therefore hadn't been able to remove the wads of silk from her bodice. Madelyn inwardly cringed. She should have gone with her, but then Rothbury had come along and muddled up her mind.

"Wolverest," the earl said in greeting. "I see you've chosen to mingle with your guests this evening. Quite shocking, really."

Gabriel responded with a heavy sigh and continued to stare Rothbury down.

"If you'll excuse me," Lord Rothbury said, finally showing some good sense. He bowed slightly over Madelyn's gloved fingers. "Although I long to dwell in the presence of the enticing Miss Haywood, I've promised this dance to one Miss Belinda Fairbourne and would not have her accuse me of an incivility by hastily retrieving her for the dance. Until we meet again, Miss Haywood," he finished, his predatory gaze unashamedly raking her from top to bottom.

And with his lips twisting with a grin of smug satisfaction, the earl sauntered away.

Tension hung heavy and thick as Madelyn and Gabriel were left with no other distractions but one another. Unable or unwilling to meet his stare—she wasn't sure which—Madelyn swallowed and found a strange interest in the small section of parquet floor between her and Gabriel.

When he finally spoke, his low voice washed over her. "You look exceptionally beautiful this evening."

Her head jerked up at his softly spoken words. Warmth, pleasant but uninvited, enveloped her as she stared into his sparkling blue depths. She loved him, of that there was no doubt. But there was something new and strange in his eyes that spoke to her. It was something she'd never seen before, and her mind searched to give it a name. In another moment it came. What she discerned in his gaze was vulnerability. And she didn't like what it did to her insides. Feeling disarmed, his expression made her want to embrace him and forgive him for his insulting proposal instead of stomp on his toes and call him a pompous cad.

Instead she said, "You look quite handsome." And she smiled like a ninny when he acknowledged her compliment with a small nod.

Actually, saying he looked handsome was the understatement of the year. He was so austerely striking in his formal black evening wear, it almost pained her to look at him. Indeed, it was a good thing he'd never be her husband. He was so sinfully attractive with those eyes and ink-black locks, she'd probably stare at him all day and end up walking into walls and closed doors.

"I must admit," he began, taking a step closer to her, "I didn't expect you to be here this evening."

"Thought I'd hide in my room, I suspect," she said coolly.

"Quite frankly, yes."

"Well," she said, her shoulders lifting in a small shrug, "as long as we are being frank, I didn't expect to see you here either."

"At my own ball?" he asked incredulously. He ducked his head close to her ear. "You expected me here. Admit it, love. You've been scouring this ballroom for a glimpse of me ever since you set your pretty little foot inside it."

She rolled her eyes. Arrogant man. Perceptive, but completely arrogant.

Gabriel presented her with his right hand. "Will you do me the honor, Madelyn, and dance with me?"

A familiar prick of alarm skittered across her nerves, just as it always had when some brave and sympathetic soul asked her to dance. And, as in the past, her gaze sought and unerringly found Priscilla in the crowd. She was speaking with Bernadette Fairbourne, but her stepmother's eyes were on her. Hope flared in Priscilla's gaze as it flitted back and forth between herself and Gabriel.

Turning his head, Gabriel followed her gaze. Priscilla bowed her head in acknowledgment of his attention, but he ignored her, turning back to Madelyn.

"Don't you dare do this for her," he muttered. "If you take my hand, do it because it is your desire and your desire alone."

Looking up at him, Madelyn wanted to refuse him, but that accursed vulnerability was lingering in his gaze. Reaching out, she placed her hand inside his large one. But the pain of his words the day before clanked in her ears like a hammer on a brass bell.

Gabriel led her across the room to where the other dancers awaited the first strains of a waltz. The crowd parted before them. Onlookers gaped with curiosity, chaperones and hopeful mamas of the *ton* crowded behind their fans, whispering, speculating.

"Are you sure you want to tempt the odds, sir," Madelyn asked, her voice tight. "Chances are most unfavorable for you and your toes." She felt him grow rigid at her side, but she couldn't seem to stop herself. "Would you like to consult your aunt before we proceed?" She smiled sweetly at him when he turned his head to look down at her, his light eyes smoldering with a dark promise. She paid it no heed and went on. "Perhaps Lady Eugenia could suggest a dancing instructor."

The music began as soon as they reached the other dancers. Scowling, Gabriel turned to face her, a dark lock tumbling forward to partially cover one of his eyes. Taking her hand in his left, he settled his right hand at the small of her back instead of her waist and gave her a little, unnecessary, push. She managed to stop herself just short of pressing against his tall, lean-muscled form.

As he eased her into the steps of the waltz, he smiled at her, his lips holding about as much warmth as a frozen pond. "My tactless aunt's comments were trifling compared to how society could, and most probably would, shred your spirit."

"Humph. They would hardly say such things to a duchess."

"Perhaps not in your presence, but definitely behind your back." His expression softened. "Their comments would come to you, and the pain they would inflict would be no less than if they said it to your face." He stared at her for a long moment. "I was only trying to protect you, Madelyn."

She didn't know what to say to that, but she did know what his words did to her resolve and her stand on why she could not marry him. Annoyed with herself, she looked away.

All around them the paired dancers twirled and spun in perfect precision. A wave of light-headedness nearly shook Madelyn off balance as she took in the sight. The ballroom had quite suddenly turned into a swirling kaleidoscope.

She blinked back a surge of dizziness. The faces of the guests observing the dance melted into indiscernible blurs.

"Gabriel," she whispered frantically, "I'm going to stumble."

"I won't allow it," he assured her.

"No, Gabriel. I'm really going to fall." Her knee seemed to give out for a moment, but his unwavering support never faltered and she maintained her rhythm. To her, it was nothing short of a miracle.

"Look into my eyes," Gabriel murmured. "Trust me, Madelyn."

Reluctantly, she complied, knowing he was asking her for much more than to have faith in his ability to keep her from falling flat on her face.

Out of the corner of her eye she saw Charlotte spiral past with Lord Tristan, her friend giggling in delight.

"Your brother is going to break Charlotte's heart. The girl will cry for days, no doubt, and forever shy away from the idea of finding true love. And it will be all your fault for holding this ridiculous ball."

His eyes darkened. "You're desperate to hit upon a reason to hate me, but you cannot find one." He gripped her waist a little tighter. "Miss Greene is an intelligent woman. She certainly knew the consequences regarding her heart before she made her decision to fall for my brother . . . unlike you."

"So now I'm stupid," she offered harshly. "Did you realize how expensive having me for wife would turn out to be? Now that you've discovered I'm an idiot, you'd have to hire a tutor for my schooling."

"What if there is a child?"

She very nearly stopped dead in her tracks. "I will know in a sennight if I carry . . . " Her voice trailed away as she quite suddenly felt deflated. Honestly, everything was happening so fast, she hadn't even considered that they might have conceived a baby. *A baby.* She hadn't realized until that very second that she even wanted one.

Rothbury and Miss Fairbourne twirled by too closely and almost crashed into them.

Gabriel gave the earl a frightening glare before returning his attention to Madelyn. "I do not care for the company you keep," he stated, a hint of dissatisfaction in his voice. "Tell me you have not promised a dance to him."

How dare he display such an act of jealousy! He had no claim on her. She had refused him. And if he should ask again, her answer would remain the same. He had certainly stolen her heart, but he had handed it back to her, trampled and misused by his careless words in the pergola.

Something inside her clicked. Be it from his tone of voice or the way he stared down at her with overt possessiveness shining in his eyes, she suddenly wanted to hurt him.

Hurt him the way he hurt you.

"I have promised the earl so much more," she replied, swallowing a twinge of regret at the hastily spoken words.

The dance came to a sudden end, and just as abruptly, Gabriel released her, his eyes cold and hard. He gave her a stiff bow and then strode away, leaving her with a swiftness that took her breath away.

"Gabriel, wait," she called out, ignoring the few shocked gasps from those who surrounded her. But he continued walking and was soon out of the room and off to who knew where.

Her chest rising and falling rapidly, Madelyn stood there alone, tears brimming in her eyes. *What on earth have you done, you stupid, stupid girl?*

She raised her chin, preparing to face the scandalized faces of the guests who had heard her utter the duke's given name. But once she gathered the courage to look around, everyone's gazes seemed to be fixed on a point across the room. Standing on tiptoes, Madelyn watched a stone-faced footman hand Lord Tristan a bouquet of dark red roses.

"Midnight. It's midnight," Madelyn muttered. She searched madly for Charlotte's face in the crowd and finally spotted her standing next to Harriet Beauchamp. The sultry brunette grinned and fluttered her lashes, her high cheekbones rosy apples in the candlelight.

Charlotte didn't look as composed. She kept giving Harriet's bodice side glances and then looked to her own, as if comparing. In the end, Charlotte stood a little straighter and puffed out her chest.

Madelyn reached her friend just as Lord Tristan approached the row of brides-to-be. In reflection, Madelyn realized that she too was supposed to be standing here as a potential bride. But somehow along the way her reason for being here had nothing to do with Lord Tristan and everything to do with Gabriel.

The various levels of murmurs and whispers in the expansive ballroom lowered in unison, then completely faded into a dreadful silence. Madelyn held her breath.

Holding the bouquet at his waist, Lord Tristan passed the Fairbourne twins without sparing them a single glance. They didn't seem to mind, Madelyn mused. The twins seemed preoccupied, craning their necks like a pair of swans to see where the duke had gone off to.

Next in line was Madelyn. He paused to give her a crooked, brotherly smile. She didn't return it, but her heart seemed to jump in her throat as his next step brought him before Charlotte. He faced her and smiled down at her while she beamed up at him. Madelyn placed a reassuring hand at her friend's back.

Then Lord Tristan looked down into the bouquet of roses almost as if he longed to pluck one bloom from the tangle of the others and present it to Charlotte. And it was that very hesitation that incensed Madelyn. He was torturing the sweet girl with his simulated indecision. Beneath her hand, Charlotte's heart thumped at a wild pace, making Madelyn want to wrest the blooms from Lord Tristan's hold and smack him with them.

One more second of this nonsense and she just might do it. And then, before Madelyn could ponder it a moment further, he took a step to the left.

And handed the bouquet to Harriet Beauchamp.

Chapter 20

An hour later Madelyn sat opposite Charlotte in the cushioned window seat in her friend's guest chamber.

Having recently alleviated their coiffures of hundreds of poking pins and traded in their constricting ball gowns for the soft coziness of their dressing gowns, the friends shared a comfortable silence, each lost in her own thoughts.

An emptiness, cold and hollow, had stretched in the pit of Madelyn's stomach ever since Gabriel had walked away from her in the ballroom. The chasm grew still, leaving her to float in painful regret of her hastily spoken words. She had behaved like a vengeful schoolgirl, and she longed to go to him and apologize. Only she was too afraid he would send her away.

And why should you care? The man is a heartless, critical, insensitive oaf. He should be apologizing to you!

Charlotte let forth a loud yawn, breaking the silence and spurring Madelyn into a yawn of her own.

"Is your mother overly disappointed?" Madelyn asked softly, hugging her knees to her chest.

"Not at all," Charlotte answered, snuggling deeper into the thick blanket she had wrapped around herself. Her nose was red from crying and her voice still held a nasal quality. "Don't know what my father might say. Truth be told, now that it's over, I've become more worried about him than the state of my own heart."

"I feel simply wretched for you," Madelyn declared. "The most important part of my purpose here was to keep you from getting hurt, to make you see Lord Tristan's true character, and I failed miserably. I'm sorry, Lottie."

"Please," Charlotte replied with a small laugh. "You must quit apologizing. I knew my chances were slim all along. That's why I ventured to try new ways to . . . revise myself, so to speak, all in the name of competition."

"I think, my dear, you should find a man who thinks you're perfect just the way you are," Madelyn remarked.

"Oh please." Charlotte waved her words away. "All is not lost, Maddie."

"Go on," she said, eyeing her friend with trepidation.

"If I've come away with anything from this whole affair, it is a renewed sense of urgency and competition. They are so many of us and so few eligible bachelors. Well, at least so few who aren't covered in age spots and old enough to be our grandfathers, anyway." Charlotte took a deep breath, the sort one took just before revealing a particular juicy tidbit of gossip. "This evening, after Lord Tristan picked Harriet to be his bride and they started the next waltz—and you were nearly dragged to the dance floor by that young lad who wore his riding breeches—who should come to my immediate rescue but Lord Rothbury."

"You say rescue," Madelyn scoffed, "I say he's a lowly scavenger who spotted a wounded creature."

"I believe he has redeeming qualities," Charlotte defended.

"Stop," Madelyn said, holding up a hand. "Your sensibilities are fragile at present and I will hear no more of this foolishness."

Charlotte straightened her spine, her voice yet altered by her stuffed nose. "He's an earl, he's handsome, he has thirty thousand a year, and it's no secret he's been looking for a bride since last Season. I hardly think setting my cap for him makes me a candidate for Bedlam."

"But Rothbury? He's worse than Lord Tristan."

Charlotte sighed.

"I guess I'm just going to have to trust you to use good judgment," Madelyn said.

"Yes, you must. After all, I can handle it . . . er, handle him, that is. I think. " Smiling, Charlotte pushed off the window seat and stretched. "Does he know you love him?"

"Who?" Taken by surprise by the sudden change of subject, Madelyn studied her fingernails, masking her expression with what she hoped looked like disinterest.

"Oh bother! Don't pretend you don't know who I'm talking about."

Madelyn sighed—she was certainly doing a lot of that this evening. "I don't suppose I ever told him," she said wistfully.

"Has he ever told you?"

"No."

"Do you *think* he loves you?" Charlotte asked softly.

"Unfortunately, I think he did, only I went ahead and ruined things as usual."

Early the following afternoon, Madelyn sat upon the settee in the morning room of Wolverest Castle. The walls of the richly furnished room were of pale yellow and white, which gave it a cheery, blithe atmosphere, serving only to magnify her somber mood.

After she had dressed that morning, she requested an audience with Gabriel. However, the butler politely informed her that the duke was no longer at home. This could have meant two things. That Gabriel was still here—and didn't wish to speak with her ever again—or he had left—because he didn't wish to speak with her ever again. She sighed. Wherever he was, she pondered with a heavy heart, the outcome was still the same. He so very obviously didn't want to be bothered with her. And that was the way it should be, she supposed. He would only marry her if she agreed to "fix" herself. And she refused to live the rest of her life scampering to catch up to another person's expectations.

From down the hall the shrill voice of Bernadette Fairbourne echoed loudly as she scolded a footman who had mistakenly packed one of her numerous valises in someone else's carriage.

With hands on hips, Priscilla tapped her foot in cadence with Bernadette's chattering. "Just what are we supposed to do while he argues with that shrew? The Greenes ordered their carriage an hour ago and still we wait."

Madelyn brushed at the folds of her lavender carriage dress with hands covered in straw-colored gloves that matched her wide-brimmed bonnet. "I should point out that neither Charlotte nor her mother have come down yet."

"Yes, that's very clear," Priscilla said angrily. "That's the trouble with traveling with others. No one is ever ready to depart at the same time." She threw her hands up in agitation. "There's no sense standing waiting here now. If we're ever to leave, I'd better see what's delaying our departure myself." And with that her stepmother swept from the room in a rustle of gray bombazine.

Standing, Madelyn was just about to stride over to the French doors overlooking a small garden and lily pond when the sound of swishing fabric came from the hall.

"Good afternoon, Madelyn," Rosalind said, her round blue eyes filled with guarded concern. Looking beautiful in a pink muslin dress and matching velvet bonnet, Gabriel's sister crossed the room and took Madelyn's hands into her own.

"Good afternoon," Madelyn replied.

"I've been looking for you." Rosalind searched her gaze for a moment, then said, "It's none of my business to know what happened between you and Gabriel, but I do so hope your disagreement is quickly resolved and feelings are mended."

Hesitating, Madelyn pressed her lips together for a moment, then said, "I asked to speak with him this morning, but was told he wasn't at home."

Rosalind only nodded in response, which squelched Madelyn's hope that his sister might expound on his whereabouts.

"I was wondering . . . " Rosalind's eyes took on a sharpness Madelyn hadn't seen since their quick little chat in the orangery. "Are you not going to visit Willowbrooke before heading back to London?"

"I don't think that will be possible. My stepmother and I are minutes from departing—"

"Whyever not?" Rosalind prodded. "You're right here in Yorkshire. When are you ever again going to have such an opportunity?"

"I'm afraid the point would be for naught." She shrugged. "It's out of my hands now . . . or rather, my stepmother's hands. She sold the property just the other day."

Rosalind's mouth gaped open with exaggerated shock. "How simply dreadful! Well, that's settles it, then. You're coming with me." Grabbing Madelyn's hand in hers, she tugged her along, heading for the French doors that led outside.

Madelyn had no choice but to follow. "Come with you? Where?"

Opening one of the doors with her free hand, Rosalind made a sound that was half sigh, half groan of frustration. "To Willowbrooke Cottage. I'd just ordered the barouche to be brought around for a ride. It's such a fine, unusually warm day, is it not?"

"Er . . . quite," Madelyn said, stumbling behind an almost running Rosalind.

"And now," Rosalind continued, rounding the lily pond, "I have a reason to be about."

Madelyn didn't miss how Rosalind's grip tightened on her hand. No doubt the duke's sister feared she would fall in. "But we can't just barge in, unannounced."

Rosalind only shrugged. "It's quite possible the new owners aren't even there yet, and if so, I'm sure they won't mind us having a look inside once we explain our case to the housekeeper. Wouldn't you like that, Madelyn?"

"Yes. Yes, of course." Madelyn bit her bottom lip, trying to tamp down a sudden surge of nervousness. "But what of my stepmother? She'll be looking for me."

Rosalind waved away her worry as they rounded a bend that led them to the front drive. "The maid will cover for me." Her footing faltered, then picked up again. "Ah . . . what I meant was . . . was that the baroness will be far too busy waking up Mrs. Greene," she said quickly. "Charlotte's mother seems to prefer frequent naps and is in the midst of quite a heavy one, I'm afraid. Don't you worry. It will all be just fine."

Madelyn wasn't so sure. Coming around to the front of the castle, a shiny carriage with the top folded down awaited them. With the help of a liveried footman, the women were handed up into the fancy barouche and sat facing one another.

"See? No worries," Rosalind chirped.

Madelyn smiled politely, casting a fretful glance at the tall rows of mullioned windows. She wondered if Gabriel was watching them. It all seemed very odd to her as the well-sprung carriage lurched into motion and rolled over the cobbled drive worn smooth by time.

As they rambled down the inner courtyard and through the two-story gatehouse, a strange feeling toyed with her mind. She couldn't place her finger on it, though, and so shrugged the feeling away.

Rosalind grabbed a thick blue blanket, whipped it open and spread it across their legs. "There now," she said with a wide smile. "Let us sit back and enjoy the ride. We'll be there sooner than you think."

After some time, Madelyn took her eyes off the passing countryside and very cautiously looked at Rosalind. The duke's sister sat leaning comfortably back on the brown leather seat, a secret, satisfied smile curling her lips while her light eyes took in the view of rolling, green velvet fields alternately bracketed by long hedges or low stone walls.

Madelyn tried forcing herself to relax, or at least to appear to be enjoying herself. Admittedly, she appreciated Rosalind's kindness and willingness to assist her in visiting Willowbrooke Cottage. It was something she was unable to do by herself. Priscilla wouldn't allow her, and she knew she couldn't very well have gone off alone. But now . . . she was so close. And after all, what did she stand to lose?

Priscilla was well and truly dissatisfied with the past fortnight's outcome and would most likely continue to make her life miserable. In truth, all she had to look forward to was for Priscilla to finally surrender her marriage ambitions and send her off to live with aging female relatives as a companion. And it couldn't be that bad of a life, she guessed. She would spend her days reading aloud, fetching blankets, chatting while perfecting her needlework . . . and pining for Gabriel and the life she might have had with him if she wasn't so blasted stubborn.

Squinting up to the sky, she noted that the bright azure hue was painfully akin to the very shade of Gabriel's eyes when he smiled down at her. A sudden sob tore at her throat and her stomach felt queasy. How in the world was she ever going to forget him? And, God forbid, how in the world was she to survive if she ran into him in town?

With her mind a turbulent sea of conflicting emotions, Madelyn tried to extinguish Gabriel from her thoughts and settle down. Truly, she tried to enjoy the warm sunshine and the sweet smell of a freshly clipped lawn, only her heart still gave a wrenching twist, as he remained in the forefront of her mind.

The road to Willowbrooke was surprisingly free

of ruts and mud puddles. Even more surprising was how quickly they got there.

At the first sight of the moderately sized two-story stone building, her heart leapt to her throat. Memories of her youth, of her healthy mother, came flooding in . . . and so did her tears.

Rosalind reached forward, grasping her hands and giving them a squeeze. "Happy or sad?" she asked quietly.

"Both," Madelyn answered.

The carriage rolled to a stop before the front gate, which now hung askew between the low stone wall. In too much of a state, Madelyn didn't bother waiting to be helped down and just hopped down by herself.

A familiar sound reached her ears and she smiled. On a field in the distance, sheep scuttled uphill, bleating and crowding together at the top.

A twitch of black caught her eye, and she noticed a horse grazing in a fenced yard adjacent to the now dilapidated stable. The beautiful beast must belong to the caretakers, Mr. and Mrs. White, she thought, or to the new owners.

"I can't believe I'm here," she said in wonder. Smiling, she turned back to Rosalind, who still remained seated in the barouche.

And then it hit her, that odd feeling she had when they departed Wolverest for the cottage.

"You never told the driver where we were going," Madelyn said, her words shaky. "You knew before you even came to fetch me that you were going to take me here. I'm right, aren't I?"

Clasping her hands together on her lap, Rosalind acknowledged her gentle accusations with a firm nod. "And I have another confession to make." She took a deep breath. "It was me."

"What was you?"

"The shoes, the posset, the letter, locking you in."

"What?" Madelyn blinked in surprise. "Why?"

Rosalind's delicately winged brows knitted with worry. "They were all designed to get you into Gabriel's company one way or another. I had hoped you would think it was one of the other ladies seeking to undermine your chances, and that you would take your problem to Gabriel. I thought once you both were in each other's company, trying to ferret out the culprit, you wouldn't be able to deny your attraction for one another." Her expression softened. "Madelyn, I think you both fell in love the second your eyes met in that garden. You belong together." She smiled then and gave a quick laugh. "You're both so very different, but complement one another. Like a pair of puzzle pieces."

"Together, we are complete," Madelyn murmured. She turned back to the house. Distractedly, she noted that the roof needed thatching and two of the upstairs windows were broken. The cottage was a mess, indeed.

Just then there was a loud crash, followed by what sounded like the shout of a man. The horse in the field picked up its head, flicking its ears. Seconds later a rolling cloud of dust puffed out of one of the broken upstairs windows.

"What in the world?" Madelyn pushed through the gate, ignoring the sharp jab on her thumb from a piece of splintered wood. She dashed toward the front door. Upon reaching it, the rumbling of a carriage sounded behind her. She turned just in time to see Rosalind's barouche hug the bend in the road and disappear.

She'd left her. Rosalind had left her here with no way back and all alone . . . well, all alone except for whoever was fumbling around upstairs.

Hitching up her skirts, Madelyn stepped inside the small front hall and looked to the left, to the first room that opened up. The familiar, almost forgotten sight of the front parlor made her feel like she was in a dream, an awful dream where her existence was wiped clean. For the room was completely empty. Gone were the cozy rugs, the paintings, the furniture, and her mother's collection of porcelain dancing figures that had stood frozen in motion on the mantelpiece.

Her heart beating wildly, she forged on, her footsteps sounding hollow as she continued down the hall, past the empty breakfast room, past her father's tiny office. It all seemed so much smaller than she'd remembered. Of course, the last time she'd stood within these walls she was much younger.

She reached the base of the narrow staircase, hesitating to ascend them. The floor creaked above her head and she looked up.

"Mrs. White?" she called out. "Mr. White?"

There was no answer, only more footsteps from

above, but this time those creaks were moving to the head of the staircase. In a minute she'd find out who was upstairs.

A tall shadow shifted above, and then Gabriel—a very disheveled Gabriel—stood at the top of the stairs. His ink-black hair looked almost white with dust. Wearing only a white shirt, sleeves rolled to the elbows, and a pair of buckskin breeches and boots, he looked adorable and kissable and . . .

"What took you so long?" he asked, scowling down at her. "I almost got myself killed."

"What are you doing here?" she questioned in return, blinking up at him. The sight of this glorious man, this man whom she loved, standing in her childhood home was almost more than she could take. She had never counted herself as someone who swooned, but she certainly felt that way presently.

He smiled, all lopsided and breathtaking, and held out his hand to her. "Come up," he said lightly. "I've something to show you."

As if suddenly bound to him by an invisible chain, Madelyn slinked up the steps. At the top, he didn't budge an inch, and she was forced to brush up next to him. His bright gaze dropped from her eyes to her lips and went back up again.

The cottage suddenly felt overly warm. She looked at his dusty hair, noting that whatever was in it was all over his shoulders as well.

"What is all this stuff on you?" she asked.

"The ceiling."

"No . . . " she gasped, drawing out the *o* in disbelief.

"Yes," he stressed with a grin. "I was hunting around in the attic when I quite suddenly fell through."

So that was the crash she'd heard when they first arrived. "Oh, my," she said, then tried to cover her smile with her hand.

"Go ahead, laugh if you will," he replied in mock offense. "Just know that I almost died without ever telling you that I love you."

Madelyn's smile wavered, then fell, then rose up again with a brilliance that nearly made her cheeks hurt. "You do?"

His hooded eyes sparkled with blue flame. "I do."

"You do?" she repeated in wonder.

"I do," he gently repeated with a smile, his eyes crinkling at the corners. "I love you, Madelyn."

Overcome with emotion, she stood on her tiptoes and went in for a kiss. But he backed away until the wall was at his back. Madelyn found herself leaning provocatively against him to keep from falling. Befuddled by his declaration, she missed the teasing light in his gaze.

She reached up for another kiss, this time holding both of his lean bristled cheeks in her hands. Closing her eyes, she pressed her soft lips to his. He didn't respond at all. Slowly, she opened her eyes while keeping her mouth inches from his own. He hadn't even closed his eyes.

"What is it?" she asked, whispering.

"Madelyn, we are alone."

"I know," she said, going in for another attempt.

He turned his head, deftly evading her kiss. "It isn't at all proper."

Unable to stop herself, she started unbuttoning his shirt. Slipping her hands inside, she caressed his flat stomach and warm chest. "So now *you're* a master of propriety?"

Sweet Lord, how badly he desired this woman. She was driving him mad with her delicate touch, but they had much to discuss, to resolve, before they went any further. Besides, there was still the subject of Rothbury to cover.

"You belong to another," he stated, knowing it wasn't true, but wanting to hear what she'd say.

"No, Gabriel," she said softly. "It was awful of me, I know, but I didn't promise anything to him."

"I know," he replied with a cheeky grin.

"You knew?" She swatted his shoulder. "And you let me believe otherwise?"

His broad shoulders lifted in a shrug. "I wanted to hear it from your lips."

"I behaved childishly and said it only to hurt you. I'm sorry."

Finally he touched her, placing his large hands at her waist, and Madelyn's entire body rejoiced.

"No. I'm sorry," he intoned. Taking her chin delicately in his thumb and forefinger, he tilted her face so he could look more intensely into her eyes. "You have captivated me from the very beginning, my love. How could I have ever thought to change you? Forgive me."

"I understand now," she explained matter-of-factly. "I could stand to use some instruction. I *am* clumsy, and graceless, and—"

"No." He pressed a finger to her lips, then kissed her forehead. "You are sweet and kind and protective and interesting and spontaneous." He kissed her nose. "You are beautiful and humble and sensitive and the keeper of my heart. I know it will take some time, growing up with a beast of a guardian as you did, but there will come a day when you no longer criticize yourself, no longer believe less of yourself, and you will come to love yourself just as much as I love you. Well, almost as much, I imagine."

"Oh, Gabriel," Madelyn said softly. "I do love you too."

He smiled, pulling her to his chest for a bone-melting embrace. She felt as if she sank into him.

"You give the most glorious of hugs, you know," she mumbled, her voice muffled by his shirt.

He chuckled softly, then added in a whisper, "And do you know a woman who is missing a ring?"

"A ring?" She pulled away from his chest just enough to look into his eyes. "Are you . . . "

"Yes. Yes, I am," he said silkily, his love and affection for her shining in his eyes.

He reached inside a small pocket sewn into the waist of his pants and made sure to tickle her in the process. He then dropped to his knees before her, and she was reminded once again of that night in his garden. This time, however, she lovingly threaded her fingers through the locks atop his head, disturbing the specks of dust.

Holding the ring in a shaft of light, he presented it to her. "Marry me, my precious, perfect bride?"

Tears in her eyes, she could only nod quickly. Smiling broadly, Gabriel peeled off the straw-colored glove of her left hand, tugging on the tips of each finger first. Her hand bared to him, he placed a lingering kiss on her knuckles, then slipped the ring on her finger.

Standing, he pulled her to him and leaned down to cover her mouth with his. Inside, Madelyn felt something loosen and was then set free. Filled with giddy enthusiasm, she returned his passionate kiss with tender eagerness.

Gabriel's hands roamed over her back and waist, promising her future delights. Cupping her bottom, he tugged her closer to him and their mouths broke on a shared gasp.

"Wait," she murmured when his fingers started unfastening her gown.

"Hmm?" He nuzzled her neck.

"What *are* you doing here?" She swallowed, looking up at him expectantly.

"Looking. I was hoping to find some of your belongings. I did find an old trunk in the attic. Trouble is, I fell through the ceiling before I could get to it."

"Are you all right?"

"Well enough, I suppose," he said, chuckling at himself.

Her brow furrowed. "But are you not concerned about the new owners? Certainly, you must have contacted them and asked for their permission before coming here?"

"Madelyn, *I* am the new owner. Well, *you* are, that is. There's still some paperwork to be shifted around, and it's definitely going to need some work, but I bought it for you."

Her breath caught in her throat. "You did?" she squeaked out.

He nodded slowly, a wolfish grin spreading across his handsome face.

"Oh, you sweet, sweet man," she exclaimed, raining kisses all over his face.

"But you know, you cannot live here," he said cautiously in between her kisses. "You're going to live with me, whether that be in the country or in London. And you'll sleep nowhere but in my arms. Ever."

She nodded happily. "Yes, of course. I cannot think of a more perfect place to be."

And then his mouth pressed onto hers for a thought-shattering kiss. Madelyn shivered in response and weaved her fingers in his silky hair. He broke their kiss to nibble her earlobe.

Blown away by the events like a leaf in the breeze, she still had more questions. "Gabriel," she said, only it came out like a moan.

"Hmm?"

"Did you know what your sister was up to?"

He nodded and pulled back to look into her eyes.

"When did you find out?" she asked.

"The day you wandered into my office, you mentioned it. I had my suspicions, and after I danced with you, I questioned her and she admitted her guilt."

"Were you angry with her?"

"Not at all," he said, giving her a quick kiss. "Although I appreciate her efforts—she did bring you to the cottage, as I ordered her to—I would have been ensnared by you without her endeavors. There was no stopping it. You enchant me."

Her eyes level with his throat, she kissed the base of his neck, right where his pulse throbbed.

He swallowed convulsively. "Where the devil did you learn that?"

"You did that to me, in your bedchamber," she whispered, then nipped at his chest.

"In *our* bedchamber," he groaned. "Oh Lord, the things I've yet to do to you. I should warn you . . . if you ever happen to wander into my private office again, you'll be well and truly ravished right there upon my desk.."

"Is that a threat or a promise?"

"Choose which ever inspires you to misbehave."

She smiled wickedly at his words, which were spoken to her in almost the same fashion as they had been during her interview when she first arrived.

"Oh, and Madelyn?"

"Hmm?"

"If you're ever angry with me, will you promise me one thing?"

She nodded, her brow rising with interest.

"Please stay away from the orangery," he replied, rubbing his forehead.

She threw her arms around his neck and agreed with a blissful laugh.

Epilogue

◦◦◦◦◦

"**A**ll hands! All hands on deck, I say," Lady Eugenia Devine called out in the cheery yellow and white morning room. Armfuls of crisp sheets, broomsticks of varying heights, lengths of rope, and an astounding array of strategically placed furniture had turned the new Duchess of Wolverest's favorite room into a formidable warship worthy of the Royal Navy.

"Get yerself aboard, ye landlubber," she continued, but was poked on the behind for her comment by a very short, fleet-footed sailor. *"Oh!"*

A paper captain's hat sitting askew atop his sooty locks, he giggled as he rounded past his doting great aunt. His bright eyes flashing, he looked over his shoulder, squealing with delight as he dove underneath a low canopy draped between two shield-back chairs—just before her outstretched hand would have closed around his ankle.

"The nerve! Why I ought to make you scrub the deck," she exclaimed in mock offense, "or at the very least put you in leg irons!"

"Do tell, what has the lad done now?" Gabriel asked from his position just inside the doorway.

"Dear me," his aunt proclaimed with a laugh, "don't scowl so. We're playing."

"Papa!" In a flurry of movement, the little sailor scrambled from his hiding place and ran to his father, arms outstretched.

Hoisting the boy up, Gabriel gave him a hearty squeeze and a kiss on the forehead.

"Eww," he said, wiping his face with the back of his hand.

"Now who taught you that? Couldn't have been me," Gabriel grumbled.

"Of course not," his aunt said, hoisting herself up from her knees with the help of an overstuffed ottoman. "With the way you and your lady go on about, you'd think you were just married instead of four years ago."

Gabriel smiled. What a remarkable change had occurred in his aunt Eugenia during the past few years. She and Madelyn had come to an agreement of sorts: to keep the hell away from one another. But with the birth of their son two years ago, his aunt found it difficult to stay away for long stretches of time. She never had any children of her own, and what better joy was there than to spoil her favorite nephew's son with love and attention.

It only took a matter of months for his wife's infectious laughter and light spirit to engage his aunt's heart. She had told him, privately of course, that she was wrong about Madelyn, that he had chosen well, that she was a good wife and a wonderful mother.

And then one day she had told a surprised Madelyn those very things herself.

"Gabriel?" Madelyn called out from the hall. "Gabriel?"

Handing his son over to his aunt, he pressed his finger to his lips, asking for silence, then slipped under the same canopy of sheets his son had emerged from earlier.

"My, my," Madelyn said with a laugh, stepping into the morning room. If not for the portrait of her mother hanging above the hearth—the very portrait they'd found in Willowbrooke's attic four years ago—she'd have thought she stepped into the wrong room.

"Did Michael make you do all this?" Madelyn asked.

"Dear me," Eugenia said. "The lad's only two years of age and barely says a handful of words. However could he have coerced me to do such a thing? You may place the blame entirely on his aunt. It's all my doing, it is."

Madelyn raised a skeptical brow. She knew blooming well how those bright blue eyes could melt hearts and persuade one to do his will. Her son was very much like his father in that respect.

Michael yawned, spurring Lady Eugenia into motion. She shuffled to the door, dipped him forward so his mother could place a kiss on his plump cheek, then announced she would take him to the nursery for his nap.

"But have you seen Gabriel?" Madelyn asked, and received no answer, as the woman left cooing over Michael, paying her no heed.

Hands on hips, Madelyn surveyed the mess. "Well, I certainly hope they had a lot of fun."

She had scooted back a small rosewood writing table to its former position under the window when she heard a shuffling sound coming from under a secluded draping of linens. Her curiosity—not to mention a sense of dread—piqued by the sound, she tiptoed over, praying Michael hadn't adopted another woodland creature and brought it into the castle.

On hands and knees she lifted the edge of the sheet . . . and was promptly hauled inside by Gabriel's strong hands clamped on her hips. Quite suddenly, she found herself flat on her back, her husband's familiar weight atop her, his warm mouth searching, exploring, and plundering her own.

After a deliciously long moment, she managed to reluctantly break free. "As tempting as staying under here with you might be . . . "

"Might be?"

" . . . the fact of the matter is, I must get up and straighten this mess. Charlotte's coming for tea in an hour."

He scowled down at her—truthfully, she would have called it a pout if not for the fact that he was a grown man—and she smiled up at him.

"No," he said, looking about their linen cocoon. "The captain of this sailing vessel has requested a private audience with you in his quarters. It seems you've a treasure map hidden on your person, and I mean to explore every inch of you until it is discovered."

"Oh, really?" she asked, giggling. He sounded so serious.

"Really." He nodded, his blue eyes turning dark with desire.

"My, you're playful," she crooned as he nuzzled her neck.

"I learned from a master," he replied, his breath hot on her skin. "But first, you must tell me what you wanted."

"What I . . . " He took her face in his hands and kissed her soundly.

"You were calling for me," he drawled, brushing his lips across her earlobe.

For a moment Madelyn didn't know what he was talking about. Desire thrummed through her in sensual waves. "Oh, yes," she said, feeling silly for forgetting. "There is something I must tell you."

He paused at the serious tone in her voice. "What is it?"

"Well, my dear, sweet man . . . we are going to have another baby."

Gabriel blinked, instant tears rimming his beautiful eyes. "Y-You are?"

She nodded happily, her own eyes growing teary.

Shifting his weight, he slid down her body and placed a kiss on her abdomen. "I love you," he whispered, returning to her.

"And I love you."

"But you're still not getting out of here just yet," he said with a roguish grin.

"Captain's orders?"

"Indeed," he muttered, sinking his mouth onto hers.